Seeker of Legends

Books by Clayton Taylor Wood:

The Runic Series

Runic Awakening

Runic Revelation

Runic Vengeance

Runic Revolt

The Fate of Legends Series

Hunter of Legends

Seeker of Legends

Destroyer of Legends

Magic of Havenwood Series

The Magic Collector

The Lost Gemini

Seeker of Legends

Book II of the Fate of Legends series

Clayton Taylor Wood

Published by Clayton T. Wood.

ISBN: 978-1-948497-02-2

Cover designed by James T. Egan, Bookfly Design, LLC

Printed in the United States of America.

Special thanks to my brothers and my wife for their invaluable advice.

And to my son Hunter, for whom this book was written.

Table of Contents

Seeker of Legends

Prologue

Countless stars shone down on the King's Road, a seemingly endless series of stone slabs suspended seven meters above the ground by massive wooden posts. The three moons of Varta, nearly full now, cast their pale glow on the forest the road cut through, casting soft shadows on the forest floor. A cool wind whipped through the trees, a prelude to menacing clouds approaching slowly from the west.

And on the King's Road, a lone carriage rolled steadily northward toward the Kingdom of Tykus, pulled by two burly horses.

Seeker Dante shifted uneasily in his seat inside the carriage, his buttocks aching from the days-long ride through the forest. The carriage was old and worn, the seat cushions stiff and uncomfortable. It was far from the usual luxury the Guild of Seekers provided. No one who managed to spot the carriage would think it was owned by the guild…or that it carried such precious cargo.

And that, Dante knew, was precisely the point.

He glanced to his right, at the other man seated in the carriage, a younger man with light brown hair and a pencil-thin mustache. It was Seeker Murin, a low-ranked Seeker Dante was mentoring. The man – practically a boy – was still green, fresh out of his apprenticeship. As with most fresh graduates, Murin's confidence far exceeded his competence. With experience, that would change.

If it doesn't, Dante mused, *he'll be dead.*

Dante sighed, looking down at the large wooden music box sitting between them on the seat cushions. It was well-made, with intricate designs carved into every inch of its exterior. A convincing counterfeit; anyone lifting the lid would find a fully-functioning machine inside. But hidden within that machine was a sealed secret compartment, nestled between its gears. And in that compartment was an obsidian container containing a very valuable artifact.

A very *illegal* artifact.

What the artifact did exactly, Dante didn't know. That was often the case with the guild when they acted as their own client. Most Seekers retrieved artifacts for private clients, giving a percentage of their profits to the guild. A few of the more skilled – and more trustworthy – Seekers ran missions for the guild itself, retrieving artifacts that High Seeker Zeno felt were necessary to strengthen the guild. These artifacts were sacred indeed; the traits stored within them were almost guaranteed to increase the powers of all the Seekers, making them stronger, faster, or smarter.

Each artifact brought them one step closer to the Founder's grand vision: the Ascension.

Seeker Murin stirred, glancing at Dante.

"That was some weird shit, huh?" he said, shaking his head. "The Kingdom of the Deep, I mean."

Dante said nothing, not meeting the man's gaze. He recognized the statement for what it was…a banal conversation-starter. Silence made Murin nervous. It was a weakness of the young, and it betrayed a lack of self-confidence. All signs of a low-level Seeker. Assuming he was ever promoted, Murin would be exposed to a stronger form of the Founder's will, through an upgraded Seeker medallion. This would cure his weaknesses eventually, even if experience did not.

"If you ask me," Murin continued, "…they're all a bunch of freaks." He smirked then. "Ever wonder how they, you know?"

"No, I don't," Dante grumbled.

"How they do it," Murin continued. "Especially the guy who sold us that," he added, gesturing to the music box. "I mean come on, the guy was *huge*."

"Like I said," Dante stated coolly, "…I don't."

"They're not even human anymore," Murin pressed, oblivious to Murin's unspoken sentiment – that he didn't want to talk. "They're like…*animals* there."

Dante ignored the younger Seeker, closing his eyes and resting his head back against his seat. They'd traveled from the Kingdom of the Deep, passing through the Glade of the Deep to reach the King's Road. Then they'd taken the road all the way to the Fringe, the last few kilometers of forest before the Deadlands…and the Kingdom of Tykus. A vast wasteland, the Deadlands was all that remained of the old Outskirts, a city once filled with peasants. Peasants that, under the leadership of the Original, had risen up to start the great Civil War a half-century ago.

Tykus had driven the peasants – and the Original – out, laying waste to the old Outskirts, digging the tainted earth of the ruined city up and tossing it into the ocean.

Dante stifled a yawn. It would only be another hour before they reached the Deadlands, and not much longer than that before they made it to the great wall surrounding Tykus. Going through customs would be risky, as usual; if they were caught transporting illegal artifacts, they would be tried and convicted of treason. Thus the necessity of building the music box around the obsidian container housing the artifact; customs officials would not break apart such a delicate machine to find the artifact, and the wood of the music box would insulate the traits emitted by the artifact, making them difficult to sense.

Dante had been through the process countless times, and had never been caught. A skilled smuggler like himself was exceedingly valuable to the guild…a fact that had made him a wealthy man.

Customs would use the guild's own Seekers to test the artifacts, as was the protocol. These Seekers were trained differently than the rest, of course. None carried the Founder's will. The kingdom tested each of these "false" Seekers by having mentally deficient, weak-willed people called Testers spend time with them, absorbing their wills. Then the Testers were extensively questioned by the kingdom. Any anti-Tykus sentiments a person might have would be absorbed by the Testers, and as they were simple-minded, they would not think to hide them.

A *real* Seeker would not stand up to such scrutiny.

"Wonder what that thing is," Murin mused, breaking the silence. His eyes were on the music box.

"If you're smart," Dante grumbled, "…you'll never find out."

"Why's that?"

"You should know why," Dante retorted. It was well-known that artifacts from the Kingdom of the Deep were often *wild* artifacts, those containing traits that weren't human. In the Kingdom of the Deep, humanity was not valued as it was in Tykus, and it was perfectly legal to expose oneself to wild traits. In Tykus, such a thing was forbidden. Preservation of one's humanity was the sacred mission of the Acropolis, the great fortress where the highest nobles lived…and King Tykus himself.

"I wonder if this came from the Deep," Murin mused. Dante glanced at him.

"Doubt it."

"Why's that?" Murin pressed. "What is the Deep, anyway?"

Dante sighed.

"What did I tell you about asking questions?" he stated wearily. Murin grimaced.

"Don't ask more than one at a time."

"You know it," Dante stated. "So *do* it."

"Right," Murin muttered. He shifted uneasily in his seat. "So what is the Deep?" he pressed.

"No one knows," Dante answered. "Except maybe High Seeker Zeno. All I know is the Great One went there a long time ago."

"What was what, a hundred years ago?"

"Hell of a lot longer than that," Dante corrected.

Suddenly there was an ear-splitting shriek.

Dante's gaze jerked forward, and he spotted the horse on the right through the front window of the carriage. It reared up on its hind legs, then bolted leftward, slamming into the other horse. The driver shouted something unintelligible, yanking back on the reins. But the horse ignored the driver, breaking out into a gallop, veering off to the left…and bringing the carriage with it.

"What the hell?" Murin blurted out.

Then Dante saw what'd spooked the horse: an arrow was sticking out of its right flank.

"Get out," Dante ordered, shoving Murin toward the rightmost door of the carriage. "Go!"

Both horses veered to the left, bring the carriage rolling straight toward the leftmost edge of the King's Road…and the sheer, twenty-foot drop to the ground below.

"Get out!" Dante shouted, shoving the music box off the seat and diving rightward toward Murin's door. He grabbed the door handle and pulled it, shoving the door open…just as the carriage's front left wheel rolled off the edge of the road.

Shit!

Dante scrambled over Murin's lap toward the open door…and felt the carriage tilt to the left, making him slide toward the opposite door. His back slammed into it, and he grunted, bracing himself. He saw the horses plunge off the side of the King's Road, then felt his stomach lurch as the carriage entered into free-fall.

His Seeker instincts kicked in.

He curled into a ball, ducking his head in his arms, every muscle relaxing, going limp. He felt the carriage accelerating downward, time slowing as it careened toward the ground seven meters below. The carriage driver leapt from his seat outside of the carriage, falling to the right of the horses. As Dante watched, the horses slammed head-first into the ground, the driver hitting moments later. The driver's seat struck next, disintegrating as it smashed into the forest floor. The front of the carriage *exploded*, pieces of wood and stone flying toward Dante. He closed his eyes, remaining limp.

And then there was darkness.

* * *

Dante groaned, opening his eyes.

He found himself lying on his back, staring upward at the seat cushions of the carriage. He frowned, wondering how they'd gotten up there…then realized that he was lying on the ceiling. The carriage had flipped upside-down.

He heard groaning, and turned to see Murin lying beside him, a deep gash in the man's forehead. Blood poured from the wound, forming a puddle under their heads. Dante grimaced, sitting up, feeling pain in his back and arms as he did so. He looked down, seeing pieces of glass and wooden splinters jutting out of his forearms…and his legs. Sharp, stabbing pain shot through the left side of his chest with each breath, and he grunted, putting a hand on his ribs there. The merest touch brought him agony.

What the hell happened?

It took him a moment to remember, and when he did, he swore.

"Get up," he ordered Murin, rising to a crouching position, ignoring the pain the movement caused. He lent the younger Seeker a hand, pulling him to his feet. Murin looked dazed, his eyes glassy. Concussed.

"What…" he began, but Dante cut him off.

"They're coming," he growled. "Go out that way," he added, gesturing to the still-open door nearest the man. "I'll go the other way."

"Who-"

"Shut up and go!" Dante hissed, shoving Murin toward the door. He turned to *his* door, yanking at the lever to open it. But it didn't budge. He swore.

They're watching, he knew. Whoever had shot the horse. If they saw his door open, they'd know he was trying to escape. Hopefully Murin stumbling out of the carriage would be distract the enemy. The kid was useless now, except as bait.

Dante waited for Murin to get clear of the carriage, then braced himself, kicking his door just below the handle. It burst open.

A fresh jolt of pain shot through his ribs, and he held his breath, his eyes watering. He waited for the pain to lessen, taking shallow breaths. Eventually it did.

He peered outside.

Pieces of the shattered carriage were strewn across the forest floor, lined by pale moonlight. The carriage had struck front-first, then tipped over onto its back. Which explained why it was upside-down. He spotted a man lying in a broken heap nearby…the driver.

If the man wasn't dead, he would be soon.

Dante drew his longsword from its scabbard slowly, turning so that his body was blocking the blade from view. Otherwise whoever had shot them down might see the moonlight flashing on the blade. He peered into the darkness, seeing nothing but trees and bushes.

Then he heard footsteps behind him.

Crunch, crunch.

Dante spun around, then relaxed. It was Murin; the man was limping into the forest, his sword in plain sight, moonlight shimmering off the blade. Exactly as Dante had hoped.

Idiot.

Murin jerked back suddenly, an arrow protruding from his chest.

Dante broke out into a run toward a large tree ahead. He reached it, ducking behind it, keeping his sword down low. He felt panic rising within him, and suppressed it, trying to focus. Panic would get him killed. He needed to think.

The arrow came from straight ahead, he reasoned, recalling the angle it'd struck Murin at…and the horse earlier, on the King's Road. That meant that the archer had to be to the right of the road. Dante circled around the tree trunk until it was between him and the carriage. His ribs hurt terribly, and his hands were slick with the blood trickling down the countless wounds in his forearms. The hilt of his sword felt slippery, and he wiped his hands on his pants one at a time, then gripped the hilt of his sword tightly.

He had to kill whoever ambushed them, he knew. If he didn't, whoever it was would get their hands on the artifact. His hand went to his chest, reaching for his Seeker medallion, but of course it wasn't there. He'd left it at the guild, as he always did when going out to transport illegal artifacts. Couldn't have the enemy getting ahold of his medallion, after all.

There could be more than one archer.

The thought made the hair on the nape of his neck stand on end, and he glanced out from behind the tree, peering into the woods. He still couldn't see anything; a dense mist hung in the air just above the ground a few dozen meters away. There was no way the archer could have shot Murin through that haze. Which meant…

Pain lanced through his left leg, and he cried out, dropping his sword and falling onto his back on the hard ground. He looked down.

An arrow was sticking out of his shin.

He scrambled to his feet, then saw something burst out of the mist ahead. A man in a black cloak, their face hidden in the shadows thrown by the hood over their head. Holding a bow, sprinting right at him!

Shit!

Dante reached down, retrieving his sword. The cloaked man dropped the bow, unsheathing a sword from their hip in one smooth, quick motion. Moonlight danced off the silver blade, and the man reached Dante within seconds, swinging their sword at him with terrible speed!

Dante felt his Seeker reflexes kick in, and he blocked the blow, their blades ringing with the impact. He counterattacked without thinking, without needing to think. He'd spent years absorbing the skills of the finest Seekers who'd ever lived, some of the most skilled swordsmen in the world.

He thrust at the cloaked man's chest with perfect technique, aiming unerringly for their heart.

The man dodged to the side at the last second, then slashed at Dante's neck!

Dante parried the blow…or tried to. The man pulled the attack back at the last minute. But the feint caused the enemy to lose his balance, stumbling backward. Dante lunged forward, slashing at the guy, but the man dodged easily, scooping dirt from the ground and flinging it right into Dante's face. He closed his eyes automatically, turning his head to one side…

…and felt a horrible pain in his belly, shooting right through to his back.

Dante gasped, opening his eyes and looking down. At the sword buried to the hilt in his abdomen. He gasped, staring at it in disbelief, his sword slipping out of his hands and falling to the ground beside him.

The cloaked figure lifted one black boot, kicking Dante in the hip. Agony burst through his belly as he lurched backward, the sword sliding free from his body. He fell onto his butt, his back slamming into a tree trunk behind him. He stared up at the cloaked figure, clutching his belly with both hands. There was a dagger at his hip, but he didn't bothering reaching for it. It was futile, he knew.

He was already dead.

Dante stared up at his attacker, feeling hot blood pour from between his fingers. The cloaked man stood there, facing him silently. Then they reached up with one hand, grabbing the edge of their hood and pulling it back.

Dante's breath caught in his throat.

It was a young man, he realized. With skin nearly as dark as the night sky, and black eyes that glittered in the moonlight. His hair was so short he was almost bald.

"You've just attacked two Seekers," Dante growled, grimacing as a fresh wave of pain shot through his belly.

"Damn right," the man agreed. He raised the tip of his sword, pressing it against Dante's breastbone.

"You must have a death wish," Dante muttered. "They'll find out about this," he added. "You'll have to face the entire guild now."

The man's lips curled into a smirk.

"That's the idea."

"You're a dead man," Dante promised. When the man didn't respond, he grimaced, shoving the tip of the man's sword away from his chest with one hand. "What are you after?" he added. "The artifact?"

"That," the man answered, "…and information."

"What information?" Dante pressed. Not that it mattered…he wouldn't live to relay the information. But he was curious.

"About the guild," he replied. "And a certain artifact they stole."

Dante gave the man a smug smile.

"Over my dead body," he muttered.

The man shrugged, flipping his sword around so he was carrying it backward, gripping the blade with both hands.

"Works for me."

And then he swung his sword over his head, chopping downward at Dante's face.

CHAPTER I

Hunter knelt before the Seeker he'd killed, ignoring the ache in his thigh as he did so. Even after two weeks, the two gashes he'd suffered there hadn't fully healed. The pain was a constant reminder of Traven, the Seeker who'd tried to kill him...and who'd killed his best friend Vi.

He closed his eyes, the image of Traven's warhammer coming down at his head flashing in his mind's eye. The last thing Vi had seen before her death. A memory he'd absorbed from her, just as readily as he was able to absorb emotions from others, or skills. Or any other trait, for that matter. For unlike on Earth, in this world *all* traits were potentially transferable.

Hunter opened his eyes, staring down at the dead Seeker. At the deep, ugly wound he'd made in the guy's skull. He'd killed Traven the same way, after the guy had double-crossed him and Vi. After Traven had betrayed them both to get the severed head of the leader of the Ironclad, the prize Duke Dominus had hired Vi and the Seekers to retrieve.

And it had been Dominus that'd ordered Vi's death...and Hunter's.

Hunter felt an all-too-familiar pang of grief, and forced it aside, gritting his teeth. He'd wasted enough time wallowing in self-pity. Hell, he'd spent most of his life playing the victim. Grieving over losing his mother when he was eight, blaming his alcoholic father for ruining his life. Letting the kingdom turn him into a sex addict. He refused to be a victim anymore, to let people push him around.

What was done was done. Dominus and the Seekers had screwed Vi over, and left Hunter for dead. And that would prove to be their biggest mistake.

Get the head, Hunter recited to himself. *Take back what they killed Vi for. Get stronger. Then kill them all.*

He rummaged through the Seeker's pockets, finding a few coins and not much else. The Seeker wore a half-dozen rings on his fingers; Hunter pulled these off, stuffing them in his cloak. He had no idea what kind of traits the rings contained, but they might be valuable. *Any* artifacts were potentially valuable, if absorbing their traits made him stronger. Faster.

Better.

He finished searching the man, finding nothing more of value. He didn't bother taking the guy's weapons, knowing that his own were far superior. They'd been owned by Vi, after all...the best fighter he'd ever met. The best in the world. Nothing else could compare.

Hunter paused, staring at the man. Then he lowered himself to his hands and knees, turning the dead Seeker's head to one side, hiding the ghastly wound in the guy's forehead. He closed his eyes, bowing down and pressing his forehead against the man's temple. Almost immediately, images flashed before his mind's eye, coming to him in rapid succession. He didn't bother trying to process any of the images, letting them come and go as they pleased. They were the Seeker's memories, he knew. Fragments of memories, anyway. Incomplete, many of them uninterpretable.

And now they're mine.

Hunter felt the images fading, and lifted his forehead from the man's temple, rising to his feet. He turned to the fallen carriage, striding up to it. Both doors were open, revealing the cabin inside. It was strewn with broken glass and splintered wood; he ducked inside, looking around. The Seeker had mentioned an artifact...

He spotted an ornate wooden box lying next to the door, and knelt down, picking it up. He turned it in his hands, then focused his awareness inward. Studying himself. *Monitoring* himself.

No change.

The box had no effect on his emotions, then. If it'd absorbed any emotion, he would've known it. He was incredibly sensitive to emotion; merely being close to an object that had absorbed someone else's emotion would cause him to start feeling that emotion.

He studied the box, suddenly knowing that it contained an artifact. An illegal artifact, in fact, from the Kingdom of the Deep. It was not *his* memory, of course...there was no way he could've known that. It was the Seeker's. But it *felt* like his memory. It was still confusing, this new ability of his. A power he hadn't even noticed he'd had at first, but that was growing over time. According to Vi, it was an exceedingly rare gift, one that no one had possessed for over a century. Until now.

It wasn't just people that he could absorb memories from. He could absorb those of animals as well, even after death. And their deaths were usually their most powerful memory...a fact that had quickly converted him to a vegetarian.

Hunter stuffed the box into a large pocket in the inner lining of his cloak, walking through the carriage to the opposite door. He spotted a body lying on the ground nearby, the man he'd shot through the chest. Another

Seeker, probably. He stripped the man of his coins and a few trinkets, then leaned over, pressing his forehead against the man's temple. Again, images flitted by in rapid succession in his mind's eye.

Then he lifted his head, yanking the arrow from the man's chest and returning it to his quiver. He walked back to the first Seeker, pulling the arrow from the man's shin. He retrieved his bow, slinging it on his back, then strode away from the carriage, toward the three moons high above.

Two down, so many more to go.

* * *

By the time Hunter reached the edge of the forest, the sun was starting to peek out from above the horizon, its rays casting the clouds above in brilliant orange-red. He left the trees behind, walking forward into the clearing beyond, until the ground gave way suddenly, ending in a steep drop-off. Beyond, a massive, cylindrical canyon lay, dropping hundreds of feet to a lake below. He gazed down at it, spotting two small islands in the center. There was a house on the larger island, and a smaller building on the other one. A long wooden bridge connected the larger island to the shore of the lake, a crescent of rocky ground at the bottom of the canyon. A much shorter bridge connected the two islands.

He felt a pang of nostalgia then, remembering the first time he'd seen this canyon. The awe he'd felt.

Of course, he hadn't been alone then.

Hunter sighed, turning left to follow the edge of the canyon, eventually reaching a narrow path that spiraled down the side of the canyon wall, all the way to the bottom. He followed it, glancing over the edge as he went, remembering the fear he'd felt when he'd gone down it the first time. Vi had saved him from himself then, lending him her preternatural calm. He had no need of it now, of course. He had nothing to fear anymore; the worst that could happen to him had already happened to him.

And most of it was *his* fault.

He forced the thought out of his mind, knowing all-too-well where it led. He'd spent enough time wallowing in self-loathing. Not that he didn't have a good reason for it. He'd unwittingly killed his own mother after she'd mortally wounded Vi. And he'd murdered his brother the day he'd arrived in this terrible world, blowing the guy's face off with a revolver. A brother he'd never even known he had, one somehow transformed into a monster. One of the Ironclad.

Stop it.

Hunter focused, realizing he'd reached the bottom of the canyon. He veered rightward toward the long bridge, crossing it to reach the island where Vi's house was. He'd repaired the front door as best as he could, after it'd been smashed in by one of the Ironclad. Huge beasts with black armor and two pairs of arms, he'd thought of them as monsters...as the enemy. Until, that is, he'd gone into the Ironclad lair with Vi, and realized that his mother – the very person he'd traveled to this strange world to save – was their leader. Now Hunter knew who the *real* enemy was.

The Kingdom of Tykus...and Duke Dominus. And the guild.

Get the head. Get stronger. Kill them all.

He turned away from Vi's house, walking across the short bridge to the smaller island. This is where Vi had built her storehouse, a small building designed to hold powerful artifacts without contaminating the nearby environment. It'd been badly damaged by the Ironclad; Hunter had spent the last couple of weeks repairing it, replacing each brick and using clay from the lake as mortar. He'd rebuilt the walls, but had found the roof trickier to re-create. He was going to need the storehouse if he was to become a Seeker like Vi.

Hunter stopped before the storehouse, retrieving the wooden box from his cloak. He set it down on the ground, then got to work prying the thing apart. The Seeker's memories he'd absorbed were correct – the box contained a hidden obsidian container within, perhaps a foot long and half as wide. He withdrew this, opening it and looking inside.

There was a bone there, a long, narrow shaft. It looked like an upper arm bone...a humerus. It was thicker than he imagined a human's would be, with large, prominent bumps on the ends. He stared at it, waiting for a memory to be triggered. One of the Seeker's memories. But nothing came. The memories he absorbed were like that...fragmentary, incomplete. It seemed like the most powerful memories and most recent ones were the clearest; he certainly didn't absorb *all* of a person's memories. Just bits and pieces.

He paused, then picked up the bone, holding it in his hand. He closed his eyes, turning his focus inward.

No emotions came to him.

That meant that the bone contained traits other than emotions. He absorbed emotions the best, and skills a little above average. Physical traits he absorbed poorly, as best he could tell, and he didn't appear to absorb anyone's personality at all. He had a strong will, Vi had told him...one that resisted being changed. It'd been nearly as strong as Vi's.

Hunter opened his eyes, then walked up to the storehouse. There was a narrow moat surrounding it, filled with water from the lake. The water served to carrying away any traits that might radiate from an artifact held within, preventing those traits from being absorbed by the ground beyond the moat. This prevented contamination of the environment by particularly powerful artifacts. He climbed over the wall of the storehouse, dropping through an incomplete section of the roof. There was a square platform immersed in a half-inch of water inside, and he landed on it, then placed the bone upon it. That done, he climbed out of the storehouse, walking back across the small bridge.

He glanced at Vi's house, having the sudden urge to go inside. To feel Vi's presence again.

Don't do it.

He hesitated, stopping before her house, eyeing the front door. It'd been at least a week since he'd given in to the temptation. He'd promised himself that he wouldn't do this anymore, that he'd leave her be. Even though she was dead, her will lived on in the places she'd been, absorbed by the things she'd spent the most time near. All he had to do was go inside, and she would be there.

She's dead.

He was about to turn away when he spotted something in the air above her house. A black bird carrying something in its talons. It landed on her roof – on the chimney-like structure there – and dropped something into it. Then it flew away.

A carrier pigeon, Hunter realized. Vi had received a contract from a client from a carrier pigeon a few weeks ago, before they'd gone back to Tykus.

He hesitated for a moment longer, then walked up to the front door, opening it and stepping inside.

Everything was just as he'd left it.

A small bed sat in one corner, dolls and stuffed animals all around it. Vi's childhood possessions, filled with her essence. She'd kept them to restore her humanity after experimenting with wild artifacts. Weapons hung from the walls, each filled with the skills of ancient warriors. Only one was missing…the mace he'd taken two weeks ago, after returning from the Ironclad lair.

His gaze fell to a small opening in the wall, where the chimney-like structure – a mail chute – met the floor. There was a rolled-up piece of parchment there. He bent over to grab it, peeling off the wax seal and unrolling it. There was writing on the page, letters that resembled English, but were different enough to make reading them difficult. He studied it, interpreting as best he could:

> *V –*
> *Need to speak with you. New job, usual perks.*
> *– C*

Hunter stared at the page, feeling a burst of excitement. It was one of Vi's clients, that was certain. Without the support of the Guild of Seekers, and without knowing any of Vi's clients, he'd resorted to staking out the King's Road, waiting for carriages to pass and intercepting them in hopes of retrieving artifacts. He'd had to wait a few days for the last carriage to come, and he'd been lucky that it'd been a Seeker carriage. The last two carriages he'd ambushed hadn't carried anything of value at all. Two weeks of hunting, and he had very little to show for it. Sooner or later word would get out that someone was attacking the carriages, and he had no doubt that soldiers would be sent to patrol the road. It wouldn't be long before he'd have to abandon that strategy…and he hadn't come up with a backup plan yet.

But if he could get access to Vi's clients…

He rolled the paper back up, then paused, bringing it to his forehead. Vi's client's memories might have been absorbed by the parchment, after all. He waited.

An image came to his mind's eye, of a woman lying curled-up in a bed. The vision dissipated rapidly, far too quickly for him to make sense of it.

Damn.

Still, he had an initial – C – and he'd absorbed some of Vi's memories, as well as this client's. A woman, he knew, without knowing how. It might be enough to find this client. And if the client could point him in the direction of Vi's other clients, he might just have a chance at accumulating a lot of powerful artifacts like Vi had. Artifacts that would make him stronger, faster, and more skilled. Powerful enough to take on Duke Dominus…and the Seekers.

Hunter nodded to himself, shoving the paper into one of the pockets in his cloak. He left the house, closing and locking the door behind him. Then he walked back across the long bridge back to the shore, to his makeshift bed near the narrow path winding back up the canyon. He laid down on the dirt and leaves, holding his sword – *Vi's* sword – in his arms, and his bow. The more time he spent with them, the more of their skills he would absorb.

He closed his eyes, feeling suddenly exhausted. He'd been sleeping during the day for the last week, and hunting during the middle of the night, in the cover of darkness.

Somehow he knew that he needed to go west from the canyon to get to this woman's house…no doubt from the memories he'd taken from Vi, or from this client. He'd have to start his journey after he woke up, and trust that their memories would guide him through the forest. If not, he'd just go back to Vi's place. He couldn't afford to leave Vi's house unguarded for too long, of course…not with the veritable treasure trove of artifacts she'd collected. But a few days wouldn't hurt.

Maybe, just maybe, this client would be able to help him get his revenge.

CHAPTER 2

Dominus sat up in bed, squinting against the bright light shining through the windows of his bedroom. He waited for his eyes to adjust, putting a hand on the sheet covering him.

To his surprise, he found that it was dry.

He was even more surprised that he'd woken up at all. High fevers had wracked his body all day yesterday, coming in terrible waves, their arrival heralded by uncontrollable shaking. He only remembered bits and pieces of the last few days, the infection that had spread from the bones of his right leg to his bloodstream having made him delirious. In the few moments of lucidity he'd been granted, he'd expected the worst: that he was going to succumb to his illness. That those terrible moments would be that last of his life.

He frowned, then threw off the sheet covering him, exposing his legs. He stared at his right leg, unable to stop himself from grimacing. Bandages were wrapped around it from the knee down, those covering his foot stained with pink and yellow secretions. He waited for the stench of rotting flesh to assault his nostrils. But none came.

Interesting.

He leaned over, untying one end of the dressing from his leg, then unwrapping it, exposing his mutilated foot. He grimaced again, staring at what remained of his limb. The toes amputated, a deep ulcer on the bony knob on the right side of his ankle. A consequence of his dread disease, the flesh rotting as its lifeblood was choked off bit by bit. Yesterday, the gangrene – wet, black flesh – had extended halfway up to his knee, angry red streaks winding up his leg to his groin, where painful lumps had grown. But now…

His breath caught in his throat, gooseflesh rising on his arms.

The red streaks were gone…and the skin at his shin was no longer completely black. Islands of pink flesh had grown there.

Dominus stared at them, hardly believing his eyes.

It's working.

He looked at his foot, at the stumps of his midfoot. To his surprise, he saw pink flesh growing from around the exposed bone there…and tiny blood vessels growing within the thin, transparent membrane covering those bones. Even the ulcer on the side of his ankle was a bit shallower, new flesh visible at its base.

Dominus smiled, a chuckle escaping his lips. Then he began to laugh, tears brimming in his eyes and dripping down his cheeks.

It's working!

He turned then, to look at the rug before his bureau. A trapdoor lay hidden beneath, to a small cubby that held an obsidian chest. The very chest that Edgar, the Seeker, had retrieved for him. Inside this was the head of a very special Ironclad, one with a unique gift. The ability to regenerate…to heal from any wound.

And now, after weeks of exposure to its flesh, it had finally given that gift to him.

Dominus laughed again, finally allowing himself to have hope. Hope that he might survive this horrible disease, that he might live for a while longer, to find a suitable heir to the Duchy of Wexford. His son Conlan was dead, his protégé Axio now in line for the throne. With little time left to live, Dominus had resorted to securing a lackluster heir, a relative of meager will and ability. Like so much of humanity, the man was a disappointment.

Now he had a chance to do better…to secure the future of the Duchy, and that of the kingdom itself.

There was a knock on the door.

"Yes?" Dominus called out.

"Are you all right, your Grace?" a voice inquired from beyond his bedroom door. It was Farkus, his loyal servant.

"Quite alright," Dominus replied. "Come in," he added.

The door opened, and Farkus stepped through. He was older even than Dominus, in his late seventies. He'd been tall once, but now his back was stooped with age. He had long silver hair, and his face was smooth-shaven, in the manner of all servants. Farkus gave a short bow, his gaze then drawn inexorably to Dominus's right leg. To the man's credit, he said nothing.

"Send two dozen of my soldiers to Vi's home," Dominus ordered.

"At once, your Grace," Farkus replied. But he did not leave, knowing full well that Dominus was not finished. After spending over three decades with his master, Farkus had absorbed Dominus's superior will, becoming so much like him that anyone seeing them for the first time would assume they were brothers.

"Tell them to retrieve all of her artifacts," Dominus continued, "...and destroy her house."

"Of course, your Grace," Farkus replied.

"That is all," Dominus stated.

Farkus bowed, then hesitated, glancing at Dominus's leg again.

"Shall I retrieve your will, your Grace?" he inquired. Dominus smirked.

"Yes."

Farkus left him then, and Dominus sighed, throwing the sheet back over his legs. There was a great deal for him to do in the coming days, not the least of which was dealing with the aftermath of Vi's death...and the consequences of his actions against the Guild of Seekers. He'd bought off one of their Seekers, after all, and stolen the head of the Ironclad from them. It was perhaps the most valuable Ossae ever discovered, and the guild knew it. They would undoubtedly send Seekers to retrieve Vi's personal possessions, wanting nothing more than to gain her incredible skills. And Dominus had a suspicion that High Seeker Zeno – the leader of the guild – would be terribly eager to retrieve the Ironclad's head as well.

The guild would be stupid to go against Dominus, of course. He was the Duke of Wexford, second only in power to King Tykus himself. But Dominus knew that it was folly to underestimate his opponents. He had to assume the worst, and plan for it.

There was another knock at the door, and Farkus returned, carrying a rolled-up piece of parchment in one hand. He walked up to the side of the bed, handing it to Dominus...along with a small glass tube. Dominus smiled.

"Thank you Farkus."

"Do you require anything else, your Grace?" Farkus inquired.

"No."

Farkus bowed, then left, closing the door behind him. Dominus set the metal tube on the bed, then turned to the rolled-up parchment in his hand, unrolling it and glancing at the large, perfect letters at the top. "Last Will & Testament," it read.

Dominus stared at it for a long moment, then got out of bed, crumpling the document into a loose ball and throwing it in a metal wastebasket. He retrieved the tube from the bed then; there was a syringe at the top, with some tinder visible at the bottom of the tube. It was a fire piston, technology reverse-engineered from a similar device brought by an Original hundreds of years ago.

He depressed the plunger quickly, compressing the air inside...and superheating it. The tinder at the bottom of the tube burst into flames, and Dominus pulled the plunger out of the tube quickly, tipping the tube over the wastebasket, spilling the burning tinder into it.

Then he watched as the flames grew, devouring his Will. One future ending in fire, with the promise of something new rising from the ashes.

He waited until the flames died away completely, ignoring the smoke filling his room. He hardly cared that it stung his eyes, or that its stench would taint his fine bedding. Farkus would see to their cleansing.

Dominus turned away from the embers of his will, limping up to his nightstand and grabbing the cane that was leaning against it. Hidden within was a spring-loaded sword, a weapon that, in his hands, was exceedingly deadly. He turned to gaze out of his bedroom window, at the huge expanse of his gardens far below. He'd been given a second chance, one that he had no intention of wasting. There was no telling how much time he had left; he needed to act quickly and decisively.

He turned away from the window, limping toward his bedroom door.

It was time for him to write a *new* future.

* * *

The sun had reached its peak in the sky overhead by the time Hunter made it through the Fringe, emerging into the deep forest beyond. Everything was a little different here, he found. The flora of the Fringe resembled foliage one might find on Earth. But here, everything was…mixed up. The grass underfoot had a thin layer of bark at the base of each blade, and crunched under his boots. There were still trees, of course, but some of them had leaves that resembled huge blades of grass. Bugs crawled on the ground, many of them hard to spot because of their woody carapaces. Some of the trees even had spikey hairs on their bark, reminding Hunter of porcupine quills.

It was all very strange…and the deeper he went into the forest, the stranger it got.

Some trees were segmented, like a centipede, with branches coming off at different angles from each segment. Others went up, then arched over to plunge into the ground, rising back up to form more arches, like a serpent. He'd even spotted something that looked like a walking bush…an animal the size of a large dog, with six spindly legs and branch-like things sprouting from its back. Hunter had kept his distance, but to his relief, the creature had paid him no mind.

It was, he realized, the logical result of the bizarre laws of this world, that each organism could give its traits to nearby creatures. Why the Fringe had little of this variation, he had no idea…but there had to be a reason.

Hunter grimaced at the dull ache in his legs as he walked, particularly in his shins. He was in much better shape than he'd been even when Vi had been alive, but he was still no match for her. He had a long way to go before he gained her strength and endurance…which he had every intention of doing. To become as good as Vi, he needed to train like her. He had to be better every single day.

He focused ahead, spotting a large hill in the distance, the trees starting to thin out. They gave way gradually to huge blades of grass, nearly half the height of the trees themselves. He reached these, having to part the blades with his hands as he continued forward. It was like walking through a corn field back in Wisconsin, where his dad had been born. Eventually, the grass grew shorter and shorter as he went, dwindling to a relatively normal height ahead…and giving him a better view of the hill.

Hunter slowed, feeling a sudden sense of déjà vu.

I've been here before.

That, of course, was impossible. It had to be a memory he'd absorbed…Vi's, or this client's. Or maybe even from one of the Seekers he'd killed. He knew that he should go rightward, following the edge of the hill. Why, he had no idea…it just seemed right. Back on Earth, he would almost certainly have ignored this intuition, but now he let it guide him.

Onward he went, staying on a natural path at the foot of the hill, following it as it curved leftward. He spotted something moving off to his right, and froze. It was another one of the animals he'd seen before, the creature that'd looked like a walking bush. This one was considerably larger, about the size of a deer. It had only four legs, and limped along slowly, like a sloth. It paid him no mind, but still he waited for it to pass further into the trees before he started walking again.

Eventually the path led *through* the hill, dipping down to form a valley of sorts that split the hill in two. Vertical cliff walls some twenty feet high flanked the path, casting a shadow over it. Hunter hesitated, retrieving the letter once again and putting it up to his forehead for a moment. He put it away then, staring at the path, waiting to feel something. But he felt nothing…no memory was jogged, no sense of déjà vu. All he felt was a sense of unease…but was that an emotion he was absorbing, or his own feeling?

He grimaced, glancing back the way he'd come. There was no other way for him to go now, and his absorbed memories had led him here. He had no desire to backtrack, especially if it meant risking that he'd lose his way. He had to stay the course.

Hunter continued along the path, and after a few minutes it opened up into a large clearing, the short grass underfoot starting to crunch under his boots. He paused, kneeling down, and found that there was bark on the shafts of each blade…and that on some, tiny leaves sprouted from the stem. He stood, gazing forward. The grass-tree hybrids grew taller further out, eventually leading to a huge tree in the center of the clearing, some sixty feet away. It had a wide trunk with silver bark that looked like the skin of an elephant, and thick branches that extended outward almost horizontally. Its leaves were silver on the bottom and green on top, and its roots extended outward in all directions, covered with thick bark. All around the tree grew other trees with similar bark, but these were smaller and misshapen, with twisted trunks and stunted branches. There was barely any room between each tree, so densely had they grown together.

Hunter eyed the trees, then the steep cliff walls flanking the clearing. There was just enough room between the two for him to squeeze by the densely-packed smaller trees. He continued forward, staying close to the rightmost wall. Reaching the first of the trees, he stepped between it and the wall, squeezing past. He passed another tree, then another.

Something grabbed his shoulder from behind.

Hunter spun around, jerking his shoulder away, his sword somehow already in his hands. But when he looked, no one was there…just one of the trees he'd squeezed past. He took a step backward, his sword in front of him, his eyes darting from tree to tree. But he saw nothing.

Huh.

Then a branch of the tree in front of him swayed downward with a sudden breeze, touching him on the shoulder. He took a step back, and it slid off. He sheathed his sword, shaking his head.

Spooked by a tree, he mused. *Some warrior I am!*

He was about to turn around when the branch swayed down again, barely missing him. It stayed down then, and he stared at it.

There'd been no breeze this time.

His eyes went to the tree itself; it was deformed like the others, with two trunks rising a couple of feet to merge into a single trunk. Three branches sprouted from this, one on either side and one in the middle. There were knobby growths on the central branch, at its base…and something else.

Hunter leaned forward, peering at it. There were two small holes at the base of the central branch, and a deep gash below these. Something white was visible deep within that gash; he walked up to the tree to get a closer look, then jerked backward, his breath catching in his throat.

They were *teeth.*

He stared at them, then at the two holes above. Something glittered within each of them. A chill ran down his spine as he realized what they were.

Eyes…staring right at *him.*

He took a step back, staring at the twin trunks, unable to help noticing the slight bend in the middle of them. Or the bits of fabric poking out of a few clefts in the bark.

The gash moved suddenly, almost imperceptibly, a sound coming from it. Clear liquid drooled out of one corner of the gash, dribbling down the bark.

Hunter swallowed in a dry throat, staring at the thing, dread coming over him. He had the sudden urge to run, to sprint away from this clearing and go back the way he'd come.

I never should have come here, he thought.

It made the noise again.

Against every impulse, he stepped forward, leaning in. The gash moved again, a faint whisper coming from it.

"Kill…" it wheezed.

Hunter stared at it, hardly believing his ears.

"What?" he asked.

"Kill…" it repeated.

Hunter backed away from it, drawing out his longsword and holding it before him. He glanced at the other trees surrounding him, half-expecting them to turn and attack him.

"…me."

He blinked.

Those two glittering eyes stared at him, more drool dripping from the corner of the thing's mouth. For that was what it was…a mouth. His eyes went to the thing's two main branches, each bent in the middle, like arms. Twigs sprouted from the end of each branch like fingers.

"Kill…me," it rasped.

Hunter felt goosebumps rise on his arms, and he took another step back, holding his sword between himself and the…thing.

"Why?" he asked.

The tree said nothing, merely staring at him. He hesitated, then reached out with one hand, touching one of its branches. All he felt was cool, dry bark; no images came to him, no memories. He withdrew his hand, staring at the thing's eyes. Then he leaned in, placing his forehead just above those eyes.

And felt immediate, overwhelming terror.

Get out!

He jerked his hand away, backpedaling quickly, his heart pounding. Though he'd only touched the tree for a moment, he knew without a doubt what it was.

This thing is human!

Hunter had the sudden, powerful urge to get the hell out of here. To go back the way he'd come, to go back home – to Vi's home – and never come back. He resisted it, knowing full well that urge was not coming from him. It was coming from this tree.

He closed his eyes, recalling the memories he'd been given. They felt like his own, indistinguishable save that it didn't make sense for them to be his. He…or rather, the thing in front of him…had been a man once. He'd been following this path when he'd come up to the big tree in the middle of the clearing. There'd been fewer smaller trees then – it'd been nearly a year ago – and he'd been exhausted. He'd decided to set up camp by the big tree, and had curled up next to it, falling asleep.

And when he'd woken the next morning, something had been terribly wrong.

He'd tried to get up, but his body had been terribly stiff. He remembered looking down, seeing his skin covered with thin bark. He'd smashed his arms and legs against the ground to crack the bark so he could move better, and blood had oozed from the wounds. After what'd seemed like an eternity, he'd managed to get to his feet, and he'd started walking away. Slowly, painfully. One step at a time, each step taking hours.

But with each hour that'd passed, the bark on his limbs had grown a little thicker, making it harder and harder to move. After a few days – or maybe longer – he'd stopped at this very spot, unable to move at all. Over the weeks that had followed, roots had sprung from his legs, plunging into the dirt, anchoring him here for eternity.

Hunter opened his eyes, staring at the tree's twisted face.

"Kill..." it rasped. "...me."

He hesitated, gripping the hilt of his longsword with both hands. If he did kill this thing, he'd be taking the life of an innocent man. Or at least what had once been a man. But to *not* kill him would be to sentence the guy to a fate worse than death. The man was trapped in his own body, unable to escape. He had no quality of life whatsoever. It would be cruel to not grant him his wish. But it would be murder if he did.

Hunter grimaced, knowing that with each minute that passed, he was putting himself at risk of suffering the same fate. He glanced at the big tree in the center of the clearing, knowing without a doubt that it was a Legend. A living being with a will so powerful that it could change everything around it into something like itself. He'd never imagined that a plant could be a Legend, but the man before him was proof that it was possible.

Hunter took a deep breath in, steeling himself. Then he nodded.

"Okay," he agreed.

He strode up to the tree, tightening his grip on his longsword, the hilt feeling slippery in his sweaty palms. He planted his feet, then swung his sword as hard as he could, aiming for just below the tree's open maw. He threw his hips into the motion, his blade striking true. It sank an inch into the bark, then stopped, lodging there.

The tree screamed.

Hunter yanked the blade free, stumbling backward. Thin, reddish sap poured from the gash made by his sword, and the tree screamed again, the awful sound echoing through the clearing. Hunter took a step back, then turned to run.

"Kill...me!"

He stopped, turning to face the tree again. Its eyes were locked on him, bloody sap still seeping from the wound below its mouth. Hunter swallowed past a lump in his throat, wiping one sweaty hand, then the other, on his pants. There was no way he'd be able to chop through the tree's neck in one blow. Or two, or even three.

"I'm sorry," he stated, shaking his head. "I can't."

"Do…it," came the raspy reply.

Hunter clenched his jaw, tightening his grip on his sword. He couldn't just leave the man here, wounded and in pain. Hunter knew all too well the power of his conscience. It never forgot, nor did it forgive easily. If Hunter didn't put this tree…this *man* – out of his misery, it would be a decision that would follow Hunter wherever he went, haunting him for the rest of his life.

He set his jaw then, taking a deep breath in, then letting it out.

"I'm sorry," he repeated.

And then he charged forward, swinging his sword as hard as he could. The blade struck true, hitting the tree exactly where it had the first time, sinking deeper into its woody flesh. Sap flew out with the force of the blow, splattering Hunter's clothes.

The tree *howled.*

Hunter grimaced, bracing himself and yanking his sword free. He swung again, chopping deeper into the tree. Again and again he swung, ignoring the tree's agonizing screams as his blade sank further into its flesh.

At length, his blade chopped through a hollow tube in the trunk, and mercifully, the screaming stopped.

Still, those glittering eyes stared at him, wide with pain. He could *feel* the man-tree's terror, and knew that it was still alive. Again he swung at it, his arms burning now, his muscles tiring quickly. He resisted the urge to stop, knowing that every second he gave himself to rest, he would prolong this poor creature's suffering.

So he continued, long past the point of exhaustion, until at last the deed was done.

When he'd finished, Hunter stumbled away from the severed head, his sword slipping out of his hands and falling onto the ground. He fell against the angled cliff wall, leaning on it, his breath coming in ragged gasps. Sliding to his buttocks, he looked down at his cloak, finding it covered with bloody sap.

Bile surged up into his mouth, and he vomited.

The nausea passed quickly, and he tried wiping the sap away with his hands. But it was no use; he took the cloak off, tossing it aside. He hesitated, then leaned over to grab it, using the inner layer to wipe off his face and hands. Then he threw it away again, rising unsteadily to his feet. He resisted the urge to glance at the severed stump, grabbing his sword and wiping the blade on the grass underfoot. Then he sheathed it, turning away from the trees and continuing forward down the path. Eventually the clearing ended, the cliff walls gradually closing until they were only a dozen feet apart from each other. His muscles felt like lead, every step a herculean effort.

A sudden pang of fear gripped him, and he looked down at his hands, half-expecting them to be covered with thin bark. But he saw only his skin.

He pulled up his sleeves, running a hand over one forearm, and found the skin smooth and soft.

Thank god.

Still, he felt a little stiff, and couldn't help but wonder if the tree's influence was already working its power on him. He chided himself, knowing that it was probably all in his head. He was fine. He was strong-willed, after all. Vi herself had said he resisted change…in his physical appearance as well as his personality.

You're fine, he told himself.

Or was he?

Hunter continued forward, getting as far away from the Legendary tree and its victim – or victims – as he could. Whether or not the tree had changed him, even in the slightest, he'd probably never know. But it was clear that it was possible. The memories he'd so casually absorbed from the people he'd touched – Vi, Traven, and the Seekers he'd killed, not to mention that tree – had *already* changed him. It was hard enough trying to remember which memories were his and which were not….and it would only get harder with each additional memory he absorbed. Sure, he might have a strong personality, but what would that really matter if he lost track of which past was his?

He knew one thing for sure: if he wasn't careful about who and what he exposed himself to, he was going to deeply regret it.

Chapter 3

The triple moons of Varta shone overhead, the lesser light of countless stars struggling to penetrate the dense clouds approaching from the west. To the human eye, these pinpricks of light would be dull, barely visible, and the forest they looked down upon would be frightfully dark.

But Xerxes was not human…and he was not afraid.

To him, the moons shone like lesser suns, the stars shimmering like diamonds in the infinite blackness of the night sky. Their light bathed the forest in a silver glow, every detail of the trees – their rough bark, their leaves – visible with a sharpness and contrast that would amaze any human.

Xerxes strode through the forest, this place the humans called the Fringe. Grass, leaf litter, and twigs crunched under the thick black plates of armor covering the soles of his feet, smashed into pieces by his formidable weight. Creatures hiding in the shadows spooked at the sight of him, bolting away as quickly as they could. And they were wise to do so; at over eight feet tall, his entire body covered in thick black armor, and two pairs of powerful arms, Xerxes was an Ironclad…one of a race of creatures so dangerous that few would dare stand against them.

And of all the Ironclad, Xerxes was by far the most dangerous. Except of course for the Queen.

He felt his tail twitch, swinging to one side, then the other irritably. A thick, translucent membrane extended from the top of his head and all the way down his spine, terminating in a broad-based tail that ended at knee-height. Filled with glowing blue gel, the thing seemed to have a mind of its own. He could control it if he wanted to, but if not, it did what it pleased. And to those wise enough to watch it, it showed them exactly how he was feeling.

He heard the *thump, thump* of dozens of other Ironclad behind him, and quickened his pace, not bothering to turn around to see if they would do the same. They were his soldiers, loyal to him without question. He was the son of the Queen, after all. They all had a piece of her will within them, molding them into her image. They lived and died at her command…and she had commanded them to obey *him.*

Xerxes spotted a break in the forest ahead. It was the end of the tree line…they were almost there. He continued forward, putting up one hand and flashing a few rapid hand signals.

"If he attacks you," he signed. "Do not fight back."

They obeyed, staying well behind him. They would not risk getting too close, as doing so would expose them to his aura. The Queen forbade it.

He continued forward as silently as possible, giddiness coming over him. The same feeling he'd had when he'd seen a young man appear out of thin air in the Deadlands a month ago, falling to the ground, his limbs jerking uncontrollably. A man with dark skin. Xerxes hadn't known for sure who the man was, but the few vague memories he'd absorbed from his mother had made it clear who the stranger *could* be. Someone they'd been waiting for for nearly half a century: Hunter.

My brother.

And despite impossible odds, it *had* been Hunter. But the Kingdom had gotten to him first.

Xerxes felt an all-too-familiar anger grow within him, and he let it, grinding his teeth as he walked to the edge of the forest. He passed the end of the tree line, emerging from the forest. The Kingdom had taken everything from him and his mother. From their people. When they'd taken Hunter…

I'm coming, brother.

He felt a burst of elation at the thought, of finally reuniting with his brother. Of being able to speak with him at last, without interruption. Without anyone or anything getting in the way. To be able to tell Hunter everything that had happened to them, and to finally get to know his brother.

To be a family again.

It wasn't long before Xerxes found himself standing near the edge of a cliff, a few dozen meters beyond the forest line. He stopped, gazing downward to see a familiar sight: a large, cylindrical canyon a hundred or so meters below, with a lake at the bottom. Countless waterfalls cascaded down the sides of the canyon in a huge circle, rivers emptying into it in an endless stream.

He spotted the two small buildings sitting on islands in the middle of the lake below. And something else…tiny orange lights forming a long line across the bridge spanning the lake.

He clenched his four fists, his eyes widening.

They were soldiers, he realized. Nearly twenty of them, almost certainly from the Kingdom. Carrying torches and moving toward the house on the larger island.

Toward *Hunter.*

Xerxes bolted to the left, sprinting along the edge of the cliff toward a narrow path hugging the canyon wall, one leading downward toward the shore far below. He ran as fast as he could, hardly fearing the hundred-meter drop a fraction of a meter to his right. With his glowing mane and tail, the enemy would be sure to spot him in the darkness, but he didn't care. Faster he went, pushing his body to the limit.

The soldiers reached the end of the bridge, rushing toward the house in the distance. One of the soldiers reached the front door, taking a warhammer out and winding up to swing it at the door.

Xerxes roared, the sound echoing through the canyon. He pivoted, leaping over the edge of the path, hardly caring that he was only halfway down. Free-fall gripped his gut, the wind shrieking past him as he accelerated toward the rocky shore, still fifty meters below.

Downward he plunged, the ground rushing up to meet him.

And then he smashed into the ground, the world going black.

He fought the void, clutching on to consciousness. Pain tore through him, agony beyond description. His vision returned quickly, and he saw himself lying on the ground on his belly. Saw one of his arms outstretched, bent at an impossible angle, white bone protruding from his shattered armor, blood spurting from the wound.

And as he watched, the bleeding slowed, then stopped.

The torn flesh knit together rapidly, starting from the edges, near the undamaged tissue. His arm straightened, the ends of his bones realigning, the armor covering it sloughing off, replaced by a thin layer of fresh, new armor. This thickened as he watched, his pain peaking, then quickly abating.

He grunted, pulling his arms underneath him and pushing himself up from the ground. He stood then, hunks of shattered armor falling from his chest and belly, already replaced by smooth armor underneath. Glancing across the wooden bridge, he spotted the soldier near the door swinging his hammer against the door, which burst open under the impact. Soldiers rushed into the house, their weapons drawn.

Hunter!

Xerxes roared again, bursting forward, bounding up to the bridge. A few soldiers were still standing on it, near the middle. They turned at the sound of his voice, their eyes widening as they saw what was coming for them. But the soldiers who'd gone into the house didn't come out.

Xerxes closed the gap between himself and the nearest soldier, lunging at the man. The soldier backpedaled, swinging his warhammer awkwardly. But he was too slow; Xerxes rammed his shoulder into the soldier, sending the man flying into the lake.

Another soldier rushed him, chopping down at his chest with their warhammer.

Xerxes didn't bother to block the blow, letting it strike him full-on. The hammer bounced off his thick armor, the ricochet making the soldier stumble backward.

He grabbed the soldier by the upper arms, lifting the man off of the bridge and slamming his armored forehead into the man's face. The soldier's head snapped backward, blood spurting from his shattered nose. Xerxes threw him down so hard he bounced off the bridge, careening into the lake.

Then he turned to the soldiers huddled at the other end of the bridge, charging at them.

They backpedaled rapidly, forming a loose "U" around the end of the bridge, their warhammers at the ready. Xerxes sprinted right at them, reaching the end of the bridge and charging at the nearest soldier. The man backed away, the soldiers flanking Xerxes forming a circle around him. He ignored them, barreling forward, his eyes on the house ahead.

Something smashed into the back of his leg, throwing him down onto his hands and knees on the ground. He grunted, turning to see a warhammer chopping down at him…right before it struck his temple.

Pain exploded through his skull, his vision blackening.

Anger turned to rage.

Another blow slammed into the middle of his back, then another, and he roared, lashing out blindly with one arm. He felt it strike something, and he clung on, rising to his feet. It was one of the soldiers' warhammers, he realized.

He tore it out of the man's hands, swinging it in a wild circle as if the massive weapon weighed nothing, striking one of the soldiers in the temple. Their head snapped to the side in a spray of blood and brain matter, the sheer force of the blow sending the man flying through the air.

He landed on the packed dirt, never to move again.

Xerxes swung the hammer again, smashing it into another soldier's skull. He tossed the hammer away then, feeling more blows rain down on him. He allowed it for a moment, the pain feeding his rage, stoking his bloodlust. It built up within him, bringing him to a place beyond thought or reason.

To ecstasy.

He roared, grabbing the nearest soldier by the arms and lifting them clear off the ground. Xerxes forced the man's arms out to the sides, using his second pair of arms to pummel the man's chest over and over again. Ribs caved in under his fists, organs rupturing with the sheer power of the blows. He yanked the soldier's arms out to the sides as hard as he could then; the man's shoulders tore out of their sockets, tendons popping loudly.

Then the skin tore, one the man's arms ripping free from his body, blood spurting from the gaping wound.

Xerxes tossed the man at another soldier, knocking him flat on his back. Xerxes leapt on the man then, tearing at the soldier's face with his fingers, ripping the flesh from the man's bones. The bloodlust peaked, its power nearly orgasmic.

He grabbed the man's butchered face, slamming the back of their skull against the ground over and over again, until they moved no more.

A hammer smashed into the back of Xerxes' skull, snapping his head downward.

He leapt to his feet, swinging in a blind fury, using all four arms to smash or grab anyone nearby. His fist collided with a soldier's head, shattering the man's skull. He grabbed another soldier's hammer, tearing it from their hands and tossing it aside, then grabbing their head and plunging his massive thumbs into their eye sockets. They shrieked as their eyeballs ruptured, clear fluid pouring down their cheeks.

Pain shot through his left knee as a warhammer smashed into it, the armor there cracking. He fell to his knees, then lunged at the soldier who'd attacked him, shoving the man to the ground and landing on top of them. Xerxes' fists rose and fell, pummeling the man's face and body again and again. Then he rose to his feet, his knee already healed.

The remaining soldiers backed away from him, their eyes wide with terror.

He lunged at them, tearing through them one by one. Some turned to run, others tried to fight.

They all failed.

He beat them, tore at them. Snapped their limbs and smashed in their skulls, until there was no one left to kill…not even the soldiers that'd rushed out of the house to attack him.

And when he was done, Xerxes stood a few meters from that house, covered in the blood of his enemies, his heart pounding in his chest. His rage – that wondrous, incredible rush – faded slowly, and he looked around, wanting nothing more than to feed it a while longer, to lose himself in the pleasure it promised. It was then that he saw his Ironclad striding across the bridge toward him, staring at the carnage he'd wrought.

One of them stopped a few meters before him, fingers of one hand moving rapidly.

"Hunter?" it signed.

Xerxes turned to the house, striding up to the door and ducking down to step inside, the top of his head still scraping against the ceiling. He saw no one there…just a bed, some weapons on the walls. He grimaced, stepping back outside to face his men.

"Not here," he signed back, feeling profoundly irritated. He suddenly wished he'd ignored his mother and come for Hunter sooner, before his wounds had fully healed. She'd forbidden it, and now Hunter was missing. He clenched his fists.

If his brother was dead, it was *her* fault.

Xerxes grit his teeth, pushing the thought out of his mind. He felt his anger draining away, and he missed it, wanting nothing more than to feel it again. To have the bloodlust take over, and make him lash out and destroy anything in his way.

"A survivor," one Ironclad signed, pointing at one of the soldiers lying on the ground. The man was badly injured, his face bloodied and one arm bent at an impossible angle. Xerxes grunted, striding up to the man and signaling for an Ironclad to pick him up. They did so, hauling the man to his feet.

The soldier screamed, his broken arm dangling limply at his side.

Xerxes stepped right up to him, looking down at the man. Nearly a meter taller than the soldier, Xerxes towered over him…and when the soldier looked up at Xerxes, his eyes widened in terror. Wetness spread over the front of his pants.

"Please," the soldier pleaded. "Don't kill me!"

Xerxes stared down at him, saying nothing.

"Please," the soldier begged, tears dripping down his cheeks. The man was shaking, sweat beading up on his skin.

"WHERE IS…HUNTER?" Xerxes demanded, his voice deep and raspy. Each word took effort to produce, forcing each sound from his throat. He'd been able to speak well once, like mother. Before he'd changed.

The soldier's jaw dropped, no doubt shocked that Xerxes could speak. They all reacted the same way. So predictable. Except for that one woman, the one who'd cut off his head.

"WHERE?" Xerxes repeated, glaring at the man.

"I don't know," the soldier answered. "We came here to grab Vi's stuff."

Xerxes stared at the man, then sighed, turning away and staring at the empty house. Of course the Kingdom would want the woman's things. She'd been a far better warrior than anyone he'd ever met. The only one who'd ever bested him in one-on-one combat.

He lowered his gaze to the ground, imagining himself bashing this soldier's face in. But the thought no longer interested him. He raised one hand, flashing rapid signals to his Ironclad. Then he began walking away, toward the long wooden bridge in the distance.

Behind him, the soldier screamed, the sound echoing across the canyon, piercing through the endless roar of the waterfalls all around them.

CHAPTER 4

Sukri groaned, rubbing her eyes. She heard the familiar sound of a bell ringing from outside – the second time it had rang – and opened her eyes. The ceiling was less than a meter above her head, bare wooden cross-beams holding up the wooden planks of the ceiling. She sighed, and would've sat up, but she'd made that mistake before, banging her head on one of the cross-beams. She rolled onto her side instead, gazing outward.

She was in a small room, not much bigger than her room in the Outskirts back home, laying on the top bunk of a bunkbed set against one wall. Opposite this was another bunk bed set against the far wall a couple meters away. Only the bottom bunk was occupied, a very large man sleeping there.

Sukri closed her eyes, feeling utterly exhausted. She's slept like shit, as usual. Every night brought the same dream. Of a blond-haired boy on his knees before her, his face a bloody mess. Of the knife clutched in her hand.

Of him begging for his life.

An image of that knife slicing through the boy's pale neck came to her, of his flesh parting, blood spurting from the ghastly wound.

Her eyes snapped open, the tolling of the bell stopping suddenly.

Fuck.

Sukri sighed, rolling onto her belly, then swinging her legs over the edge of her bed and dropping down to the floor. Something she would've been nervous to do a week ago, after the cast on her leg had come off. She landed with a *thump*, and the big man stirred.

"Come on, Gammon," she grumbled, walking up to his bed and shaking his shoulder. "Time to get up."

Gammon groaned, rolling onto his back and opening his eyes. Over two meters tall, Gammon was huge…the biggest man she'd ever met, in more ways than one. He had an impressive belly, a testament to his love for food.

Gammon was her gentle giant, a man who wouldn't hurt a fly, unless it was to protect his friends.

"Hey big guy," she greeted, forcing herself to smile. He smiled back.

"Hey Sukri," he greeted.

"Let's go," she urged. The large bell in the bell tower at the top of the guild had rung twice already, and that was all the warning they were going to get. If they weren't at class in another ten minutes, they'd pay dearly for it. The Guild of Seekers did not tolerate laziness in its Seekers…especially the apprentices. As lowly initiates, they'd been allowed to live in their apartment in the Outskirts, coming to the guild at noon for their lessons. But now that they'd passed their three Trials, they had to live in the guild itself, sleeping in dormitories on the far end of the massive seven-story building. For the last two weeks, they'd spent every minute of every day in the guild, eating and sleeping and training here. Contact with the outside world was forbidden. The guild was their world now.

They weren't Sukri and Gammon anymore; they were Seekers.

Gammon rolled out of bed and stood up, towering over Sukri. He pulled on his apprentice uniform – a simple gray shirt and pants, halfway between the white of an initiate's uniform and the black and gold Seeker uniform. Sukri looked down at her Seeker medallion, a triangular hunk of silver-colored metal resting on her chest. It was surprisingly heavy for its size, three symbols engraved into its surface near each of the three points: an eye with rays shooting out from it, a skull, and a human heart. She stuffed it down the front of her shirt, then lifted her shirt up, taking it off. Her medallion hung between her bare breasts, which were ample. Gammon's face turned red, his eyes widening, and he nearly tripped over himself in his haste to turn away from her.

"Aww, don't be shy," she said. "You can look, you know," she added, smirking at him. She took a perverse pleasure in teasing Gammon. He was chivalrous to a fault, far more protective of her modesty than she was. She didn't have much use for modesty, hardly being ashamed of her body. It was no secret to her anymore that he was in love with her, and had been for a very long time. A fact that she'd only recently discovered…and one that she was still coming to terms with.

"I'll wait," he mumbled.

"Afraid you'll get hard?" she pressed, grabbing her gray top and pulling it on. Gammon ignored the comment, clasping his hands in front of him. She wondered if he *was* hard.

She put on her gray pants, slipping back into her shoes.

"You're safe," she called out. Gammon hesitated, then turned around, clearly not trusting her. Which she supposed was fair enough. She'd pranked him one too many times.

"I wish you'd stop doing that," Gammon muttered.

"But you turn such pretty colors," she retorted, grinning at him. She stood up on her tip-toes, punching him in the upper arm. "Grab your shit," she added. "I don't want to be late."

He nodded, walking to the far end of the room and grabbing his longsword and his warhammer. The traditional weapons of a Seeker, they were supposed to wear them at all times. Partly to absorb the skills the weapons exuded, and partly to get used to the warhammer's formidable weight. Well, formidable to Sukri, anyway.

She grabbed her weapons, strapping her belt to her waist, the longsword at her left hip. Then she lifted her warhammer, strapping it to her back with some difficulty. Gammon offered to help, of course, but she declined. She had to get used to doing it by herself, after all. That done, Gammon opened the door for her, gesturing for her to walk through to the hallway beyond.

Always the gentleman, she mused, stepping into the hallway. It was a shame she'd always been attracted to bad boys. As much as Gammon cared for her, she had a hard time imagining him as a lover. It wasn't his size…not really, anyway. Sure, she liked a hard body, but it wasn't a necessity. Gammon was just…meek.

Except when he isn't, she thought, remembering their battle with the Ironclad weeks ago. And their third Trial.

For a moment she felt the hot spray of blood strike her face, as it had when she'd slashed Udeln's throat. She flinched, forcing the thought out of her mind.

Glancing out of one of the windows in the hallway, Sukri spotted a long line of people in the courtyard below, arriving early for the next round of Seeker tryouts. She wondered if any of them would've shown up if they knew the price they'd have to pay to become a Seeker. Wondered what *she* would've done if she'd known.

Too late to go back now, she thought glumly.

Gammon cleared his throat behind her, snapping her out of her morbid thoughts. She continued forward down the hallway, Gammon following behind her. They walked down the long hallway, turning right at the end and continuing forward down another. Eventually they came to an open door on the left, and Sukri stepped through into the room beyond. It was much larger than their dorm room, maybe five meters squared, with chairs facing a desk at the far end. Seated at this desk was an old man in a well-worn Seeker uniform. He had to be at least seventy or even eighty, his head mostly bald save for some wispy white hair at his temples. His skin was liver-spotted, deep wrinkles lining his face. He was Seeker Hanlen, and his sharp blue eyes followed Sukri and Gammon as they entered the room, walking to their respective seats at the back. The other seats were filled with other Seeker apprentices, ones that had passed their Trials months before Gammon and Sukri. These apprentices had already taken a few other classes – ones Suki and Gammon would take next year – but everyone was taking *this* class for the first time.

"That's all of you then," Seeker Hanlen stated in a clear, if slightly raspy, voice. "Good morning, my young Seekers," he greeted. "Today we will continue our exploration of the world of transference."

Sukri fidgeted in her chair. Transference was the technical term for the transfer of qualities – emotions, personality, physical traits, skill, and so forth – from one thing to another. She absorbed emotions extremely well, experiencing them quite powerfully. She'd always considered it a curse, but she'd learned that it could also be an extremely useful gift. The ability to absorb emotions allowed her to sense danger around her…things in the environment that others had been hurt by. Their fear remained within the vicinity of the threat, and when she drew near, she too would feel it. It'd saved her from certain death during her second Trial…and it had saved Gammon.

"As we've discussed," Seeker Hanlen continued, "…the greater one's ability to absorb a category of transferrable energy, the less likely you are to transmit that energy." He gestured at the class. "Some of you absorb emotional energy very well…and for those that do, you transmit very little of your own emotion. The opposite is also true. Those that absorb poorly tend to transmit very well."

Sukri nodded. She absorbed emotions very well, but barely transmitted them. Gammon, on the other hand, was impervious to the emotions around him, but transmitted his quite powerfully. His preternatural calm had helped her on many occasions.

"Today," their teacher declared, "…those of you that absorb emotions well will be tested by those who transmit them. Pair up; the goal is to transmit anger to your partner…so much so that you get them to strike you."

"Wait, what?" one of the more senior students, a young man named Sen, blurted out. Seeker Hanlen smiled.

"As a Seeker," he explained, "…those of you who transmit emotions well can use this gift as a weapon. Simply trigger yourself to feel a particular emotion, and those around you will absorb it. Those of you who transmit well can manipulate people in this way, priming them to feel a certain way, to make them do what you want."

Sen clearly didn't appreciate this explanation. He was more like Gammon, after all, able to transmit emotion. Apparently he didn't relish the idea of being punched. Sukri glanced at Gammon, who shrugged. He clearly wasn't as concerned about being punched as Sen was. Sukri had to take a little credit for that; she punched him all the time.

"Go on," Seeker Hanlen prompted. "Stand up and pair up."

Sukri nodded at Gammon, who stood from his chair. She did so as well, walking up to face him. She smirked at him, knowing that he would have a hard time dredging up enough anger to get her to attack him. She wondered how he would do it.

"Begin," Hanlon ordered.

Sukri stood there, staring at Gammon. The big guy closed his eyes, frowning slightly. Sukri focused inward as she'd been taught, concentrating on how she was feeling. Relatively neutral. A bit hungry. This was her baseline…the emotional state that was *hers*. Any change from it meant that she was being manipulated by outside sources.

She felt a sudden flash of fear, and almost took a step back, staring at Gammon. That wasn't the emotion he was supposed…

And then it hit her.

Suddenly she wanted nothing more than to tear into Gammon. To smash him in the temple, to knock him onto the ground and stomp on his face. She pictured herself slamming her heel into his forehead, over and over and…

Emotion is temporary, a voice inside of her said. Calm, soothing words. *Action is forever.*

She resisted the urge to lash out at her friend, feeling herself dissociating from her anger. It wasn't hers, after all. It was an alien thing, an imposter that would leave eventually, but only if ignored. She waited, allowing the rage to swell within her.

Within moments, it passed.

"Huh," Gammon mumbled, clearly disappointed. Sukri relaxed her shoulders, letting them slump. Her fists were clenched, she realized; she forced them to relax as well.

"Damn big guy," she said, shaking her head. "Almost got me there."

"You did well," he admitted.

"Lucky for you I *always* want to punch you," she quipped, grinning at him. Still she felt his disappointment. "I've been practicing," she added. "You did good."

She heard someone yelp, and turned to see Sen getting slapped in the face by his partner, a tall young woman with auburn hair. She was Jasmin, an apprentice who'd graduated with Sen…and just happened to be dating him. Jasmine glared at him.

"Asshole," she spat. Sen stepped back, holding his hands up.

"Take it easy," he protested. "I was just following directions!"

"Uh huh," Jasmine shot back. "So was I."

"Very good," Seeker Hanlen interjected. "You can see how useful this technique might be. While you all have been trained to resist the influence of emotions, most people have not. You'll find them quite easy to manipulate…and not just with negative emotion. You can make people like you – or even love you, temporarily – by utilizing this technique." He smiled at them. "Any questions?"

Sukri shook her head, stealing a glance at Gammon. Seeker Hanlen was right; she'd experienced firsthand the effects of Gammon's love for her, after all. She'd felt an intense love for *him*, at least for a short time. Somehow he'd managed to hide his feelings for years…a testament to his incredible self-control.

"Those of you who absorb emotions," their teacher continued, "…can use it to manipulate people as well. Most people will not be able to hide their emotions from you, no matter how hard they try. By sensing the emotions they transfer to you, you can sense their emotional state…how they're feeling at any one moment. You can also detect how your actions *change* their emotions…whether or not you're angering them, or pleasing them, and so on. By figuring out what a person responds positively to, you can coerce a positive outcome in your interaction with them. Or you can find out what upsets them, and force them to have negative emotions."

"Sounds a lot harder than what these guys can do," Sukri commented, gesturing at Sen and Gammon. Hanlen nodded.

"It is," he agreed. "But trust me…a truly gifted Empath – someone who absorbs emotion extremely well – has incredible power. The power to know what everyone around them is feeling, and how their own actions can influence that."

Sukri said nothing, and Seeker Hanlen raised an eyebrow at her. She must've looked skeptical.

"I suggest you start thinking of being an Empath as a gift," he counseled. "Not a curse. Some of our greatest teachers are Empaths," he added with a wink.

"Is it a gift to be easily manipulated?" Sukri pressed. "I'd rather be like Gammon."

"A great gift," Seeker Hanlon replied, "…often comes with a price. Remember that Gammon cannot sense emotions like you can," he added. "He is a Polarizer. You each have a gift the other lacks."

"A Polarizer?" Sen asked.

"That's right," Seeker Hanlen stated. "A Polarizer is someone who forces anyone near them to feel what *they* feel. If you make yourself feel angry," he added, gesturing at Sen, "…everyone around you will start to feel angry. And so on."

"Got it," Sen mumbled.

"Alright then," Seeker Hanlon stated. "It's time I showed you Empaths and Polarizers how to make use of your gift!"

* * *

The sun shone directly overhead by the time Hunter made it to the top of a large hill, its hot rays making him sweat in his leather armor. He'd had to stop on more than one occasion to take a drink from the big flask of water in his pack, one he'd refilled twice already in one of the streams he'd passed on his journey. After what'd happened at the clearing with the Legendary tree yesterday, he'd spent the rest of the day and night trekking through the woods, finding himself eyeing everything around him suspiciously. Looking for clusters of trees that all looked the same, or animals that looked like trees, and so on. The ordeal had made him paranoid, and rightly so. Vi had mentioned that the forest could be dangerous, but he'd assumed it was because of deadly monsters, not because of the influence of powerful wills.

Needless to say, he'd spent a great deal of time that night searching for a safe-looking place to sleep…and had slept terribly anyway, half-expecting to wake up rooted to the ground. Thankfully he'd woken to find himself…well, himself. He'd continued his long trek, but had stopped getting flashes of déjà vu. Without knowing where to go, he'd climbed up the hill he was on now, in hopes of using the elevation to look down on the forest, and maybe find something that would jog his memory. Or rather, someone else's memory.

Hunter spotted a large boulder in a clearing at the top of the hill, and removed his pack, placing it on the ground. He scaled the boulder then, having little difficulty climbing it. Whether it was the skills he'd absorbed from Vi or her weapons, or a result of his daily workouts, he didn't know. At the top, he had an unfettered view of the miles and miles of land all around him, and he spun in a slow circle, studying the terrain. There was a long chain of mountains in one direction – with the sun directly overhead, he couldn't tell what direction it was in – and a wide river opposite them, miles away from where he stood.

He peered at the river's shore. There was something familiar about it.

He traced the contour of the shore carefully, then spotted something: a clearing, with a huge building built along the river. It had a red roof, and was many stories tall, shaped like a huge "U." A long stone wall surrounded a large amount of farmland around the building, and beyond that, grassland gave way to forest.

Hunter stared at the building, knowing without a doubt that *that* was where he needed to go.

Alrighty then, he thought.

He scanned the area between himself and the building, memorizing landmarks that he could use to guide his way. Then he climbed down from the boulder, grabbing his pack and slinging it over his shoulders. The urge to stay here and rest came over him, but he ignored it, knowing that he had a long way to go before he reached his destination. If he could get there before nightfall, he wouldn't have to sleep in the forest again.

Onward he went, trekking down the hill toward the wide river miles in the distance.

* * *

The sun was approaching the horizon by the time Hunter spotted a break in the forest a few hundred feet ahead, dense trees giving way to a wide-open grassy field. Beyond that, he saw a tall stone wall…the same wall he'd spotted from atop the hill hours ago. He strode toward it, leaving the relative cool of the shadows thrown by the trees above and stepping onto the grass. The wall ahead was maybe twelve feet high, made of fieldstone mortared together with something else. They were bones, he realized. *Human* bones…just like the ones in the great wall surrounding Tykus. He saw a tall, wrought iron gate at a break in the wall a few dozen feet away, a wide path made of crushed stone leading to it.

He stared at the gate; something about it was terribly familiar. Was it a memory he'd absorbed from Vi? Or from the letter he carried? Or was it from the man-tree he'd met yesterday? There was no way to know.

Hunter walked onto the path, following it to the closed gate ahead. It was made of two tall doors that locked in the middle. The doors were as tall as the wall itself, made of black metal rods with sharp tips at the ends. There were spikes at the top of the stone wall as well. Whoever lived here clearly didn't appreciate uninvited guests.

Beyond the gate, he saw a man standing there, a guard clad in blood-red leather armor and a shiny silver breastplate. A black serpent-like emblem was painted in the center of his breastplate, and he wore a red and silver helm.

And he was staring right at Hunter.

"Your name?" the guard demanded. Hunter stopped before the gate, nodding at him.

"Hunter," he answered. "Evening," he added.

"Your business?"

Hunter reached into his pocket, retrieving the rolled-up letter. He unrolled it, holding it out for the guard to see.

"I'm a Seeker," he explained.

"This letter is addressed to Vi," the guard stated coolly.

"I work with Vi."

"Oh really," the guard shot back. "As I recall, she doesn't work with anyone."

"She does now."

"Right kid," the guard grumbled.

Hunter hesitated, then glanced down at his sword, sheathed at his left hip. *Vi's* sword. He looked up at the guard.

"I have her sword," he offered, drawing it from its sheath. The guard stepped back, putting a hand on the hilt of their sword. Hunter held the blade out, displaying it for the guard, who peered at it.

"How did you get that?" the guard demanded.

"Vi gave it to me," Hunter lied.

"I sincerely doubt that, kid."

"What, you think I killed her and took it?" Hunter shot back. The guard considered this.

"The Lady didn't send for you," he replied at last. "She sent for Vi."

Hunter frowned, wondering who the Lady was. But he didn't want to seem ignorant.

"Well I'm all she's going to get," he stated. "Vi was…injured. She won't be making it."

The guard eyed Hunter for a long, silent moment, then sighed.

"Stay here," he ordered. "I'll be back."

The guard left, walking out of view. Hunter peered through the gate, spotting the crushed stone path continuing onward toward a huge building beyond, rows of crops growing on either side of that path. It was the same building he'd seen from the hill earlier that afternoon. It was constructed of pure white stone, elegant designs carved around numerous large windows. Tall statues flanked a short stairway going up to the large double-doors leading into the mansion. The building was five stories tall, topped by a roof made of curved red shingles…the same shade of blood-red as the guard's armor. To the right of the path was a huge statue wrought of dull gray stone amongst the crops, carved into a serpent-like form coiled upon itself, innumerable small legs sprouting from its sides like a centipede. It rose high above the crops surrounding it, easily twenty feet tall.

Minutes passed.

Hunter fidgeted, getting irritable.

Damn guard is going to make me stand out here forever, he thought.

He found himself focusing inward, as Vi had taught him to do whenever he felt a negative emotion. Was it really his? If so, why was he feeling this way? It was easy to blame the guard, but he'd learned to question his assumptions. Within moments, he found the answer: his stomach grumbled, having been fed only once this morning.

He shook his head, smiling at himself. He was hungry, of course. And like his mother, he was a bit of an asshole when he was hungry.

At length, the guard returned, striding up to the gate and unlocking it. He opened one of the gate doors, swinging it inward.

"Follow me," he ordered. "The Lady will see you."

Hunter did as he was told, following behind the guard, who led him across the long path toward the mansion in the distance. Looking to the left and right, he studied the long rows of crops growing in the large field of dirt on both sides. Some he recognized, like corn stalks, but most were unfamiliar to him. His dad had loved to garden, back before Mom disappeared.

He felt a pang of homesickness, wondering how Dad was doing. He'd left his father back on Earth, a man broken by the loss of his wife. Not for the first time, he hoped Dad would come after him.

But if Dad did, Hunter would have to explain what'd happened to Mom. What *he'd* done to her.

He felt a familiar, crushing guilt come over him, and forced himself to snap out of it, concentrating on the guard ahead of him.

Get the head. Get stronger. Kill them all.

They made it to the mansion, walking up the short stairway to the front double-doors. They were blood-red, with black serpents painted on them, similar to the statue he'd seen earlier. Two guards wearing the same armor as the first flanked the entrance. They nodded, then opened the doors, stepping to the sides to allow Hunter in. Hunter stepped through the doorway, his eyes widening as he crossed the threshold.

Damn, he thought.

He found himself in a large foyer, a huge, glittering crystal chandelier hanging from the ceiling twenty feet above his head. The floor was made of polished cherry, the walls on either side painted a deep red. Huge red wooden beams spanned the pure white ceiling, and thick red beams extended from the floor to the ceiling in regular intervals, lanterns bolted to their sides. Intricate designs were carved into each beam.

It was clear that whoever owned this mansion was incredibly rich.

"Come," the guard ahead of him urged, walking down the foyer toward another set of double-doors at the other end. More guards flanked these doors, opening them as Hunter approached. He stepped through into the next room; it was like the first, but smaller, with curved staircases ascending to meet each other in the middle one story up. The guard stopped suddenly, turning to face Hunter.

"Your weapons," he prompted, holding out one hand.

"Excuse me?"

"No visitors may be armed around the Lady," the guard explained. "You'll get them back afterward."

Hunter hesitated, then handed over his longsword, mace, and a dagger he'd stolen from one of the Seekers.

"The bow and quiver as well," the guard added.

Hunter handed these over as well, and his pack when prompted.

"Wait here," the guard instructed. "The Lady will be with you momentarily." He left then, ascending the stairs and disappearing through a door. Hunter watched him go, feeling naked without his weapons. If anyone decided to attack him now, he doubted he'd be able to fight them off…unless he'd somehow managed to absorb hand-to-hand fighting skills from Vi's sword.

He waited, seconds passing into minutes.

Then he saw her.

A tall woman appeared above the staircases, stepping down the rightmost one. She wore a long, blood-red dress, her pale legs showing through slits that extended all the way to her upper thighs. Her slender waist was cinched in by a darker red corset, which was studded with rubies that glittered with ever step she took. She was quite buxom, evident from the deep V-cut in the front of her dress. She wore a silver choker around her neck, adorned with even more rubies, and matching anklets and armbands. She appeared to be in her late thirties, or early forties at most. She had long black hair tied into a tight ponytail that hung all the way down to her buttocks, and deep green eyes that contrasted with her pale skin. Fine lines and a few gray hairs were all that betrayed her age; she was strikingly beautiful, with high cheekbones that reminded him of Vi, and she walked with an elegant confidence, her eyes locked on his as she came down the stairs toward him. She reached the bottom, walking right up to him. It was clear that she was not at all threatened by him; that might have had something to do with the man who followed behind her. A man dressed from neck to toe in a tight red and black leather suit, his face hidden behind a mask carved into a monstrous, grotesque expression. Only his striking silver eyes were visible, and the long metal staff strapped to his back.

The woman stopped before Hunter, eyeing him from his boots upward, arching one eyebrow.

"Hunter, is it?"

Her voice was a little deep, and slightly husky.

"Yes ma'am," he answered, bowing his head slightly. He smelled a faint perfume, sweet but not overwhelming…and quite pleasing. He felt uneasy in her presence; despite the fact that she was probably old enough to be his mother, she was without a doubt the most attractive woman he had ever met.

"I am Lady Camilla," she introduced. "Owner of this estate. This," she added, gesturing at the masked man who'd stopped behind her, "…is Dio, my bodyguard."

"Hey," Hunter greeted, nodding at Dio. The man didn't respond, standing as still as a statue.

"I understand you claim to be Vi's apprentice," the Lady stated.

"I was," Hunter confirmed. She frowned slightly.

"Was?"

"It's a long story," he admitted, kicking himself for using the past tense. Lady Camilla crossed her arms under her bosom.

"How convenient," she replied. "I've got time."

"Well," Hunter stated, clearing his throat nervously. He had a hard time concentrating around this woman. Where to begin? "Vi took me in after I was attacked by an Ironclad."

"Vi isn't in the habit of taking in strays," she stated, looking him up and down. She clearly disapproved.

"I got that," Hunter admitted. "Guess we had something in common."

She just stood there, waiting.

"We both didn't belong," he explained.

"Clearly," she agreed, gesturing at him…and his chocolate-colored skin, no doubt. Still, it was obvious she didn't fear him the way the people of Tykus did.

"I'm an Original," he confessed. She raised an eyebrow.

"An Original?" she asked. "Really."

"Yes," he confirmed. He explained how his mother had gone through the Gate years ago, and how he'd gone after her. How the Kingdom had taken him in, and the Seekers. And then how Vi had rescued him, taking him in and training him.

"My guard says that you claimed Vi was injured," Lady Camilla stated after he was done. "Is she alright?"

Hunter hesitated, grimacing. He lowered his gaze, then shook his head. He swallowed past a lump in his throat.

"No," was all he could manage.

"Where is she?" Lady Camilla demanded. "I'll send my physician to her at once."

"It's too late," Hunter confessed, shaking his head again. "She's…they killed her."

Lady Camilla's eyes widened.

"*What?*"

"They killed her," he repeated, his eyes brimming with moisture. He wiped it away quickly, hardly wanting to cry in front of this woman.

"Impossible!" she retorted, glaring at him. "No one could kill her."

"I saw it myself," Hunter insisted.

"Explain," she commanded, her tone suddenly ice-cold. "If you lie even once to me," she added, "…or if I find out you've lied later, I'll have you hanged."

Hunter felt the blood drain from his face, and he cleared his throat, his heart pounding in his chest. There was no doubt in his mind that she would do exactly as she threatened.

"All right," he agreed. He explained everything – how Vi had trained him, how the Ironclad had attacked them at Vi's place, and their doomed mission to the Ironclad lair. He described their battle with the Ironclad – and their Queen – leaving out the fact that she was his own mother, the Legend who'd started the Civil War in Tykus half a century ago. And leaving out how he'd killed her, realizing who she was only after it was too late.

He finished by describing how he'd found Vi dead outside of the Ironclad lair, and how he'd managed to absorb her last memories. How he'd hunted down and killed her murderer, and how he'd vowed to destroy the Guild of Seekers. And Dominus, the Duke of Wexford…the man who'd betrayed her in the first place.

Lady Camilla listened silently while he spoke, her face expressionless throughout. When he was done, she turned away from him, taking a deep breath in, then letting it out slowly. She stared off at nothing in particular, looking for all the world like a statue.

After a long, uncomfortable silence, she finally turned back to face him. Her expression was stony, but her green eyes glittered with moisture.

"I see."

"I'm sorry," he mumbled, lowering his gaze.

"Were you lovers?" she asked, her tone blunt. Hunter glanced up at her, shaking his head.

"God no," he answered. Her eyes narrowed, and he held up both hands. "I mean, she would never…she didn't like people like me."

"Like you?"

"Guys," he clarified. "She preferred women."

"Ah," she replied, relaxing visibly. "But you clearly cared for her."

"I did," he confirmed. "I loved her," he added. "She was my best friend."

"You only knew her for a few weeks," Lady Camilla countered. Hunter shrugged.

"I can't help how I feel."

"Clearly," she agreed, eyeing him. "You're an Empath, aren't you?"

"A what?"

"A sponge for emotions," she clarified.

"How did you know?"

"You don't emit as much emotion as most," she explained. "Therefore you must absorb it quite well."

Hunter nodded. She was correct, of course.

"I do," he confirmed.

"Why are you here?" she inquired.

"I want to avenge Vi," Hunter answered. "To get the Ironclad head back, and to get revenge on the guild and Dominus."

"Why get the head back?" the Lady inquired.

"Because Dominus wanted it bad enough to kill Vi for it," he replied. "So I'm gonna take it from him."

"I see. And what makes you think I would help you?"

"All I want is work," Hunter replied. "I'll be your Seeker."

She arched one eyebrow, giving him a withering look.

"You?" she scoffed. "You're no Seeker."

"Tell that to the Seekers I killed," he retorted. The corner of her mouth twitched.

"Killing does not make you a Seeker," she countered. Still, she seemed pleased with his answer. "Suppose I do hire you," she stated. "What's in it for you?"

"I get to absorb skills from artifacts," he replied. "So I can get good enough to get my revenge."

"Ah," she murmured. "Like Vi."

"That's right."

"You'll never be as good as Vi," Lady Camilla declared.

"Maybe not," he conceded. "But I'll get as close as I can."

She stared at him silently for a long moment, then nodded.

"Very well," she decided. She turned about then, walking back up the stairs. "Come."

Hunter followed her up the stairs to the floor above, the masked man – Dio – following behind him. Hunter found himself studying the Lady's figure, which he found equally compelling from behind. He tried not to stare, though she would not have known he was doing so, but found himself incapable of resisting the urge to. They walked leftward down a short hallway to another flight of stairs leading up to the next level, then made their way through a labyrinth of hallways, eventually reaching a set of red double-doors at the end of a long, wide hallway. There were two men flanking the door, each dressed similarly to Dio. Their masks were different, however, and each wore long, curved swords sheathed at their hips instead of Dio's metal staff.

The two men bowed as the Lady approached, opening the doors for her. She stepped through, Hunter and Dio following behind her into a large room.

It appeared to be a library, this room. It was of similar construction as the rest of the mansion, but shelves lined the walls, and various items lined those shelves. Mostly books, but also chalices, various weapons, and even human skulls. And some animal skulls. Each item, save for the books, was held in a glass display case. The display cases appeared to be multilayered, with at least three layers of glass surrounding each object.

On the far wall of the room hung a large map, roughly ten feet squared. The Lady walked up to it, then stopped, turning to face Dio.

"Scan him," she ordered, nodding at Hunter.

Dio stepped up to Hunter, patting him down roughly. Hunter tolerated this, and, apparently satisfied, the man stopped. He removed one red glove then, placing his bare hand on Hunter's forehead. Hunter resisted the urge to jerk away from the man's touch, forcing himself to remain still. He felt a chill run through him...along with an icy, almost inhuman calm. Images of monstrous creatures flashed in his mind's eye, and a young woman with green eyes reaching down for him, her hands covered in blood.

Hunter jerked away, taking a step back.

Jesus!

Dio lowered his hand, turning to the Lady and nodding.

"Leave us," she ordered.

The man bowed, then left, closing the door behind him. Lady Camilla turned to Hunter then.

"I don't believe I've welcomed you to my home," she stated. "My apologies; I have a well-deserved distrust of strangers."

"I can understand that," Hunter replied. And he could, especially after everything Tykus had done to screw him and his friends over. "So…what is it exactly that you do here?" he inquired.

"I do as any Lord or Lady does," she answered. "I manage my estate and provide for my people."

"So you're a noble."

"Of course," she confirmed.

"Are you with the Kingdom?" he asked. She smirked.

"Hardly," she replied. "I'm an…independent, if you will. My family was once part of Tykus," she admitted. "But we split nearly fifty years ago, during the civil war."

"Ah."

"Suffice it to say that I now act as an independent contractor of sorts," she continued. "I do business with Tykus, the Kingdom of the Deep, and several other governments."

"What kind of business?"

"Oh, the usual," she answered. "The sale of crops, other goods…and artifacts and Ossae, of course." She gave him a significant look. "Hence my letter."

"So you have a job for me?"

"Perhaps," she replied. "Although not the job I intended for Vi." She hesitated. "This will require some background knowledge, and I'm afraid I don't have time to fill you in completely."

"What do you mean?"

"If you're truly an Original," she replied, "…then you'll need a basic understanding of where you are…and how things came to be." She smiled. "How lucky for you that my ancestors were great historians. I inherited their passion."

She gestured at the room around them.

"This is my library," she explained. "The books you see are hundreds of years old, and many are copies of texts that are thousands of years old." She turned to the map, gesturing at it. "This," she continued, "…is a map of Varta."

"Varta?"

"Short for Svartálfaheimr," she explained. "The world you now find yourself in," she added. "The original world – your world – has many names. The first documented settlers called it Miogaror."

"We call it Earth now," Hunter offered.

"So I've heard," she replied. "According to ancient texts, there have been numerous waves of settlers that have come through the Gate over the millennia. We have no record of the oldest settlers, the original men and women who came here. Our earliest records show that a wave of settlers from your world arrived roughly six thousand years ago. When they arrived, they found themselves in a vast city. Utterly abandoned, save for strange, black monsters that attacked them on sight."

"Monsters?"

"Creatures with long arms and legs, and thin, skeletal bodies. Extremely quick and vicious and, according to all reports, possessed of an insatiable appetite."

"Oh."

"These settlers managed to fend off the creatures with great difficulty, and settled the city. They believed the creatures to be Svartálfar, or dark elves. They thought this world was Svartálfaheimr, the world of the dark elves…one of nine worlds in the universe."

"Wait, so there are more than two worlds?" Hunter asked.

"Perhaps," she replied. "We assume that these settlers were merely attempting to describe this world in the context of their existing mythology. In any case," she added, "…they settled the city, and built a massive fortress on top of an existing structure in the center of it. A large crypt of sorts. The original name for this fortress is lost to time, but future waves of settlers named it the Acropolis."

"So Tykus was built around this original city," Hunter deduced. Lady Camilla nodded.

"The original city of humans," she agreed. "For, despite the creatures they found living there, the bones within the crypts that the Acropolis was built upon were unmistakably human. We can only assume that these humans were earlier settlers, and were overrun by the Svartálfar."

"Okay," Hunter replied. "What does that have to do with the job?" She gave a slight smirk.

"Everything," she answered. "You're young," she added. "But if you live long enough, you'll realize just how important the past is."

Hunter grimaced, realizing he'd sounded impatient.

"Sorry," he mumbled.

"Quite alright," she replied. She walked up to the map then, retrieving a long wooden pointer from below it. It was easily eight feet long, and she wielded it expertly, pointing at the top of the map, at a small peninsula.

"This is the location of the Gate," she explained. "The first city was constructed around it. Now it leads to the Deadlands, of course, but it used to bring Originals to the center of Tykus." She slid the pointer downward, well into a forest. "This is where you are now, by the River Ormr." She slid the pointer downward and to the right, stopping at the base of a mountain range. "This," she continued, "…is the location of the Crypt of Zagamar."

"The what?"

She lowered the pointer, placing it back under the map. Then she turned back to Hunter.

"The Crypt of Zagamar," she repeated.

"What's that?"

"The oldest known crypt in the world," she answered. "Are you familiar with crypts?"

"Just that they have dead people in them," Hunter replied cheekily. She smirked.

"When Legends die, they're buried in elaborate crypts," she explained. "Vast underground labyrinths that prevent others from being exposed to them. Can you imagine why?"

"So that people aren't changed by them?"

"Correct," she replied. "When Legends die," she stated, "…their bodies continue to influence everything around them. If people were allowed near a Legend's Ossae, they would slowly turn *into* that Legend, at least an inferior version of them. People would lose their souls to the Ossae, and everyone would start becoming the same person."

"Ah."

"So Legends must be dealt with," she continued. "Buried deep within the earth where no one can get to them. Other Legends are kept in vaults, as I suspect Tykus is. All Legendary Ossae – the bones of Legends – are protected, and highly valued."

"Why valued?"

She arched one eyebrow.

"Can you imagine what would happen if the Kingdom of the Deep managed to steal the Ossae of Tykus?"

Hunter considered this. If that happened, Tykus's legendary influence would wane, and the kingdom would lose its very identity. He imagined that the kingdom would pay dearly to have the Ossae returned. He said as much.

"Correct," she agreed.

"So what about this Crypt of Zagamar?" Hunter inquired.

"When the settlers first repopulated the city now known as Tykus," she replied, "…they sent scouting parties to the surrounding lands to survey them. One party found a crypt at the base of a mountain range, and a few scouts attempted to go in." She paused for a moment. "They went insane and killed themselves."

Hunter raised an eyebrow.

"Since then, many have attempted to get in the crypt," she continued. "Over the millennia, many have tried. A few centuries ago, a man managed to get into the outer rooms of the crypt, and retrieved an artifact…a medallion."

"What happened to him?" Hunter asked.

"He went insane," she answered. "But was still sane enough to bring it back to Tykus. The medallion had a name inscribed on the back."

"Let me guess," Hunter replied. "Zagamar?"

"Correct."

"So what is it you want me to do?" he inquired.

"I want you to go to the Crypt," she replied, "…and retrieve the skull of Zagamar."

"Wait, what?"

"I want you to retrieve his skull," she repeated. Hunter frowned.

"But I thought you said anyone who tried to go in the crypt went insane."

"True," she agreed. "But you have an advantage that no one else has."

"And what's that?"

"You're an Original," she answered. Hunter blinked.

"How is that an advantage?" he pressed. She smiled, putting a hand on his shoulder, then sliding her fingers down the side of his arm.

"Have you ever wondered," she replied, "…why everyone around you is so frightened of you?"

"They're afraid I'll change them," he answered. She nodded, dropping her arm to her side.

"But you remain unchanged," she stated. "Why?"

"I have a strong will."

"Perhaps," she conceded. "Perhaps not."

"What do you mean?"

"Originals aren't like everyone else," the Lady explained. "Not at first, anyway. You see, you're from another world. Your…substance is foreign to Varta."

"I don't get it."

"We believe," she continued, "…that when an Original passes through the Gate, his or her body is slowly transformed. Its very substance is converted – over time – to the substance of this world."

"You mean my body is changing?"

"Indeed," she confirmed. "As you take in the air of this world, the water, the food, your body is being replaced. At first, you'll barely have any effect on others around you, no matter how weak or powerful your will. And others will have little effect on you. You see, your original flesh cannot absorb or transmit traits. It must be made of the substance of *our* world in order to do so."

Hunter considered this. It certainly explained why Trixie had no effect on him the day he'd arrived…and how he didn't seem to be changed by anyone or anything around him. Vi had mentioned that he was only average at absorbing skills.

"Different parts of your body are converted at different rates," Lady Camilla continued. "Clearly the part of your brain processing emotions was converted first, you being an Empath."

"And my skin," Hunter guessed, remembering how he'd changed Trixie's skin color slightly after every night he'd been with her. Skin was replaced relatively quickly, he knew. Again, it made sense.

"Perhaps so."

"How exactly will this help me retrieve the head?"

"Most of your mind is still of your world's substance," she answered. "You'll be relatively immune to the Crypt's defenses."

"But how can you be sure?" he pressed.

"Your mother," she replied, "…came through the Gate half a century ago. When she did, she was brought into Tykus as you were, and housed in the Outskirts with the weak-willed rabble."

"I know."

"She was a Legend," Lady Camilla continued, "…but it took months before anyone realized it. Months for her body to be converted to the substance of this world, at least enough for her to start to show her true potential. And well over a year for her to reach her full power." She paused. "You've been here for how long now?"

"A month and a half, maybe?"

"Then we must hurry," she replied. "Every day you spend here, your body is changing…and your mind. If you want to succeed at retrieving the head of Zagamar, you'd better do it soon."

"What's in it for me?" Hunter asked. Lady Camilla smirked.

"If you retrieve the head of Zagamar," she answered, putting a warm hand on his cheek, "…then I will help you as my grandparents helped your mother…and I will give you everything you need to exact your revenge."

Chapter 5

Dominus crouched before one of the large pallets resting in a large grassy clearing in his gardens, upon which a number of wooden boxes had been placed. Each box contained many wooden frames; Dominus pulled one out, studying the small wax cells his bees had built within its borders. Perfect hexagons in an orderly array. He marveled – as he often did – that these simple creatures were capable of such perfect creations. To him, it was no less marvelous than the incredible architecture of the Acropolis in Tykus. An expression of their orderly natures, these cells. Each bee had a task, a reason for being. Each bee executed its task faithfully, without question. There was no room for doubt in a bee's mind, no resistance to its nature. While humans were plagued with sloth, self-doubt, and a bewildering array of other derangements of the mind and soul, bees were not. They just did. They just *were.*

There was no doubt in his mind which creature was superior.

He stared at the cells, feeling uncharacteristically antsy. He replaced the frame, ignoring the bees that landed on his white beekeeper uniform, stinging its thick fabric. A futile effort, suicidal even. For these bees could only sting once, and to do so was to die.

He regarded the doomed bees, struck with a sudden disgust. There was a price to pay for simplicity; humans were at least capable of anticipating the futility of a plan of action, while bees could not. For all their weaknesses, for all that they strayed from the order imposed on them, humans had the great power of adaptation.

Dominus grabbed his cane from the grass beside him, then stood, barely needing it to support his right leg. He'd woken to find more pink tissue growing from the stumps of his toes, the ulcer on the side of his ankle nearly filled in. The last of the gangrene had sloughed off, revealing more fresh, vital flesh underneath. He'd even spotted pearly white bone protruding from the new tissue. New bone, building upon the old.

It'd sent chills down his spine.

Dominus sighed, staring down at the various boxes laying on their wooden pallets on the grass. His hives, ones he'd tended to for the greater part of his lifetime. As had his father, and his father's father before him. Again, he felt antsy. Unsettled. He usually treasured these moments, his time working with his bees. But now he wanted to do anything *but* this. Glancing upward, he spotted dark, ominous clouds hanging low in the sky. They were almost directly overhead.

A storm was coming.

He turned, spotting Farkus, ever faithful, standing nearby and watching him silently.

"Let's go," he stated, beginning the walk through his gardens back to the castle. Farkus bowed slightly, limping behind Dominus, keeping his distance. Hardly necessary, given how long the servant had been exposed to Dominus's will. They were like brothers now. Still, he appreciated the gesture.

When the last of the bees had given up on attacking him, Dominus removed his hood, walking through his gardens, limping only slightly. He tried exaggerating the limp, knowing that to walk normally would arouse suspicion when he inevitably went back to the kingdom. The last thing he needed was for his fellow dukes – or Axio – to discover his miraculous recovery. Such a thing would immediately expose his dabbling in forbidden artifacts, a crime for which there was only one sentence.

Death.

The special Ironclad's head had saved him from his terrible disease, and that fact alone made his crime worthwhile. But he could not afford to expose himself much more. For he knew that, even as it imparted its gift of extraordinary regeneration, it was also changing him in other ways. Ways he hadn't yet discovered. If he strayed too far from his ancestors, from the unbroken chain of loyal stewards of the kingdom of Tykus…

"I'll be sleeping in the shrine tonight," he stated suddenly. His ancestral shrine – where the Ossae of his ancestors lay – would cleanse him of his impurities. He would drink of the sacred water of the great fountain there, and sleep within the shrine, surrounded by the powerful wills of his forefathers.

"I'll arrange for the bedding, your Grace," Farkus replied.

They walked past rows of flowers, blossoms of various colors having bloomed at regular intervals. His ancestors had designed them such that as one species' flowers wilted, another's would bloom, ensuring a continuous display of natural beauty…and an ever-changing fragrance to the air. It was a feast for the senses, one that reminded him of his childhood. Strange that odors had such a powerful gift, to conjure memories so vividly. In that respect, no other sense compared.

A droplet struck his forehead, and he glanced up again, seeing a flash of light deep within the thunderclouds above. Seconds later, a deep rumbling echoed through the air.

He heard shouting in the distance.

Dominus frowned, glancing across his gardens, to the inner curtain – the tall stone inner wall surrounding his gardens. His eye went to the large, wrought-iron gate at the far end, nearly a hundred yards away.

It was open.

More shouting, followed by another flash of lightning.

Boom.

"Are we expecting visitors?" Dominus asked, already knowing the answer.

"No sire."

He saw a few of his soldiers making a mad dash toward the open gate, their swords in their hands.

What in hell…

Then he spotted them. Shadowy figures spilling through the open gate, swarming into the courtyard. They engulfed his soldiers, overwhelming them in seconds. His men fell in a chorus of screams.

Rain pelted Dominus's scalp, and he swore, breaking out in an awkward run, limping despite the use of his cane.

"To the vault!" he cried.

He ran faster, a dull ache building in his calves with the effort. A jagged bolt of lightning struck just beyond the castle's outer walls, an ear-splitting *boom* blasting through the night air. He was fast approaching the castle; he turned a sharp left, following parallel to it, the castle to his right. There was a secret door in the castle wall twenty meters ahead, camouflaged to be indistinguishable from the wall itself. A long row of tall bushes was set half a meter from the wall, with a narrow gap between the two.

The shadowy figures swarmed toward the castle, a few of them breaking off and running right toward him.

Damn!

He pushed himself, feeling a dull pressure in his chest as he did so. He hugged the castle wall, peering ahead. It was impossible to see what the figures were in the darkness, but he had to assume the worst.

Ironclad.

They're coming for me, he thought. *Coming for revenge.*

The storm intensified, the wind howling in his ears, tearing at his clothes and soaking him to the bone. He held one arm in front of him to shield his face, reaching the row of bushes and squeezing into the gap between them and the wall. He could hear the enemy sprinting toward him, only a few dozen meters away now. He could stay and fight – he'd absorbed considerable skill from the artifacts Vi had procured for him, after all – but if they were Ironclad…

He pushed forward toward the secret doorway, countless branches scraping against his beekeeper suit. The door was only a few meters ahead, barely distinguishable from the wall. That was by design, the door made of stone blocks in the same pattern as the rest of the wall; only he and a few of the servants knew of it.

He heard shouting from the other side of the bushes…then saw a large, shadowy figure chopping at the bushes with a curved silver blade, trying to open a gap big enough to squeeze through.

Dominus cursed, reaching the door and pushing against it. It resisted his efforts, cracking open, then stopping, its hinges undoubtedly rusted from lack of use. Dominus glanced back, seeing more shadowy figures squeezing between the bushes and the wall.

Damn it!

He rammed his shoulder into the door, but it barely budged. He stepped back, then rammed it again, ignoring the pain in his shoulder as it struck the unforgiving stone. The door jerked open a few centimeters, a faint light visible beyond it.

Come on!

Dominus rammed the door again, and this time it swung open all the way. He stumbled through the doorway into a small, dimly lit room beyond, catching his balance with his cane, then spinning around. Farkus hurried in after him.

"Shut the door!" Dominus urged, but of course Farkus was already doing it. The door closed, and Farkus gripped the sliding wooden cross-beam to bar it.

There was a shout from beyond the door, and suddenly it jerked open a few centimeters, throwing Farkus backward. Dominus caught the servant, then rushed forward, slamming the door shut and bracing himself against it. He felt the door shudder once, then again.

"Farkus!" he shouted.

Farkus recovered quickly, rushing to the door and grabbing the cross-beam again, sliding it to bar the door from opening.

"Let's go," Dominus ordered, turning away from the door. The room they were in was small, with a single lantern hanging from a chain from the ceiling. It was always lit, thank goodness; his servants saw to that. Opposite the door they'd come through was another door – one that was always guarded. Dominus walked up to the door, then hesitated. Only a small contingent of the enemy had broken away to attack him. The rest had almost certainly stormed the castle itself. He could not assume that his guards were still alive.

He gripped his cane tightly, his thumb hovering over the hidden trigger on the head of it. A deadly blade was stored within, the shaft of the cane serving as a scabbard. With a touch of his thumb, the spring-loaded blade would be freed. It was a fine weapon, but it would prove useless against the thick armor of an Ironclad. He needed to get to his vault, one of the most well-protected rooms in the castle. But first he needed to retrieve the Ironclad's head.

If they find me before I get to the vault…

He pushed the thought away, gripping the handle of the door and pulling it open. Or at least he tried to. It didn't budge. He paused, then knocked on the door in a specific rhythm. Moments later, the door opened, revealing a guard beyond.

"Your Grace!" the guard blurted out, bowing quickly. Dominus strode through the doorway into a long hallway beyond, Farkus following behind him.

"The castle is under attack," Dominus stated tersely. "Lock this door and get me the captain of my guard. I want an escort to the vault."

"At once," the guard replied, locking the door and rushing away. Dominus turned to Farkus.

"I…"

A blood-curdling scream echoed through the hallway. Dominus turned his head, seeing the guard slump to the floor twenty meters away, blood spurting from his neck. And beyond them, a half-dozen men in black and green leather armor, wielding long, curved blades in each hand. Dominus's eyes widened, his breath catching in his throat. He knew exactly who these men were: Seekers.

From the Kingdom of the Deep.

Dominus cursed, limping down the hallway away from the men, Farkus right behind him. The Seekers sprinted after them, and Dominus grimaced, running as fast as he could. There was no way he was going to be able to outrun them. He would have to fight…and while he was possessed of formidable skill, these creatures – these Seekers of the Deep – had been exposed to wild artifacts beyond anything Dominus would ever think of touching. There was no way of knowing what they were capable of.

The hallway ended, splitting into a hallway going left and another going right. Dominus turned left, hearing the muted sound of a bell tolling in the distance.

"The vault!" Farkus protested, pointing rightward. Dominus pulled the servant to the left alongside him.

"I need to get something first," he explained. "From my room."

They're after the head, Dominus realized.

It was the only explanation. Somehow, the Kingdom of the Deep's spies had discovered Dominus's betrayal of the Guild of Seekers. Somehow they knew of the Ironclad head. Of course they would risk anything to get it. To have its power.

Dominus continued down the short hallway, hearing footsteps rushing behind him, getting closer by the second. He glanced back, seeing the Seekers turning the corner, rushing right at them. Turning forward, he saw the hallway curving to the right ahead, and followed the inside wall, his calves aching terribly. Pressure was building in his chest again, a dull ache that shot up the left side of his neck. The stairs leading up to the second floor – and his bedroom – were close.

I'm not going to make it.

The hallway straightened out, and he saw the staircase ten meters ahead, to his left. He pushed himself as hard as he could, the pressure in his chest intensifying, his breath coming in short gasps now. Sweat trickled into his eyes, making them sting.

I'm not going to make it!

He reached the stairs, climbing up the first few, then spinning around to face his pursuers. The six Seekers – each armed with two of those strange curved blades – rushed toward him.

"Your Grace!" Farkus cried, continuing up the stairs until he was behind Dominus. Dominus faced the Seekers, pressing down on the head of his cane. The shaft sprung free, falling down the stairs with a clatter, the exposed blade of his cane-sword glittering in the light from the lanterns on the walls.

The first of the Seekers sprinted right at him, slashing at Dominus's legs!

Dominus reacted instantly, his sword intercepting the blow and counterattacking without hesitation, thrusting at the Seeker's chest. The Seeker parried the blow with his second curved sword, slashing at Dominus's throat with the first. Dominus jerked backward, the blade missing his windpipe by mere centimeters. The Seeker followed a split second later with another attack using his other sword, moving with terrifying speed.

Dominus intercepted the attack, but only barely.

He stumbled up a few steps, dodging another rapid series of attacks. There was shouting from above, and soldiers – *his* soldiers – ran down the stairs from the second story toward him.

"Get back, your Grace!" one of them cried.

Dominus felt hands grabbing him from behind, felt himself being hauled backward up the stairs. Soldiers rushed past him, coming between him and the Seekers. An archer stood at the top of the stairs, nocking an arrow and letting it fly at the group of Seekers at the bottom of the stairs.

The arrow slammed into a Seeker's abdomen, throwing him to the floor.

Two soldiers stood back with Dominus, pulling him and Farkus further up the stairs. The archer drew another arrow, firing it. A second Seeker dropped.

"Get me to my bedroom," Dominus commanded the soldier hauling him up the stairs.

"It's not defensible, your Grace," the man protested. "We…"

"Don't question me," Dominus snapped. The soldier hesitated, then nodded.

"Yes your Grace."

They reached the top of the stairs, and Dominus glanced down, seeing one of his soldiers fall as a Seeker slashed his throat, blood spurting down the staircase. The soldier tumbled down the stairs. One of the Seekers drew their arm back, whipping it forward. A knife whirled through the air up the staircase, slamming right into the archer's chest.

The archer dropped.

Dominus turned away, limping alongside the soldier aiding him, continuing down a short hallway. It took a left turn, then a right, leading to a large door at the end, less than ten meters away. He heard screams from behind, then footsteps coming up the stairs. He looked over his shoulder, spotting three Seekers rushing down the hallway after him, their curved blades shining a dull silver in the lantern-light.

"Hurry!" Dominus shouted, trying to move faster toward the door, now only a few meters away. His legs ached terribly, threatening to give out from beneath him. The pressure in his chest was almost unbearable now, accompanied by a deep, gnawing pain that traveled all the way down his left arm. He gasped for breath, sweat pouring down his flanks. The same insidious disease that had robbed his leg of its lifeblood was choking his heart.

If he didn't rest soon, he was going to die.

He struggled to reach the door, his vision starting to blacken.

"Duke!" he heard someone cry. He felt hands encircle his waist from behind, felt himself being lifted off the ground. A soldier shoved the door open, and Dominus was carried through, into the room beyond.

His bedroom.

The soldier slammed the door shut behind them, locking it. Dominus barely heard the shouting from beyond, hardly registered the *bam, bam* as Seekers rammed into the door over and over. His vision went utterly black, and he felt himself being lowered onto something cool and soft.

He lay there, clutching at his chest, gasping for air.

"Your Grace!" a voice shouted. He grit his teeth against the agony in his chest; it was as if a horse was standing on it, the pressure was so intense. His whole body felt utterly drained, and even the thought of speaking was suddenly too much to consider. He lay there, unable to do anything else.

I'm dying, he realized. A primal terror seized him, the realization that this was the end. Not by the sword, but by his cursed disease. It was claiming him at last.

More shouting, and then a loud *bang*. The sound of wood splintering, then of men rushing into the room.

Dominus thought of the Ironclad's head beneath the trapdoor by his bed. Imagined these Seekers stealing it away. Or even worse, the Seekers failing, and the other Dukes finding it after he died, and realizing how far he'd strayed. His legacy tarnished forever, the Duchy torn from his family.

In that moment, he hoped desperately that these Seekers succeeded in finding it.

His vision began to return, spots of color growing before his eyes. He blinked, seeing the ceiling above him. He was lying in his bed, drenched in sweat; the two soldiers were facing off against three of the Seekers. Farkus was standing beside the bed, staring down at him with terror in his eyes.

"Your Grace," Farkus urged.

Dominus stared back mutely, too exhausted to speak.

One of his soldiers screamed, blood spurting from a large gash in his chest. The Seeker battling the wounded soldier slashed at the man's belly, and it gaped open in his spray of blood, a loop of intestine protruding from the wound. The soldier fell…and the other soldier leapt in front of his fellow, thrusting his sword into the Seeker's abdomen.

Just as another Seeker attacked, slashing at the second soldier's neck!

The second soldier fell, clutching at a gaping wound in his neck. Blood sprayed from between his fingers, his breath gurgling in his throat.

The two remaining Seekers turned to face Dominus and Farkus, their blades dripping with fresh blood. Slowly, deliberately, they approached the bed, shoving Farkus out of the way.

Dominus stared at them, his limbs feeling like lead. The pain in his chest had subsided somewhat, but he was still utterly exhausted.

Get up, he ordered himself, gritting his teeth.

He gripped the hilt of his cane-sword tightly, taking a deep breath in as the two Seekers reached the foot of the bed. One of them stepped to the left side of the bed, staring down at Dominus. The thing's face – for the people of the Deep could not be called human – was hidden behind a green and black mask, only its glittering eyes visible.

Blue eyes.

The Seeker lifted one sword above its head, then brought it down in a vicious arc. Right at Dominus's neck.

Dominus cried out, willing himself to roll *toward* the Seeker, and bringing his sword up to intercept the blow. The blades clashed in a sharp *clang*, and Dominus slashed at the man's exposed throat. The flesh parted, blood spraying outward from the great arteries of its neck. It stumbled backward, then fell to the floor, clutching at its throat.

Dominus heard a shout, and turned to see the remaining Seeker lunging at him from the other side of the bed. Dominus continued his roll, falling off the edge of the bed and landing on his left shoulder. He heard a *crack*, felt a horrible pain burst through his shoulder.

He didn't even have time to cry out before the Seeker was upon him.

It leaped over the bed, landing beside Dominus, slashing downward with one sword. Dominus brought his blade up to block the blow, but he was too slow. The Seeker's sword continued past his parry, deflected only a few degrees, its cruel edge sinking into the wooden floor centimeters from Dominus's nose. Dominus's sword went flying, clattering on the floor to his left. The Seeker yanked at its blade, trying to pull it from the floor, and succeeded, stumbling backward.

Dominus lunged for his sword, reaching out for it. But he couldn't grasp it. He stared at his right arm, seeing it end at his wrist, twin jets of blood spurting from it in irregular pulses.

Then he looked at his sword, spotting his disembodied hand lying beside it.

He heard a grunt from above, and rolled onto his back just in time to see the Seeker walking up to him, its twin curved blades hanging at its sides. It stared at him from behind its mask, standing over him.

Then the Seeker raised one sword high in the air, bringing it down on Dominus's neck.

CHAPTER 6

The merciless sun beat down on Hunter's shoulders as he hiked through the forest, his boots making a steady *crunch, crunch* as they crushed countless dead twigs and leaves on the forest floor. He wiped the sweat beading up on his forehead for the umpteenth time, struck with an almost overwhelming urge to stop and drink every last drop of the water from the flask in his pack. He'd put it there – instead of hanging it on his belt – to make it harder for him to get at. There was no telling when he'd come upon the next stream or river, after all…and he didn't trust water from a pond. A bad case of vomiting and diarrhea was an annoyance back on Earth. In the middle of the forest, miles from civilization, it might very well be deadly. He didn't have anything he could boil water in…a mistake he wouldn't make the next time he went off into the wilderness.

Two days had passed since he'd left the Lady's mansion, embarking on his journey to the Crypt of Zagamar. He'd been given a map, as well as advice on dangerous areas and monsters to avoid. And there were plenty of the latter, apparently. A crash-course in wilderness fauna had been sobering indeed. The Ironclad were the most dangerous creatures near the Fringe, but they paled in comparison to monsters of the deep forest. And as he'd learned on his trip to the mansion, the flora could be deadly as well.

He sighed, ignoring his thirst as best he could, keeping his eyes on the forest ahead. The ground sloped upward, making the going difficult. His legs burned with each step, and he ignored this as well, having become accustomed to the discomfort. His legs were getting stronger, he knew. He remembered Vi's powerful, well-muscled legs, and imagined that if he kept this up, his would eventually grow to match hers.

Forward and upward he went, until the forest floor leveled off. He was on top of a hill now, and it gave him a pretty good view of the land ahead. He slowed, retrieving a rolled-up piece of parchment from his front shirt pocket. It was a map Lady Camilla had given him. He unrolled it, studying it, then looking at the scenery before him.

There was a chain of mountains ahead, the nearest of which was perhaps a mile away. They were, he realized, the same mountains he'd seen earlier, from atop the hill before he'd made it to the mansion. The closest mountain, according to the map, was his destination. At the base of the mountain was the Crypt of Zagamar, an underground tomb. Almost nothing was known of it, save for the mad ramblings of the men who'd attempted to venture inside. Even Legends had attempted to plumb its secrets over the millennia, to no avail. Tykus himself hadn't dared make the attempt, at least according to the Lady.

Which begged the question of how the Lady even knew that there *was* a man named Zagamar, or that his head was in the Crypt.

He'd asked her, of course. No one could be certain, she'd admitted, but other ancient crypts had been discovered in the past, and all had contained the bodies of powerful men and women. Not to mention that the medallion retrieved from Zagamar's crypt had apparently contained rather powerful traces of his will. A triangular artifact fashioned from pure platinum, it was the only object ever retrieved from the place.

Hunter tried not to think of what might happen to him in that crypt. Sure, he was an Original, but was that *really* going to protect him? Or was the Lady simply trying to get rid of him?

He grimaced, shoving the thought away. Picking up his pace, he rolled the map back up, putting it in his pocket. There was no point in second-guessing himself; he was going to do this, and that was that. After all the terrible things he'd done, his life was forfeit. He owed Vi that much. And his brother.

And Mom.

He fought down a sudden exhaustion, the feeling he got whenever his mind wandered back to his unfortunate past. The forest floor began to slope downward as he reached the end of the small hill, and he followed it, his eyes on the base of the mountain ahead.

The Crypt of Zagamar was near, and he was going to retrieve the man's head.

Even if it killed him.

* * *

By the time Hunter reached the base of the mountain, the sun was hovering just above the treetops behind him, throwing his shadow several yards ahead of him. The trees ahead stood on the shallow slope of the base of the mountain, appearing strikingly different than those around him. They had black bark, for one, and their trunks were a bit smaller in diameter. But they were much taller, with countless spindly branches that twisted upward and to the sides. Dark green leaves grew in remarkably dense clusters on each branch, at least on the trees that were still alive. Most were dead, their branches bare. The ground was covered in a thick bed of black branches that had fallen to the ground.

He slowed, staring at the trees ahead warily.

There was something *off* about them. Something wrong. Whereas he might have forged onward without much thought a few days ago, after his harrowing experience with the Legendary tree, he had a newfound respect for the power of the forest. An abrupt change in flora or fauna might mean that powerful, invisible forces were at play…another Legendary creature might be nearby, or might have influenced this area.

Hunter glanced to the left and right, spotting the black trees extending to either side as far as he could see. He'd have to go a considerable distance around to avoid them. The fact that there was such a large swath of them – and not just a circular patch like with the Legendary tree earlier – meant that it was unlikely that there was a single, powerful tree nearby. Luckily, the black trees didn't extend very far ahead; they gave way to bare rock and sparse grass that climbed further up the base of the mountain. He'd only have to hike a few hundred feet before being clear of them.

He remembered what Master Thorius had taught him, back at the Guild of Seekers. Transmission of traits depended on proximity to that which exuded the trait, the strength of the trait, and the duration of exposure. If he could limit the duration of exposure, he'd probably be fine. Especially if Lady Camilla had been telling the truth, and his status as an Original would protect him.

Only one way to find out…

He took a deep breath in, then burst forward, sprinting toward the blackened trees.

The carpet of dead branches crunched underfoot as he ran, and an immediate feeling of foreboding came over him. A primal fear that wrapped its fingers around his gut, twisting slowly. He had the sudden urge to turn back, and nearly did so. But Vi's training kicked in, and he dissociated himself from the feeling, studying it.

This emotion is not mine.

He continued forward, weaving around the blackened trees, lifting his knees high as he ran to avoid tripping on the fallen branches. Within moments, he passed the trees altogether, bursting past the forest to the bare rock beyond. Still he ran, until he was well clear of the trees. Only then did he slow, eventually coming to a stop.

The fear gradually faded, but did not leave completely. It remained in the back of his mind, present but manageable. So far.

Hunter glanced back at the forest, then turned forward. The base of the mountain sloped upward at a sharper angle here, making the going more difficult. He looked to his right, spotting a narrow dirt path a few hundred feet away. A path that wound up the mountain at a shallower angle, cutting through the stone around it, which formed short rocky walls on either side. He recalled what Lady Camilla had told him…that the entrance to the Crypt of Zagamar was at the end of a path that extended a short way up the base of the mountain.

That had to be the path she'd mentioned.

He stared at the path, feeling another pang of fear. It had to be residual emotion he'd absorbed from the bizarre trees…or was it? Lady Camilla had mentioned how dangerous this place was. How men had entered and never returned. The fear might very well be his.

He took a steadying breath, clenching his hands into fists.

It doesn't matter who owns this fear, he told himself. *Emotion is temporary, action is forever.*

And if he didn't take this path, he'd never get a chance at exacting his revenge.

Do it for Vi, he told himself. *Do it for Mom.*

He strode toward the path, forcing himself to put one foot in front of the other. As he drew nearer, he spotted stark white objects lying at the beginning of the path, half-covered by dirt. They were bones, he realized. He stopped before them, examining them.

They weren't human…that much was clear. It looked like a deer-sized animal, with four legs and a long skull, like a dog's. There was no flesh on the bones, which he supposed meant they'd been here for some time. He looked ahead, further along the path, and spotted more bones there. Lots of them, scattered on and around the path. And bodies, with dried, rotting flesh on them. Many appeared to be dead birds, while others were larger animals.

He stared at them, feeling a chill run down his spine.

What happened here?

Maybe there was some creature that had killed all these animals…but that didn't make much sense. Animals hunted to eat, and the corpses that still had flesh on them didn't look like they'd been munched on. Which meant that they'd died from something else.

He returned his gaze to the half-buried skeleton before him, then knelt down, lowering his forehead to press it against the creature's skull. He closed his eyes, and waited.

There was fear – a fresh spike of it that shot through his chest – but nothing else.

Hunter continued to wait, ignoring the fear, knowing that it was coming from this animal. It was powerful, this fear. The last emotion this creature had felt before its death. The fear grew within him, and he felt his heart start pounding in his chest. The air felt thin suddenly, as if the oxygen had been pulled out of it. His heart raced faster, and it took everything he had to stop himself from jumping to his feet and running back the way he'd come. He stayed put, gritting his teeth, his forehead still pressed against the beast's skull. Sweat trickled down his armpits to his flanks.

He felt himself running, saw black trees all around him. He looked down, seeing white fur covering his arms. No, his *legs*. He was running on all fours, black hooves where his hands should be.

His only thought was fear. A dread so powerful that it allowed nothing else.

He burst through the forest within unnerving speed, galloping toward the base of the mountain. He saw a path ahead, and ran toward it blindly. Faster and faster he galloped, his breath coming in short gasps, his heart nearly bursting out of his chest. He ran straight for the path, only fifty or so feet away now.

Have to get it out.

And there was only one way to do it.

He ran right up to the path, then veered left, toward one of the short rock walls bordering it. Faster he went, lowering his head, aiming right at the wall.

Get out of me!

And then pain exploded through his forehead, and the world went black.

Hunter gasped, his eyes snapping open. He shot to his feet, stumbling backward from the skeleton.

Jesus!

He forced himself to take deep, slow breaths. It was the creature's memory he'd experienced, not his own. But he'd never experienced an animal's memories so vividly.

It killed itself, he realized. Indeed, now that he looked, he noticed a large dent in the front of the creature's skull. It had smashed its own head against the rock wall.

He felt a bug land on his cheek, and swatted it away. But there was nothing there; it must have flown away before he hit it.

Jesus.

He took another deep breath in, letting it out slowly. If he could absorb an animal's memories, that meant that he could very likely absorb *any* creature's memories. But he'd touched quite a few trees in the past, and not felt anything. That made sense, he supposed; trees didn't have brains, after all, and couldn't make their own memories. They could only absorb the memories of things that had touched or been near them…and with each transmission, traits – including memories – grew weaker. That was why it was easiest to absorb traits directly from their source.

Okay, he thought. *This could come in handy.*

He stepped over the skeleton, following the path as it continued forward and upward. Rock walls almost as tall as he was flanked him on either side, the path only ten or twelve feet wide. The farther he went, the greater the density of bones lying on the path, and scattered atop the rock walls. He felt his fear return. No, *their* fear. The combined terror of countless creatures who had died here.

He felt another bug land on his forehead, and swatted it away. Again, there was nothing there. But he could still *feel* something. Something tickling his skin, as if an ant was crawling there. He slid his hand across his forehead, but didn't feel anything.

Weird.

He ignored the sensation, focusing on the path ahead. It wound to the left, revealing even more bones. They littered the ground so thickly that he could barely see the dirt of the path, and crunched under his boots with each step, the sound making his skin crawl. He noticed something else then, something *on* the bones.

Tiny black bugs, so small that he had to concentrate just to see them. They were *spiders*, he realized. Crawling over the bones…and his boots. They swarmed up his legs, quickly reaching his knees.

Shit!

He brushed them off quickly, striding faster down the path. He *hated* spiders, a loathing he'd inherited from his mother. It took everything he had to continue forward. Still, he couldn't help but glance at his legs again…and he saw more tiny spiders crawling back up his boots, swarming up to his thighs.

"Oh, come on!" he complained, brushing his legs off again. He felt a tickling sensation on his hands, and saw more tiny spiders crawling over them, running up his forearms.

For the love of…!

He sprinted forward, the *crunch, crunch* of his boots on the carcasses below sending a crawling sensation up his back. Or maybe it was the spiders. Crawling on his back. Crawling *under* his clothes.

He swore, slapping at the spiders as he ran. But the crawling sensation continued, moving up his spine, then the back of his neck. He felt a tickling sensation in his scalp then, crawling over his ears.

Crawling *into* his ears.

"Shit!" he swore, jabbing his fingers in his ears, then swatting at his scalp. "Damn fucking god-damn…!"

He felt a crawling sensation on his forehead again, and slapped his forehead with one hand. But the crawling sensation only intensified.

What the…

He pressed his fingers against his forehead, feeling something there. Something under his skin. Something *moving.*

Oh shit oh shit…

Hunter felt a similar sensation in his arms, and yanked up one sleeve, seeing small bumps on his skin. *Moving* bumps.

They're under my fucking skin!

He cried out, swatting at his arms and his head. But the sensation continued, that horrible crawling feeling. There was a sudden, gnawing pain deep within his forehead; he swore again, running blindly down the path, his heart practically beating out of his chest. He slammed the heel of his hand into his forehead, ignoring the pain. But the gnawing pain didn't stop. It grew stronger, deeper.

And then he felt a *pop*.

The crawling sensation spread across the front of his skull, expanding from the center of his forehead. But it wasn't on his skin, or under it. It was *inside*.

In his *brain*.

Hunter screamed, tearing at his skull with his fingernails, shrieking as he ran blindly. His shoulder slammed into one of the rock walls, and he ricocheted off, barely keeping his balance. Bones crunched underfoot as he ran down the path, blood trickling down his forehead and into his eyes, casting his vision in a crimson blur.

They ate a hole in my head, he realized. *They're in my brain!*

He screamed again, clawing at his forehead, his skin slippery with blood. His foot caught on something, and he fell forward, landing onto his belly on a thick pile of stark-white bones. The impact knocked the wind out of him, and he gasped for air, pushing himself onto his hands and knees. He crawled forward, seeing the path end ahead in a sheer rock wall…with a huge hole carved into it. An arched entranceway some twenty feet wide and equally tall, leading to pitch-blackness beyond. Two massive stone statues flanked the entrance, of scrawny humanoid creatures with unnaturally long legs and arms, faces twisted in a silent scream.

And tiny spiders swarmed over them. Over the path. Over *everything*.

Hunter scrambled to his feet, stumbling toward the entrance, his forehead burning. More blood dripped into his eyes, and he wiped it away with one sleeve, then looked down, spotting the hilt of his longsword – *Vi's* longsword, sheathed at his left hip. He grabbed it, sliding the sword free, then brought the blade up to his forehead, pressing it against his skin. He grit his teeth, feeling that awful crawling sensation in his skull. There was only one way to get the damn bugs out.

He gripped his sword tightly, pressing the blade harder against his skin.

He had to *cut* them out.

Do it, he ordered himself.

He took a deep breath in, letting it out. Steeling himself.

Do it!

He felt something then. Something soothing. Something calm. It was familiar somehow. It felt like…

Vi.

He hesitated, lifting the edge of the sword from his forehead, staring at it. The silver blade was stained with blood. His blood. But that didn't bother him.

His heart slowed, the crawling sensation under his skin – and in his skull – fading. He looked down at his free hand.

There were no bugs. Nothing crawling under his skin.

He looked back at the sword, catching his reflection in the blade. There were claw-marks on his forehead, with blood beading up from the wounds. But there was no hole in his skull. No bugs there.

He lowered the blade, staring at the bones around him.

No spiders.

Then he felt a spike of fear. Felt the crawling sensation return with a vengeance. He stared at his free hand, seeing faint bumps under his skin. Moving.

Shit!

He nearly dropped his sword…then froze, staring at the blade. He raised it again, pressing the cool metal against his forehead. Almost immediately, the crawling sensation vanished, the fear replaced by a soothing calm. A familiar calm…the same feeling he'd gotten after freaking out when walking down the path into the canyon to get to Vi's house for the first time. After standing close to Vi.

It was *her*. Her preternatural calm, absorbed by her sword after years of being close to her.

Hunter kept the side of the blade against his forehead, realizing that the spiders had vanished again.

They're not real, he realized.

A chill ran through him, and he swallowed in a dry throat, goosebumps rising on his flesh.

I almost cut open my own damn skull!

And he knew beyond a shadow of a doubt that, if it hadn't been for Vi – for her emotion absorbed into this sword – that he would have done it.

He closed his eyes, remembering the animal smashing its skull into the rocks. Trying to kill the things crawling in its brain. The spiders.

Hunter looked around at the countless bones around him. Thousands of corpses. He didn't need to touch them, didn't need to absorb their memories to know how they'd died. They hadn't been killed by a beast, or by poison.

They'd killed themselves.

Jesus.

He turned to the entranceway carved into the rock wall at the end of the path, keeping Vi's sword firmly against his forehead. If it hadn't been for Vi, he'd be dead now. Killed by his own hand. She'd saved him once again, even in death.

Thank you, he mouthed silently.

He stared at the entrance, knowing that it was the way forward into the Crypt of Zagamar. For the first time since he'd started the trip, he seriously considered turning around and going back. He hadn't even gotten into the crypt itself, and he'd nearly died. What chance would he have of surviving whatever horrors lay within?

It doesn't matter, he told himself. *Not after what you did.*

He'd killed his mother and his own brother, and his best friend was dead. His life was forfeit now. If he didn't finish this mission, he didn't deserve to live anyway.

Get the head. Get stronger. Kill them all.

He took a deep breath in, then strode forward, toward the gaping, pitch-black maw that marked the entrance to the Crypt of Zagamar.

CHAPTER 7

Dominus lay on his back on the floor beside his bed, staring at the blood spurting in irregular pulses from the stump of his right wrist. He turned his gaze upward, seeing the green and black-masked Seeker's curved sword rise into the air over its head.

The blade gleamed in the lantern-light.

The Seeker grunted, chopping downward with all its might, the cruel edge of its sword slicing through the air.

Aiming right for Dominus's neck.

Dominus didn't have time to bring his arm up to block the blow. Didn't even have time to be afraid. He closed his eyes, waiting for the end.

There was a sharp *clang* inches from his head, followed by a muffled grunt.

Opening his eyes, Dominus saw a broad band of pure silver across his line of vision. It was a blade, he realized…his cane-sword. It'd intercepted the Seeker's sword.

His cane-sword swung upward, flinging the Seeker's blade to the side, and the Seeker stumbled backward, the back of its legs striking the bed behind it. Dominus followed the cane-sword with his eyes, seeing a hand grasping its hilt. An old, wrinkled hand.

His eyes widened.

"Farkus!" he cried.

It *was* Farkus, his trusty servant. The man rushed at the Seeker, thrusting Dominus's sword at the Seeker's chest with unnerving speed, his technique perfect.

How…

The Seeker barely managed to block the blow with one of its swords, slashing at Farkus with the other one. Farkus dodged the attack effortlessly, thrusting forward again, this time at the Seeker's throat. Again the Seeker blocked, but Farkus pulled the attack back at the last minute, thrusting at its chest. The blade sank into its armor, and it grunted, taking a step backward.

Farkus thrust again and again, the blade striking its belly, then its upper thigh, then its groin, his attacks almost too quick to follow. Then he whipped the blade across its neck, severing its windpipe.

The Seeker stumbled into the bed, falling backward onto it.

Farkus climbed up onto the bed, his feet straddling the Seeker. He switched his grip on Dominus's sword, holding it with both hands, point-down. Then he thrust the blade downward, burying it in the Seeker's chest.

Farkus let go of the sword then, stepping down from the bed with some difficulty and kneeling at Dominus's side.

"Your Grace!" he cried in horror, his eyes going to Dominus's bleeding stump.

"Staunch the bleeding," Dominus ordered, his voice strangely calm. "Apply a tourniquet at once."

"Yes your Grace," Farkus replied, rushing to the bed. He yanked a pillowcase from one of the pillows, twisting it, then kneeling down and wrapping it around Dominus's forearm.

"Tighter," Dominus snapped. "Until the bleeding stops."

Farkus obeyed, tying the tourniquet so tightly that it was painful. Dominus grimaced, but did not complain, staring at his stump. The spurting stopped, blood dribbling from the two arteries there.

"There may be more of them," Dominus warned. "Lock and barricade the door." But Farkus was already doing so, locking the door, then sliding a chair up to it, leaning it so that the seat-back rested just beneath the doorknob. When he was done, he turned back to Dominus, who sat up with some difficulty, rising unsteadily to his feet. He felt a wave of lightheadedness, and steeled himself against it, waiting for it to pass.

"Your Grace?"

Dominus didn't reply, closing his eyes. The pressure in his chest had mostly subsided, vitality having returned to his limbs. To his surprise, his amputated limb and almost assuredly broken shoulder didn't hurt…yet. It was only a matter of time before they did, he knew. He went to his nightstand, opening one of its drawers and retrieving a small, corked glass vial. It was filled with a clear fluid…opium, just enough to dull his pain without overly dulling his mind. Dominus popped the cork with his thumb, pouring the fluid into his mouth and swallowing. It was terribly bitter; he resisted the urge to throw it back up.

"What now, your Grace?" Farkus asked. Dominus turned to the old man.

"My sword," he ordered.

Farkus walked to the bed, pulling the sword from its fleshy scabbard and handing it to him. Dominus held it in his left hand; even with his nondominant hand, he would be more skilled than Farkus. Something was lost any time a trait was transmitted from one person or object to another. Farkus's skills would never match Dominus's, unless the servant absorbed them directly from his master's collection of artifacts.

Suddenly there was pounding at the door. Dominus spun around.

"Your Grace?" a voice called out from behind it. He recognized it immediately…it was the captain of his guard.

"Stay back," Dominus ordered Farkus. The captain could be at the Seekers' mercy, forced to call out to Dominus or be killed. He needed to speak with the captain, however, to organize the castle's defenses. And to better understand the remaining threat.

"I am here," Dominus called out.

"The castle is secure," the captain stated. "Are you well?"

Dominus considered this. The captain hadn't immediately requested entry into the room; that meant it was less likely the man was acting under duress, at the command of the Seekers. He nodded at Farkus, who opened the door, revealing a tall man in chain mail armor, a half-dozen more soldiers behind him. He saluted sharply when he saw Dominus…then noticed Dominus's severed hand.

"Your Grace!" he cried, his eyes widening in horror. He turned to one of his soldiers. "Summon the doctor at once!" he ordered.

"Debrief me," Dominus commanded.

"The castle is secure," the captain repeated. "Nearly fifty Seekers dead," he continued. "And twice as many of our men," he added darkly.

"How did they gain entry?"

"Unknown," the captain admitted. "We're working on it."

"Send a courier with an armed escort to Tykus," Dominus ordered. "Relay news of the attack, and request replacements for the soldiers lost."

"Yes your Grace."

"Secure the perimeter," Dominus continued. "Prepare for a second attack." He sighed, glancing back at the bed, the dead Seeker splayed across it. "I'll be sleeping in the vault tonight."

"Understood, your Grace."

"Good work," Dominus told the captain. "You and your men have done a great service to preserve the Duchy." He gave a rare smile, handing his cane-sword to Farkus, then putting a hand on the captain's armored shoulder. It was an almost unprecedented gesture; for a member of the aristocracy to touch a commoner was to expose them to a hint of the combined wills of the most powerful men in history of Tykus. It was a great honor…perhaps the greatest honor the captain had ever been bestowed.

The captain accepted this silently, his eyes downcast, his lower lip trembling.

"Go now," Dominus ordered.

The captain exited at once, and Dominus closed the door. He sighed, then turned to the body of the Seeker lying on the bed. He walked up to it, staring down at its green and black mask. The unmistakable uniform of a Seeker of the Kingdom of the Deep.

But why would they attack him?

Tykus and the Kingdom of the Deep had no love for each other, it was true. But they were not at war, and neither party would dare provoke the other. Of course, the prospect of an Ossae as powerful as the head of the Ironclad – and the incredible ability it offered – might prompt the Kingdom of the Deep to risk war.

Still, something was bothering him.

If *he* were to attempt such an attack on an enemy, he would not send men dressed in his official regalia. It was asinine to so readily disclose one's identity to an enemy. A covert operation such as this required anonymity…it was pointless to advertise the source of such a mission.

Unless…

He grabbed the mask, pulling it from the Seeker's face…and frowned.

It was a man. A bald man with blue eyes and a brown goatee. He was not completely human – his skin texture was too rough, his ears abnormally small – but he was far more human than Dominus had expected. Far too human for a Seeker of the Deep.

Interesting.

He stared at the man's face, considering the possibilities.

The goal of the attack was to kill him, that much was clear. But why try to kill him? He had no shortage of enemies, it was true, but no one from Tykus would dare move against him. Or at least no one from the Acropolis.

Dominus turned away from the Seeker, staring at the floor.

The only other person that used Seekers trained in the Kingdom of the Deep was Lady Camilla. But she would never act against him, for fear of upsetting the delicate balancing act she'd managed between the two kingdoms.

His eyes wandered, going to the rug hiding the trapdoor, where the Ironclad's head was stored.

Of course!

He turned to Farkus.

"Double our resources on the surveillance of the Guild of Seekers," he ordered. Farkus bowed.

"Yes, your grace."

The man turned to leave, but Dominus stopped him with a gesture, eyeing the man for a long, silent moment. Then Dominus walked up to his faithful servant, putting his remaining hand on the man's frail, bony shoulder. Farkus's eyes widened, his body stiffening. It was the first time Dominus had ever touched him.

"Thank you Farkus," Dominus stated. Farkus swallowed visibly, bowing his head.

"Of course, your Grace."

"I owe you my life," Dominus declared. Farkus said nothing, clearly uncomfortable with this praise. Dominus lowered his hand from Farkus's shoulder, turning to look at the Seeker lying on the bed. "You fought well," he observed. A fact that still surprised him; the man had no training in the use of weapons. Farkus had clearly absorbed more than Dominus's personality. Much more.

"I didn't know I could," Farkus admitted.

"Yes, well," Dominus muttered. "You'll have your reward."

Farkus bowed deeply.

"That you live," he replied, "…is reward enough, your Grace."

Chapter 8

The air cooled instantly as Hunter stepped through the massive arched entrance of the Crypt of Zagamar, the sun not daring to cast its warming rays into that formidable, gaping maw. The stone floor beyond was littered with skeletons, as the path leading to the crypt had been. Gray stone walls surrounded him on either side, forming a broad hallway, the ceiling lost to darkness high above his head. Beyond, there was pitch-blackness.

He stared into that void, the side of Vi's blade still pressed against his temple. Despite the calming influence of her weapon, he felt a trickle of fear.

Slipping his backpack from his shoulder, he set it on the ground, keeping the sword against his head. He opened the pack, finding a small lantern inside. It was an oil lamp; it would last him a few hours according to Lady Camilla. She'd provided him with it and a small amount of replacement oil. He retrieved the lamp, then some flint and a small steel file. He lowered his sword for a moment, setting it aside, then used the flint and file to light the lamp. He retrieved his sword quickly as a wave of panic threatened to overtake him, and pressed the blade against his forehead again. The panic subsided as quickly as it had come, and he packed everything up, picking up the lamp with his left hand and holding it ahead of him.

The lantern cast its golden light forward, piercing through the darkness ahead. The wide hallway narrowed gradually, ending at a set of massive double-doors forty feet away. He strode toward them, studying them carefully. The doors were made of a silver metal, and they were so tall that they were swallowed by the darkness above. One of the doors was slightly ajar; Hunter walked up to it, putting a hand on the metal. It was cold to the touch, and he felt an immediate spike of fear as he rested his hand on it. He withdrew his hand quickly, cursing silently.

Don't touch anything.

As Master Thorius had taught him, absorption of traits depended on proximity. The closer he was to an object, the more powerfully he would absorb its traits. Touching anything in this cursed place could be extremely dangerous…or even deadly. As long as he kept Vi's sword against his skull – close to his brain – and didn't touch anything else, he should be safe.

Or so he hoped.

The rightmost door had been opened just enough to allow him to squeeze through, for which he was immensely grateful. There was no way he'd have been able to get those doors open himself. If they'd been closed, this would've been the end of the line.

Hunter peered through the gap, shining his lantern through it. He saw a stone floor littered with bones piled high, almost up to waist-level…and beyond that, darkness.

He hesitated, then squeezed through the gap, his chest and back scraping against the doors. Even that short contact made the fear return, more powerfully this time. He hurried through, emerging on the other side, feeling the fear abate. He tried not to imagine what he'd be feeling if it wasn't for Vi's sword.

Jesus, he thought. *Place is friggin' cursed.*

Hunter held the lantern in front of him, finding himself in a short, narrower hallway. While there had been a few skeletons lining the floor on the other side of the door, here they were piled up so high against the door that he had to practically wade through them. He grimaced, peering ahead; the pile of bones sloped downward quickly to meet the gray stone floor, maybe twenty feet ahead. It seemed like every one of the long-dead bodies was facing the door.

Wading through the pile, he continued onward down the hallway, following it until it opened up into a large, dark chamber…one so large that the light from his lantern was only able to illuminate a fraction of it. Most of the chamber seemed to consist of a huge pit, one so deep his lantern-light couldn't reach the bottom. The floor split into three stone ledges five feet wide each, suspended over the huge pit; one continuing forward, vanishing into the darkness twenty feet ahead, and two ledges on either side, jutting out from the rear wall of the chamber…and dropping off abruptly into that pit.

Hunter hesitated, then stepped forward onto the ledge directly ahead, peering through the darkness. The narrow stone platform extended forward as far as he could see, surrounded on either side by the pitch-black pit. A few skeletons lay strewn across the narrow ledge.

Three options: left, right, or forward.

He took another step forward, then froze.

Take your time, he told himself. *Think about this.*

If he went forward, he'd be stuck on a narrow platform, with a drop on either side into God-knows what. The light from his lantern extended about twenty to thirty feet ahead, meaning that there was at least a twenty-foot drop on either side of the platform…enough to kill or seriously injure him. All it would take is a slip-up, or a particularly strong radiated emotion – say one that made him freak out, or feel dizzy, or whatever – and he'd be as good as dead.

All right, he decided. *Not forward then.*

He looked left and right, but there was no difference between the two. Just ledges five feet wide, with a wall on one side, the black pit on the other.

Eeny, meeny, miney, moe…

Then he had an idea.

He took a few steps down the right ledge, then stopped, setting his lantern down and placing his palm on the wall to his right.

Fear.

He continued forward, switching his sword to his left hand and grabbing the lantern, hooking it on his upper arm and keeping his right hand on the wall as he went. The fear grew, twisting his guts. Sweat trickled down his sides.

Still forward he went.

The path continued ahead as far as he could see, the gaping maw of the pit to his left. He kept as close to the wall as possible; with only a couple of feet between him and that pit, he knew that one slip-up, one mistake, and he'd be a dead man.

Turn back.

He stopped, pulling his hand away from the wall, waiting for the panic to subside. It did, more slowly this time. Turning around, he walked back to the leftmost ledge, continuing down it, switching his sword to his right hand again, and placing his left hand against the wall.

Again, the fear.

Forward he went, one foot in front of the other. His fingertips slid against the cold, smooth stone, making faint lines in the dust covering it. The air was musty as well, tickling his throat. He resisted the urge to cough, continuing down the path, hugging the wall. The fear was there, as before, but less intense, less urgent.

This must be the way.

The ledge went on for another dozen yards or so, ending at a tall, narrow doorway at the corner of the huge room. Hunter stepped through the doorway, finding himself in a wide hallway that continued rightward. The walls on either side were so tall that they vanished into the darkness high above; ahead, he spotted a huge stone statue standing against the left wall. It was identical to the ones he'd seen flanking the entrance to the crypt, taking up half the width of the hallway. He stayed close to the rightmost wall, stepping past the statue. Unlike the statues he'd seen outside of the entrance to the crypt, this one had bones embedded within. Skulls.

Countless skulls, all facing outward, their empty eye-sockets staring lifelessly, their jaws open in a silent, eternal scream.

Hell of an interior decorator.

There was another, identical statue further ahead, this time standing against the rightmost wall. He went to the left, passing it. More skulls staring at him.

One of them turned as he passed, its eye sockets following him.

He blinked, stopping abruptly and staring at the skull. It was facing outward, not staring at him. Which made sense, because skulls couldn't move. Especially skulls embedded in stone. His eyes were clearly playing tricks on him.

Hunter shook his head, continuing down the hallway. It wasn't long before he came upon a third statue, on the left-hand side again. He passed this, keeping his eyes straight ahead. No point in freaking himself out again. Still, he could *feel* dozens of eyes upon him, following him as he passed.

Don't look, he told himself. *Just gonna freak yourself out.*

The hallway ended ahead in another right-hand turn, and Hunter followed it, seeing another tunnel extending into the darkness. His right arm was burning from having to keep his sword up against his forehead; he switched the lantern and sword, then continued forward.

To his relief, there were no more statues ahead…just plain stone walls on either side.

It wasn't long before the hallway ended again, turning to the left this time. He turned with it; there were stairs leading downward ahead, rougher-looking rock walls on either side. Going down the stairs, he reached the bottom some ten feet below, leading to another fork in the path…a hallway to the right, and one to the left.

He repeated the same process he'd used last time, going down the right path, his hand on the wall as he did so. Again, the fear…and the farther he went, the more intense it got.

Wrong way…shouldn't have gone this way.

He felt a sudden, powerful sense of regret, and stopped in his tracks, doubling back. It had to be someone else's memory, absorbed into the wall. He continued down the left hallway, doing the same as before. Fear…but less intense. This had to be the right way.

The path took a left turn, then another, and suddenly the hallway opened up, the leftmost wall ending, replaced by another pitch-black pit. Hunter paused, kneeling at the edge of the pit and lowering his lantern into it.

Below – far below – he could barely make out something. Orange light reflecting off row after row of…things. He peered at them.

They were spikes. Long, very sharp, spikes.

He stood, backing up quickly. Looking up, he saw only blackness.

There was a sudden rumbling sound to his right.

He turned toward it, seeing the wall there. Something was wrong. Very wrong.

It was moving. Toward *him.*

He stared at the wall, watching in disbelief as it inched toward him…and the pit. Watched as the ledge he was standing on steadily narrowed.

"Oh come on!" Hunter complained. He shoved his shoulder against the wall, but it was no use…it kept moving, pushing him toward the pit…and the deadly spikes far below. He was forced to take a step back, then another, until one of his heels was hanging over the edge of the platform.

Shit!

Turning to face the wall, he held his sword flat against it, shoving the hilt into the wall with one hand, and the flat of the blade with the other. He dug his boots into the floor, pressing against the wall with every bit of his strength. But it was hopeless…the wall continued to shove him backward, slowly but surely, toward the spike-laden pit behind him.

He was forced to take a step back with his other foot, both of his heels hanging off the ledge now.

Hunter cried out, pressing his whole body against the wall now, his temple shoved against the cold steel of Vi's blade. He felt the wall press forward, felt one of his feet slip off the platform. He squeezed his eyes shut, knowing that he was about to die.

And then the wall seemed to vanish.

He stumbled forward, catching his balance and opening his eyes.

The wall was five feet away from him, the platform he stood on back to its original width. He looked down, realizing he was standing at the very edge of it, inches away from falling into the spiked pit. He swore, stumbling forward and pressing himself against the wall, half-expecting it to start moving again.

And then it did.

He braced himself, then froze.

Your sword!

Lifting it up, he pressed the flat edge of the blade against his forehead, ignoring the wall. Moments later, it stopped moving, instantly returning to its original position.

Holy shit.

It'd all been an illusion. He'd forgotten about keeping Vi's sword against his head, and had nearly thrown himself into the spiked pit. If he hadn't pressed his temple against the blade at the last minute by accident, he'd be dead.

God damn.

He stood there, sweat pouring down his sides, his heart pounding in his chest. He swallowed in a dry throat, knowing that he was alive only through sheer, dumb luck. The urge to go back – to leave this god-forsaken place – nearly overwhelmed him.

Calm down, he told himself.

He waited, taking deep breaths in, then letting them out slowly. His heart gradually slowed, the terror easing. He kept Vi's blade against his head, absorbing its calm. Vi's calm.

Then he steeled himself, continuing forward down the platform.

It wasn't long before he saw something in the pit to his left…large stone columns rising from the darkness. He followed them upward, seeing that they were supporting a narrow platform one story above. It was, he realized, the platform he'd seen earlier, near the entrance to the tomb…the one the stairs had led down to. He could only imagine what awful delusions had been absorbed by it, to make an unwitting victim leap to their own death. Lady Camilla had mentioned that the men who'd attempted to enter the Crypt of Zagamar had all gone mad. Perhaps this Zagamar had forced actual madmen – men with schizophrenia, or some other delusional disorder – to stay here. The stone walls would've absorbed their madness, transferring it to anyone that passed near.

That explains the narrow platforms and hallways, he deduced. It forced people to stay near the walls. Absorption required proximity and duration; that explained all the intersections. Each time someone went the wrong way and had to double back, it increased the duration of exposure.

Clever bastard, this Zagamar.

He continued forward, and eventually the platform ended in a sheer stone wall ahead. To the left, over the pit, was a narrow staircase spiraling downward. It was the only way to go, unless he wanted to turn back. But he had a feeling this was the right way. How he knew that, he could only guess…but he'd learned to trust his intuition. More often than not it was absorbed memories that were guiding him. He'd be a fool to ignore them.

Hunter followed the stairs downward, making sure to stay as far away from the edge as possible. The stairs spiraled downward, bringing him down through the floor of the spiked pit. He paused to study the spikes on the way down; they were a few feet long and made of rusted steel. There were more than a few bones wedged between them.

Could have been me, he thought with a shudder.

He continued down the spiraling staircase, descending into another room one story below. The floor of the spiked pit was the ceiling of this new room; peering through the darkness, he saw an irregular, rocky floor at the bottom of the stairs. Bones were strewn across it, almost as thickly as they'd been outside the crypt. He slowed, stopping a few steps above the bottom of the stairs, holding his lantern ahead of him and peering into the darkness.

An endless sea of bones littering the floor, and nothing else.

Keeping Vi's sword against his forehead, he stepped down from the last of the stairs, bones crunching under his boots. The air was thick with dust, tickling his nose. He sneezed, trying to hold it back for some reason, but failing. A silly attempt…there was no one here to hear him after all.

No one alive, anyway.

He strode forward, careful not to trip over the bones as he went. So many bones, extending as far as the lantern's light allowed him to see. Still he walked, until he spotted a wall ahead. There were bones there as well, embedded into the stone.

Human bones.

Hunter stayed well clear of the wall, hardly wanting to suffer whatever influence those bones might have on him. The ones at his feet were far away from his head – much farther than Vi's sword, at least – which was probably why he couldn't feel their influence. Or not very strongly, at least; he did feel a slight trepidation.

Dust tickled his nose, and he sneezed again. The sound echoed through the large chamber.

The wall extended to the left and right as far as he could see, vanishing into the darkness beyond. He decided to go right, walking parallel to the wall, staying a few yards away from it. It curved to the left as he went, ever-so-slightly. He followed the curve, his boots crunching on the bones underfoot.

Seconds passed, then minutes. Still the wall curved, ever-leftward.

How big is this damn room?

Hunter walked for few more minutes before stopping and staring at the wall, a frown on his face. He'd been walking for at least a quarter mile, if not a half-mile. There was no way the room could be that huge. He inspected the wall more carefully; there were occasional symbols carved into its surface, one every few yards. A skull, a heart…the anatomical version, not the standard Valentine's day one. He strode forward, spotting another symbol, at eye-level: a brain.

Hunter resumed walking, still following the wall, but studying its surface. More symbols…a human hand. Then a tree. A man standing in water, his arms raised to the heavens. Long, spindly arms, with long, thin fingers.

Onward he went.

There were fewer carvings now, spread farther apart…and never repeating. A book. A crowd bowing before the same long-limbed man. And then a long stretch with no symbols at all.

Huh.

A minute passed, and then he spotted something familiar…a carving of a skull. Then a heart.

He slowed, then stopped. The symbols were identical to the ones he'd seen before. Beyond them, he spotted a symbol of a brain. At eye-level, just as before.

I'm going in a circle, he realized.

He shook his head, kicking himself mentally. Of course he was…the wall was curving to the left…and that meant it was making a circle. A huge circle. Which meant that this room had a huge circular wall in the center of it, and he was just going around and around it. There was no way to get inside the circle that he could see. Maybe if he followed the exterior wall of the room, he might find a way forward.

Hunter turned away from the wall, walking perpendicular to it. It wasn't long before he came to another wall…flat, not curved. He turned left, following perpendicular to it. Eventually it ended at a ninety-degree angle, turning left. He turned with it, coming to another left-turn a minute later. He repeated this a few more times before he realized that he was going in circles. Or rather, squares.

Well shoot.

He stopped, thinking it through…and ignoring a constant, low-level anxiety that had gripped him ever since he'd descended into this room. As far as he could tell, the room was a huge square, with a walled-off circle in the center of it. He'd only spotted one staircase going up, which was the one he'd come down through. That meant that this room was a dead end.

But it *felt* like he was going the right way. What was he missing?

He walked back to the circular wall in the center of the room, studying the surface of the wall more carefully. There were occasional bones embedded into the surface, and the symbols he'd seen before. Glancing upward, he noticed that the wall was curving away from him as it went up, vanishing into the darkness high above his head. He held his lantern higher, but still couldn't see where the wall met the ceiling. But it was pretty clear that the wall wasn't just a wall.

It was a dome.

Why would they put a dome in the center of a room?

The dome was huge, of that he was certain. Maybe sixty feet in diameter, or perhaps even bigger. He looked down, noticing that the skeletons lying on the floor were piled up a bit higher at the perimeter of the dome.

Strange.

He switched his sword to his left hand, his lantern to his right, giving his right shoulder a break…but making sure to keep Vi's blade against his forehead, so that he could continue to absorb…

His eyes widened.

Memories!

He stepped closer to the dome, kneeling and setting his lantern on the floor. Then he reached out, picking up a skull. He hesitated, then set Vi's sword aside, lifting the skull until it pressed against his forehead. He closed his eyes.

Images of men sitting all around him. Men with grotesquely gaunt faces, their eyes sunken into their skulls. More men lying dead on the floor, looking for all the world like skeletons save for a thin layer of flesh draped over their bones.

He looked down, seeing his own bare belly, ribs and the bones of his pelvis clearly visible. His clothes barely held up by a long piece of cloth wrapped around his emaciated waist. He was holding a knife, and crouching before a young, emaciated man lying on the floor, one too weak to move anymore. The man stared up at him, his eyes wide with terror.

He held the man's arm down by the elbow, plunging the knife into his bicep, severing the tendons securing it to his bones.

The man screamed, a pathetic mewling that echoed through the room.

He ignored the sound, freeing the hot, bloody muscle, then bringing it hungrily to his lips.

Hunter eyes snapped open, and he jerked back, dropping the skull and bolting to his feet.

Jesus!

He looked down at himself, relieved to see his own body again. Then he gazed at the countless skeletons on the floor, a chill running down his spine.

They all starved to death.

His eyes went to the dome in front of him, and he knew – without knowing how – that there was a way inside. That the man who had built this crypt was inside of the dome. The man who had trapped him…trapped these people, rather…inside of this cursed tomb.

Zagamar.

But these people – whoever they'd been – hadn't known the way inside the dome. And the double-doors far above – at the entrance to the crypt – had been sealed shut when these people died. A memory of countless men crowded by those doors, pounding on them, came to him. Screaming for someone to open them.

They'd been tricked. Left to die with their master.

Hunter shook the memory away, knowing it was not his. He couldn't help but picture the bones piled high against the doors at the entrance to the crypt, the ones he'd had to wade through.

Goosebumps rose on his arms.

He took a deep breath, letting it out…then quickly retrieving his sword and pressing it against his head. He stood there, considered his options. It was clear that these people – these skeletons – on the floor hadn't know the way into the dome. But *someone* must have. The question was, who?

He stared at the wall, his eyes resting on one of the symbols there.

A brain.

Hunter hesitated, then stepped forward, stopping a foot from the wall. He reached out with his free hand, touching the symbol and waiting.

Nothing.

He leaned in then, lowering Vi's sword and pressing his forehead against the symbol. The stone was cool and dusty, and he stifled another sneeze, holding his breath.

Sudden, intense despair…and nothing else.

Hunter took a step away from the wall, bringing Vi's sword back up to his forehead.

Well shit.

Frustration mounted within him, and he resisted it, trying to think. There was no point in getting upset…that would be a waste of time.

He glanced to the left, spotting another symbol on the dome…the skull. There was something very familiar about it. Which wasn't surprising; he'd seen it before, after all. But still…

He walked up to it, pressing it with his left hand. The symbol sank inward a fraction of an inch, forming a small circular depression.

Click.

"All right," he murmured, smiling to himself. "Now we're getting somewhere."

He glanced at the symbol of the heart, then the brain, walking up to the latter and reaching out to touch it. But something didn't feel right; he lowered his hand, continuing rightward, following the perimeter of the dome. The next symbol was of the man standing in water, then the one of a hand. He touched the latter, then pressed on it. Another *click.*

Continuing rightward, he saw the next symbol, the tree…and passed it. Again, it didn't feel right. Next was the symbol of the book. An open book, tiny symbols etched into the pages. His hand hovered over it.

Nope.

The last symbol was the crowd worshipping the man; he passed this, circling around again. At length he came back to the symbol of the skull, then the heart. Then the brain. He hesitated, staring at the last one, sliding his fingers over it. This time, it felt right. He pressed on it.

Click.

"Two more," he murmured. And he knew without a doubt that he was right. He walked leftward this time, circling back to the symbol of the man standing in water, and pressing on it. Another *click.* He immediately went rightward, stopping at the symbol of the crowd worshipping the man and pressing on it.

Click.

A deep, low rumbling sound echoed through the darkness, the floor vibrating under his feet. Dust fell from the ceiling, sliding down the dome walls and covering Hunter from head to toe. He took a step back, pulling the neck of his shirt up to cover his mouth. Even so, he coughed, the musty air irritating his lungs.

Then the rumbling stopped.

Hunter stared at the dome, his eyebrows furrowing.

Now what?

Something had happened, that was certain. Something had moved. But what?

He resumed walking, circling around the dome slowly, lighting the way with his lantern. It was eerie, being surrounded by darkness, and complete silence, save for his own breathing. If it hadn't been for Vi's presence – through her sword – he was sure he'd have gotten claustrophobic.

Eventually he spotted something: passage through the dome. One that hadn't been there earlier. It was three feet high, and just as wide. He stopped before it, kneeling down and peering through. The lantern light illuminated a stone floor beyond in a narrow ray; the floor sloped sharply downward. It was too dark to see much further. He hesitated, glancing back, seeing only darkness.

"Guess I don't have a choice," he grumbled.

He got on his hands and knees, crawling through the opening. The dome was a full foot thick; he passed through the small passage, standing up on the other end. He raised his lantern, taking in his surroundings.

He was in a large, domed room. The lantern-light allowed him to see twenty or so feet ahead…not enough to take in the whole room at once. The walls of the dome curved upward, eventually obscured by darkness, making it impossible to see the ceiling. The floor sloped sharply after a few feet; beyond that, he spotted something rippling…a pool of dark, murky water. The air was terribly muggy, in stark contrast to the dryness of the rest of the crypt.

Hunter peered ahead, seeing the pool extending forward as far as he could see. Beyond that, there was darkness.

He turned rightward, circling around the perimeter of the pool. Eventually he spotted the same doorway ahead…the one he'd come through. Nothing else…except for the large pool. Which meant that if there was anything in here, it had to be in the center of the pool.

Alright then, he decided. *Time to get wet.*

Stepping to the edge of the platform before the pool, he peered into the water. It looked to be a about foot deep…not too bad. He took another step, dipping his foot into the pool, feeling nothing until the water rose above his waterproof boots. Then he felt chilly water soak into his pants and socks, spilling into his boot. His foot touched bottom, the water up to his knee. He stepped in with his other foot, then strode forward carefully. The floor of the pool sloped downward gradually, and as he waded, the water rose all the way up to his groin. He grimaced, taking a sharp breath in.

"Oh yeah," he muttered as the icy water bathed his tender bits. "That's the stuff."

Continuing forward, the bottom of the pool continued to get deeper, the water rising to his hips now. And to his backpack, he realized; he hardly wanted to get it – and everything in it – wet. He turned about, wading back to the edge of the pool and setting his pack on the floor. The he resumed his foray into the pool, aiming for the center of the domed chamber.

The pool deepened, the water rising to his bellybutton.

Better not get much deeper, he thought. If he had to swim, he wouldn't be able to hold both his sword and the lantern. God only knew what horrible things might happen to him if he didn't have Vi's sword...and he'd be blind without the lantern. But he didn't have to worry for long; he spotted something ahead, the light of the lantern illuminating something black protruding from the water. As he drew closer, he saw that it was a large circular platform. Life-size statues lined the perimeter of the platform, save for directly ahead of him. They appeared to be human, these statues, carved from black stone. Some were kneeling, others were bowing.

Hunter felt the floor of the pool angle upward, and realized that the floor was ramping up to the platform. He strode up it, studying the statues. They weren't *exactly* human, he realized; their faces were off somehow, their arms and legs a bit too long. And they were beyond gaunt, their ribs showing, their eyes sunken.

And all of them were facing the center of the platform, their mouths open in a silent, agonizing scream.

Hunter took the ramp up to the platform, squeezing between a statue on either side of him and peering ahead. The platform was about forty feet in diameter, and in the center of it was...something. Something *huge.* His eyes widened, his jaw going slack.

"Holy shit," he breathed.

A huge statue stood there made of the same black stone, but dwarfing the others. The base of it was a huge skull made of the same stone as the platform. The twin caverns of its eye sockets, each large enough for Hunter to crawl through, stared outward at him. The top of the skull was flat, and there were stairs between its eyes – where its nose should be – going from the platform up to the flat surface. Beyond the stairs was a large stone bowl, and standing behind that bowl was a second statue, also made of black stone, rising up from the top of the skull.

A very tall statue.

It was of a man, its nude groin endowed with an enormous member preserved at half-mast, extending slightly downward so that its bulbous head hung directly over the large bowl. It had a narrow torso, the muscles of its abdomen defined by deep furrows in that black stone, veins crawling up on either side of its core. A muscled chest, the thick slabs of its pectorals leading to equally muscular arms that extended upward in a "V" high above its head. Arms that were too long to be human, with equally long fingers that ended in short, sharp claws barely visible in the shadows above.

Hunter's eyes went to its face.

It was human, again…although not completely. Its face was slightly too long, its eyes slightly sunken. Its mouth was open in a silent scream, its face twisted in eternal agony.

Triumphant in its pose, yet tortured by that triumph.

Hunter stared a moment longer, then stepped up to the staircase between the skull's eyes. He took the stairs upward; they led to the floor of its open cranium, a flat, black stone surface. He stood before the large bowl positioned below the bulbous head of its engorged member.

"Someone's over-compensating," he grumbled.

In the center of the bowl was a human skull embedded in a block of solid, transparent crystal, fused to the bowl. The dome of its skull emerged from the crystal, glowing a faint yellow in the light of his lantern.

He stared at it silently, feeling a grumbling in his stomach.

Hunter ignored the sensation – he hadn't eaten in hours – and stepped up to the bowl, staring down at the skull. He felt a powerful sense of déjà vu, a chill running through him.

Setting the lantern down, he reached for the skull.

Za-ga-mar!

A force slammed into his consciousness, so powerful that he nearly stumbled backward. He cried out, feeling a sudden pain in his abdomen, as if giant fingers had plunged into his belly, gripping his intestines and twisting them.

Za-ga-mar!

He squeezed his eyes shut against the pain…and saw a flash of blinding light.

He opened his eyes, finding himself standing on a stone balcony, facing a huge courtyard far below. Thousands of men stood in that courtyard, kneeling before him. They stood then, as one, their eyes raised to him. Pumped their fists in the air, chanting in unison, their voices echoing through the courtyard.

Za-ga-mar!

The pain in his belly grew, a sharp, cramping pain that demanded his attention. He cried out, opening his eyes…and finding himself standing before the bowl again, before that skull embedded in its crystalline tomb. His mind began to race, his vision sharpening. He took in the details of the skull, every suture connecting its bones, every glittering facet of the transparent crystal. He spotted an unbroken horizontal line in the base of the skull immediately above the crystal, where the top of its skull protruded.

The pain in his abdomen intensified, forcing him to double over. He closed his eyes, gritting his teeth against that agony, feeling something else.

Hunger.

Images flashed in his mind's eye in rapid sequence, one after the other in a seemingly endless parade. A huge pool of black water. An army of men standing before him in a town square, the burnt-out husks of shattered buildings all around him. Bodies lying all around him…women, children. Babies strewn across the cobblestones with shattered skulls.

Za-ga-mar!

One moment he was standing in a massive chapel, men kneeling before him. He looked down at his hands, seeing a jewel-encrusted crown clutched in his long fingers. The next moment, he was lying in bed, surrounded by nude women. Young women, their hands all over him. One woman lay between his legs, her hot mouth engulfing his member. His hips bucked, and he cried out in ecstasy, feeling a rhythmic pulsing as she brought him to orgasm.

More pain. More hunger, insistent now. Demanding to be fed.

He heard his men shouting his name. The sound echoing through the air. The name of a conqueror. Of a man who had become God.

Za-ga-mar!

Hunter gasped, his eyes snapping open. He clutched at his belly, the pain gripping it forcing him to his knees. Vi's sword fell from his hand, striking the ground with a clatter. He grit his teeth, reaching out and grabbing the lip of the stone bowl with one hand, then the other.

Hunger consumed him. Ravished him. A hunger so powerful that nothing else mattered.

Za-ga-mar!

He pulled himself to his feet, his heart pounding in his chest. He opened his eyes, seeing the skull there, its empty eye sockets staring back at him.

Feed.

Hunter stared at the horizontal line in the skull, at the base of the dome. He reached out with both hands, his fingers trembling. Rested his fingertips on that cool, smooth bone, a chill running through him. His heart beat faster, thumping powerfully against his breastbone, blood pulsing in his ears.

He pulled upward at the dome of the skull, feeling it resist. Then he felt a *pop*, saw the dome open like the lid of a chest. The inner surface of the skull was lined with a silver metal that glimmered in the light of the lantern.

And within its hollowed base, a light brown liquid filling it to the brim.

Za-ga-mar!

Hunter stared at it, feeling a sudden dull, aching sensation in his hands. His hunger grew, insatiable now, a mad desire that threatened to consume him.

FEED.

He stared at that brown liquid, his fingers trembling, that aching pain in his hands spreading to his wrists and forearms.

A voice inside his head screamed at him. Told him to run.

He dropped to his knees, gripping the stone bowl on either side, lowering his face to the base of the skull. His lips stopped a fraction of an inch from the surface of the brown liquid it held, trembling as they parted.

He knelt there, the hunger lashing out at him. A deep voice boomed in his skull, demanding to be obeyed.

FEED!

He closed his eyes, his whole body trembling now.

Za-ga-mar!

And then he lowered his lips to the cool, thick liquid, and drank.

Chapter 9

Sukri stood in the Sparring Room, a large room in the basement of the Guild of Seekers, standing on a ten-by-ten-meter mat. Gammon stood to her left, and Sen, Jasmine, and a few other Seeker apprentices stood to her right. All were facing Master Thorius, who had just finished teaching the newest batch of initiates, and had come to supervise the apprentices' battle training. Master Thorius was only slightly taller than Sukri, and rather stocky, with a salt-and pepper goatee and short, light brown hair. A long scar ran down his left cheek, rippling as he spoke.

"Good afternoon," he greeted.

"Good afternoon, Master Thorius," the class droned.

"Today we test your progress in the martial arts," Master Thorius declared, clasping his hands behind his back. His eyes darted from apprentice to apprentice. "To see how well you've absorbed the skills held within your medallions."

Sukri nodded, glancing at Gammon. They'd both wondered why neither of them had ever been formally trained to fight. Seekers had a reputation for being incredibly skilled swordsmen, after all. She hadn't realized that skill was thanks to exposure to the skill of the greatest swordsmen in history, absorbed into the medallions Seekers wore at all times. A far more efficient way to train, she supposed.

"Sukri, step forward," Master Thorius ordered. "Jasmine, step forward."

They both obeyed, and Master Thorius gestured for them to grab one of the long wooden practice swords stacked on the edge of the mat, then stand in the middle of the mat, a meter away from each other. Sukri faced Jasmine, studying her. She was taller than Sukri, and irritatingly slender, with long, slightly tanned limbs. She was pretty, but boyish; her dark hair was short, a pixie cut really, compared to Sukri's long dirty-blond hair. An advantage for Jasmine, Sukri knew. If she got a hold of Sukri's hair, she would pull it…and that would hurt like hell. And knowing Jasmine, she would do it if she got the chance. She beat up her boyfriend Sen all the time, after all. Whipped little bitch that he was.

"No strikes to the head," Master Thorius ordered. He stepped back, then nodded. "Fight."

Sukri barely had time to register his command; Jasmine lunged at her, thrusting her sword at her chest. Sukri barely blocked it in time, knocking Jasmine's sword to the side. She hadn't even thought of blocking it…it'd just happened, purely on reflex.

"Good," Master Thorius stated. "Follow-up with a counter-attack next time."

Sukri nodded, circling Jasmine, her sword held before her. Jasmine smirked, and Sukri felt a sudden burst of irritation. It was Jasmine's emotion, of course.

She's better and she knows it.

Jasmine had been exposed to her Seeker medallion for longer, having become an apprentice a month before Sukri. It was hardly a fair fight.

Jasmine lunged forward again, then pulled back, making Sukri flinch. Jasmine smirked again.

Bitch.

Sukri swung at Jasmine's neck, but Jasmine blocked the attack, knocking Sukri's sword aside and thrusting at her belly. Sukri blocked the blow – again on reflex, and found herself counterattacking, thrusting the tip of her sword into Jasmine's belly. Jasmine grunted, bending over and clutching her abdomen, and shooting Sukri a nasty glare. Sukri glanced at Thorius; it was an unnerving feeling, performing techniques that she'd never even practiced. She felt out of control, like she was fighting purely on faith.

"Better," Master Thorius said. He glanced at Jasmine. "Again."

Jasmine recovered, standing up straight and circling Sukri again. She looked pissed.

Wiped the smirk off your face, Sukri thought. But she hardly took comfort in that fact. Jasmine was still better than she was…and now the skinny bitch wouldn't hold back. Sukri circled even as Jasmine did, waiting for the inevitable assault. She didn't have to wait long; Jasmine cried out, thrusting at Sukri, who blocked the attack with a loud *thwack*. Jasmine didn't skip a beat, slashing at Sukri's shoulder. Sukri tried to dodge the attack, but she was too slow; the blade clipped her shoulder, throwing her off-balance. She stumbled backward, and Jasmine lunged at her, thrusting the tip of her wooden sword right into Sukri's belly. Hard.

Sukri crumpled, falling onto her butt, then rolling onto her side, clutching at her stomach. Tears blurred her vision, and she fought back a surge of bile, swallowing it down. She refused to puke in front of Jasmine…and Master Thorius.

"Enough," their teacher ordered. "Help her up," he added, nodding at Jasmine, who walked up to Sukri, offering a hand. She was still smirking, and Sukri slapped her hand away, rolling onto all fours, then standing up slowly. She fought back another wave of nausea, shuffling back into line next to Gammon. The big guy put a beefy hand on her shoulder, looking down at her worriedly.

"You okay?"

"Shoulda hit her harder," she muttered. "Would've put my sword right through her."

"You did good."

"Bullshit," she retorted, still holding her belly. She'd gotten her ass handed to her and she knew it.

"You're progressing," Master Thorius said, facing Jasmine. "You lost the first round because you were cocky."

"Yes Master Thorius," Jasmine muttered.

"Get back in line."

Jasmine did so, and Master Thorius pointed at Gammon, then Sen.

"You're up."

Gammon smiled at Sukri, then took her sword, striding to the center of the mat and turning to face Sen. Gammon was easily a third of a meter taller than Sen, and while Sen was wiry, Gammon was massive, his protuberant belly nearly closing the gap between them. Sukri chewed her lower lip nervously; Sen was faster and more experienced than Gammon…and Gammon was the gentlest man she had ever met. He wouldn't hurt a fly. Sen, on the other hand…

"No strikes to the head," Master Thorius ordered. "Fight."

Sen attacked, slashing at Gammon's belly. He moved so quickly his sword was a blur, and Gammon barely managed to block the blow in time. Sen immediately followed up with another slash, and Gammon backpedaled, again only barely managing to intercept the blow with his own sword. Sen attacked a third time, stabbing Gammon in the belly. This time Gammon didn't block in time; he grimaced as the tip of Sen's sword jabbed him.

"Good," Master Thorius stated. "Sen, keep applying pressure. Gammon, you need to fight back."

"Yes Master Thorius," Gammon replied. He and Sen walked back to the center of the mat, facing each other again.

"Again," Master Thorius ordered.

Before the words finished leaving Master Thorius's mouth, Sen went after Gammon, slashing viciously at the big guy. Gammon blocked, but Sen kept after him, slashing again and again. Gammon blocked blow after blow, backing away as he did so, until one of Sen's slashes made it through his defenses, the wooden blade slamming into Gammon's upper arm.

Gammon grunted, lowering his sword, waiting for Master Thorius to stop the fight. But he didn't. Sen took the opportunity to thrust his sword into Gammon's gut, and Gammon slapped Sen's blade aside, shoving him back with one meaty palm. Sen stumbled backward, catching himself, then grinning at his opponent.

"Come on fat boy," he jeered. "Might wanna try hitting me at some point. You know, with your sword."

"Back to the center," Master Thorius ordered. They both obeyed, Sen's grin vanishing. They faced each other, swords held before them. "Go," Master Thorius ordered.

Sen burst forward, swinging at Gammon viciously, the *thwack, thwack* of their swords striking echoing through the room. Again, Gammon backed up, put on the defensive. And again, Sen eventually got through, slamming the dull edge of his sword into Gammon's shoulder. He followed up with yet another thrust to Gammon's gut.

"Who knew you'd be such a big fat pussy?" Sen jeered. "Your girl has bigger balls than you."

"Back to the center," Master Thorius ordered. Sen smirked, walking back to the center of the mat, then watching as Gammon made his way over. Master Thorius scowled at Gammon, folding his arms over his chest. "I told you to fight back."

Gammon lowered his gaze.

Master Thorius stared Gammon down for a long moment.

"If you don't win this next round," he declared, pointing right at Sukri, "...I'll break her leg."

Sukri felt the blood drain from her face. Her leg had just healed, after being broken by the Ironclad. She had no doubt that Master Thorius would do exactly as he promised. He always followed through on a threat.

Always.

"Yes Master Thorius," Gammon muttered, glancing at Sukri. His eyes were moist.

"You can do this big guy," Sukri encouraged, with a lot more confidence than she felt.

"Better man up fat boy," Sen warned, grinning at Gammon.

"Ready?" Master Thorius stated. "Begin!"

Sen lunged for Gammon, thrusting his sword right at the big guy's chest!

Gammon swatted the blade away, and Sen followed up with a vicious chop down at Gammon's shoulder. Gammon grabbed Sen's wrist, stopping the blow, then stepped in, smashing his forehead into Sen's face.

Sen's head snapped back, blood spurting from his nose.

Gammon shoved Sen backward, throwing him onto his back on the mat. He strode up to his fellow student, bending down and grabbing Sen by the leg and the arm, then lifting him up over his head.

"Gammon!" Sukri cried in horror.

Gammon threw Sen down on the mat as hard as he could. So hard that Sen bounced. The loud *thwap* of the impact echoed off the walls.

Sen lay there, utterly limp, his eyes wide, gasping for air.

Gammon reached down again, picking Sen up by the throat with both hands, lifting him until his legs were dangling above the mat.

"What the hell are you doing?" Jasmine shouted. "Stop!"

She burst forward across the mat, reaching Gammon in seconds, swinging her sword at the back of his knees. He took the hit with a grunt, then tossed Sen at her. They collided, tumbling to the mat in a jumble of limbs.

Gammon strode toward them, his face red, his mouth set in a grim line. His huge fists were clenched so hard his knuckles were white.

"Stop," Thorius commanded. "Gammon, stop!"

But Gammon didn't stop.

Thorius burst toward him, moving so quickly that Sukri could barely register what was happening. A second later, Gammon was on his belly on the mat, his arm locked behind his back and Master Thorius's knee grinding into the back of his head.

"Yield!" Thorius shouted, his voice piercing through the air.

Gammon struggled for a moment longer, then went limp.

"Yes Master," he mumbled. "Sorry."

Master Thorius released Gammon, checking up on Jasmine and Sen. Jasmine had gotten up, and was kneeling over Sen, tears streaming down her cheeks. She looked terrified.

"He's not waking up!" she cried, looking up at Master Thorius as he approached. "Help him!" she pleaded.

"Step aside," Thorius order, kneeling over Sen. Gammon stood up, staring down at them, his expression unreadable. Sukri walked across the mat to him, grabbing his arm. He flinched, and she let go, taking a step back.

"It's me," she said. "Gammon, it's okay."

He stared at her silently for a long moment, then glanced at Sen's bloodied face. He shook his head.

"No," he replied. "It isn't."

* * *

Hunter felt the cool liquid in the skull he was kneeling before on his lips, felt it course over his tongue as he accepted it into himself. It was thick and creamy, and terribly salty. He held it in his mouth, hunger consuming him, demanding release.

Don't do it, a voice within him cried.

He knelt there, withdrawing his lips from the skull, rolling the liquid in his mouth with his tongue, tasting that awful saltiness.

And at the same time, relishing it.

No!

He swallowed.

The liquid coursed down his throat, and he gagged, gritting his teeth against a sudden wave of nausea. He resisted the urge to vomit, desperate to feed his hunger. To be rid of it.

The fluid trickled down his esophagus, and he felt it in his upper chest as he forced it downward. Felt the sensation vanish as the liquid entered his stomach.

He stared at the remaining liquid in the skull, suddenly hungry for more. *Desperate* for more.

Za-ga-mar!

Hunter leaned in, lowering his lips to the surface of the liquid again.

Then pain exploded in his skull, lancing through the back of his eyes.

He screamed, reaching out blindly, feeling his hand strike something. The lid of the skull; it snapped shut, the sound lost in the echoes from his tortured cry. He stumbled backward, nearly losing his balance and falling down the staircase behind him.

The pain in his head abated…then returned, like a spike impaling his skull over and over again.

He cried out again, falling onto his knees, cradling his head in his hands.

Oh god what have I done what have I done…

He moaned, reaching out with one hand, feeling it strike something. His lantern. He clutched at it, turning to spot Vi's sword lying on the ground to his right. His heart pounded in his chest, so quickly that he thought it would burst.

Oh god oh god oh…

He grabbed Vi's sword, bringing it to his forehead, feeling its cool metal against his skin. Waited for its absolution, for Vi's powerful will to take this pain away.

Nothing happened.

Another burst of pain shot through his skull, and he grit his teeth against it. Grabbing his lantern, he turned around and stumbled down the steps to the platform below. He broke into a run, his heart beating ever faster, his breath coming in short gasps. The hunger – that terrible, ravenous *need* – struck him again, and he nearly doubled over. It was all he could do to keep going, descending down the ramp to the dark waters of the pool ahead.

Got to get out of here!

He stepped into the water, felt it engulf his legs, then his groin, rising all the way to his belly.

And then there was darkness.

Hunter froze, blinking. Pitch-blackness surrounded him, the afterimage of the pool fading rapidly. He closed his eyes, forcing himself to remain calm, and opened them.

Utter darkness.

Oh god no, he thought. *No no no!*

He stood there in the water, terror gripping him.

You're going to die here, he told himself. *You're going to die you're going to…*

A part of his mind broke away then, splitting from his consciousness. It was cold, calculating. Frighteningly fast. He felt it analyzing the problem, ticking through the possibilities with inhuman precision.

The lantern.

He lifted it, feeling it rise from the pool, hearing the sound of water dripping from it. In his haste, he'd failed to raise it above the pool. Another wave of fear came over him; without his lantern, he'd never make it out of the crypt alive. But even as he panicked, that other part of his mind kicked into gear, plotting his course in a fraction of a second, moving so fast he couldn't hope to follow it.

Get to your pack. Drain the lantern. The oil inside is dilute, drain it and refill it with your spare. Find the flint and re-light it.

He obeyed, wading through the water, trying to walk in a straight line. If he didn't, he'd end up at the edge of the pool, but not where his backpack was.

Doesn't matter, he knew. *It's a circle. Follow the edge until your reach the pack.*

He felt that alien part of his brain monitoring every step he took, calculating his course. Correcting any deviation. Somehow, he knew that he was going straight. His mind calculated the distance of every step, comparing it to his memories of the pool before the lantern had gone out.

Seven meters to go, he knew, taking another step. *Six-and-a-half meters.*

He saw the domed chamber in his mind's eye, fully lit, as if he were looking at it from above. Saw himself wading through the water. He was close to his pack now, only a dozen feet away.

The floor of the pool sloped upward, the water receding as he made his way to the edge. He looked down, *seeing* his backpack in his mind's eye, recalling its exact position. Knelt before it, reaching for the zipper and finding it exactly where he expected it to be despite the darkness. He opened it, finding the flint instantly, and the steel rod. He lowered his sword to the floor.

Don't need it anymore, he knew.

He emptied the lantern, opening it and reaching inside, dumping the oil. He found the replacement vial, opening it and pouring it in the lantern's well, hardly concerned about spilling it. He knew exactly where it was, knew exactly when he should stop pouring, when it was full.

It was *obvious.*

He used the flint and rod to light the lantern, getting it on his first try.

Light bathed the dome.

Hunter grabbed his sword, sheathing it, then threw his pack over his shoulder, grabbing his lantern.

Could've gotten out anyway, he thought. And he knew beyond a shadow of a doubt that he could have. A vision of the entire crypt appeared in his mind's eye, every centimeter of it measured, the number of steps it would take to get out of it already calculated. He was already planning his return to Lady Camilla's estate. Their inevitable conversations.

The skull!

He looked over his shoulder, realizing that he was supposed to retrieve it. Still, he hesitated, something holding him back. His mind – cold, calculating, moving so quickly his thoughts were a blur – considered the consequences. Ticked through the two possible futures. Get it, don't get it.

Don't.

He turned around, crawling through the exit of the dome, emerging into the room beyond. Saw the innumerable skeletons lying on the ground. That part of his mind began counting, tallying up the victims.

They died for their god.

He felt no grief at the thought. They would have gladly slit their own throats to appease him.

Hunter walked through the darkness, finding the staircase in moments and ascending the steps to the narrow ledge above. The spiked pit was to his right, stone wall at his left. He strode forward without fear, knowing that the wills of the madmen he'd buried within the wall could have no influence over him…not until the liquid he'd swallowed ran its course.

And maybe never again.

He strode forward, turning as the platform ahead turned rightward, walking through the long tunnel and turning right again. He found the stairs leading upward to his right, taking them to the next level up.

The hunger within him grew ravenous, his heart beating even faster now. So fast that he was afraid it would leap out of his throat.

Hurry, that other part of his mind urged. *You don't have much time.*

He grimaced, clutching his aching belly, resisting the urge to stop, to double over. Onward he went, following the hallway beyond, passing the tall statues protruding from the walls. He turned left at the end of the hallway, then left again, seeing the pit to his left again.

Almost there.

He felt a dull ache in the back of his head, growing stronger with each step he took.

Ignore it, he told himself. *It's not real.*

His head began to pound, and he grit his teeth, pushing forward. A sharp pain lanced through his forehead, as if someone were holding a nail to it, then hammering it into his skull. He cried out, dropping the lantern and clutching his head in his hands. Another invisible nail drove into his forehead, then another.

Fuck!

He lowered his hands, finding himself suspended in utter darkness. He'd dropped the lantern into the pit!

More pain…and that awful hunger, so intense that it made him double over. His legs wobbled, threatening to give out beneath him.

Get out, that cold, calculating part of him ordered. *Or die.*

He stumbled forward blindly, his hand on the wall to his right, focusing on walking in a straight line. His mind raced, thoughts coming one after the other in rapid sequence, so quickly he couldn't follow.

Thirteen meters until the entrance. Sundown two hours and sixteen minutes ago. Make fire, make shelter. Camp site with no dangerous wills four hundred meters from entrance. Go to Vi's place? No, high probability Camilla knows where Vi's home is. Duke Dominus might too. Need new home base.

The future opened up before him, possibilities forking in his mind, each decision with its consequences, each consequence snowballing as it led to more consequences.

Get out!

He rushed forward, breaking out into a run, his fingertips sliding across the wall. Then they slid off the wall, plunging into open space. He turned right, seeing the entrance to the crypt in his mind's eye, sprinting toward the double-doors he knew were ahead. There was no fear of running into something. He'd calculated perfectly.

Another burst of pain shot through his forehead, nearly stopping him in his tracks.

Hunter pushed through the agony, reaching the doors in the utter darkness. He waded through the bones piled against it, sliding between the doors. Then he burst forward, seeing a faint light ahead.

Starlight shining on the bones of those long dead, victims of the millennia-old curse of the Crypt of Zagamar.

He ran toward it, his boots crunching on the bones underfoot, his heart fluttering in his chest. He gasped for air, his lungs on fire, pain lancing through his skull again and again in and endless rhythm. Onward he went, bursting into the starlight, emerging onto the winding path leading down the foot of the mountain.

The voices of men called out all around him, of men long dead. Men standing victorious in city after city, town after town, leaving nothing but fire and misery in their wake.

Za-ga-mar!

He followed the path to its end, spotting the black, twisted trees ahead…and beyond them, the relative safety of the forest. Sprinting up to the black trees, he wove between them, his mind racing, scanning and processing his surroundings with incredible speed. Faster even than before.

Black trees absorbed my will. Excess absorption leads to death, trait combinations not survivable. Trees that live selected for by ideal combination of traits. All living things selected for in this way. The Deep creates new combinations. Most die, few live. This is the origin of species.

A bright light flashed before his eyes, glowing, multicolored geometric shapes bursting to his left.

Za-ga-MAR!

His right hand began to twitch, then his arm.

Za-ga-MAR!

And then he stumbled, and darkness claimed him.

Chapter 10

Two days had passed since the attack on Castle Wexford, and Duke Dominus's plentiful staff had seen to it that all evidence of the ambush had been erased. The bodies of the Seekers had been studied and discarded, those of the guards cremated, their ashes stored and sent to Tykus for processing. Ashes of men of the finest character would be used to instill these qualities in future soldiers of the kingdom, while lesser men would have their ashes thrown in the sea.

All part of the glorious system, every detail accounted for, every action having its purpose, no resource wasted. A perfect machine made of imperfect parts.

Dominus sat at the edge of his bed, marveling at the fact that his shoulder – broken only two days ago – seemed to have mostly healed, hardly hurting him at all. He lifted his right leg to pull off his sock, exposing his foot. To his surprise, there were short nubs growing from the stump where his toes had been severed. Five pink, fleshy bumps. They hadn't been there the night before. He'd checked.

His eyes went to his right wrist. To the stump there, covered in bandages.

He tore the bandages off, exposing the flesh underneath. New flesh, pink flesh, growing from the stump of his wrist, extending past the exposed ends of the two bones of his forearms. And new, pearly bone visible, growing from those two bony ends, covered in a thin skin teeming with tiny blood vessels.

A laugh burst from him, and he allowed it, staring at his wrist in wonderment. Then his eyes went to the trapdoor where he kept the Ossae of the Ironclad.

My god.

He was suddenly grateful for sending his doctor away two days ago, after the attack. The man had insisted on operating, on sawing off the ends of his forearm bones and closing the flesh with sutures. Dominus had refused, unable to give up hope that he might gain his hand back with the power of the Ironclad's incredible regeneration.

And that I will, he thought, breaking out into a smile. *That I will.*

His smiled faded quickly when he remembered how a few of his soldiers had seen his amputated hand…including the Captain of the Guard. He'd have to figure out how to deal with that problem eventually.

He sighed, pulling his socks back on, then replacing the bandage on his arm. A considerable task with one hand, he discovered. That done, he rested, staring off at nothing in particular.

He'd spent the last two days contemplating the attack on his person, trying to tease out the source and the reason for it. Of course, the source of the attack would reveal the reason.

There were three possibilities.

The first was that the Kingdom of the Deep had indeed sent its Seekers to kill him. If their spies had discovered the existence of the Ironclad's unique powers, they would stop at nothing to acquire it. But these had been no Seekers of the Deep; they'd been too human, and had fallen to Dominus's soldiers too easily. A real Seeker of the Deep could have killed four to six men before being felled. His attackers had killed an average of only two.

The second possibility was that another entity had attempted to frame the Kingdom of the Deep for the attack, with the purpose of starting a war between the two kingdoms. Lady Camilla, a supposedly neutral party, would gain a great deal by doing so, increasing the demand for illicit artifacts and Ossae to fuel such a war. But it was also incredibly risky, upending the delicate balance she'd maintained for so many decades, one that had ensured her survival.

The left the third possibility…the Guild of Seekers.

Dominus stood up, grabbing his cane leaning against the bed. He walked to one of the windows, protected by thick iron bars, and looked down at his gardens. At the beehives sitting on the wooden pallets, bees already starting their day, buzzing about with militaristic discipline. A discipline that each bee was born with, not needing to be taught. Nature did not suffer sloth; it was only in humans, so removed from the pressures exerted by Nature's hand, that weakness was allowed to exist.

To breed.

Throw them all out into the wild, Dominus knew, and most would die. The lame, the stupid, the lazy. The delusional. Those crippled with anxiety and the urge to kill themselves. These leeches, who sucked the blood of the kingdom, demanding food, water and shelter without having to earn it, would find themselves having to fend for themselves. Without the tools to do so, they would be the first to die.

The forest would teach them or kill them. That was its way.

Dominus blinked, then turned away from the window, frowning at himself. He shook his head, trying to clear it.

The forest is the enemy, he reminded himself. It threatened the most valuable thing of all: humanity.

And the kingdom of Tykus, that perfect machine, had been designed to withstand the imperfections of lesser humans, to work despite them. It was the humans of the Acropolis, those steeped in the wills of the greatest of men, that were worth protecting. Worth preserving.

There was a knock on the door.

Dominus flinched, his heart leaping into his chest. He spun to face the door, then looked down, realizing that his cane-sword was unsheathed, the blade held before him.

He took a deep breath in, forcing himself to calm down.

"Come in," he called out, re-sheathing his cane-sword, then resting on it. The door opened, and Farkus appeared. "What is it?"

"Your Grace," Farkus greeted. "The soldiers you sent to Vi's house haven't returned."

"What?"

"A scout returned just now," Farkus explained. "He says that Canyon Falls is crawling with Ironclad."

Dominus stared at the man.

"Ironclad?" he blurted out. That didn't make any sense. Why would Ironclad…?

He closed his eyes, thinking it through. Farkus said nothing, knowing better than to interrupt Dominus's train of thought.

"How many?" Dominus demanded.

"They counted dozens, your Grace."

Dominus grimaced. Canyon Falls – the canyon Vi had built her house in – was extremely well-protected, with only one way in…a narrow path that would only allow one man at a time. A small force of Ironclad could easily defend the canyon, and they knew it. He would have to abandon his efforts to pilfer Vi's artifacts, at least for now.

"Very well," Dominus stated. "That is all."

Farkus bowed, turning about and closing the door behind him.

Dominus sighed, turning to look out of the window once again. He thought back to the attack, the ambush that had nearly succeeded in assassinating the most powerful duke in the kingdom of Tykus. The man second in power to king Tykus himself.

Only one man would have the audacity to attempt such a thing. A man who claimed fealty to the crown, but whose true loyalties were unknown.

A man whose organization had been allowed far too much leeway by the Acropolis, in exchange for artifacts of incredible power.

High Seeker Zeno, leader of the Guild of Seekers.

Dominus smiled grimly, gripping the head of his cane tightly.

Well played, Zeno, he mused.

But now it was *his* turn.

* * *

High Seeker Zeno strode down the broad hallway leading away from the second-story balcony overlooking the great hall of the Guild of Seekers, ignoring the Seekers who bowed as he passed. He kept his eyes forward, not making eye contact, knowing that his Seekers would not dare attempt to interact with him. No one wanted to risk being the target of his ire…and everyone feared him.

As well they should.

He reached an intersection, turning right down a narrower hallway, then taking stairs up to the third floor of the guild. A massive building, the guild was seven stories tall, save for the bell tower, which was nine. It contained well over a hundred rooms, not including the labyrinth of chambers below-ground…secret tunnels that led to vaults hidden from prying eyes. Vaults that contained riches beyond the imagination of the majority of his Seekers, and even the nobles of the Acropolis, who had no idea the vaults existed. If they – or King Tykus – ever realized the extent of the guild's collection, or how far the guild had strayed from the ideals of the kingdom…

He ignored the thought, secure in the knowledge that such a thing would never happen. His was not a mind that fell prey to fear. Fear paralyzed. It too often created the very thing that one feared, by preventing action to prevent a bad outcome. And bad outcomes could be planned for, the damage mitigated.

If the kingdom ever did discover the guild's treachery, then so be it. He and his predecessors had already planned for such a contingency.

Zeno strode down another hallway, finding yet another stairwell going upward. He took this, ascending to the fourth floor. His office was on the seventh story of the guild, restricted to himself and the highest-ranking Seekers below him. It too contained rooms hidden behind secret walls.

Secrets within secrets. A shadow government hiding in plain sight of the kingdom.

The guild had taken great pains to hide their nature from Tykus, withstanding yearly inspections and surprise inspections. The Acropolis sent men to sample water from the narrow moat surrounding the guild, testing it for improper traits. Not knowing that it was all for nothing; the underground chambers containing the guild's illegal artifacts were well-insulated. Corrupted water passing over these artifacts flowed in secret channels below ground, separate from the moat, and drained into underground tunnels that led to the ocean. This water absorbed any residual traits from the illegal artifacts, preventing the earth around the guild from becoming contaminated.

Through the will bestowed upon the Founder, they had thought of everything.

He continued through the hallways of the guild, expertly navigating them. They were designed to be maze-like, appearing identical to each other, without seeming order or reason. Designed to confuse. The stairwells leading to the uppermost levels were well-hidden. The door to the fifth floor required him to go down a flight of stairs, find a secret lever to open a door indistinguishable from a wall, ascend two flights, then use a key – given to a select few – to open the door at the top of the stairs. All while avoiding hidden traps along the way.

Zeno took this route, navigating it expertly.

At length, he reached the seventh floor, making his way to his office. It was small – far smaller than one might expect for a man of his station. Prominent displays of his status were well and good for the public to see, but were mere distractions for the purposes of his work. Only that which was useful could be found in his office: a desk, a chair, and a few cabinets. Paper stacked neatly on his desk, with a quill pen and an inkwell, a bowl of sand for soaking up excess ink, and wax for the seal.

The most powerful tools of all…those of communication.

He'd barely managed to sit down at his desk when there was a knock on the door.

"Come in," he stated briskly.

The door opened, revealing a short woman wearing the black-and-gold uniform of a Seeker. The insignia at her left breast – and the medallion resting on her sternum – identified her as Grand Counselor of the guild, Zeno's second in command.

"High Seeker," she greeted, bowing before him.

"Grand Counselor Nova," he replied with a nod.

"The mission failed," she stated bluntly.

Zeno took the news in. His men had failed to retrieve the head of the Ironclad. So be it.

"Our secondary target?"

"Alive, we assume," Nova answered. "There's been no move to bring his body to the Acropolis for burial. We're awaiting confirmation."

"Casualties?"

"All but three," she informed.

"Kill them."

To her credit, Nova's expression didn't change.

"Yes High Seeker."

"That will be all," Zeno stated.

Nova bowed, then left. He sighed, knowing that – despite her lack of expression – she'd been taken aback by his order to kill his own Seekers. He'd sensed the emotion emanating from her. It was the most compelling reason why she would never be fit for the office of High Seeker.

Zeno had come to the conclusion long ago that humanity was of the idiotic belief that the greatest forces in the world were wealth, or military might…or even knowledge. How blind they were, clueless as to the most powerful force of all: the opinion, perceived or actual, of others.

A blessing that he was not burdened by such concerns.

Nearly all of Man's behavior was governed by this invisible force. It was the reason he could order men to their deaths. The reason why they didn't squat in the middle of the street to take a shit. Why they combed their hair, took to the baths, and tolerated conversation they found boring or inane. Why they wore matching clothes, and engaged in all of the expected behaviors of polite society. The most powerful men in the world were subject to it. Only a small fraction of the insane were free from this overwhelming power…and a few men that were created without the ability to feel its forces.

Like me, he thought.

A great gift, that. It was as if all men were subject to the law of gravity but him…but his gift was far more useful. He could not expose that he possessed it, not without inciting horror in his fellow Man. He had to pretend to be under the influence of public opinion, to be swayed by it like all the rest.

But only when others were watching.

Zeno pushed aside these thoughts, realizing that he was woolgathering. He took in a deep breath, focusing on the matter at hand.

The mighty Dominus, Duke of Wexford.

Zeno would of course operate under the assumption that the man was still alive. And that he hadn't been fooled by his assassins' disguises. Dominus knew that the Guild of Seekers was the culprit, and that the head of the Ironclad was the goal.

Very well.

The news did not bother him. He'd already planned for such a contingency, after all. Only a fool failed to plan for failure.

He found himself fingering the medallion laying on his chest. A triangle made of pure platinum, the densest of metals. Able to absorb wills more completely than any other substance. A fact that its creator had most assuredly known.

He gazed down at it, seeing the three symbols carved into its surface, at each point of the triangle: a skull, a brain, and a human heart. Staring at it, he was struck with a rare wistful feeling. There was very little in this world he could not have, were he to ask for it. But he lacked that one rare gift the

Founder had possessed. A gift bestowed upon so few that no one had possessed it for generations.

Zeno lifted the medallion, holding it to his forehead and closing his eyes. He was too much like its maker now to be able to feel its power…it had already transformed him as much as it would. An incomplete transformation, he knew, regrettably. There was no man, alive or dead, he wanted to be other than himself.

Except for one.

He pressed the medallion harder against his forehead, as if he could shove it through his skull and into his brain. How he wished he could retrieve the memories stored within…the memories the Founder had absorbed!

He sighed, letting the medallion fall against his chest.

Stop woolgathering.

Dominus would be dealt with. He felt no fear at the prospect. No matter how formidable the old man was, Dominus's will paled in comparison to the will trapped within Zeno's medallion. A will that the Founder had used to create the Guild of Seekers, the most powerful entity within the kingdom. More powerful than Duke Dominus – or even King Tykus himself – could ever imagine.

The Guild of Seekers would retrieve the head of the Ironclad, and complete its sacred mission. A mission given to the Founder by a singular, god-like will. A being beyond anything modern Man had ever known.

Oh, how they'd thought the Founder to be insane, when he'd returned from his sacred journey! Thought him a madman.

Zeno smiled, retrieving a sheet of paper, then dipping his quill pen into the well of ink.

The world would soon realize how very wrong they'd been.

CHAPTER 11

Hunter opened his eyes.

He found himself lying in a large bed, a red sheet covering him from the chest down. The ceiling high above his head was pure white, with wooden beams painted blood-red supporting it. The walls were red as well, as was the sheet draped over him.

He was, he realized, naked.

Hunter turned his head to the left, and nearly jumped. A young woman was sitting in a chair beside the bed, wearing a plain white dress. She was looking down at something in her lap; a half-knitted piece of cloth. But instead of knitting needles, she was using a single golden rod with a small hook at the end. She must have noticed him stirring; she looked up at him, her eyes widening.

"Oh!" she exclaimed, bolting up from her chair and setting the knitting down. "You're awake!"

"Uh, yeah," Hunter mumbled, his voice cracking. He cleared his throat looking around. "Where am I?"

"I'll get the doctor," the woman stated, turning away and leaving the room through a door opposite the bed. The door closed behind her, and Hunter stared at it, feeling utterly confused.

Where am I, he wondered. *What happened?*

He tried to remember the last thing he...well, remembered. But his mind drew a blank. Moments later, the door re-opened, and a hefty-looking man in long red robes entered, the young woman following behind.

"Ah, good," the man declared, walking up to the right side of the bed and looking down at Hunter. He had short gray hair and chubby, flushed cheeks, glasses with thick black rims magnifying his eyes like a fishbowl. "When did he wake?" he asked, glancing at the woman.

"Just now, doctor," she answered.

"Where am I?" Hunter repeated, this time asking the man…the doctor.

"I am Dr. Phelbus," the man introduced. He frowned then. "Where do you think you are?"

Hunter sat up a little, looking around, taking in the red walls, the white ceiling. The deep cherry floor.

"Lady Camilla's place," he guessed. The doctor nodded approvingly.

"Correct," he agreed. "Can you tell me the date?"

"No idea."

"Hmm," Dr. Phelbus murmured. "What's the last thing you remember?"

"That's what I've been trying to figure out," Hunter admitted. "I remember being here before," he continued. "And leaving for…" He paused, unsure if he could tell the doctor the details of the mission the Lady had given him.

"You have significant retrograde amnesia," the doctor concluded. "A result of your seizures, I imagine." He turned to the young woman. "The post-ictal state does not allow for formation of new memories, you see. Quite common in those with epilepsy or significant trauma to the skull."

"Excuse me?" Hunter asked.

"You've been having seizures," the doctor explained, turning back to Hunter. "Have you suffered them previously?"

"No."

"Are you sure?" Dr. Phelbus pressed. Hunter nodded.

"Pretty damn sure."

"Acquired seizures," Phelbus murmured, rubbing his jowls thoughtfully. He turned to the woman. "All men are allowed one seizure unprovoked by means of trauma or fever. Any more than that is diagnostic for epilepsy."

"Yes doctor," she murmured.

"So we must inquire as to whether his seizures are provoked or not," Dr. Phelbus reasoned, eyeing Hunter critically. "No external signs of trauma. But he was feverish on arrival. He may not have epilepsy after all."

"Then what does *he* have?" Hunter asked, irritated that the man continued to talk about him as if he weren't there.

"I would have presumed infection, given the fever," Dr. Phelbus replied, clearly oblivious to Hunter's ire. "But the time course is wrong. You've been here only thirty-six hours."

"Wait, *what?*" Hunter blurted out.

"Most infections have a longer course," Phelbus explained.

"I've been asleep for a day and a half?" Hunter pressed incredulously, sitting up straighter. The sheet covering him slid down to his waist, revealing his nude torso…and a hint of something else. The young woman's eyes widened, and he quickly covered himself.

"Oh no," the doctor confirmed. "You've woken before. We've spoken before, in fact," he added. "But each time, you suffered another seizure. These of course erased your memory of our conversations."

"Oh," Hunter mumbled.

"Notice how lucid he is," Dr. Phelbus observed, glancing at the young woman. "I suspect he's turned the corner, so to speak."

"You suppose so?" the woman pressed, looking hopeful.

"By virtue of my considerable experience," Phelbus declared authoritatively, "...I would say it's quite probable."

"Hold on," Hunter interjected, feeling irritated again. "What happened to me? How did I get here?" Dr. Phelbus turned to him.

"I regret that I don't have the answer to your question," he confessed. "You'll have to ask Lady Camilla." He shook his head. "It would be useful for me to know," he added with a scowl, facing the young woman again. "I can't deduce the etiology of his illness with incomplete information."

"Can I speak to her?" Hunter requested. Dr. Phelbus frowned.

"Pardon?"

"Can I speak to Lady Camilla," Hunter clarified. Phelbus hesitated, then nodded.

"She hasn't come the last few times you've woken," he admitted. "On account of you having a seizure and forgetting. But as I've predicted, you seem to have turned the corner." He glanced at the woman. "Fetch the Lady."

"Yes doctor," the woman replied, leaving the room at once.

"Who's she?" Hunter asked.

"My nurse," Phelbus answered.

"Ah."

"How are you feeling?" the doctor inquired.

Hunter frowned, focusing internally. His muscles were sore and stiff, and the sides of his tongue throbbed a bit. He said as much.

"Quite expected," Phelbus reasoned. "Muscular inflammation from the seizures."

"And I'm starving," Hunter added, his stomach growling so loudly that even the doctor could hear it. Phelbus frowned.

"Fluids only for the time being," he commanded. "Your risk of aspiration if you have another seizure is too great. Can't have you catching pneumonia."

Just then, the door opened, revealing someone very familiar: Lady Camilla. She wore a long black dress with a black corset, slits at either leg traveling all the way up to her hips. Her neckline plunged down to her corset rather scandalously, revealing substantial cleavage. Again, he was struck by her beauty...and the regal way she held herself. She walked up to the foot of his bed, smiling down at him, the nurse behind her. He found himself, as before, unable to take his eyes from her.

As always, a masked man followed behind her. The man with the silver eyes. Dio, if Hunter remembered correctly. As usual, the man carried his metal staff on his back. It had, Hunter realized, short, sword-like blades on either end.

"Will he seize again?" the Lady inquired, glancing at Dr. Phelbus.

"I cannot be certain," he confessed, adjusting his glasses. "But he has improved greatly, my Lady. When he resumes eating, I recommend a diet of meat and fat only," he added.

"Leave us," Lady Camilla commanded. The doctor and his nurse bowed, leaving immediately. Lady Camilla smiled at Hunter again, walking up to his left side and sitting on the edge of his bed, twisting to face him…and offering him a stunning view of her profile. He cleared his throat, pulling the sheet up to his belly.

"Hello," he greeted rather lamely.

"Good morning," she replied. "Do you recall our previous conversations?"

"No," he admitted. "The last thing I remember is leaving here. How did I get back?"

"I had my men follow you," she replied. "All the way to the forest before the Crypt of Zagamar."

Hunter stared at her, a chill running down his spine.

Za-ga-mar!

Memories flooded his brain, his harrowing journey coming back to him. Of nearly sawing through his own skull into his brain, the madness that had nearly convinced him to leap into a pit of spikes.

The massive statue standing before the bowl. Liquid pouring into his mouth.

Za-ga-mar!

He looked down, realizing he was gripping the sheets so hard his knuckles were white. Sweat beaded up on his forehead, his heart pounding in his chest.

"Are you alright?" she asked, putting a hand on his bare shoulder. He swallowed in a dry throat.

"I remember," he whispered.

"Remember what?" she pressed. Her hand was warm on his shoulder, and her touch helped to ground him. To calm him.

"The crypt," he answered, not wanting to say that name.

"What happened?"

Hunter recalled his experience, telling the Lady of his trip to the crypt, the madness that had nearly killed him. Described the crypt itself…and the massive statue, with that skull embedded in solid crystal. Of how he'd sipped from it. And then…and then…

He couldn't remember.

"You say you drank this brown liquid," the Lady stated. He nodded. "How did you feel when you did this?"

Hunter frowned, thinking it over. He remembered the incredible hunger, the visions that had assaulted him. Visions of his men all around him, chanting his name…

"Hunter?"

He snapped out of it, glancing up at the Lady.

"Sorry," he mumbled. "I felt…hungry. So hungry that it hurt. And I saw…visions."

"Describe them."

He hesitated, then did so, to the best of his ability to recollect them. The Lady listened until he was done, then stood up, turning away and staring off into space.

"Sorry I didn't get the skull," he apologized. "It was stuck in a block of crystal, and…"

"Yes yes," she interrupted, waving the apology away. She turned back to him, eyeing him with an expression he couldn't read. He squirmed under her gaze, feeling suddenly exposed, and pulled the bedsheet up to his chest.

"What?" he asked.

"You've accomplished something no one has ever managed to do, Hunter," she replied. "You entered the tomb of Zagamar and lived to tell the tale."

"I thought one other guy did that," he countered.

"He looted a single medallion from the outer crypt," she replied dismissively. "And emerged a madman, babbling about the ascendance of Man. Spent the rest of his life obsessing over hoarding artifacts. You," she added, sitting back down on the bed and putting a hand on his shoulder again, "…made it all the way to Zagamar's tomb…and came out alive, and sane."

Hunter grimaced at the "Z" word, hearing that name echo in his mind. The sound of thousands of men chanting it over and over.

"So why was I having seizures?" he asked.

"I don't know," she admitted. "But I have a few ideas." She stood again, starting to pace before his bed. "There have been other crypts – pre-historic ones like Zagamar's – that our ancestors managed to study in full. None as deadly as Zagamar's, of course."

Hunter grimaced again, and Lady Camilla paused.

"What's wrong?"

"I…that name," he explained. "I don't like hearing it."

"Why not?"

"I can't explain," he replied. "It just…makes me uncomfortable."

"Ah, well," she continued. "These crypts have a similar overall design. The outer portions are steeped in the wills of madmen, the inner portions defended with physical and psychological traps. Zaga…the crypt you entered is different. We suspect it employs the Ossae of Legends. Madmen Legends, an enormous number of them, built into its structure." She shook her head. "The fact that he had the resources to collect so many Ossae of Legendary madman is a hint at his influence."

"In any case," she continued, "…each crypt has a tomb, almost always of a long-dead Legend. We can only assume that ancient Legends did not want just anyone to access their Ossae. The tombs were a sort of trial, only allowing other Legends – those powerful enough to overcome the defenses of each crypt – to access them."

"For what?" Hunter inquired. "I mean, why would anyone want to get to these tombs?"

"Well, you're aware of Tykus the Legend."

"Yeah."

"His Ossae reside in the Acropolis," she explained. "Each king exposes themselves to his Ossae, absorbing his Legendary will until they are for all intents and purposes Tykus himself."

"Right," Hunter stated. He'd heard it all before.

"But none of them *is* Tykus," the Lady continued. "None of them is the original. None are Legends themselves."

"So they're *almost* Tykus."

"Correct," Lady Camilla agreed. "As close to the original as possible…or so we assume."

"What do you mean?"

"Well," she replied, "…there are some cultures – primitive ones – that still practice cannibalism…the consumption of the flesh of their enemies, and of their ancestors."

"Okay…"

"They believe that, in eating the flesh and drinking the blood of their ancestors and enemies, they might absorb their traits more completely than by exposing themselves to Ossae."

"Is it true?" he asked. Lady Camilla shrugged.

"We don't know," she admitted. "Cannibalism is strictly forbidden…and great pains are made to ensure that our food supply is from weak-willed livestock and plants."

"So you don't turn into animals," Hunter reasoned, remembering the Legendary tree…and what it had done to that poor man.

"Correct."

"What does that have to do with that stuff I drank?" Hunter pressed. Lady Camilla sighed.

"I'm not certain," she admitted. "Zagamar's tomb clearly carried his Ossae…and you obviously felt his influence. Your sudden compulsion to drink from his skull is certainly concerning. Clearly he wanted whoever managed to make it into the tomb to do so."

"But why?"

"That fluid has been resting in his skull for millennia," she reasoned. "Absorbing his will, and perhaps dissolving a small portion of his skull into itself. Perhaps Zagamar was part of a cannibalistic society as well."

"But the inside of the skull was lined with metal," Hunter countered. "It wouldn't have absorbed anything."

"Hmm," the Lady murmured, clearly vexed. "Then I don't know." She stood then, smoothing out her black dress. "I need to think," she added. "I'll spend more time with you later this afternoon."

"What do I do?" Hunter asked.

"Rest."

"I can't just stay in bed all day," he protested. "I have things to do."

"Such as?" she inquired, arching an eyebrow.

"You know."

"Ah yes," she replied. "Your revenge." She sat back down on the bed, leaning over to put a hand on his cheek. He was surprised at her touch, and smelled the now-familiar scent of her perfume as she drew close. It was intoxicating, that scent…as intoxicating as the view. His eyes dropped to the deep V-cut of her dress; her leaning over gave him an intriguing view of her cleavage, and he found himself staring. He glanced back up at her eyes, feeling his cheeks flush…and hoping that, with his dark skin, she wouldn't notice.

And that she wouldn't look down at his lap and notice his rapidly growing…problem.

"You've been through a great deal," she murmured, sliding her hand down his cheek to his neck, then resting it on his bare chest. "We need to make sure you're not having any more seizures before you go out for your revenge."

Hunter swallowed, taking a moment to focus on what she'd just said. Then he nodded grudgingly. It was a fair point.

"Rest," she urged, withdrawing her hand and smiling at him. "And eat," she added, her eyes dropping to his body. He bent his knees reflexively, hoping to hide his reaction to her closeness. "You've lost weight."

"Okay," he mumbled.

"I'll return," she promised, standing up. "I assure you that while you're here," she added, "…you'll be afforded every comfort."

She turned then, walking out of his room. He watched her go, his eyes drawn to her hourglass figure, her pale legs flashing through the slits in her dress with each step. Watched her pass through the doorway, followed by Dio, who closed the door behind them. Then he lay back, staring up at the ceiling. It took some time before the pressure in his groin abated, for his body to recover from her presence. He couldn't help but think of Trixie, the prostitute who'd turned him into a hopeless sex addict back in the Outskirts. She'd done so by virtue of her extraordinary aura, one she'd developed over a lifetime in a brothel. Just by getting close to Hunter, Trixie had been able to seduce him time after time.

This woman – Lady Camilla – had no such aura, he assumed. But she had the same effect on him, if not even more so. Which meant that his attraction to her – overwhelming and intoxicating – was very real.

Be careful, he told himself.

And then the door opened, and the nurse returned, wheeling a tray of food up to his bed. He sat up quickly, staring at the plates on the tray, filled to the brim with steaming meat. His hunger returned with a vengeance, his stomach growling painfully.

"The doctor says you can eat," the nurse declared.

"Don't have to tell *me* twice," Hunter replied, sitting up and rubbing his hands together eagerly.

And that she most certainly didn't.

* * *

It was late afternoon by the time Hunter woke from a long post-breakfast nap, the sun casting long shadows of the furniture in his room. His nurse had returned, sitting in the same chair as before. He'd been immediately struck by a ravenous hunger, and thankfully his nurse was quick to see to his needs. After stuffing his face, he'd needed to take a piss. She'd shown him the way, and he'd gone to the bathroom, thankfully clad in a plain white shirt and pants that he'd been given after breakfast. He'd peed for what seemed like forever, enjoying the release.

That done, he'd returned to his bed, sitting down on the edge of it. And that's when Lady Camilla entered, as promised.

"Good evening," she greeted, stepping into the room. She was wearing the same dress as before, and Hunter again found himself staring at her. She moved with a casual grace, a confidence that reminded him a bit of Vi, but more overtly feminine.

"Evening," Hunter replied. "Where's Dio?" he asked. The creepy bodyguard was nowhere to be seen.

"Come," she ordered, gesturing with one hand. Hunter stood obediently, walking up to her side, and she led him out of the room into a wide hallway. He felt lightheaded, and swayed a bit as he walked.

"Are you alright?" she inquired, stopping. Hunter stopped with her.

"A little lightheaded," he admitted. She took his hand, pulling him closer and wrapping his arm around her slender waist. Her perfume tantalized him, warmth radiating from her body. She was nearly as tall as he was, and supported his weight surprisingly well.

"Lean on me."

He allowed this, and she led them up a flight of stairs, to a familiar set of double-doors. Passing through them, he found himself in the large library he'd been in a few days ago, with the huge map of Varta on the wall. Again, red-masked men guarded the room, leaving when Lady Camilla waved them away. She turned to Hunter then, disengaging from him.

"I brought you here to show you something," she explained. "Something I think you'll appreciate."

"What's that?"

"This," she stated, walking up to one of the tables in the periphery of the room and gesturing at it. A hollow, columnar metal object lay atop it. "It is the bracer worn by a famous brawler forty-five years ago…Tykus's top champion in hand-to-hand combat at the time." She picked it up, handing it to Hunter. "It's yours."

"Wow," Hunter replied, turning it over in his hands. It was made of dull-looking metal, and was riddled with small dents. "Thanks."

"I promised to help you get your revenge," she stated with a smile. Hunter grimaced.

"Yeah, well I didn't exactly keep my end of the bargain," he countered. As much as he wanted the skills the bracer offered, he couldn't accept the gift while giving nothing in return.

"Nonsense," she retorted. "You didn't bring back Zagamar's skull, it's true," she added. "But you brought back his essence…more than anyone in history has ever accomplished."

"I thought someone else brought back a medallion," he countered. "I didn't bring back anything but myself."

The Lady's expression soured.

"Yes, a man did bring back a medallion – Zagamar's medallion – from the crypt," she agreed. Then she sighed. "His name was Jakar. He was a Seeker from Tykus before the Guild of Seekers existed."

"How long ago was that?"

"Centuries ago," Lady Camilla answered. "Back then, my ancestors were nobles of Tykus, a respected family. We were historians, then as now, with a focus in artifacts and Ossae. In fact," she added, "…we were the greatest single source of information on important Ossae and artifacts in the kingdom."

"But not anymore?"

"That's a long story," the Lady admitted. "Suffice it to say that, back then, Seekers were all independent contractors, and came to my family for information about artifacts they wanted to seek out for their clients. And clients came to us for information about artifacts that might be useful for them to acquire. We had a monopoly on such information."

"Ah."

"Jakar was hired by a high-ranking noble in the kingdom to get the medallion," she continued. "He refused to use us. He thought he was powerful enough to enter the Crypt of Zagamar…to do what no man had ever done before. To bring back the Ossae that must lie within. He figured that a crypt as well-protected as Zagamar's – more protected than any crypt ever discovered – must contain something of extraordinary value."

"What happened?"

"Jakar went to the crypt," she answered. "The doors were already open from previous attempts. He made it in, but not as far as you. When he emerged, he gained the medallion – but lost his sanity."

"He went crazy?" Hunter asked, recalling what had happened to him. It wasn't hard to imagine someone going insane after venturing near the place.

"In a way," she agreed. "He became obsessed with immortality," she added, "…and the Deep."

"The Deep?" Hunter pressed. He recalled Vi having talked about it, but couldn't remember any specifics.

"A place far from here," Lady Camilla replied. "Near the Kingdom of the Deep. It is a region where the forces of this world are magnified…and twisted beyond recognition. No one truly understands the Deep."

"So why was this guy obsessed with it?"

"He thought that he could use the Deep to gain immortality," she answered. "Jakar became convinced that he had some horrible disease…that he would die young. He was by all accounts in quite good health," she continued. "But apparently he thought the Deep would cure his illness, and grant him everlasting life."

"So what'd he do?"

"He demanded information from my family," she answered. "But he was poor, and refused to sell the medallion, or even to let us study it. So he resorted to breaking into our archives and stealing the information." She crossed her arms below her bosom. "He was caught and jailed," she continued. "His delusions grew stronger, until he went utterly mad and killed himself."

"Ah."

"My family gained the medallion as compensation for his crime," Lady Camilla explained. "For a time."

"What happened to it?" Hunter asked.

"Jakar had a son," she answered. "Who grew up to be a very successful businessman. Rich beyond the fortunes of many nobles, in fact," she added. "Back when such a thing was possible. He used his considerable influence to insist that Tykus's Seekers be trained and operate under a single unifying body."

"The guild," Hunter guessed. The Lady nodded.

"Precisely," she confirmed. "Under the pretense of standardizing training and operations to improve the quality and consistency of Seekers. His true purpose, however, was to directly compete with my family. To gather his own intelligence about artifacts and Ossae, and to build his own network of clients."

"He succeeded," Hunter stated. He had to have. The Guild of Seekers had a monopoly on Seekers in the kingdom.

"They did," she agreed. "By offering considerably lower prices, and by arguing that a monopoly on such information gave my family undue influence."

Hunter couldn't help but smirk at that.

"Bit ironic," he opined. She smirked back.

"Isn't it?"

"So the Guild of Seekers won," he concluded. "What happened to your family?"

"We endured," she answered. "For centuries we endured. We had something the Seekers didn't…a store of knowledge collected over millennia. The guild still used us, but demanded insultingly low prices, and the return of Jakar's medallion. We had no choice but to agree to their terms."

"Because they controlled all the Seekers."

"Correct."

"But you're not part of Tykus anymore," Hunter pointed out.

"Also correct," she agreed. "When your mother arrived in Tykus, we saw her potential. We approached her to do as you did…to explore the Crypt of Zagamar. But she refused."

"Why?"

"She wasn't interested in helping any of the nobles," the Lady replied. "Neesha assumed we were like everyone else in the Acropolis."

"And you weren't?"

"My ancestors were historians," she explained. "They didn't hold the same prejudices as the rest of Tykus. Those who understand history are less swayed by the biases of the present."

"So what happened?"

"As I said, over the next two hundred years, my family grew less and less influential as the Guild of Seekers expanded their base of knowledge. When your mother started the Civil War, my grandparents took the opportunity to secede from Tykus, withdrawing to this estate," she added, gesturing at the room around her. "They formed an alliance with the Kingdom of the Deep, allowing that kingdom's Seekers access to our family's archives…for a price, of course."

"Tykus must not have liked that," Hunter guessed.

"Indeed," Lady Camilla agreed. "But they were hardly in a position to stop us, given the war. Your mother nearly took down the kingdom, you know."

"Really?"

"Oh yes," she replied. "Neesha was a Legend, of course. Legends have a habit of turning their staunchest critics into loyal allies…and she turned the entire Outskirts – and many of the lower nobles – against the Acropolis. If it weren't for Tykus and Duke Dominus, she might have succeeded."

"What did they do?"

"They coordinated the defense of the Acropolis," she explained. "...slaughtering nearly every last citizen of the Outskirts, and even some of the nobles in Hightown she corrupted. Tykus ordered a third of the kingdom to be set ablaze."

"Damn."

"It worked," Lady Camilla continued. "Neesha was chased out of the kingdom with the few survivors from the Outskirts, and she fled past the Fringe. Duke Dominus ordered his men to hunt her down, but she – and her people – were never found."

"I see," Hunter mumbled. He'd found his mother, of course...although she'd hardly been as he'd remembered. Somehow, she'd turned into a beast...the queen of the Ironclad.

"So here we are," the Lady stated. "And I find myself standing before the son of a Legend, the only man to successfully enter the tomb of Zagamar and drink of his flesh."

Hunter frowned.

"Wait," he protested. "You said I drank some water from his skull."

Lady Camilla hesitated, then shook her head.

"Doubtful," she replied. "You said the fluid was thick."

"Yeah."

"From what we've gathered," she stated, "...the ancients stored their Ossae in tombs, like we do," she explained. "But they were not satisfied with mortality. They liquified and preserved their brains, so that someone worthy might drink them."

Hunter stared at her silently, feeling a chill run through him.

"By consuming their flesh," the Lady continued, "...a person would incorporate the will of the Legend into themselves...theoretically a direct, one-hundred percent transfer. The matter of their brains would become – to some extent – incorporated into the drinker's body."

"Wait," Hunter stated. "Are you saying..."

"Zagamar's brain is inside of you," she confirmed. "His flesh is part of you now. His mind lives within you."

Hunter swallowed in a dry throat, his heart starting to pound in his chest. He felt suddenly queasy, and swallowed again.

"I don't feel any different," he protested.

"I know," she replied. "Your will is strong, and much of your flesh is still made of the matter of your world, not ours." She put a hand on his shoulder. "Time will tell what affect Zagamar will have on you."

Hunter processed this silently, feeling the Lady's eyes on him. He had a hard time concentrating under her gaze, and lowered his.

"How are you feeling?" she inquired.

"Terrified," he admitted. He shook his head, looking up at her. "I don't want him to change me."

"I understand," she replied. "But what will be will be."

"What's going to happen to me?"

"I don't know," she admitted, giving him an apologetic look. "That's why it's so important that you stay here."

"What for?"

"To keep you safe," she answered. "Dr. Phelbus can continue to treat you, and my Seekers can help to monitor any changes that happen to you."

Hunter hesitated.

"What's in it for you?" he asked bluntly. He immediately regretted it, realizing how rude he sounded. But to his surprise, she smiled.

"That," she replied, stepping closer and placing a hand on his chest, "…is something you should have asked the first time we met."

He stood there, staring at her, smelling her perfume and feeling the warmth of her touch. Her eyes transfixed him, pinning him in place. He found it difficult to concentrate.

"So what's in it for you?" he pressed. She slid her hand off his chest, but didn't back away.

"You and I want the same thing," she answered.

"And what's that?"

"The Guild of Seekers nearly ruined my family," she explained. "And you," she added, putting a hand on his cheek, "…are going to get me my revenge."

Chapter 12

Nearly a week had passed since the attack on Castle Wexford, with reinforcements from Tykus having just arrived to replace the soldiers lost during the battle. Dominus' health had continued to improve a little each day, and he'd spent each morning marveling over the changes the prior night's sleep had brought him. The pressure he'd been experiencing in his chest with anything more than modest exertion was still present, but improving. And his toes were clearly regenerating, having grown past the first joint. The ulcer on his ankle was gone, and even his severed hand was regrowing, his wrist having regrown completely. The bony nubs of his fingers were starting to show, poking out of the pink flesh surrounding them.

It was remarkable, this progress. Every day brought a new miracle…and hope for a future he'd given up on long ago. But miracles came with a price…and his was pain.

It was incessant, this pain. The newly regenerated tissue throbbed terribly, and itched where the healing was nearly complete. A blessing that Farkus saw fit to provide the narcotic potion that dulled this pain, making it bearable. There was a price for this as well…one that Dominus particularly disliked. For the narcotic dulled his intellect, and bound his bowels terribly.

Still, it was all very much worth it.

Now, with the castle properly staffed, and his wounds on the mend, Dominus could focus on his next mission: to confirm who had ordered his assassination, and utterly destroy them. He'd spent the last hour in his office on the first floor of the castle doing just that…until the knock on his door. He looked up from the surface of his desk, leaning back in his chair.

"Come in," Dominus stated, feeling a flash of irritation at having his train of thought interrupted. He turned his focus inwardly, recognizing the source immediately: he was hungry.

The door opened, and Farkus stepped in, bowing deeply.

"A courier has arrived from Tykus with the reinforcements, your Grace," he declared.

"Bring him in."

Farkus bowed again, then left, returning moments later with a tall man with long blond hair and blue eyes, wearing the white and gold uniform of a noble. A uniform in which countless teeth had been sewn…the bones of the man's ancestors, shielding the courier from the foreign influences of the Fringe. The courier stopped a good three meters from Dominus, out of respective for Dominus's considerable will, and bowed deeply.

"Your Grace," he greeted.

"What is it?" Dominus snapped. He saw the courier swallow. The man clearly knew of Dominus's reputation…and his utter distaste for having his time wasted.

"King Tykus requests an audience with your Grace," the courier declared.

Dominus stared at the man, digesting the implications of that statement.

King Tykus requests…

That meant that Axio, Dominus's former protégé, had completed the transition to kingship, exposing himself to Tykus's Legendary will until he had all but become the long-dead king. The boy he'd known was essentially dead, his soul destroyed.

A waste.

It should have been my son, he thought bitterly. An image of Conlan lying next to Tykus's bed came to him, slumped over in a pool of his own blood.

Dominus forced the image away, focusing on the courier.

"When?" he pressed.

"Tomorrow, your Grace."

Dominus turned to Farkus.

"Prepare my entourage," he commanded. Farkus bowed.

"Consider it done, your Grace."

"Leave me," he stated, waving the men away. They did so quickly, leaving him alone in his office once again. Dominus sighed, staring at the papers stacked neatly on his desk. Staring *through* them. He felt a sudden pang of fear…an emotion he rarely suffered.

King Tykus requests an audience…

He hadn't planned on returning to the Acropolis so soon. Hadn't prepared himself for the scrutiny such a trip entailed.

The fear gripped his innards, twisting them slowly.

No man could enter the Acropolis without being Tested. Without having a Tester – a weak-willed imbecile – expose themselves to Dominus's will. Any concerning deviation from the acceptable traits of the aristocracy might be detected…and such a deviation, if found to be due to consorting with forbidden artifacts, would bring charges of treason.

He closed his eyes, an image of the Ironclad's grotesque face coming to him. Somehow still well-preserved after all this time, despite not having been embalmed.

Damn.

Dominus opened his eyes, taking a deep breath in, feeling his heart pounding in his chest. He wiped his clammy hand on his pants, forcing himself to focus. To think.

The shrine.

It was the only solution, of course. His ancestral shrine – hidden in catacombs beneath the castle grounds, the entrance known only to himself. It housed the Ossae of his ancestors going back thousands of years…and served as the wellspring of his family's virtue. He would have to spend the rest of the day – and night – in that shrine, absorbing the cleansing will of his ancestors. Drinking of the waters of his ancestral fountain, water steeped in the bones of the most virtuous men in his family's history.

He would have to bathe in it.

"Farkus!" he yelled. Within moments, the door to his office opened, and Farkus stepped in. "Clear my schedule," Dominus commanded. "I'll be spending the night in the shrine."

"Yes your Grace," Farkus replied. To the servant's credit, he asked no questions.

"Bring me food," he ordered, remembering his hunger. "Now."

"Of course, your Grace."

Dominus watched Farkus leave, then stood from his desk, turning to look out of his office windows at the gardens beyond. At the pallets where his beehives had been stacked.

The beekeeper must return to his hives, he mused.

He frowned then, staring at them for a long moment. A thought came to him then, one that he'd never considered before.

The beekeeper is not a bee.

He turned away from the window, feeling uneasy. He thought back to the Ironclad's head, and knew that he could not expose himself to it any more. But he couldn't very well risk having it stolen from the castle while he was away.

The beekeeper cannot *be a bee.*

He felt a chill run through him, and shoved the thought away, horrified that he'd even considered it.

I've strayed too far.

He clenched his left fist, feeling the nubs of his regenerating right hand contracting as best they could. He'd strayed far too far from the ideals of the Acropolis recently, inviting forbidden traits to corrupt his soul. They were twisting his mind, making him think unacceptable thoughts.

Shame came over him, followed by immediate resolve.

Humanity needed him, it was true. And he'd done terrible things to ensure that he would survive to serve them.

Humanity needed him, but now *he* needed his humanity.

Dominus snatched his cane from where it rested against the side of his desk, then strode out of his office, starting the long journey to his shrine. He felt pressure growing in his chest, and grimaced, slowing down.

"Farkus!" he shouted. Moments later, the servant arrived.

"Yes your Grace?"

Dominus hesitated, eyeing Farkus for a long moment. It was forbidden for anyone but the men of Dominus's family to enter his shrine. But there was little chance he'd make the journey in his current condition. He needed help…and Farkus, weak-willed as he was, would not pose any harm to the shrine. And he would never dare to tell anyone of its secrets.

"Come with me," he ordered.

He walked beside his loyal servant, making his way slowly to the front entrance of the castle.

* * *

High Seeker Zeno leaned back in his chair, crossing his arms over his chest and gazing across his desk at Nova, his second-in-command.

"So Dominus lives," he stated. Hardly surprising news, but not the ideal outcome. Reality, of course, hardly cared about his expectations. "Very well," he stated. "We must assume he will plot against us. Relocate the forbidden artifacts and Ossae, then seal the tunnels."

"Yes High Seeker."

"Send out all true Seekers," he continued. "Keep the false Seekers within the guild."

"And the apprentices?" Nova inquired. Zeno sighed. The true apprentices were already too indoctrinated to risk being Tested by the kingdom…but too new to survive in the field.

"Send them all out," he decided.

"To the field?"

"Yes."

"As you command," Nova agreed. She hesitated then, and Zeno frowned.

"Yes?"

"One more thing, High Seeker," she stated. "Our spies spotted a man in the Cursed Wood."

Zeno leaned back in his chair, steepling his fingers together. *That* got his attention.

"He…struggled with the first Trial," she continued. "And won entry into the Crypt."

"And?"

"He emerged over an hour later, High Seeker," Nova replied. "Stumbling to the woods. He had a seizure."

Zeno stood from his chair, leaning over his desk.

"Where is he now?" he demanded. "Is he alive?"

"He was taken by Lady Camilla's men, High Seeker," Nova answered. "There were too many of them for our spies to intervene. He was taken back to her mansion."

Zeno grimaced, then sat back down, taking a moment to compose himself. No man had dared enter the Crypt for centuries…and only one man had emerged alive, and sane. If Lady Camilla was behind this…

"Retrieve this man," he ordered. Nova nodded.

"Yes High Seeker." She hesitated. "He had dark skin," she added. "We have reason to believe he was the Original."

Zeno nodded; of course he was. They never should have wasted that boy…or his mother. The guild had sent several other Originals to the crypt, all without success, but even still, Master Thorius had been a fool to act without consulting with him. A chance like this happened once in a lifetime…and Lady Camilla had clearly taken advantage of it. And if the Original had truly had a seizure, it was almost certain that he'd succeeded in the task she'd given him.

"Is that all?" he asked. Nova nodded.

"Mobilize the guild," he stated. "And get me that boy."

"Yes High Seeker."

"And Nova," he added, staring into her eyes, his expression suddenly hard. He saw her swallow nervously.

"Yes?"

"I want the Ironclad's head," he replied. "And failure," he added, "…is not an option."

CHAPTER 13

It was late afternoon by the time Lady Camilla led Hunter from her library back down to his room, and when he walked through the doorway into it, he found a small circular table sitting before the bed, two chairs around it placed opposite each other. The table had been set with silver platters covered with ornate silver lids, two plates, a bewildering array of silverware, and several large bottles of red wine. Lady Camilla walked up to one of the chairs, standing beside it.

She glanced at him, arching one eyebrow.

Hunter grimaced, rushing to pull her chair back from the table, then gesturing for her to sit.

"Such a gentleman," she murmured, giving him a smirk, then sitting down. He pushed her chair in a bit, after which she gestured at the chair opposite his. "By all means," she added, "...join me."

He did so, and moments later a man in a crisp red uniform walked into the room, lifting the lids off the silver platters, revealing steaming meats and vegetables. He doled these out to Lady Camilla and Hunter, then popped the corks on all of the wine bottles. That done, he turned to the Lady.

"Anything else, my Lady?"

"That will be all," she replied. The man bowed, then left as quickly as he'd come. Lady Camilla turned to Hunter, gesturing at the food. "Eat," she urged. Hunter did so eagerly, his hunger having returned despite having pigged out earlier that day. He wasn't quite as ravenous as before, but still, he had to stop himself from shoveling the food into his mouth.

"So what's your plan?" he asked in-between bites.

"I assume you mean for revenge against the guild," she replied, chewing a piece of meat, then swallowing. "A straightforward attack will never work. We need to frame them."

"Frame them?"

"Tykus has zero tolerance for illegal artifacts," she explained. "If we can show that the guild is trading in such artifacts, they will be shut down by the aristocracy."

"Ah."

"If my sources are correct, the newest heir to the throne is already fully converted to Tykus's will. This means that the king is in charge now instead of the dukes."

"Go on," he urged, continuing to eat. The food was delicious – far better than anything he'd had since arriving in this forsaken world. A hell of a lot better than the slop they'd fed him in the community center back in the Outskirts.

"I also happen to know that Duke Dominus has been trading in illegal artifacts with the Kingdom of the Deep," Lady Camilla revealed. Hunter's eyebrows rose.

"How do you know that?"

"I do business with the Kingdom of the Deep," she explained. "Unlike Tykus, they appreciate my family's millennia of stored knowledge. They even provide Seekers for me," she added.

"The men in the masks," Hunter guessed. She nodded.

"Men *and* women," she corrected.

"If Dominus is dealing in illegal artifacts, can't we frame him too?" Hunter asked. The Lady smiled.

"Of course," she replied, taking another bite of meat. "But that seems like an awful amount of work, don't you think?"

"Maybe," Hunter replied.

"Far better to let them destroy each other," she opined. Hunter frowned, leaning back in his chair.

"How do we do that?"

Lady Camilla smirked, leaning forward and giving him a conspiratorial look. This happened to give him a rather intriguing view down the deep V-cut of her dress.

"Already begun," she revealed.

Hunter raised an eyebrow, and Lady Camilla leaned back, much to his disappointment.

"That Ironclad head you retrieved," she stated, "…was meant for the guild. According to my spies, Duke Dominus happened to divert it."

"Where?"

"To himself," she answered. "At the Castle Wexford." Hunter's eyebrows rose.

"Oh," he murmured. If that was true, it was good news. Retrieving the head from the Seekers would've been nearly impossible, requiring him to infiltrate the kingdom and the guild. Getting it from the Castle Wexford, on the other hand…

"The guild is none too pleased," she continued. "In fact, they would do anything to get it back." She smiled then, pushing her plate away. "Imagine what would happen," she added, "…if a group of Seekers happened to attack Duke Dominus in his castle, and try to retrieve the head?"

"He would destroy the Guild of Seekers," Hunter deduced. Lady Camilla nodded.

"One does not dare attack the most powerful duke in Tykus," she agreed.

"You said you'd already begun," Hunter recalled.

"Oh, *I* haven't done anything," she corrected. "Haven't needed to. The guild sent Seekers to kill Dominus about a week ago."

"How do you know?" Hunter asked. She gave a little smile.

"I have spies everywhere," she answered. "And not all of them are…human. Dominus has no idea they exist."

"Ah," Hunter mumbled. He remembered the Legendary tree he'd encountered, and the strange creatures he'd seen before reaching it. The ones that had looked like walking bushes. If they hadn't been moving, he would never have known they *weren't* plants. Maybe the Lady's spies were like that.

"Time will tell if the attack succeeded," she continued. "But of course the Seekers were disguised…apparently as Seekers of the Deep."

"Huh?"

"Seekers from the Kingdom of the Deep," she clarified. "They're framing the Kingdom of the Deep, of course."

"Why frame them?"

"The Kingdom of the Deep is the nearest foreign kingdom to Tykus," she explained. "And Tykus despises them, not the least because they deal in wild artifacts."

"How do you know it *wasn't* the Kingdom of the Deep?" Hunter pressed.

"Because I deal with them all the time," Lady Camilla answered. "And believe me, if they wanted Duke Dominus dead, they wouldn't send Seekers to do it." She leaned back in her chair. "The Guild of Seekers has the motive and the means to kill Dominus," she stated. "It must be them."

"So what now?"

"If Dominus is still alive, he'll see through the ruse," she replied. "He's no fool."

"And then he'll destroy the guild," Hunter realized. She nodded, clearly pleased.

"Exactly."

Hunter glanced down at his plate, realizing that he'd finished his food. He raised his gaze to Lady Camilla.

"What does this have to do with me?" he inquired.

"You," she replied, "…are my secret weapon."

"How so?"

"You drank the flesh of Zagamar," she explained. He frowned.

"I don't understand," he admitted. "What does that have to do with anything?"

Lady Camilla sighed, then reached for a bottle of wine, pouring some into a glass beside her plate. She reached for his glass then, pouring a generous portion of wine, then setting the bottle down. She picked up her own glass, gesturing for him to do the same.

"That," she stated, "…is for another day."

Hunter glanced at his glass, then crossed his arms over his chest.

"Why can't you tell me now?"

"Because everything has its time," she answered. "And now is not it."

"You're hiding something," he accused. She smiled.

"Of course I am," she agreed. He felt irritated by her answer, and had the urge to stand up from his chair.

"It sounds like you don't need me at all," he decided. "I have to get back to Vi's house anyway," he added. As the best Seeker in Tykus – and maybe even the best Seeker period – Vi's collection of artifacts was an easy target for potential looters. He'd already been gone longer than he'd wanted.

"I wouldn't do that," Lady Camilla warned, her voice remaining calm. Hunter's brows furrowed.

"Why not?"

"Vi's canyon has been overrun by Ironclad," she answered. "I sent scouts to her home after you claimed that she'd been killed. They found the canyon teeming with Ironclad…and the corpses of Duke Dominus's men."

Hunter stared at her, a chill running down his spine.

The Ironclad!

"If you go back to Vi's house," she stated, "…they'll kill you."

Hunter lowered his gaze. She might be wrong. The Ironclad hadn't killed him…even after he'd killed his own mother, their queen. The question was, why had they swarmed Vi's place? And why had Dominus's soldiers been at Vi's?

"We'll see about that," he replied at last. Lady Camilla sighed.

"Very well," she stated, her tone suddenly weary. "You may go if you like. But it will be safer to go tomorrow morning," she added. "And you need to pack provisions for your trip."

Hunter considered this, then nodded grudgingly. She was right, of course.

"Alright," he agreed. "I appreciate everything you've done for me," he added hastily. "I don't want you to think…"

"I know," she interjected, smiling at him. "If you change your mind…"

"I'll let you know."

"Good," she replied. She raised her glass of wine then, gesturing at his glass. "A toast?"

"To what?" he inquired, picking up his glass.

"To our revenge," she stated, clinking glasses. She sipped her wine then. Hunter did the same; it was quite sweet, to his surprise, with only a hint of dryness. It burned pleasantly on the way down, making his belly feel warm.

"To our revenge," he agreed.

"You'll return if the Ironclad are still there?" she asked. Hunter nodded.

"I will," he agreed. "As long as you tell me what my role in all of this is." She arched one eyebrow, then leaned forward, her eyes twinkling mischievously.

"You're learning," she observed. His gaze fell to her substantial cleavage, milky white against her black corset. Again, he was struck by her sheer beauty, barely marred by age. He found himself staring, and felt a stirring in his groin. His cheeks flushed, and he looked up, finding her gazing at him.

"Hmm?" he mumbled.

"I said you're learning," she repeated. When Hunter didn't respond, she sat up straight, taking another sip of her wine, then set her glass down. "A good vintage," she opined. "I like my wine sweet."

"Me too." he agreed.

"I never understood the dry wines," she mused, swirling the wine in her glass, then taking another sip. "Why suffer for your pleasure?"

Hunter shrugged, tasting the wine again. The same sweet taste greeted him, and that pleasant burning.

"Hunger is the best spice," he replied, feeling warmth spread through him. "Maybe suffering makes pleasure feel all the better."

"Granted," Lady Camilla conceded, nodding approvingly. "You're not a brute at all, are you."

"Only sometimes."

"I'm curious," she confessed. "What were you, before you went through the Gate?"

"A student," he answered.

"Of what?"

"Of everything," he clarified. "Where I come from, you don't pick a profession until you're in your twenties."

"Hmm," she murmured, leaning over and resting her chin in one palm, gazing at him curiously. And giving him another view of her spectacular bosom. He found his eyes drawn inexorably to it.

Damn, he thought. *Just…damn.*

He'd only ever been with one woman in his life – Trixie – and she'd been as young as him, and skinny and angular, with small breasts. He couldn't help but be curious about what it'd be like to be with someone like Lady Camilla. The thought was intriguing, and he found himself imagining the possibilities…and quickly felt himself growing against the front of his pants.

Bet she's more experienced.

"That seems like a waste of time," she stated. He glanced up at her, realizing she was still looking at him.

"Hmm?"

"Not choosing a profession until your twenties," she clarified. "I knew of my future profession – as landowner and researcher – when I was four." She took another sip of wine, then smiled at him. "Feeling the wine I see," she murmured.

"Little bit," he admitted. He felt only a slight buzz, having drank barely half of his wine. He took a larger gulp, savoring the sweetness. "I don't drink much."

"Clearly," she agreed. "You needn't worry about a hangover," she added. "There's very little alcohol in the wine…it's absorbed the sensation of pleasant drunkenness, and that's what you're feeling."

"Really?"

"Really," she confirmed. "The more you drink, the more pleasantly drunk you'll feel. And unless you drink all of these bottles and more," she added, "…you won't pay dearly for the experience."

"Why suffer for your pleasure," Hunter murmured. Lady Camilla chuckled – for the first time since he'd met her.

"Well said," she murmured, giving him a mysterious smile. She stood then, sliding her chair over until it was next to his, then sitting back down.

"I thought you didn't know how to move chairs," Hunter accused. She laughed, a low, raspy sound.

"Oh you're just precious, aren't you?"

She slid her wine over, finishing it in one gulp. Then she lifted her arms, taking a small black band from her wrist and pulling her hair into a long ponytail. He took the opportunity to appreciate her profile, which was extraordinary. But to his chagrin, she caught him looking, and lowered her arms, *tsk*ing at him.

"Caught in the act," she murmured, hardly seeming displeased. Hunter shrugged nonchalantly, feeling rather bold.

"Can you blame me?"

"Not really," she replied with a smile. "You've done quite well hiding your furtive glances," she added.

"I'm guessing this isn't the first time you've caught me," Hunter ventured. She smirked.

"I'm not blind."

Hunter finished his own wine, enjoying the warmth it gave him, and realized that he was now pleasantly drunk. She glanced at his empty glass, then gestured at a fresh bottle of wine.

"Are you going to refresh us?" she inquired. Hunter did so, pouring them both another generous portion. They clinked glasses again.

"To being caught," he toasted, grinning sheepishly. She arched an eyebrow.

"To the hunt," she replied, taking a gulp of her wine. He hesitated, a part of him wondering if it was a good idea to drink so much…and wondering where that might lead. He imagined the possibilities…and felt himself straining against his pants.

He took a gulp of his wine, then another, his heart starting to race. The thought of losing control with this woman – of letting go and seeing what might happen – was tantalizing. He remembered the night he'd spent with Trixie so long ago, when she'd seduced him. When he'd thought she was another girl, and he'd struggled to break free of her hold on him, only to inevitably give in. How amazing it'd felt.

Fuck.

"Where did *you* go?" Lady Camilla inquired. He blinked, realizing she was staring at him.

"Huh?"

"I lost you for a bit there," she explained.

"Sorry," he mumbled. She put a hand on his knee.

"So where did you go?" she pressed. He hesitated, feeling the warmth of her hand, then took another gulp of his wine. Warmth spreading through his belly…and his loins.

"Somewhere pleasant," he confessed, flashing her a rueful grin. Her eyebrows raised.

"Oh really?" she replied. "Do tell."

Hunter didn't even hesitate, his head swimming pleasantly now. His eyes fell to gaze at her…the curve of her breasts, her slender waist. He didn't care if she saw him look anymore.

"I'd prefer to show you," he replied at last, his heart pounding now, a flash of fear running through him. At the realization that he'd crossed a line…and that there was no going back.

"Hmm," she murmured, her hand sliding up the inside of his leg, stopping on his inner thigh, inches from his aching groin. He wanted nothing more than to shift in his chair, to meet that hand, to feel its warmth and pressure on him. But he stayed where he was…and so did her hand. "You would, wouldn't you."

"Mm hmm."

She slid her hand up a little, then down, her fingers trailing a fraction of an inch from his groin now, massaging his inner thigh gently. He felt the pressure in his member grow stronger, felt every beat of his heart in it. He shifted in his chair, trying to make her fingers slide onto his groin, but she moved with him, her fingers remaining on his inner thigh.

God damn, he thought.

"I'm far too old for you," she murmured, cocking her head to one side, her eyes boring into his. A slight smile played on her full lips. "It wouldn't be proper now, would it?"

"I've never been proper," Hunter countered. She smirked.

"Well, I'm a Lady," she retorted. "My mother taught me to be proper." Then she leaned forward, her lips brushing up against his ear. Her touch sent a shiver down his spine. "You know what else she taught me?" she whispered.

"What's that?"

"Proper," she murmured, her fingertips trailing up his thigh to his lower belly, then sliding down until they rested just above the bulge in his pants, "…has no place in the bedroom."

Hunter turned, glancing at the bed near their table, then turning back to Camilla.

"I like her already."

"In the bedroom," she continued, her lips trailing down to the side of his neck, brushing against it. Goosebumps rose on his arms. "…anything goes."

"Anything?"

"Anything," she murmured, pulling away from him – while keeping her hand on his belly. She smiled at him, her eyes twinkling, and took another drink of her wine, downing the remainder of it in one gulp. He did the same, the wine burning in his belly, the sensation spreading over his entire body. He stared at her, at this marvelous woman, and had the sudden, mad urge to kiss her. To pull her in and crush her against his body, to feel every inch of her under his fingertips. He wanted to take her, to make her his.

"More wine?" she offered, gesturing at the last bottle. Hunter glanced at it, then back at her. He cleared his throat.

"I shouldn't," he said at last.

"Why not?" she inquired.

"Because I might not be able to help myself afterward."

"Are you afraid of losing control, Hunter?" she asked, pouring wine into his glass, then into hers. He stared at his glass, at the wine filling it to the brim, and licked his lips nervously.

"I am."

"Good," she replied, raising her glass. "Fear," she added, "…can make such a wonderful spice."

"Pardon?"

"Proper has no place in the bedroom," she replied. "And I," she added, lowering her hand, her fingertips sliding over his erection, "…am going to break you down, inhibition after inhibition, until you've done things you never imagined."

Hunter's breath caught in his throat, his member pulsing under her touch. He waited for her to place her palm on him, but she kept her fingers there, trailing up, then down, slowly, with the barest of pressure.

It was maddening.

"You *should* be afraid," she murmured, bringing her lips to his neck again, brushing them against his skin ever-so-lightly. Then she raised her lips to his ear, biting his earlobe just hard enough to hurt a little. "Your choice," she whispered, pushing his wine glass closer to him.

He stared at it, his heart hammering in his chest. Sweat trickled down his flanks, and he licked his dry lips, reaching for the glass, feeling its cool surface. Her fingertips went up and down his shaft, painfully slowly, as light as a feather. His hips bucked reflexively, but she moved with him expertly, never applying more than the slightest of pressure.

Hunter raised the glass, staring at the red liquid within, then bringing the rim to his lips.

And then he closed his eyes, and drank.

Chapter 14

Sukri stepped into her small bedroom, seeing Gammon already there, taking his shirt off. She closed the door, looking around. Moonlight shone through the window at the other side of the room, casting the twin bunkbeds in a silver glow. Gammon barely acknowledged her, nodding slightly when she entered. He'd been quiet all day, not that he was a man of many words to begin with. But he'd said almost nothing since waking up this morning, and every time she drew near him, she felt glum. Depressed. He'd been this way since the sparring match with Sen. Hell, ever since they'd become apprentices…which made sense, considering what they'd been forced to do during their graduation ceremony. But it was much worse now.

She faced him, putting her hands on her hips.

"What's wrong?" she asked. Gammon didn't make eye contact.

"Nothing."

"Bullshit," Sukri retorted. "You've been moping all damn day," she added. "For the last few days, actually."

He just stood there.

"Come on Gammon," she urged, forcing herself to use a gentler tone. She put a hand on one beefy arm. "Talk to me." She felt the glumness lessen a little, felt a twinge of affection amidst the darkness.

"I'm just tired," he mumbled. She smiled up at him, stepping in closer, and felt the affection grow stronger. And something else…a sad wistfulness.

"You can tell me," she urged. Gammon hesitated, then turned away. She felt the affection cut off instantly, and in its place…nothing.

"Don't manipulate me," he growled.

"I'm not," she protested. "Gammon, come on," she pleaded. "I'm your best friend. I just want to help."

Gammon's shoulders rose, then slumped, and he turned to face her again.

"I almost killed Sen," he muttered.

"You made a mistake," Sukri soothed, putting a hand on his arm again. "And Sen's fine." She smirked then. "If you ask me, he had it coming."

"That's not the point," Gammon retorted.

"Then what is?"

"I..." he began, then stopped, grimacing.

"You what?"

"I...wanted to," he confessed.

"He provoked you," Sukri countered. "And Master Thorius threatened you."

"He threatened *you*," Gammon corrected. Sukri smiled.

"You wanted to protect me," she replied. "Thanks for stopping him from breaking my leg, by the way. I don't think I could stand another six weeks in that damn wheelchair."

"Yes," Gammon conceded. "I wanted to protect you. But I also wanted to kill Sen. And..."

He stopped, his jawline rippling, and sat down at the edge of his bunkbed, resting his elbows on his knees.

"I'm listening," Sukri stated.

"I wanted to kill everyone else too."

Sukri stood there, staring at him.

"What?"

"You heard me," he replied.

"Why did you want to kill everyone?" she pressed.

"I don't know," he answered. Then he sighed. "I'm changing," he admitted. "We're changing." He stared at her for a long moment. "*They're* changing us."

"People change," Sukri countered. "That's normal. Think of everything that we've been through. Everything we've had to do."

"I did it willingly back then," Gammon retorted. "I did it for you."

Sukri thought back to their third Trial. A vision of Gammon slicing Udeln's throat flashed in her mind's eye, blood pumping from the severed vessels of their fellow initiate's neck.

"I know," Sukri replied. "And I know you did what you did to Sen for me too," she added.

He stared at her, then shook his head slowly.

"No," he countered. "You don't."

"Yes I do," she insisted. "You love me."

He lowered his gaze, and she reached under his chin, forcing him to look at her. She smiled.

"I think I know how to make you feel better," she said, taking a step back. She reached down, grabbing the bottom of her shirt and pulling upward, stripping it off. She flung her shirt to the floor, standing before him with her breasts exposed.

He turned away, his cheeks flushing a bright crimson. She flashed him a grin.

"Ooo, it's working," she said. And it was; she could feel his depression lifting, replaced by embarrassment…and something else she couldn't quite read. "Told you it would work."

"Sukri…" Gammon protested.

"When's the last time you jerked off?" she inquired. Gammon's face flushed an even deeper red, and he grimaced.

"I'm going to bed," he muttered.

"Well?" she pressed. "Answer the question."

"Goodnight Sukri."

"Answer the question," she pressed. "A guy's got to get release, you know. Can't go walking around with all that pent-up energy inside you."

"I haven't."

"Why not?" she teased. "Afraid I might hear you?" He sighed, laying down on his mattress and turning away from her. She laughed, sitting down on the edge of his bed and leaning over him, putting a hand on his shoulder. "*I've* done it, you know."

"Sukri…"

"Well?"

"Because I might…influence you," Gammon answered at last. Sukri frowned.

"What?"

"If I get…aroused," he clarified. "I might…get you the same way."

"So?"

"I don't want to do that to you."

"Well that's why we haven't done it," she retorted, pulling away from him and standing up. "You can't just be all passive and expect anything to happen, you know."

He rolled onto his back, looking her in the eye. After stealing a glimpse of her bare chest, she noted.

"I'd be a lot more attracted to you if you…you know, were more aggressive."

"That's not me," Gammon retorted quietly.

"Like hell it isn't," she countered. "I saw what you did to Sen. And what you did to that Ironclad back in our first Trial."

"That was different."

"Yeah, well it was sexy as hell," she retorted.

"I can't feel something for you without making *you* feel it toward me," he pressed. "If I let myself…if I…"

"If you got horny around me?" she ventured. He blushed.

"Then you'd be forced to feel the same way, and it wouldn't be right."

"Gammon, you think too much," she admonished. "You're a Polarizer," she added. "Does that mean you can't have a relationship with anyone ever?"

"I can with another Polarizer."

"But not me," she concluded.

"Right."

Sukri sighed, walking to the other side of the room to grab her shirt, then pulling it back on. She hardly felt slighted – she didn't really want a relationship with Gammon – but he'd killed any playfulness she'd been feeling. And any chance that she might sleep with him just to get some. She had no qualms about sex without a relationship, but Gammon clearly did. He was one of those people that couldn't separate his emotions from the act.

"Well, I *was* going to make you feel better," she grumbled.

"Thanks," Gammon replied. "But you can't."

"Why not Gammon?"

"Because it's too late," he answered.

"Too late for what?"

Gammon sighed, turning away from her, laying on his side in his bed. She waited for him to answer, but he didn't. It wasn't long before she heard him snoring. She sighed, climbing up to the top bunk of her bed, then laying down. She rolled onto her side, staring down at the big guy…then noticed something odd about the back of his neck. It took her a moment to realize what it was.

He wasn't wearing his medallion.

She glanced at his nightstand beside his bed, spotting a slightly open drawer there. Gammon must've taken the medallion off and put it in the drawer. But why?

She rolled onto her back, chewing on a fingernail.

They were supposed to wear their medallions at all times…those were the rules. Master Thorius himself had demanded it. To violate that rule…it was unthinkable.

He's just going through a phase, she reasoned. *He's scared of it changing him.*

She'd gone through the same fear, back during their final Trial. Hell, she herself had had the urge to stop wearing her own medallion. But she hadn't dared, for fear of bringing Master Thorius's wrath upon her.

She forced herself to stop biting her nails, trapping her hands between her thighs. Gammon was going through a rough time, especially after what he'd done to Sen. She wouldn't rat him out to Master Thorius…not yet, anyway. In all likelihood, he'd be better in a day or two, and start wearing his medallion at night again.

But if he didn't, she was going to have to have a talk with Master Thorius.

* * *

Sukri followed Gammon into Seeker Hanlen's classroom, rubbing the sleep from her eyes. Sen, Jasmine, and the other Seeker apprentices were already there, sitting at their desks facing the front of the classroom, where Seeker Hanlen was seated at his desk. Neither Jasmine or Sen greeted them as they entered, which was hardly surprising. They hadn't forgiven Gammon for what he'd done to Sen, and as for Sukri…well, she was guilty by association. Sen had been lucky to get away with a concussion and a few broken ribs. If Master Thorius hadn't stopped Gammon…

"Good morning," Seeker Hanlen greeted, gesturing for Sukri and Gammon to take their seats. "That makes all of us, I think. Let's begin."

He stood then, walking up to Sen's desk, stopping and eyeing his student. Sen's face was still black and blue, his nose swollen from being head-butted by Gammon.

"Are you alright?" Seeker Hanlen inquired. Sen grimaced, lowering his gaze.

"Fine," he muttered.

"I think not," Seeker Hanlen countered. "You're ashamed that Gammon here beat you," he added. "And you're furious with him for it. You never want to talk to him again…and you were just fantasizing about beating the crap out of him the next time you two spar."

Sen's eyes widened, and he shrank into his seat. Seeker Hanlen smiled, raising his gaze to the rest of the class.

"You see," he stated. "As an Empath, I can sense the emotions of anyone nearby. And, as Sen here is sitting in the front row, I happened to sense his emotions as you two," he added, gesturing at Sukri and Gammon, "…came in. I sensed the change in his emotions, and was able to deduce exactly what had happened to him…and how he felt about it…without anyone having to tell me."

Sen stared at the top of his desk, his face pale.

"That," Seeker Hanlen declared, "…is the power of an Empath. Knowledge. Awareness of the emotional state of everyone around them." He looked down at Sen. "No one can hide their emotions from an Empath, save for a fellow Empath. Understood?"

"Yes Seeker Hanlen," Sen mumbled.

"We have a tendency to believe that Polarizers – those who transmit emotion – are more powerful than Empaths," Seeker Hanlen continued. "After all, a Polarizer can control another person's emotions, yes? But there are two sides to every coin, and one side is not more valuable than the other. Understood?"

"Yes Seeker Hanlen," the class droned.

"This is the way of the world," he explained. "That for every trait there is its opposite. For every strength there is a weakness. Even a Legend," he continued, "…who transmits only – and does not receive – is blind to the state of the world around them. They cannot sense emotion, or absorb skills, or better themselves in any way through possessing artifacts. For all their considerable power, they have only two gifts: to be forever themselves, and to force everyone else around them to become them."

Sukri glanced at Gammon, who met her gaze for a split-second. It was practically heresy to say anything negative about a Legend, after all. At least it was in the rest of the kingdom. The Guild of Seekers, however, was different. Their initiation ceremony had proven that.

"Empaths are those who can see," Seeker Hanlen lectured. "Polarizers are blind. Empaths are easily manipulated, while Polarizers are not. Therefore, it is imperative that Empaths learn to dissociate from their emotions. To observe – to *experience* – without acting. Thus the mantra?"

"Emotion is temporary," the class droned. "Action is forever."

"Precisely," Seeker Hanlen agreed. "If you stay within the river of your emotions, you'll be carried away by its current. You must learn to separate from yourself, and become *two* selves. The watcher and the watched." He turned to Gammon then. "Polarizers must do the opposite. They must lose themselves to their emotions. Like an actor on a stage, they must be able to play a role, to actually *feel* an emotion that they want to transmit. They must jump into the river of emotion, and let it carry them away."

Seeker Hanlen walked up to Gammon's desk then. Sukri saw Gammon shrink back into his seat – as much as the big guy could – eyeing his teacher warily. Hanlen smiled.

"Now now," he chided. "See how nervous he is?" He turned to the rest of the class. "An Empath has great power, but it is limited. I cannot read Gammon's thoughts…only his emotions. And only the emotions he's having right now. It takes a great deal of skill to piece together his emotions over time, to weave a story about them. Right now, for example, all I feel is fear."

There was nervous laughter at that, and Seeker Hanlen turned back to Gammon.

"An Empath is a detective. Gammon is afraid of my sensing his emotions, so he must therefore have something to hide. Something he is ashamed of. Finding out what precisely that might be requires manipulation. By asking the right questions, I can sense which ones intensify his fear. Those are the questions that will lead to the root of his fear."

Hanlen smiled down at Gammon, then turned away, gesturing at the class.

"We all have something to hide," he stated. "We all have hidden shame that must not be revealed. That must be kept secret at all costs. This shame eats at us, erodes our happiness, yet we protect it with all our being." He raised an eyebrow. "Empaths can uncover this shame, and use it to their advantage. Tell me," he added. "If nearly everyone has a secret they will do anything to hide, how can that be of use to us?"

Sukri raised her hand, and Seeker Hanlen nodded at her.

"Blackmail," she answered, giving Gammon an apologetic look.

"Correct," Hanlen agreed.

"So what about Polarizers?" Sen asked. Hanlen turned to him.

"Polarizers have great power," he replied. "Imagine what might happen if a Polarizer stood in the middle of an angry mob, and exuded calm? Or if he were to stoke his own lust, making a woman he was dining with lust for him? Or if he were to exude murderous rage near two men having a simple argument? Or suicidality near a man standing at the edge of a bridge?"

"But wouldn't people be able to sense their emotions being manipulated?" Jasmine asked.

"For the most part, no," Seeker Hanlen answered. "Most people are slaves to their emotions, having no clue as to what might have triggered them, nor how to manage them. There is no end to the mental contortions a man will undergo to explain away an unpleasant emotion."

"What do you mean?" Jasmine pressed.

"Well, say Sen here forgets to close a cabinet door," Hanlen proposed, gesturing at Sen. "You get angry with him, and have an argument about it. How many times have you told him to close the cabinet doors after he's done with them?"

Sen smirked at Jasmine, who glared at him.

"Now, you may *think* that the cabinet door being open triggered your anger," Hanlen continued. "But in reality, you were merely hungry, and this made you irritable. After a good meal, your anger fades away, and you forgive poor Sen for his infraction." He walked back to his desk, sitting down. "All the while never realizing the root cause of your anger."

Damn right, Sukri thought. She was a god-awful bitch when she was hungry. But at least she realized it.

"A Polarizer can manipulate everyone around them," Seeker Hanlen concluded, "...without most people being ever the wiser. Only trained individuals will be able to sense a Polarizer's influence...and the only people who receive such training are Seekers and the aristocracy."

Sukri raised her hand.

"Yes?" Hanlen inquired.

"Why are we learning this?" she asked. "I mean, I thought Seekers were supposed to collect artifacts, not manipulate people."

"Most Seekers *are* mere collectors," Hanlen agreed. "Or warriors. Tell me...have you ever wondered why you're all taking this class together?"

Sukri glanced at Gammon, then shrugged.

"Because you're special," their teacher explained. "Powerful Empaths and Polarizers such as yourselves are very rare indeed," he added. "You'll become a...*different* kind of Seeker, assuming you complete your training."

Seeker Hanlen cleared his throat then, gesturing at a stack of rolled-up papers on his desk.

"With that in mind, I have a mission for each of you," he declared. "You are all called to the field effective immediately." He called each apprentice up to his desk one-by-one, handing a paper to each of them. Sukri was last to be called, and grabbed her paper, walking it back to her desk and sitting down. "Read it now," he instructed.

Sukri peeled the golden wax seal from her roll of parchment, then unrolled it, scanning it carefully.

Apprentice Sukri,

Lady Camilla is a former noble banished to the deep forest during the Civil War. She has kidnapped Hunter, the Original.

Your mission is to rescue Hunter using any means possible. You must retrieve him alive and whole. A carriage will take you across the King's Road to the deep forest in three hours. Meet the rest of your team at the Wall.

If the opportunity presents itself, kill Lady Camilla.

If you fail to retrieve the Original, kill yourself.

There was a map drawn below the text, and Sukri stared at it, committing it to memory.

"After you have committed your mission to memory, return it to my desk and I shall destroy it," Hanlen continued. "Understood?"

"Yes Seeker Hanlen," the class replied.

"Good," Hanlen stated. "Class dismissed."

CHAPTER 15

Hunter opened his eyes.

He found himself lying on his back in bed, red sheets strewn haphazardly across the mattress. He yawned, rubbing his eyes, then staring up at the ceiling high above. At the wooden beams against that white ceiling. It took him a moment to remember where he was.

The Lady's place.

He glanced left, then right, realizing he was alone in the bed. Images from last night came unbidden to his mind's eye, of everything that he'd done. And everything that had been done *to* him.

Jesus Christ.

Hunter grunted, sitting up…and grimacing. His abs were sore, and his inner thighs. And…other places.

He looked beyond the edge of the bed, seeing the table there as it'd been last night. There was fresh food on it…all meats and cheeses, it appeared. And only one chair. He stared at that food, his stomach grumbling, and slid off the bed. Naked. Staring down at himself, he spotted more than a few bruises, and some scratch marks. He shook his head.

She'd been more experienced than Trixie. *Oh* yeah. He found himself still trying to process exactly what'd happened. She'd seduced him, driven him crazy. Played him like a musical instrument, drawing it all out for what seemed like hours. Eventually she'd gotten him to the point of a kind of madness, where he'd eagerly done anything she wanted. And let her do anything she wanted to *him*.

It'd felt amazing, better than anything he and Trixie had done. But now he found himself picturing everything she'd made him do, and felt…dissociated. Like it'd happened to someone else.

When she said anything went in the bedroom, he mused ruefully, *she meant it.*

He broke out of his trance, walking up to the table and grabbing a wedge of cheese. He bit into it, savoring the sharp flavor. Hell of a lot better than back on Earth. He finished it quickly.

Probably should get some clothes on, he thought, glancing at the closed door leading out of his room. No point in scaring the poor nurse if she happened to barge in. He searched around the bed, finding his clothes strewn across the floor in various places. He got dressed, then frowned. His weapons and his pack were missing; he'd forgotten to ask for them back yesterday. He was going to need them for his trip back to Vi's house.

Hunter walked up to the door, opening it. Beyond, he saw the long, wide hallway…and two guards standing there facing him.

"Hey," he greeted. "Can I speak to the Lady?"

The guards said nothing.

"I need to speak with her."

Still nothing.

Okay, he thought. He strode forward, trying to pass between them. But they blocked his way, shoving him backward. He stumbled, then caught himself, staring at the two.

"What the hell?" he complained. "I need to get my stuff."

"Get back in your room," one of the guards ordered.

"Why?" Hunter shot back. The guard strode toward him, unsheathing his sword. Hunter backpedaled, holding his hands out before him. "Whoa, whoa!" he blurted out. "Take it easy!"

"Turn around," the guard commanded, "…and get in your room. And don't," he added, "…come out."

Hunter stared at him incredulously, realizing he'd backed up into his room. The guard slammed the door shut, and Hunter heard the *click* of a lock.

The hell?

He tried the doorknob, but it didn't budge. The door was locked…from the outside. Which meant that this room was designed to keep people *in.*

He swore, slamming the door with his palms.

Damn it!

It was the Lady, of course. She hadn't wanted him to leave. Had stopped him from leaving last night. It'll be safer to go tomorrow morning, she'd said.

"Bitch," he swore, slamming the door again. He turned then, around, staring at the table, then at the bed. It'd been her plan all along, to keep him here. And she had his sword, and the rest of his stuff. "Well played, Lady," he muttered. Although he had a hard time thinking of her as a lady after everything they'd done last night.

Now what?

He wracked his brain, trying to come up with a plan. Without weapons, he wouldn't have much luck against her guards…assuming her guards were competent, which was almost certainly the case. Unless he could disarm one of them, and grab their sword…

He heard a *click*, and the door opened. He spun around, seeing the two guards standing there…and Camilla. She was wearing a long golden dress, low cut as usual. He stared at her, watching as she smiled at him.

"Good morning Hunter," she greeted. She frowned. "You look upset."

"I want to leave," he stated, crossing his arms over his chest.

"Ah yes," she replied. "About that. I don't think it's a good idea, Hunter."

"I don't care," he retorted. "I'm leaving."

She sighed.

"Hunter, you're far too important to me," she countered. "I can't risk you being killed out there…by the Ironclad, or by anyone else. I need to keep you safe."

"I can take care of myself."

"I can't rely on that," she insisted. "You're not from this world," she added. "You don't understand all of its dangers." She stepped up to him, putting a hand on his shoulder. "Stay here," she urged. "I can see that you're properly trained…and that you have time to absorb the skills you need to get your revenge."

He hesitated, staring at her silently, feeling the warmth of her hand on his shoulder. Remembered last night, the sweet torture of her seduction, the…

"Stop it," he blurted out, stepped back. Her hand slipped from his shoulder. "Don't play with my emotions."

She smiled, nodding approvingly.

"You're learning," she said. "That's good."

"You're not going to let me go," he stated bluntly. He knew it suddenly…as suddenly as he knew that she had no real desire to train him. An image of her ordering her guards to keep him here came to him. And an image of himself…of him lying on his back in bed. Of looking down at himself past large, pale breasts, long black hair splayed over them, bouncing rhythmically as…

"Not yet," she replied, snapping him out of it. He blinked, realizing he'd been reliving her memories of their night together. It made sense, of course; they'd spent hours together, and he'd absorbed some of her memories.

"What do you want with me?"

"I want *you*," she replied, putting a hand on his cheek, then sliding it down to his chest. She smiled, slipping her hand down until it was inches from his groin. "All of you."

"Thought you already had that," he retorted. Still, her touch had its effect, and he felt a stirring in his groin.

"Oh, I want more," she replied, her eyes twinkling mischievously. "So much more."

"I need to go," he insisted.

"What's the rush?" she countered, sliding her hand down, cupping his groin gently. Her palm was warm, the pressure causing his manhood to swell. Within moments, he was hard, his member straining against the front of his pants, more than filling her hand. She had to have felt it, because she smiled broadly, leaning in and brushing her lips against his earlobe. Goosebumps rose on his flesh. "Stay a while," she whispered.

He found himself wavering, remembering everything they'd done. The incredible intensity of it, the hours of…

"I can't," he blurted out, pulling away from her. He remembered Trixie, how she'd played him. Made him her slave. He couldn't risk that again…no matter how much he wanted it.

Emotion is temporary, he reminded himself. *Action is forever.*

She gazed at him for a long moment, her expression unreadable. Then she smiled.

"Playing hard to get then," she murmured, her eyes twinkling again. "Oh, how I enjoy the hunt." She turned to the guards. "Tie him down," she ordered.

"What?" Hunter blurted out. The guards strode forward suddenly, grabbing him by the arms and throwing him back onto the bed. There were restraints tied to each bedpost from the night before; they tied his wrists, then grabbed his legs. "Hey!" he yelled, kicking at them. But it was no use; they forced his legs down, tying them as well.

"Spread him," Lady Camilla ordered, gazing down at him.

"Stop it!" Hunter shouted, struggling against the restraints. But the guards obeyed, pulling on the ropes binding him until his arms and legs were taught, his legs spread wide apart. "Hey!"

"Leave us," the Lady commanded, making a dismissive gesture. The guards complied, exiting the room. The Lady stared down at him, standing at the foot of the bed. Then she sat down on the edge, displaying her profile. Try as he might, he couldn't resist the urge to stare at her curves. She must have noticed, because she smirked.

"Let me go," he ordered.

"And miss out on all the fun?" she replied. "No no, Hunter. Trust me, I'm going to make you *very* happy." She leaned over, giving him a view of her cleavage, and placed a hand on his belly, her wrist resting on his groin. Which had shrunk considerably.

"Only if you let me go."

"Mmm," she murmured, sliding her hand down until her palm rested on his groin again. This time, his body didn't respond. She withdrew her hand, turning to the table and grabbing something from it. She turned back to face him; she was holding a knife.

"What are you doing?" he blurted out, yanking on his restraints. She walked up to the edge of the bed, the knife's blade glittering in the sunlight. "No!"

She said nothing, climbing onto the bed on her hands and knees, then kneeling between his legs. She smiled, lowering the tip of the knife to his belly.

"Wait!" he shouted. "Don't!"

She slid the tip down, until it was resting just above the waistline of his pants.

"I think I'll cut something off," she murmured, gazing at his groin. She smirked then. "Something *big*."

Hunter swallowed in a suddenly dry throat, his heart pounding in his chest.

"Don't do it," he urged. "Please, I'll…"

"Shhh," she interjected. "Don't say anything." She pressed the tip of the knife into his belly, making the skin there dent inward. "Please."

He swallowed again, then nodded silently.

She released the pressure on the knife, but kept it there, just above his pants. Blood formed a small bead where the tip had violated his flesh, staining the tip of the blade. She moved the tip to the right, then grabbed the waist of his pants with her other hand, pulling up and sliding the knife underneath. His breath caught in his throat, and he nearly cried out.

She glanced up at him, a smirk curling her lips.

Then she flipped the knife around, so that the edge was against his pants, the dull side pressing against his upper thigh. She sawed at his pants, the serrated blade cutting through the thick fabric with surprising ease. Then she set the knife down, grabbing both ends of the cut fabric and pulling. The fabric tore straight down, all the way to his ankle, and she picked the knife up again, sawing at the last bit of cloth holding the pant leg together. It split, exposing his entire leg.

"One more to go," she murmured, bringing the knife back up to his waistline. She repeated the process on the left side, exposing the other leg. Then she yanked on the pants, pulling them off completely, leaving him in his underwear.

She gazed at his naked legs for a long moment, then set the tip of the knife back down on his bellybutton.

"Tell me you want me," she ordered, leaning over to display her bosom. He turned his head to the side, keeping his mouth shut. He felt the knife press into his bellybutton, and grimaced at the sudden sharp pain there.

"I want you," he muttered, turning to glare at her. She frowned.

"Now now," she scolded. "Don't be difficult. I've seen how you look at me," she added with a smirk. "The hunger in your eyes."

Hunter said nothing.

"You wanted me last night," she continued, reaching one hand up, to the laces that held her corset together. She untied them, causing her corset to pull apart slightly, exposing a little more of her large, pale breasts. He caught himself staring, and turned away quickly. But not quickly enough.

She chuckled, then slid the tip of the knife down to the waistband of his underwear.

"You just can't help yourself, can you?" she murmured, sliding the blade to the left. She sawed at his underwear over his thigh then, and it came apart quickly, the blade cutting all the way down, exposing his skin. She repeated this on the right, until only a flap of fabric was covering his privates.

"Why are you doing this?" he demanded. She gazed at his groin, then lifted her gaze.

"Because I enjoy it," she answered. "I want to see you lose control, Hunter. I want to watch your face when you break…the moment you can't help yourself anymore, when you give in." She smiled. "When you go from hating it to *wanting* it."

"You won't get that from me."

"Oh Hunter," she replied, leaning over and putting a hand on his cheek. He jerked away from her touch. "I'm going to get *everything* I want from you. You," she added, "…are going to give me your seed."

"What?" he blurted out. "What's that supposed to mean?"

She arched an eyebrow, then glanced down at her belly, rubbing it slowly. Then she got off the bed, setting the knife back on the table, then turning to face him.

"Now," she stated, pulling the laces of her corset free. It fell to the floor, exposing her full, ample breasts. They were perfect, and she knew it. "There's no reason why you can't enjoy this."

He looked away.

"Hunter, Hunter, Hunter," she scolded, crawling onto the bed again, then kneeling between his legs. She rested a hand on his groin, the thin flap of fabric from his underwear all that separated his member from her palm. He felt the warmth there, and grit his teeth, forcing himself to not get hard.

She smirked at him.

"It's only a matter of time," she continued, rubbing her hand up and down slowly. "Sooner or later, you're going to give in. And when you do," she added, "…I'm going to put you inside of me, and *make* you enjoy it." She continued to rub, and Hunter clenched his fists, pulling at his restraints. It was no use – the restraints held – but the pain at his wrists distracted him from what she was doing. What she was *trying* to do.

"You can't make me enjoy it," he retorted. She arched one eyebrow.

"Oh *really*," she murmured. She smiled then, pulling the flap of fabric off his member, then gazing at it. "I think I can."

She put her palm on it, her hand remarkably warm. He grimaced, biting the tip of his tongue and digging his fingernails into his palms.

She leaned over, her nipples brushing against his thighs, and lifted her palm, bringing her lips down within an inch of his member. She blew on it gently, the heat of her breath making him squirm.

He felt his member shift, and he bit his tongue harder, closing his eyes and holding his breath. He felt something warm and wet on him then, sliding upward.

Shit shit shit.

It slid downward, then up again, and then he felt the warmth engulf him. Blood pulsed in his groin, and he felt himself reacting, his member growing steadily. He bit down on his tongue, so hard that he tasted blood. But still he grew, his body betraying him, until he was at full mast.

He opened his eyes, looking down, and saw her head between his legs, her lips touching his pelvis. She'd taken him completely.

She pulled away slowly, letting his member free, flopping against his belly. Then she smiled at him.

"Now you're ready for me," she declared.

She crawled toward him then, until her face was level with his, only a few feet away. He struggled against his restraints, yanking at them as hard as he could, but it was futile. He tried to kick, but his legs had been pulled so taut that he couldn't even bend his knees.

She lowered her hips then, resting her groin on his. Her naked groin, he realized; she clearly wasn't wearing underwear. She slid her hips up, then down, massaging his erection.

"Don't do this," Hunter pleaded.

"Relax," she soothed, resting her hands on the bed, on either side of his head. Her breasts rested gently on his chest. "I promise you this is going to feel good."

She shifted, changing the angle of her hips, then pressing downward. He felt himself slide into her, a tight pressure engulfing him. She began to slide rhythmically up and down, grinding her pelvis into his. She closed her eyes, biting her lip.

"Mmm," she murmured.

She picked up speed gradually, and despite everything, he felt a rising pleasure in his groin. He clenched his fists harder, squeezing his eyes shut and trying to think of anything but what was happening to him.

He heard her moan, felt her grind harder against him. Felt the heat radiating from her, the grip around his member tightening. She gasped, going faster now. The pleasure between his legs mounted, becoming more insistent.

And then she cried out.

He felt her contract around him, a rhythmic pulsing as she ground into him. Despite himself, he felt his pleasure grow, until it was dangerously close to the point of no return. He held his breath, clenching every muscle in his body, trying desperately to stop himself from crossing that threshold. From crossing the line into the unthinkable.

Still she moved on him, her breath coming in short gasps, her skin slick with sweat. She moaned again, and he felt her stiffen, going even faster. She held her breath for a moment, then cried out a second time, another round of rhythmic pulsing gripping his member. He felt his pleasure rise, felt it edge closer and closer to the point of no return, until it was so close he could barely hold it back.

No!

Still she went, never stopping, never slowing. He opened his eyes, seeing her on top of him, her breasts dangling, nipples sliding up and down his chest. The pleasure grew even stronger, reaching the point of no return, then surging past it. Still it grew, and he cried out, trying desperately to hold it in, to stop the inevitable. This only made the pleasure grow stronger, until it peaked, refusing to be denied. Ecstasy overtook him, and he felt himself let go, felt the undeniable pulsing of his release. It came in a mad torrent, one after another, until at last he was spent. Even then, he felt it pulse, as if remembering what had occurred, straining to give even more.

He laid there, exhausted, sweat trickling down his flanks, staring up at the ceiling.

She stopped, pushing herself until she was sitting straight up, still straddling him. She smiled down at him, her eyes twinkling.

"Told you I'd make you enjoy it," she murmured.

She got up from him then, holding his butchered underwear to her groin, then getting off the bed. She grabbed her corset, putting it on. Then she blew him a kiss.

"Until next time," she stated.

And then she left, closing the door behind her.

* * *

Hunter laid there in bed for what seemed like hours, staring at the ceiling, his arms and legs still tied to the bedposts. Two guards had come into the room after the Lady had left, standing by the door. At first he'd felt self-conscious. Exposed. He was still naked after all, his arms and legs tied to the bed.

After a while, he stopped caring.

His stomach growled, and he ignored it, looking down at his naked body, at his groin. Stared at it. He had the sudden urge to take a shower. To scrub his skin until it was raw. Her smell was still on him, that subtle perfume, and the scent of it was making him nauseous.

He stared at his groin for a moment longer, then rested his head back on his pillow. Pictured her on him, his pleasure mounting. The moment when he'd let go, when it had overcome him.

She was right, he thought bitterly. *I enjoyed it.*

There was a mounting pressure in his bladder, not so bad that he had to go now, but it was inevitable that he would. There was a bathroom adjacent to the bedroom, but with his arms and legs tied…

He raised his head, looking across the table beyond the foot of his bed, at the guards standing by the door. Then his eyes fell to the tabletop.

There was a knife there. The knife Lady Camilla had used to…

He pushed the thought out of his head, looking at the guards.

"Hey," he called out to them. They glanced at him. "Gotta take a piss."

"Go ahead," one of the guards responded. The second guard chuckled.

"Doubt the Lady wants me smelling like piss," he retorted. This seemed to get their attention. One of them walked up to his bed, untying his left wrist, then his right, while the other guard stood back, his hand on the hilt of his sword. The guard untied his ankles, and Hunter got up slowly, watching as the guard who'd untied him returned to his buddy's side by the door.

"Go quick," the guard ordered. "Keep the door open."

"Why, you like watching?" Hunter retorted. The guard didn't take the bait. Hunter swung his legs off the side of the bed, then hopped off. He walked to the bathroom, which had a proper toilet, unlike the hole in the floors in the Outskirts. He emptied his bladder, then walked back into the bedroom, making sure not to glance at the table. He could see the knife in his peripheral vision, only ten feet away or so. He stole a glance at the guards; there was no chance of a knife penetrating their metal breastplates, but there was a gap below their helmets, exposing their necks.

"Lie on the bed," one of the guards ordered, stepping forward. "Spread your arms and legs out."

He strode toward the bed…then bolted toward the table. The guard shouted, running for the other end of the table and reaching for their sword, pulling it free.

Hunter reached the table, grabbing the knife and shoving the table back…right into the guard's belly. The guard doubled over, his sword dropping onto the table. Hunter dropped the knife, grabbing the guard's sword by the blade like Vi had taught him.

"Stop!" the other guard shouted.

Hunter held his sword by the blade with both hands, lifting it up, then chopping down on the first guard's head. The cross-guard struck the top of the man's helmet, slamming his head face-first into the tabletop. Hunter swung again, and the back of the guard's helmet caved in.

The man's arms spasmed, and he slipped off the table, landing on the floor with a *thud.*

Hunter lifted his gaze to the other guard, turning his sword around to hold it by the hilt. The guard shouted again, positioning himself between Hunter and the door.

Hunter grabbed the knife off the table with his free hand, chucking it at the guard, then sprinting toward him. The guard flinched, the knife ricocheting off his breastplate…just as Hunter reached him.

Hunter slashed at the man's throat.

The guard blocked the blow, but only barely, his sword swinging wide as it ricocheted off Hunter's.

Hunter swung again, chopping down at the side of the man's neck. His blade sank into the man's flesh, blood welling from the wound.

The guard screamed.

Hunter yanked his blade free, and the guard slumped to the ground, blood spurting from his neck. Hunter was about to reach for the doorknob when he stopped, looking down at himself…and realizing he was still naked. He went to the first guard, pulling off his armor and clothes, then putting them on. Then he turned back to the door, walking toward it.

The doorknob rotated.

Shit.

Hunter backpedaled, holding his sword in front of him. The door swung open…and a guard stepped through, over the body of the one Hunter just killed, followed by another, then another. They spotted Hunter, and drew their swords.

And then *she* walked through the door.

Lady Camilla glanced at the corpses on the floor, then lifted her gaze to Hunter. She crossed her arms under her bosom.

"Well well," she murmured. "Look what we have here."

More guards spilled into the room, putting themselves between Hunter and the Lady.

"Let me go," Hunter ordered. Lady Camilla sighed.

"Hunter, stop it," she ordered. "You're not going to escape, not like this," she added, gesturing at the half-dozen guards in front of her.

"Watch me," he growled.

"Lay down your weapon," she insisted. "We're going to strip you and tie you to the bed." She smirked. "And *then* you can penetrate me with your…sword."

"How about I do that right now," he shot back.

"Hunter, you're very important to me," she stated, ignoring his reply. "I want to help you. But you need to help me first."

"You already helped yourself," he retorted.

"I can't have you out there," she continued. "In the world, where you might be injured or killed. I need to keep you safe."

"Why?"

"You have Zagamar inside of you," she answered. "A Legend no one has been able to reach since antiquity. A mystery thousands of years old…and you are the only key to solving it."

"You want to study me."

"Of course," she replied. "I'm a researcher."

"I'm not your lab rat."

"Excuse me?"

"I won't be kept in a cage while you perform experiments on me," he clarified.

"I only locked you up to prevent you from doing something stupid," she countered. "I offer you a life here that most would kill for…luxury beyond anything you would experience outside these walls. And…other things," she added, giving a slight smile.

"Not interested."

"Hunter, you've murdered two innocent men," the Lady stated, gesturing at the two guards he'd killed. "The punishment for this is death by hanging. I'm willing to pardon you if you agree to stay."

"You'd pardon me anyway," he retorted. "You wouldn't kill your precious experiment." He grimaced. "You need my *seed.*"

She sighed.

"Hunter…"

"He's part of me now," Hunter interjected. "And you want him to be part of you." It all made sense now; absorption of traits required proximity and duration of exposure. With his seed inside of her, she would absorb his essence more quickly…and Zagamar's. And if she had a baby, they might have a bit of Zagamar in them, too.

Za-ga-mar!

The name echoed through his consciousness, the chanting of thousands of men. Calling the name of their leader. Of their god.

Hunter grit his teeth, willing that name out of his mind.

"How observant," Camilla stated. Her tone was suddenly cooler. She turned to one of her guards. "Fetch Dio, will you?"

"You want his child," Hunter continued. "You want to study me…and the child. Like some goddamn experiment!"

Camilla shrugged, a smirk playing on her lips.

"Like I said, I'm a researcher."

"I'm not a specimen," he shot back, clenching his fists.

"Oh, I'd say you're *quite* the specimen," she countered, her gaze dropping to his groin, then rising to meet his gaze again. "It won't be such a bad life for you," she added.

"Being your slave?"

"We can take turns with that," she quipped, smirking again. He blushed.

"I'm not your stud," he declared. "I'm leaving. Give me my stuff."

"Mmm," she murmured. "No."

"Fine then," Hunter replied, gripping the hilt of his sword tightly. "I'll show myself out."

"Detain him," she ordered her guards.

But before the words were finished coming out of her mouth, Hunter burst forward, kicking the guard in front of her in the belly. The man stumbled backward into the Lady, and she cried out, tumbling to the ground. Half of the other guards rushed to protect her, and Hunter sprinted around them, swinging his sword viciously at one guard who stood between him and the door. The guard blocked, but the force of the blow made him stumble to the side, and Hunter slipped past, bursting through the open door and running down the hallway beyond.

Then he skid to a halt.

There, in the middle of the hallway, was a man in a red and black leather uniform, his face hidden behind a red and black mask. He stood there, facing Hunter, his hands at his sides…and a long, curved sword sheathed at each hip.

Fuck.

He turned back, spotting Camilla's two guards spilling out of the doorway after him. Camilla appeared behind them.

"You can't run," she called out. "Don't make this harder for yourself than you have to."

"Go fuck yourself," Hunter shot back. He braced himself as the guards ran up to him, his eyes drawn to the swords sheathed at their hips. One of the guards reached for him, and he ducked low, dodging to the side at the last minute and slashing the side of the guard's neck. The flesh there parted, blood spraying from the gash.

The guard crumpled.

"Stop!" Camilla shouted.

The other guard drew his sword, but Hunter was too quick, chopping down at the man's shoulder. His blade ricocheted off the guard's armor there, but the force of the blow made the guard stumble, falling to the side onto the floor. Hunter chopped down at the man's neck, his blade sinking into the flesh, splitting his collar bone in two.

The guard *howled.*

Hunter heard footsteps from behind, and turned to see the man in red – the Seeker – striding toward him, curved blade in hand.

"Don't kill him," Camilla ordered, slipping past Hunter and backpedaling down the hallway, passing well behind her Seeker.

"Too bad," Hunter shot back.

"I was talking to *him*," she retorted.

Hunter braced himself, holding his sword in front of him…and felt something yank on his leg from behind. He fell forward, his forehead slamming into the hardwood floor. Pain exploded through his skull, his vision blackening.

"No!" he heard Camilla cry. It seemed far away, his body numb. "Don't hit his head! He's got Zagamar in there!"

The name echoed through his head, the voices of his people chanting his name.

Za-ga-mar!

Hunter groaned, trying to pick himself off the floor. He struggled to his hands and knees, his vision starting to clear. Spotted his sword a foot away, and reached for it.

Footsteps approached from ahead, the Seeker coming for him.

He reached the hilt of his sword, wrapping his fingers around it, and felt the Seeker's boot step down on his hand, crushing it against the floor. He cried out, gritting his teeth against the pain.

A vision of a hand came unbidden to his mind's eye. Olive skin, fingers unnaturally long. Tendrils of black crawling up his wrist, spreading across his palm. A horrible, burning pain searing his flesh, his heart racing in his chest. And a terrible, insatiable hunger, more powerful than any he'd ever felt.

Za-ga-mar!

He looked up, seeing the Seeker standing over him, face hidden behind that horrible mask. Felt the guard's hands on his ankle, pulling him backward. And a cacophony of footsteps coming down the hallway toward them, each footfall striking the ground in slow-motion, the sound echoing off the walls.

He felt his own heart racing, thumping madly against his breastbone, his breath coming in quick gasps. And the hunger, that terrible hunger, that he'd felt in the crypt of Zagamar. Right before he'd drank from the skull, the thick, salty fluid flowing down his throat.

Za-ga-mar!

Six guards coming, he knew. One more Seeker. He knew them by their footsteps. It was obvious.

He looked down at his hand, crushed under the Seeker's boot, his fingers still clutching his sword. Felt the pain there, but stepped back from it mentally. The pain didn't matter. It was temporary, insignificant.

All that mattered was the outcome.

His mind raced, thoughts spilling over each other in a mad tumble, too fast to follow but somehow making perfect sense.

Narrow window to escape. Reinforcements coming. No time to retrieve Vi's sword or your pack. Seekers will outclass you or outnumber you.

The exact path leading out of the Lady's mansion came to him, every step, every turn. His mind calculated the route effortlessly, along with the positions and likely patrol routes of every guard he'd seen in the last few days.

"Give up Hunter," Camilla called out. "I don't want to hurt you."

He realized she was talking to him. He smiled grimly, knowing she had no idea who she was *really* talking to.

Za-ga-mar!

He yanked his crushed hand back, ignoring the pain.

The Seeker's boot slipped forward in slow-motion, catching the man off-balance. Hunter grabbed that boot, watching as his hands wrapped around it. It was all happening far too slowly, his body unable to keep up with his racing mind.

He yanked the boot forward, forcing the Seeker to shift his weight to the other foot to keep his balance…and making it easier for Hunter to pull the boot. Then Hunter shoved the Seeker's foot to the right, crossing the man's legs up, forcing his body to rotate. At the same time, Hunter kicked his free leg, sliding his foot against his other leg, his boot scraping against the guard's hands behind him, still wrapped around his ankle.

Should've worn gauntlets, Hunter mused.

Hunter heard a shout, felt the grip on his ankle slip. He jerked his leg free, grabbing his sword and rising to his feet. To his brain, he was moving as if underwater; he saw the Seeker stumbling forward and to the right, and shoved the man's shoulder, sending him flying toward the wall.

It seemed forever ago that he'd made the decision not to kill the man.

Waste of time.

He saw the woman ahead of him – the academician – and ignored her, bolting past her. She was of no consequence, alive or dead. Her eyes followed him as he passed, wide with shock, her mouth agape. Her bosom heaved as she stumbled backward, away from him. She hardly enticed him.

He'd had so much more.

The hallway met an intersection, and he turned left down another hallway, this one with windows lining the left wall. He spotted two guards barreling toward him, swords drawn. Right where he'd expected them to be, on account of the footsteps he'd heard earlier. But instead of going after him, they went *past* him, running toward Camilla.

"My Lady!" one of them cried. "We're under attack!"

And then all hell broke loose.

The window to his left shattered, two figures smashing through it and landing in the hallway in front of him. Men in black and gold uniforms, longswords in hand.

Hunter dodged around them, his feet skidding on pieces of broken glass. He kept his balance easily, sprinting past them.

"The guild!" he heard the Lady shout from behind. "Get Dios, *now*," she ordered. "Don't let them take the Original!"

The guild's Seekers rushed after him, more windows shattering ahead of him, more Seekers spilling into the hallway. He ran along the rightmost wall, sprinting as fast as he could. Screams pierced the air behind him, but he did not bother to look back. What was happening to others was inconsequential; all that mattered was what happened to *him*.

The hallway turned right, and he followed it, spotting stairs ahead, going down. A guard was running up the stairs toward him; Hunter skid to a halt.

"I'll get Dios," he stated tersely. "You, get to the Lady!"

The guard nodded, rushing past him and down the hallway…and right into the Seekers chasing Hunter. Hunter heard the *clang* of metal on metal, then a scream. He ignored the sound, leaping down the stairs, taking them four at a time, reaching the bottom quickly.

Second floor, he knew. He counted the footsteps echoing down the hallway ahead. *Six men.*

He found himself running down another wide hallway, sunlight streaming though large windows spaced at regular intervals to his left. Sure enough, three more guards were in the middle of the hallway, all the way at the other end…and three Seekers clad in black and gold. Two of the guards fell, the third managing to impale one of the Seekers. Then he too was cut down, and the two remaining Seekers turned to face Hunter.

Two very familiar Seekers.

"Hunter!" one of them cried. A short woman with long, dirty-blonde hair tied into thick braids. And beside her, a gigantic man holding a huge warhammer.

Sukri? Gammon?

Sukri ran toward him, a huge smile on her face.

"Hunter, it's us!" she cried. "Come on, we have to get you out of here!"

Hunter hesitated, but only for a split second.

They're being used, he thought coldly. It was obvious, a pathetic attempt to gain his confidence. Still, a part of him yearned to go with them.

Za-ga-mar!

He ran toward them, moving as if in slow-motion, his mind racing ever-faster. A map of the entire estate – of the places he'd been, matched to the exterior portions he'd seen so many days ago – came to his mind, perfect in every detail. The idea that his understanding of the mansion had been so vague moments before, that his memory had been so fuzzy, his mind so pathetically slow, was contemptible.

No surprise, a rebirth within a fool.

He ran straight for Sukri and Gammon, watching as they ran toward him, the gold on their uniforms glittering as they passed through the sunbeams slanting through the windows. He passed by one window, then another, charging toward the two, shoving his feelings aside. The boy was no longer in control.

Third window. Fourth.

He was only five meters away from Sukri and Gammon now, and closing fast.

Fifth window.

He veered left suddenly, and Sukri moved with him, intercepting him.

Hunter grabbed Sukri by the shoulders, throwing her backward into the window. It disintegrated in a shower of glass, and Hunter leapt right into it, passing through the cascade and into the cool morning air.

Glittering shards flew all around him, falling slowly toward the packed dirt four meters below. He saw Sukri a meter below him, arms flailing in slow-motion as she entered into free-fall. Right toward a tall hedge just under the window, precisely where Hunter had known it would be. Where he'd remembered seeing it from the hilltop days ago, when he'd first laid eyes on the mansion from kilometers away.

Sukri plunged into the hedge, and Hunter joined her. Innumerable branches scraped at his body, and he felt himself lurch to a stop, slamming into Sukri and shoving both of them deeper into the hedge. Pain shot through his chest, but he ignored it, reaching down to unsheathe her longsword, then scrambling off of her and bursting through the bushes. He sprinted across the huge dirt field toward the closed gate ahead; A single Seeker stood guard there, having no doubt anticipated that he might escape.

He charged toward the Seeker, who quickly unsheathed their sword, widening their stance to brace for his attack.

He reached the Seeker, swinging Sukri's sword at the man's neck. The Seeker blocked the blow, but Hunter kicked at the man's knee at the same time, forcing it to lock. The Seeker's body bent forward at the waist, and Hunter snapped at the hips, elbowing the man in the temple. The Seeker's head snapped to the side, and he dropped like a stone.

Waste of time to kill him.

Hunter stepped over the man, opening the gate and jogging through. The forest began where the grassy field ended, and Hunter ran toward it, knowing that no horse would be able to navigate the dense trees quicker than he could run.

He was free.

But then he felt the hunger rise within him once again, that overwhelming lust for sustenance. Felt his heart racing, sweat pouring down his body. He realized his breath was coming in short gasps.

Damn this pathetic body!

He cursed under his breath, realizing he only had so much time before his body gave out on him. If he didn't find some place to hide – and soon – then his escape would be for naught.

They'll send dogs after me.

The tree line was less than a dozen meters away now, and he ran for it. It was difficult to pace himself, his body still seeming as if it were moving in slow-motion, his mind far outpacing his flesh. But he knew it was only a matter of time until he mastered this. He'd mastered everything he'd put his mind to.

He entered the forest, trees passing him, leaves rustling sinuously, as if an underwater current had passed through them.

Water!

He veered leftward, spotting the river ahead…the same river he'd seen from so far away days ago. The Lady's mansion was on its shore. The

Serpent's Tail, whose winding body led to great black spires rising from the forest. A kingdom at the mouth of the Potestatem Magnum, the Great Power.

There was shouting in the distance.

Hunter ran parallel to the tree-line for a while longer, then cut leftward, bursting through the trees onto the grassy shore of the river beyond. He went right in, water seeping through his pants and spilling into his boots. He waded for a short distance, then unbuckled his belt, tossing both swords aside. He pulled off his breastplate, then leapt forward, plunging through the water. Ice-cold wetness enveloped him, forcing his breath to catch in his throat. There was more shouting behind him, but he did not turn around to see how far away his pursuers were. It was a waste of time; the guards would sink if they tried to swim in their armor, and the Seekers wouldn't be able to swim without discarding their weapons.

He relaxed into the water, taking a breath out and feeling himself sink below the surface. He held his breath, letting the current carry him forward under the water.

They won't risk archers, he knew. *They need me alive.*

He kicked, lifting his head above the water, taking a few breaths, then plunging below the surface again. His heart began to slow, the feverish racing of his mind gradually abating. A sudden exhaustion came over him, and he resisted the urge to give in to it, to let the swirling darkness lull him to sleep.

Rising to the surface, he took another few breaths, then went under again.

Hunter felt himself return, as if he were stepping forward within his consciousness, that alien part of him – the *other* – slowly fading away. Time sped up, returning to normal. And at the same time, his thoughts slowed, feeling sluggish and scattered. The incredible precision and utter certainty he'd known was gone.

But the hunger…that incredible lust for food, that *need* for food…remained.

He lay there in the water, letting the current bring him downstream, shivering as the cool water drained the heat from him. It was all he could do to stay awake, to resist the exhaustion threatening to pull him deeper into the river. But he had no fear. He'd done what he needed to do. Now the river would bring him where he needed to go.

It would bring him home.

CHAPTER 16

Sukri's stomach lurched as she entered into free-fall, shards of glass twirling around her as she plummeted from the shattered window. Faster and faster she fell, the exterior wall of the mansion a blur before her. Hunter leapt through the window after her, falling directly above her.

She didn't even have time to scream.

There was a sharp jolt, and suddenly she was surrounded by countless small branches. She felt a sharp pain in her back, and realized she'd fallen into a bush. A split-second later, Hunter slammed into her, the impact blasting the air from her lungs and shoving her deeper into the bush. She gasped for air, feeling something tugging at the sword at her left hip.

Then the weight on her vanished, and Hunter was gone.

Sukri lay there for a moment, struggling to take a breath in. After what seemed like an eternity, she did, sucking air into her lungs hungrily. Then she grimaced, rolling onto her belly, then scrambling out of the bushes and onto the packed dirt beyond, seeing row after row of crops all around her. To her left, she saw the giant statue of the snake-like thing, and ahead she spotted Hunter sprinting across the dirt field to the path, making his way to the gate at the front entrance. A single Seeker stood there, blocking his path. Sukri got to her feet, running after them, sharp pain seizing her lower back with every stride.

Hunter!

She saw Hunter charge at the Seeker, swinging his sword so quickly it was a blur. The Seeker blocked the attack, but only barely, and Hunter kicked him in the knee, then elbowed him in the side of the head.

The Seeker collapsed.

Sukri sprinted across the field toward Hunter, shouting after him.

"Hunter! Wait!"

But Hunter ignored her, opening the gate and sprinting through toward the tree line in the distance. He reached the trees, then veered left, and Sukri ran after him, struggling to keep up. He was moving fast – incredibly fast – the distance between them increasing rapidly.

"Hunter!"

She was about to reach the gate when she heard a whizzing sound by her left ear, and saw an arrow fly past her, bouncing off the wall ahead.

Shit!

She spun around, seeing guards sprinting after her…and Gammon running after *them.* She reached for her sword, but it wasn't there; Hunter had taken it.

Fuck!

The nearest guard reached her, thrusting his sword at her chest. She felt herself dodge out of the way, grabbing his arm and using his momentum to pull him off-balance. He tumbled to the ground…just as another guard reached her, slashing at her neck!

She found herself stepping *into* the attack, blocking the base of the guard's blade with her forearms. The sharp steel sank into her flesh, throwing her to the side. She tumbled to the ground, pain shooting across the backs of her forearms.

The guard stood over her, raising his sword high into the air, point down. He grunted, stabbing downward, right at her chest!

She screamed, squeezing her eyes shut and throwing her arms out in front of her.

There was a *thump*, followed by a shrill scream.

Sukri opened her eyes. The guard was gone…and his place, a huge man loomed over her. It took her a moment to realize who it was.

"Gammon!" she cried.

He reached down, grabbing her arms and lifting her to her feet. She cried out, pain shooting through her forearms. Gammon let go, staring down at her arms. They were soaked with blood, a deep gash on the back of each forearm.

"Watch out!" she warned; two guards faced them, swords drawn. Gammon stepped between them and Sukri, his huge warhammer in his hands. One of the guards leapt at him; Gammon swung his hammer, striking the guard in the left flank, sending him flying. The other guard rushed at Gammon, thrusting his sword at the big guy's belly. Gammon blocked the blow with the long handle of his hammer, then thrust the head of his hammer into the guard's face. Blood spurted from the guard's nose and mouth, and he dropped to the ground. Gammon lifted his hammer up over his head, then smashed it down on the guard's face again.

The guard's head exploded.

More guards spilled out of the front door of the mansion, rushing toward them. Way too many of them.

"Where are the others?" Sukri asked, her voice rising in fear. Gammon faced the oncoming guards, his mouth drawn in a thin line.

"Inside," he answered tersely.

"But…"

"Go," he ordered.

"I'm not leaving you," she retorted, reaching down and retrieving a sword from one of the fallen guards. Or at least she tried to; her hands were clenched, and wouldn't open. She stared at the deep cuts in her forearms, at the severed ends of the rust-colored muscle exposed there. "Gammon…" she blurted out, her voice rising in panic. "My hands!"

"Run Sukri," he ordered. "I'll hold them off."

"No Gammon, you can't…"

She stopped as he put a hand on her shoulder, feeling a familiar calmness drape over her like a warm blanket. Her fear was snuffed out instantly, replaced by a profound sense of peace. She stared at her mutilated arms, the wounds no longer bothering her.

Everything was going to be okay.

She relaxed, gazing up at Gammon, then at the approaching guards.

"Think you can kill those fuckers?" she asked. Gammon stared at the approaching guards – there were six of them – and assumed a wide stance, gripping his warhammer tightly.

"Yes."

"Liar," she murmured. She put a hand on his chest then. "You know, if you don't, they're going to do a lot worse than break my leg again."

Gammon grimaced, and she felt a bolt of fear penetrate the peacefulness.

"Gammon?"

"Yes?"

"I'm gonna need you to be real sexy for me."

Gammon took his hand off her shoulder, then wrapped his big hands around her waist, lifting her off of the ground until they were face to face. He stared into her eyes for a long moment, then pulled her into him. Her lips crushed against his, and she closed her eyes. Her skin tingled, euphoria washing over her. His mouth opened, and hers did as well, accepting him into her.

For a moment the world vanished.

Then there was shouting, and Sukri felt Gammon disengage, lowering her to the ground. She opened her eyes, seeing the guards nearly upon them. Gammon shoved Sukri away, toward the open gate in the distance.

"Run!" he shouted.

Three of the guards ran up to them, sunlight gleaming off their swords. Sukri stumbled away from Gammon, then bolted for the gate. She heard shouting, then footsteps coming up quickly from behind. She turned around just in time to see one of the guards leap at her, slamming into her back and throwing her headlong into the ground.

"Gammon!" she screamed.

She scrambled to her feet, turning to see the guard standing behind her, sword held high above his head. Before she could even scream, he swung the blade downward at her skull!

And then there was a loud *whump*, and he was thrown violently to the side, tumbling on the dirt. He came to a stop, his limbs twitching, a massive dent in the side of his skull.

And where he'd once been, Gammon stood, his huge warhammer dripping with blood.

"Watch out!" Sukri cried. The other two guards were right behind Gammon; one of them thrust their sword at Gammon's back. Gammon swung his hammer in a half-circle, knocking the sword out of the guard's hands. Then he shoved the butt of his hammer into the man's chest, knocking him clear off his feet and sending him flying into the dirt. The other guard thrust his sword at Gammon's left flank; Gammon dodged out of the way, but not fast enough. The blade grazed him, blood oozing out of a small gash in his flank.

Gammon didn't even flinch.

The big guy kicked the guard in the chest, sending him flying onto his back on the dirt. Then Gammon swung his hammer over his head, chopping downward with all his might. The hammer sank into the guard's chest, his rib cage obliterated by the sheer force of the blow.

The remaining living guard got to his feet, stumbling backward, his eyes locked on the blood dripping from Gammon's warhammer. There was more shouting from near the mansion, and Sukri turned to see four more guards rushing down the path toward them.

"Run!" Gammon shouted, glaring at Sukri. She turned to flee, sprinting toward the gate.

And then something struck her in the ankle, pain shooting up her calf.

She screamed, her ankle giving out underneath her, and tumbled to the ground, her head bouncing off the path. Pain shot through her skull, her vision blackening. She resisted the sudden urge to puke, trying to get to her feet. But there was something wrong with her right ankle. She looked down, seeing a crossbow bolt embedded in the back of it.

Fuck!

She heard shouting, and looked past her ankle to see Gammon standing less than ten meters away, flanked by two guards wielding longswords. And the third guard standing further back, a crossbow in his hands.

"Watch out!" she cried.

Gammon turned to glance at her…and then a crossbow bolt slammed into his upper thigh. He stumbled, staring down at his leg in disbelief.

The two guards flanking him attacked!

Gammon held his hammer out before him, spinning in a full circle, the head of his huge hammer slamming into one guard's temple, then smashing into the other one's shoulder. Both guards were sent flying, landing in a heap in the dirt beyond.

The crossbowman loaded another bolt, then aimed it at Gammon.

And fired.

Sukri cried out, watching as the bolt zipped through the air with terrible speed, right at Gammon. The big guy lurched to the side, the crossbow bolt shooting right at his head. It struck in a spray of blood, the bolt continuing past Gammon, whizzing right over Sukri's head, then landing in the dirt near the gate.

Gammon!

She watched in horror as Gammon stumbled, blood pouring from the side of his head. He reached up with one hand, pressing it to the gushing wound. Then he lowered his hand, staring at it for a moment, then dropping something onto the dirt. It was his ear, Sukri realized; it'd been taken clean off by the crossbow bolt.

Gammon gripped his hammer with both hands then, the veins on his head bulging, his eyes wide with fury. He sprinted forward in a mad rush, a primal scream bursting from his lungs.

The crossbowman stumbled backward, struggling to load another bolt. He finally managed to do so, raising the crossbow at Gammon just as the big guy reached him.

Gammon *threw* his hammer at the man, and it slammed into the guard's head, snapping it back and knocking him clean off his feet. He landed on the path with a *thump*, the front of his skull caved in. Gammon retrieved his hammer, then turned to Sukri, limping down the path toward her.

"Sukri!" he shouted, reaching her and kneeling before her. His eyes went to the bolt sticking out of her ankle. "I'm sorry," he said.

"What fo-" she began. Then he grabbed the bolt, ripping it from her flesh.

"*Fuck!*" she shouted, yanking her ankle away from him. "God *damn* it!"

Gammon ignored her, securing his hammer to his back, then scooping her up in his arms and lifting her off the ground. He limped toward the gate, toward the forest beyond. There was a shout from behind, and Sukri turned her head, spotting two figures spilling out of the front doors of the mansion. People in black and gold uniforms.

Seekers!

"Help!" she cried, waving at the Seekers as they rushed up the path toward them. It was Sen, she realized…and Jasmine! "Guys, help!"

Sen and Jasmine slowed as they reached Sukri and Gammon, staring at the two, then at the guards sprinting through the front doors of the mansion. Sen smirked at Gammon.

"Better man up, fat boy," he called out. "Payback's coming!"

And then they ran right past them, continuing onward through the gate, sprinting toward the forest.

"Guys? Guys!" Sukri yelled after them. "What the *hell*?"

Thump.

Gammon grunted, then fell to one knee, nearly dropping her to the ground at the same time.

"Gammon?"

She looked down then, seeing a crossbow bolt protruding from his right buttock. And in the distance, more of the Lady's guards rushing out of the mansion toward them…and a figure in a black and red uniform, face obscured by a grotesque mask.

Shit.

"Come on Gammon," she urged, tugging on his shirt. He glanced back, then grimaced, rising unsteadily to his feet. He limped toward the gate, now only a few meters away. Sukri heard a whizzing sound by her ear, and saw another bolt fly past them, striking the tall fence ahead. "Go Gammon, go!"

Behind them, the guards were running, closing the distance with terrifying speed.

"Gammon!" she warned. The guards were nearly upon them…and one of them had a crossbow. Gammon stopped, dropping her to the ground, then turning to face them, grabbing his warhammer from his back. The crossbowman stood back while two other guards unsheathed their swords…and the masked man strode toward them leisurely, still a few dozen meters away.

"Drop your weapon!" one of the guards yelled. Gammon stood there between them and Sukri, gripping his hammer so tightly his knuckles were white. "I said *drop* it!"

The masked man reached the guards, stepping between them and facing Gammon. He lifted one hand, and the guards lowered their weapons. Sukri stared at the man; he wore a red and black leather uniform, a metallic staff secured to his back. He crossed his arms, his red and black mask obscuring his face, unnervingly silver eyes staring right at Gammon.

Staring *through* Gammon.

"Gammon," Sukri said, staring at the man, then at the guards. "It's over. We can't beat them."

"I said drop it!" the guard repeated. The masked man raised his hand again, and the guard's mouth snapped shut.

"It's okay, Gammon," Sukri urged. Gammon hesitated, then let go of his warhammer, letting it fall to the ground before him. She felt a weary resignation radiate from him. He gazed down at her.

"Don't let them change you," he urged. "Be the woman I loved."

The masked man walked up to Gammon, stopping less than a meter away. He gazed up at the big guy, dwarfed by Gammon's massive height and weight. A lean, wiry man facing a bloodied giant. He stood there, as still as a statue, hardly even seeming to breathe. And then he turned away abruptly, nodding at one of the guards.

Sukri let out a breath she hadn't realized she'd been holding.

"All ri-"

The masked man spun around in a flash of silver, moving so quickly it was a blur. Blood spurted from Gammon's right knee, the flesh there separating just below the kneecap. He cried out, his leg buckling, and landed on one knee on the path.

"Gammon!" Sukri cried.

The masked man stood there, facing Gammon, a long metal staff in his hands, blood dripping from one of the double-edged blades on each end.

"What are you *doing*?" Sukri shouted, getting to her feet and limping up to Gammon, placing herself between him and the masked man. "We surrender!"

One of the guards grabbed her by the shoulders, yanking her backward and holding her from behind. She struggled, but it was no use. The guard forced her to her knees, twisting one arm behind her back and pulling upward viciously. Pain shot through her shoulder, and she bit back a scream.

The masked man ignored her, gazing silently at Gammon. They were eye-to-eye now. Sukri felt a smug sense of satisfaction, and realized it was coming from the guard holding her.

"We surrender!" Sukri repeated.

"Shut up," the guard retorted. "Hands above your head, big guy," he commanded. "Now, or I'll break her fucking arm!"

Gammon complied, kneeling on the path, his hands in the air.

The masked man turned his head slightly to face Sukri, his silver eyes boring into hers.

Then he lashed out, slashing at Gammon's forearm with one end of his staff. The wicked blade there cut clean through Gammon's wrist, his hand toppling to the ground. Blood spurted from the stump of his wrist in rhythmic pulses, splattering on the ground around him.

Gammon lowered his injured arm, staring at the stump, looking dazed.

"No!" Sukri shouted, struggling against the guard's grip behind her. "Stop it! Don't hurt him!"

The guard yanked her backward, sending more pain lancing through her shoulder. She screamed, sinking to her knees, tears welling up in her eyes.

The masked man turned away from Gammon, staring at Sukri once again, then sauntered up to her slowly. He knelt down then, his silver eyes level with hers. She felt an icy-cold calm come over her, so chilling that a shudder went through her. It was not peaceful, this calm. It was a void…an utter lack of emotion, unlike anything she had ever felt.

The man turned away from her, the eerie sensation bleeding away slowly. She swallowed in a dry throat, blinking tears from her eyes.

"Don't do this," she pleaded. "Please."

The masked man paused, turning his head to stare at her, his silver eyes unblinking.

Then he whipped his staff in a vicious arc, slashing at Gammon's throat.

"*No!*" Sukri screamed.

Blood sprayed from Gammon's neck, the flesh there gaping open. His eyes went wide, and he clutched at his neck with his remaining hand, pressing it against the wound. A horrible gurgling sound burst forth from his severed windpipe, blood pouring between his fingers. He fell face-first onto the path, then rolled onto his back, his eyes wide with terror.

Sukri felt the grip on her arm release, and she stumbled up to Gammon, pressing her palms on his throat as best as she could, putting pressure there. Sheer horror gripped her, a sense of utter, impending doom. She shook her head, tears pouring down her cheeks.

"No Gammon, no!"

Her hands slipped off his slick neck, blood spraying from the wound. She gasped, closing her eyes and pressing down again, feeling a horrible, hot pulsing under her palms. He stared up at her, his lips moving, a gurgling sound coming from his throat.

"Come on big guy," she pleaded. "Stay with me. Stay with me!"

Sweat beaded up on Gammon's forehead, his lips starting to turn blue. His chest heaved up and down, his face deathly pale. Sukri turned to the guards and the masked man.

"Save him!" she begged. "Please!"

But they just stood there.

Sukri felt something grab her shoulder, and she turned around, realizing that Gammon's hand was gripping her. He stared up at her, his eyes locked on hers. She felt his fear, his utter panic, as if she were underwater, trying to claw her way desperately to the surface. She sobbed, lowering her forehead to rest on his, then pressing her lips against his lips. She kissed him gently, once, then again, lifting her hands from his neck and cupping his cheeks.

"Thank you," she whispered. "For loving me."

Gammon smiled, putting a bloodied hand on her cheek, touching it gingerly. She felt his fear seep away, replaced by a warm calmness. She realized then what that meant. What it had meant every time he'd touched her over the years, and she'd felt that same calmness. That utterly content feeling.

And then his hand slipped off of her cheek, landing on the ground with the *thump*. His eyes glazed over, the bleeding from his neck slowing, then stopping. His chest heaved once, a rattling sound coming from deep within his throat.

And then he was gone.

Chapter 17

Scores of soldiers marched in row after row on the King's Road, suspended seven meters above the desolate waste of the Deadlands. The three moons cast their silver light on each soldier's armor, making them shimmer dully in the darkness of the fast-approaching night. The last of the sun's rays spilled across the sky, casting heavy clouds in a purple hue.

And in the middle of this sea of men rolled an ornate carriage, carrying the second-most powerful man in all of Tykus.

Dominus shifted his weight on his seat cushion, staring out of the window at the passing scenery. He was thankful that he sat alone in the carriage, the only sound the clopping of the two horses' hooves as they pulled the carriage along, and the endless *thump, thump* of hundreds of footsteps marching in unison. He found it cathartic, to let his mind wander. To fall in and out of sleep, neither aware of or caring about the time.

Especially after the previous night.

He'd slept in the ancestral shrine, as promised. And bathed in the waters of the great fountain there, steeped in the essence of his greatest ancestors. Men of pure spirit, of noble purpose. Men who had guided the kingdom of Tykus through the millennia, ensuring that, in a world where change was the greatest enemy of humanity, the kingdom remained the single constant. Amidst swirling chaos, Tykus never changed.

And oh, how a night in the shrine had shown him how *he* had changed!

He smiled, remembering the feeling he'd gotten as he'd laid in those cool waters, drinking of the fountain even as he'd bathed in it. The great calmness that had come over him, the clarity of vision. He'd had no idea how scattered his mind had been over the last few weeks...or perhaps even years. How distracted he'd become. How far the corruption had taken him from his roots.

He'd nearly sacrificed his soul – and the honor of his great lineage – for a chance to live a few more measly years.

Dominus grimaced, remembering Conlan, his late son. His only son. He'd been the start of all of this. The insufferable prick had exerted his corrupt will on Dominus, twisting Dominus's mind. Making the use of wild artifacts seem acceptable, if only for a worthy cause. Once again, the fool had tried to take everything he cared about from him.

There is no acceptable corruption, he thought, clenching his fists.

He forced himself to relax, resting his back on the seat cushion. Conlan was dead, and though his influence was powerful, the bones of the previous dukes of Wexford carried a power greater even than Conlan's twisted will. They would cure Dominus, in time. He had already vowed to spend each night for a month sleeping there, in the shrine. After he'd returned from this trip, of course.

Assuming he passed the Testers.

The carriage began to bounce a little, the turbulence signaling that he'd reached the end of the King's Road. In the distance, the great wall surrounding the city of Tykus rose nearly twenty meters above the Deadlands, the huge stone portcullis barring the entrance to the city guarded by two soldiers. The soldiers ahead of the carriage parted, creating a path for the carriage to continue forward to the gate.

Dominus sat up straighter, waiting for the carriage to stop, which it did. One of the soldiers approached the rightmost window, peering in, then bowing.

"Your Grace," the soldier greeted.

Dominus nodded slightly.

Moments later, the portcullis rose.

The carriage continued forward through the opening, into the tunnel passing through the great wall, blocked by another portcullis at the end. There was another check by the guards, followed by the inner portcullis opening. The carriage moved onward across the wide street beyond, flanked by walls several stories high. Beyond lay the city of Tykus itself, the grand stairway to the Acropolis rising over the side of the giant hill atop which the fortress had been built.

The carriage stopped before the stairs, the driver disconnecting the horses. Guards gathered around the carriage, lifting it up by posts on its sides while others removed the wheels. In this way, the guards carried the carriage up the long stairway, replacing each other as they tired. A necessity ever since the lifeblood had slowed its flow to Dominus's legs years ago. He wondered if he would be able to make the walk up the steps himself again one day. Such an experiment would arouse suspicion, of course; he was supposed to be a cripple.

At length, the carriage reached the top, and the wheels were re-attached, his guards pushing the carriage toward another wall. The wall surrounding the Acropolis, the heart of the kingdom. Another pair of guards verified his identity, and the process was repeated, the carriage passing through an outer and inner portcullis, emerging at last into the large courtyard beyond. A fresh set of horses was connected to the carriage, horses unsullied by the corruption of the outside world, and too weak-willed to pose a threat to humans.

A beautiful system, one of countless checks and balances. All designed to preserve humanity, the most precious thing in this forsaken world.

Dominus fidgeted, staring at the gardens of the courtyard as the carriage rode toward the great fortress that was the Acropolis. He felt out of place, uneasy. It was a feeling he'd never experienced here before.

It wasn't long before the carriage stopped before the double-doors marking the entrance to the Acropolis, and Dominus's door opened, a guard helping him down to the street. He stared at the doors, remembering the last time he'd been here. How he'd been convinced that it would be the last time he'd ever make this walk.

If it hadn't been for that Ironclad, he thought, *it would have been.*

He pushed the thought away, feeling his unease grow. To be reminded of what he'd done…the corruption he'd allowed to seep into him…

Never again.

He strode toward the doors, leaning heavily on his cane, though it was hardly necessary anymore. A man in a white, gold, and blue uniform was waiting just outside the doors, and strode toward him eagerly. He had long gray hair and an equally long beard, and smiled at Dominus as he approached. It was Duke Ratheburg, one of the six dukes of Tykus. A principled and just man. A fine representation of the elite of Tykus.

Ratheburg reached Dominus, leaning in to embrace him. Dominus stiffened at first, suddenly fearful that Ratheburg might sense the corruption within him, despite his cleansing the night before.

Don't be a fool, he chastised himself, forcing himself to relax.

"Welcome home," Ratheburg greeted, stepping back and giving Dominus a worrying look. "I heard about the attack, of course." His gaze fell to Dominus's bandaged hand. "Are you alright?"

"A few minor injuries," Dominus lied.

"Thank god," Ratheburg replied, clearly relieved. He frowned, regarding Dominus with a surprised look. "You look well, Dominus!"

"Indeed," Dominus replied. Ratheburg had reason to be taken aback; Dominus had been near death the last time they'd met, minutes after Dominus had been forced to murder his only son. "A stroke of luck that I survived the infection."

"Your physician must have considerable talent."

"He would love to take credit for my recovery," Dominus replied with a slight smirk. "But it would be undeserved."

"Come," Ratheburg urged, turning about and offering his arm. Dominus took it, forcing down a sudden irritation. The less he exposed others to his will, the less likely they would be to discover his deception.

Don't be a fool, he chided himself. *They'll Test you soon enough.*

And if he failed…

They reached the double-doors, which had already been opened for them, and entered the great hall beyond. The floor and walls were made of the finest marble, the ceiling – over fifteen meters above their heads – supported by massive stone columns. In the center of the hall sat a huge fountain topped with a massive statue of Tykus himself, arms raised to the heavens.

He stared at that statue as they walked toward it, his guts squirming.

Tykus has returned.

"Any developments on who might have been responsible for this attack?" Ratheburg inquired. Dominus blinked, then shook his head.

"I have my suspicions," he admitted. "But no definitive evidence."

"Do tell," Ratheburg urged. They passed the statue, continuing onward to stairs at the opposite end of the hall. Dominus grimaced.

"The assassins wore uniforms of the Seekers of the Deep," he stated. Ratheburg's eyes widened, and he stopped before the arched doorway leading to another long hallway.

"You're saying the Kingdom of the Deep is behind this?" he exclaimed. Dominus hesitated, then shook his head.

"I don't think so," he replied. "It would be a declaration of war," he added. "With little benefit to them. Besides, if they'd wanted to kill me, they would have used a much larger force."

"Agreed," Ratheburg said, rubbing his chin. He continued walking. "But who would benefit from your death?"

"The dukes of Wexford have always been tasked with protecting the kingdom from corruption," Dominus answered. "Those who would profit from the loss of that protection…"

He trailed off, hoping that Ratheburg would reach the proper conclusion himself. A theory was far more believable if one came to it themselves.

"Like who?" Ratheburg inquired. Dominus sighed inwardly.

"The assassins were corrupted," he replied, "…but not nearly as drastically as true Seekers of the Deep would be. These men were almost human."

"So you suspect another kingdom?"

"I suspect our own," Dominus countered.

Ratheburg considered this, then shook his head.

"No one in Tykus stands to profit from your death," he protested. Dominus gave a grim smile.

"No one in the Acropolis," he corrected. Ratheburg frowned.

"Tell me," he urged.

"I suspect the Guild of Seekers," Dominus stated bluntly. Ratheburg stopped again, his jaw dropping.

"The guild?" he blurted out. "But why?"

"I've been conducting a secret investigation of the guild," Dominus lied. "There have been reports of Seekers importing forbidden artifacts into the city." He gave a sour look. "*Wild* artifacts."

"Impossible!" Ratheburg exclaimed. "Everything entering the city…"

"…is tested, I know," Dominus interjected. "They've been circumventing customs, hiding artifacts within larger structures. Usually complex, multilayered wooden objects." And this was true, Dominus knew; he'd been importing forbidden artifacts in the same manner.

"You have proof of this?"

"Not anymore," he lied. "My would-be assassins made sure to destroy what proof I had," he added. "I suspect that was a secondary goal of the attack."

"This is…" Ratheburg began, then sighed. "This is highly disturbing, Dominus."

"Indeed," Dominus agreed. The guild donated Seekers to act as customs agents, testing a portion of incoming artifacts – and the rare Original – for corrupt influences. All of these Seekers were subjected to Testers, of course, but Dominus was sure the guild trained these Seekers differently, knowing that they had to pass inspection.

"We need to act on this," Ratheburg stated, "…and quickly."

"Agreed."

"We should conduct a surprise inspection of the guild," Ratheburg decided. "Perhaps we can obtain the evidence we need to convict them."

"Perhaps," Dominus agreed, smiling inwardly. But he controlled his emotions, knowing that Ratheburg would be able to sense them if they were powerful enough.

"You're relieved," Ratheburg deduced. Dominus nodded, realizing that Ratheburg *could* sense his emotion. He would have to be cautious…and use it to his advantage.

"I was worried that you wouldn't believe me," he confessed. And that much was certainly true. Ratheburg smiled.

"I trust you implicitly, Dominus," he replied. "You've proven your loyalty to Tykus, at great personal cost."

Dominus forced himself to think of his son, of the shock and grief that he'd felt when he'd realized what he'd done. That he'd killed his boy. A too-familiar pain came over him, and for a split second he accepted it.

"I'm sorry," Ratheburg apologized. He'd clearly sensed Dominus's emotion. "I didn't mean to…"

"Quite alright," Dominus muttered, shoving the memory from his mind. "I agree that we should inspect the guild, but they may have planned for such a contingency."

"What do you suggest?"

"The guild hasn't had time to export their illegal artifacts from the kingdom," he answered. "These artifacts must still be within the guild. But they will be well-hidden."

"You're suggesting they have secret rooms," Ratheburg deduced. Dominus gave a wry smile.

"Don't we all," he replied. Every duke had their archives and their ancestral shrine, well-hidden from potential intruders.

"Good point," Ratheburg conceded. "What do you suggest, Dominus?"

Dominus forced himself to remain calm, not allowing himself to feel victorious. This was exactly what he'd wanted…to steer Ratheburg into having him suggest a plan to get back at the guild. He had his fellow duke on his side now…which meant that the other dukes would fall in line behind them, assuming of course that the king approved.

"I've been pondering that ever since the attack," Dominus confessed. "And I think I have a plan."

CHAPTER 18

Sukri stared down at the lifeless body of her best friend, at his eyes gazing upward at the heavens. Unseeing, unblinking. The light of his life snuffed out. She leaned down, kissing him one last time, his lips cool to the touch. Hands gripped her shoulders, yanking her backward, and she resisted, grabbing onto Gammon's big shoulders and holding onto them.

"Let go!" she shouted. "Leave me alone!"

The hands tore her from Gammon, throwing her to the side. She fell onto her back on the unforgiving path, guards surrounding her. The masked man stepped up to her, staring down at her with those ungodly silver eyes, then nodded at one of the guards, making a gesture with one hand. Sukri was hauled to her feet, her arms pinned behind her back.

The masked man eyed her silently, his staff in his hands.

"Do it," she ordered, staring back at him defiantly. "Slit my throat you fucking coward!"

Again, she felt that cold indifference seep from him, washing over her like ice water. She shivered, her lower lip trembling.

"Come on," she urged. "What are you waiting for?"

Still, he just stood there.

"Fucking *do* it!" she screamed, lunging at him. But the guards held her back, twisting her arms painfully. She swore, lifting her legs up and trying to kick him. He stepped backward casually, his eyes never leaving hers.

There was shouting in the distance.

The guards swore, and one of them let go of her, drawing his sword and starting back toward the mansion. Sukri craned her head, spotting people pouring out of the entrance. Men in black and gold uniforms.

"Shit!" one of the guards swore. The masked man drew his swords, striding toward the group of Seekers. There were at least half a dozen of them, all sprinting down the path.

"Help!" Sukri cried.

"Shut *up*!" the guard holding her ordered, putting a hand over her mouth. She bit at it, and he cursed, punching her in the back of the head…hard. Her head snapped forward, her vision blackening for a moment. Bile pooled in her throat, and she puked, vomit splashing onto the path.

More Seekers spilled out of the mansion, joining the others as they sprinted toward Sukri and the guards. The guards glanced at the masked man, who held up one hand. The guards stood down, and the masked man strode toward the approaching Seekers, his metallic staff in his hands. The wicked blades on either end gleamed in the sunlight, the blood coating them still wet.

The first of the Seekers reached the masked man, lunging at him with their sword!

The masked man whipped his staff in a wide arc, knocking the Seeker's sword clear out of his hands. The Seeker fell forward onto his belly on the path, his head tumbling off of his shoulders in a spray of blood. It rolled toward the masked man's feet, stopping a few centimeters from his boots.

A half-dozen more Seekers rushed up to the masked man, surrounding him, their longswords bared.

"At once," one of them ordered. "Attack!"

They all lunged at the masked man.

He swung his silver staff so quickly it was a blur, knocking two of the Seekers in front of him backward. He leapt high into the air then – impossibly high – spinning 180 degrees and whipping his staff in a half-circle. It struck a Seeker in the face, making a deep gash across both eyes, rupturing them. The masked man landed, twirling his staff around him in a silver blur.

The Seeker's arms separated from his body, and then his legs. He fell to the ground on his back, blood spurting from the stumps of his limbs.

And screamed.

The masked man turned his silver eyes toward the remaining five Seekers. They glanced at their dismembered colleague, then at each other…and backed away from the masked man. Who turned away from them, walking back toward Sukri and the guards, strapping his staff onto his back again.

The five Seekers watched him go, no one daring to go after him. More Seekers came out of the mansion's double doors, rushing toward them…some of them with bows on their backs.

"Our archers are coming," one of the remaining Seekers ordered. "Wait for them, then attack!"

The masked man stopped before Sukri, then turned to stare at the approaching Seekers. He retrieved something from a pocket in his uniform then. It was a whistle; he brought it to his lips and blew. But no sound came.

The archers joined their fellow Seekers, then charged toward Sukri and her guards, who were only ten meters away now and closing in fast. Sukri cried out, earning another smack in the head. She bit back another wave of nausea, gritting her teeth, her eyes watering.

Suddenly the ground began to tremble, and Sukri heard a low rumbling sound. A few of the Seekers running toward her turned their heads to their left, then skid to a halt, their eyes widening. They backpedaled, yelling at each other and gesturing frantically.

Sukri followed their gaze, across the dirt field with its rows of crops, and realized what they were looking at: the giant statue of the snake coiled upon itself, over ten meters tall, countless small legs protruding from its sides. She stared at it, her jaw dropping.

It was *moving.*

The creature started to uncoil, its serpentine head turning to face the Seekers, its eyes opening to reveal blood-red orbs. Its huge jaws opened, twin fangs curving down, each as tall as she was. A long, forked tongue whipped out, lashing the ground before it, its eyes locking on the terrified Seekers. Its head rose into the air, almost as high as the mansion's roof, its long neck curved into an "S."

And then its head reared back, and it lunged forward with blinding speed, right at the Seekers!

The Seekers scattered, throwing themselves out of the way of the giant creature. But a few were too slow; its giant maw snapped up two of them, then reared its head backward and upward. It lifted its chin until it was looking straight up into the air, its mouth opening wide. The Seekers fell into its throat, swallowed in one gulp. Its mouth snapped shut, and it lowered its gaze to the remaining Seekers, who were scattering across the field.

Then it used its innumerable legs to scurry forward, charging after them with frightening speed. It lunged at one of the Seekers, using its head as a battering ram, smashing into him. The Seeker flew backward, landing on the dirt in a heap. The creature ignored him, turning toward another Seeker and bolting toward them. Its legs tore up the earth, crops crushed under its massive body.

The guards and the masked man stood there, watching the unholy beast as it decimated the Seekers.

"Arrows!" one Seeker shouted. He and two other Seekers drew their bows, firing at the monster. But the arrows bounced off its thick, scaly hide. It whipped its head around to face them, its jaws opening in a wicked snarl.

Then it attacked.

The Seekers ran, but it was pointless; the creature was far too quick, catching up to them and picking them off one-by-one. Within moments, every last one of them lay dead on the dirt…or within the monster itself.

Then the creature turned its blood-red eyes to Sukri, slithering sinuously toward her.

Sukri's blood went cold, her breath catching in her throat.

The masked man put the whistle to his lips, blowing into it…and again, it made no sound. But the creature stopped, staring at Sukri for a moment longer, then turning around. It slithered back to its original resting place, coiling its long body upon itself. Then it rested its head on top of one of those coils, closing its eyes. It looked for all the world like a statue again.

The front doors of the mansion opened, and four more masked figures came out…followed by someone else. A woman, Sukri realized. A tall woman in a golden dress. She stopped at the top of the short stairway leading down to the path beyond, surveying the corpses littering the field. Then she strode forward, the masked figures surrounding her as she made her way toward Sukri. She closed the distance leisurely, taking her time; when she finally stopped a few meters before Sukri, she looked her up and down, her expression unreadable.

"Where is the boy?" she asked.

"He made it to the river my Lady," the silver-eyed man informed her. His voice was flat, and something about it made Sukri's skin crawl.

"Stay with me," she ordered. "The others will go after him."

The man bowed.

"Yes my Lady."

Her eyes returned to Sukri, who stared back at her silently. This, she realized, had to be Lady Camilla.

"Well well," she murmured. "What have we here?"

"An apprentice of the guild," the silver-eyed man answered. "An Empath."

Lady Camilla frowned, considering this.

"How new are you?" she asked.

"Fuck you," Sukri spat. The Lady sighed.

"I understand you must be very upset," she stated. "Your friends are dead. But keep in mind that they attacked me first, without provocation."

"You kidnapped Hunter!" Sukri accused. The Lady blinked, looking genuinely surprised.

"I did nothing of the sort," she retorted. "I was trying to protect him from your guild."

"What?"

"My dear," she stated, putting a hand to Sukri's cheek. Sukri jerked away from her touch, glaring at her. "The Guild of Seekers wants Hunter dead. That's why he ran when he saw your friends."

"Bullshit."

"Hunter is very special," Camilla continued calmly. "I would never want to harm him. But he doesn't understand the dangers outside of my home.

The guild wants him dead…as does Duke Dominus. I'm the only one powerful enough to keep him safe."

"I don't give a shit what you say," Sukri retorted. "Just kill me already."

"There's been enough killing for today," the Lady replied. "You're a victim of the guild," she added. "They sent you here to be slaughtered." When Sukri gave her a confused look, the Lady sighed. "Do you ever wonder why they sent you here? Barely trained apprentices, sent to fight some of the most highly trained Seekers in the world?" she added, gesturing at the silver-eyed man.

Sukri glanced at him, then at the Lady.

"We weren't all apprentices," she retorted.

"No," Camilla conceded. "They really did want Hunter. But they sent *you* here because you're a liability."

"What are you talking about?"

"You're a novice Seeker," she explained. "And the guild has been engaged in some…highly illegal activities. Some of which have come to your kingdom's attention."

"So?"

"So if they sent *you* out here," she continued, "…that means they're expecting the Acropolis to audit them. To Test their Seekers for corruption. They needed to get rid of you."

"I'm not corrupted," Sukri retorted. But she remembered how Sen and Jasmine had stared at her when they'd passed by. How they'd abandoned her and Gammon, leaving them to die. Was it revenge…or were they just carrying out the guild's orders?

The Lady smiled, putting a hand on Sukri's cheek again. This time, Sukri didn't bother trying to stop her.

"My dear," she replied. "You're *all* corrupted."

Chapter 19

The night sky was overcast, moonlight barely penetrating the thick layer of clouds far above the Fringe. A meandering stream – all that was left of the small tributary Hunter had followed from the much larger river upon which the Lady's mansion had been built – gurgling as it spilled over its rocky bed. Hunter strode beside it, his legs numb, his belly painfully empty. Hunger consumed him, dominating his every thought.

The last few days had been hell.

He'd escaped the Lady's men, to his surprise. They must not have seen him enter the river, or assumed that he'd crossed it instead of letting it take him downstream. Either way, he'd given them the slip, and stayed in the water until he'd been chilled to the bone. Then he'd swam to the shore, trudging alongside the river. Occasionally he'd had to stop to drink from it, as leery as he was about doing so. He'd had no other choice; it was either die from dehydration, or die quicker from dehydration via vomiting and diarrhea. Luckily, he hadn't gotten sick…yet.

Without his pack filled with rations, and without his bow, he'd had no way to hunt for food. He didn't trust the flora of the deep forest. If the plants didn't poison him, they might have a powerful will that could transform him.

So he'd walked, drank, and starved.

He had no real idea if he was going the right way to get home, other than knowing the general direction. But it *felt* right, and he'd learned to trust his gut. His hunches were usually the result of a memory he'd absorbed, after all. They hadn't led him astray yet.

Over the last few hours, the flora of the deep forest had given way to the familiar trees and bushes of the Fringe. Confirmation that he was going in the right direction. The plants here were weaker willed than in the deep forest. They were far safer to eat, and he'd gathered a few berries and edible leaves. It'd done nothing to curb his hunger, that awful, nigh-insatiable need for sustenance that had gripped him after he'd escaped.

After Za…after *he* took over.

Hunter grimaced, pushing the thought out of his mind, afraid of what might happen if he didn't.

A jagged bolt of lightning flashed in the night sky ahead, illuminating the forest for a split-second. Moments later, the low rumble of thunder rolled through the forest. Rain began to fall, large drops pelting his head and shoulders. He grimaced as a cool breeze whipped over his wet clothes, a chill running through him.

Great.

He sighed, hugging himself as he walked, forcing his tired legs to go a little faster. Another flash of lightning, followed by a muted thunderclap…and a rhythmic *thump-a-thump, thump-a-thump* from behind. He glanced back, peering into the darkness. He couldn't see more than a few dozen feet, the trees beyond that disappearing into darkness. And that was all he saw…trees.

Thump-a-thump, thump-a-thump…

The sound grew steadily louder, and Hunter's hackles rose. He turned forward, breaking out into a jog, forcing his tired legs to carry him over the uneven terrain. Lightning shot from the heavens, zig-zagging to the earth, followed by an ear-splitting *boom,* the rain falling in heavy sheets now, soaking him to the bone.

Thump-a-thump, thump-a-thump…

He ran faster, ignoring the burning in his legs, glancing over his shoulder as he weaved through the trees. A shadow appeared in the distance, barely visible in the darkness. Growing steadily larger.

The hell?

And then he saw it.

A black horse galloping toward him, a man in a red and black uniform riding atop it. A man wearing a red and black mask, a pair of curved swords sheathed at his hips.

Shit!

Hunter veered to the right, dodging trees as he went. He spotted a fallen log in the distance, and dashed toward it, glancing back again. The Seeker was still following him, steering their huge black steed deftly through the forest. Hunter leapt over the log, and the Seeker came right for him, the horse leaping into the air, clearing the log easily. Hunter swore, veering left sharply, pumping his legs as fast as he could. Adrenaline coursed through him, terror giving his muscles newfound strength.

The Seeker turned with him, dodging around a copse of trees, then bursting forward, closing the gap between them quickly. Hunter turned again, but still the Seeker tracked him, steering their steed expertly. They were only twenty feet away now, and closing fast. Hunter spotted a break in the trees ahead…the end of the forest. And the sound of rushing water, a sound that grew louder with every second.

The canyon!

He ran even faster, his breath coming in short gasps, his lungs burning. A sharp cramp gripped his belly, and he pushed through the pain, running for the end of the tree line. Lightning flashed through the darkness ahead, illuminating what lay beyond for a split-second: a very familiar canyon, waterfalls coursing down its sides.

Thump-a-thump, thump-a-thump…

He heard the horse's loud, snorting breaths behind him, its hooves pummeling the ground. He veered again, weaving tightly around the trees, hoping to lose the Seeker, but it only barely slowed them. And there weren't many trees left; he was nearing the end of the forest. Beyond, he saw rocky land leading to the edge of the sheer drop to the canyon floor hundreds of feet below. If he could just make it to the path leading down to Vi's place, there's no way the horse would be able to…

Something struck him square between the shoulder blades, sending him flying into the ground.

Hunter's chest and belly slammed into the packed earth, breath exploding from his lungs. He gasped for air, struggling onto his hands and knees, crawling forward. The Seeker rode past him, turning in a wide circle, then stopping near the edge of the cliff, facing him. The man took something from one of his pockets – a long black tube – and loaded something into it. The Seeker put one end of the tube up to his lips.

He heard a *thck*, and looked to his right, spotting a small dart embedded into the tree beside him…inches from his head.

Hunter scrambled to his feet, running out of the forest, going parallel to the cliffside. He recognized a rocky outcropping ahead; the path leading down the canyon should only be a few hundred feet away now. He glanced back, seeing the Seeker loading another dart into the blowgun.

Then the Seeker snapped the reins, and the horse charged.

Hunter veered to the side, throwing himself out of the way of the galloping beast, but the Seeker swerved to intercept him. He heard another *thck*, and felt a sudden stinging sensation in his left buttock. The horse veered to the side, galloping past him, turning in another slow circle to face him again…this time placing themselves between him and the path.

Hunter slowed, reaching back and feeling his butt cheek. There was something sticking in it. He pulled it out; it was a dart.

Crap.

The Seeker stayed where they were, facing him silently.

Hunter threw the dart aside, jogging near the edge of the cliffside. There was utter darkness beyond, the massive canyon hidden in shadow. He glanced up, seeing the Seeker just sitting there, watching him. Waiting.

Suddenly he felt the earth *shift*, as if the ground were tipping to one side, and stumbled away from the cliffside. His boots slipped on the wet earth, and he nearly fell. Bracing himself, he felt the earth tip to the *other* side.

What…

A wave of nausea came over him, and he grit his teeth, focusing on the Seeker…who seemed to grow larger, their ghostly outline spreading outward across the sky. The huge black horse reared up, unleashing an unholy shriek that pierced through the roar of the waterfalls and the rain. It dropped to its forefeet, its eyes boring into his, glowing a faint red.

Terror gripped Hunter.

He turned around, fleeing from the Seeker and its unholy steed, back the way he'd come. The earth titled sickeningly to the left, and this time he fell, landing on his side. He got to his feet, stumbling as the earth continued to tilt, this time to the right.

Oh come on!

He ran toward the trees ahead, but with every step he took, they shrank from him, seeming farther and farther away.

Thump-a-thump, thump-a-thump…

Something struck his shoulder from behind, spinning him around and throwing him to the ground. He groaned, clutching at the wet earth, the world spinning around him. Another wave of nausea came over him.

The ghostly Seeker galloped past him, turning around and facing him once again, straddling its red-eyed steed.

Hunter got to his hands and knees, staring at the two, the world spinning slowly, nauseatingly.

Then the horse charged.

He tried to get to his feet, but his feet slipped on the wet rock, and he fell onto his hands and knees again. The Seeker's massive stead ran right for him, its glowing eyes burning with unholy fire, its mouth opening in an ear-splitting shriek. He saw the Seeker unsheathe one curved blade, the metal glowing brightly as a jagged bolt of lightning shot down from the sky.

Hunter tried to get up again, but slipped a second time, landing flat on his back. The Seeker barreled toward him, sword in hand, only twenty feet away now.

Ten.

Hunter cried out, throwing his hands out in front of him.

Without warning, something huge leapt out of the shadows, slamming into the horse's flank, hurtling it and the Seeker to the left. The horse shrieked, falling onto its side, the Seeker careening through the air. Hunter stared as the Seeker landed with a *thump*, rolling to a stop on the wet earth. Then his eyes were drawn forward…to what had struck them. A huge, shadowy figure, its outline barely visible in the darkness of the night.

It moved toward him, growing larger.

"Stop," he ordered, forcing his voice to be cold and hard. He got to his feet, feeling the world continue to spin. He braced himself, taking a step back. But still the shadow moved toward him. He spotted the outline of a head, half-visible in the darkness. And a shoulder.

"I said stop!" he repeated, his heart pounding.

Still, the figure advanced.

Hunter took another step back, glancing at the horse, who was still on its side, flailing its legs, one of which was broken. The Seeker was getting to its feet, unsheathing its remaining sword. Hunter glanced back at the shadow approaching him. Lightning shot down from the heavens, illuminating the surrounding area. Just long enough for the afterimage to be burned into his vision.

A huge figure striding toward him, skin as black as night. Broad shoulders sloping down to thick arms.

And then a second pair of arms below those.

A chill ran down Hunter's spine, his breath catching in his throat.

Ironclad!

The Seeker burst toward the Ironclad, sword in hand.

Thump-a-thump, thump-a-thump…

The Ironclad turned to face the Seeker…just as a second and third Seeker appeared, riding on black steeds. These Seekers dismounted, grabbing warhammers and rushing the Ironclad.

Hunter ran away, aiming for the cliffside overlooking the canyon. He heard a loud *thump* behind him, following by a shrill scream, and resisted the urge to look back, focusing on keeping his balance as the world continued to spin slowly around him. He followed the cliffside, hearing another scream, and spotted was he was looking for: the path spiraling down the side of the canyon!

He rushed for it, sliding to a stop at the edge of the cliff and turning left to go down the path. Then he stopped, clutching the canyon wall to his left, staring over the edge of the path only a few feet to his right. The path was narrow and wet, the sheer drop to the bottom of the canyon dangerously close. He closed his eyes, feeling the world spin, and took a deep breath in, trying to focus.

Go slow, he told himself. *Be careful.*

If he wasn't, he'd end up taking the quick way down into the canyon.

He continued forward down the path, hugging the wall as he did so, each step careful and deliberate. Another scream echoed through the air, followed by a loud *crunch*. He tried not to think of what was happening up there, instead focusing on what he needed to do. The Seekers would have to follow him on foot; there was no way a horse could make it down this path. And the path was wet, so they wouldn't be able to move quickly to catch up with him. Hopefully the Ironclad would slow them down enough to let him make it to Vi's place. Then he could arm himself, and take as much of Vi's stuff as possible.

And then what?

He grimaced, knowing the answer. He'd have to fight, and kill whatever Seekers remained. Or if that Ironclad won…

A gust of wind struck him from behind, nearly making him stumble.

He swore, bracing himself against the wall, waiting for the wind to pass. Then he continued. A flash of lightning arced through the sky, and seconds later, the low rumble of thunder echoed off the canyon walls. Rain fell from the sky in heavy sheets, pelting his face and soaking him to the bone. He continued onward, his boots sliding on the slippery, bare rock of the path. Another flash of lightning, followed almost instantly by an ear-shattering *boom*. His boots slipped again, almost sending him right off the path.

That's it, he decided. *I'm sliding on my butt.*

He was about to do just that when he spotted movement on the path ahead.

He froze.

A shadow, blacker than night. Moving steadily up the path toward him.

Shit!

His hand automatically went to his left hip, for the sword that wasn't there. He cursed, taking a step back, then another. The figure advanced, and Hunter took another step back, his foot slipping again. Without a weapon, he was a sitting duck. He looked around for a loose rock to throw, but there were none.

Lightning lit up the canyon, and he saw what was coming for him…another Ironclad.

"Get back!" he shouted, terror gripping him. He clung to the wall, his heart hammering in his chest. "Don't come any closer!"

The Ironclad ignored him, stomping up the path, the *thump, thump* of its armored feet barely audible above the rain and the roar of the waterfalls around them. It was ten feet away now, its beady black eyes staring right at him.

He turned, hurrying back up the path, his feet slipping on the slick rock. He kept his balance, managing to make it to the top of the path. Glancing back, he saw the Ironclad coming after him.

Damn it!

There was no way down…and no way forward. He had to choose between the Ironclad and the Lady's Seekers.

He hesitated, then continued forward, running back toward the tree-line. There were two Seekers there, standing over the bodies of an Ironclad and a third Seeker. They spotted him, breaking out into a run toward him.

Better the Lady than death, he decided. The Seekers wouldn't kill him, not with what he had inside of him.

He raised his arms into the air in surrender, and the Seekers rushed up to him, shoving him onto his belly on the ground, then grabbing his hands and tying them behind his back. He heard a *thck*, then felt a sharp pain in his buttock.

"Tie him to your horse," he heard a man say. "I'll take him back to the Lady."

"What do I do?" another voice asked. "There could be more of those things."

"Ride double," the first man answered. "If we see any Seekers from the guild, take him to the Lady. I'll stay behind to slow them down."

Hunter felt rope being tied around his ankles, after which one Seeker grabbed his legs, the other his shoulders. They hauled him off the ground, carrying him toward one of the horses.

Thump.

The Seeker holding his legs jerked to the side, an arrow sticking out of his temple. He crumpled, dropping Hunter's legs onto the ground.

"What..." the other Seeker blurted out. He dropped Hunter, who landed on his back with a *thud.* Hunter cried out in pain, his arms pinned between his back and the ground. He saw the Seeker unsheathe their twin blades, facing something in the distance.

Then the Seeker's head snapped back, and he fell right on top of Hunter, an arrow protruding from his eye socket.

The hell?

Hunter grimaced, trying to roll away from underneath the Seeker, but it was no use; the Seeker's body was too heavy. The world began to spin, far more violently than before. He swallowed back a surge of bile, closing his eyes against the horrible spinning. That didn't help; he still felt as if he were on a merry-go-round, going faster and faster. He opened his eyes, trying to focus, to roll away from the Seeker on top of him.

There was a flash of lightning, so bright that it blinded him, followed by another deafening *boom.*

A shadow came over him, blotting out the sky. Someone standing over him as the world rotated madly around him. He blinked away the afterimage of the lightning bolt, staring upward, but he could barely see; his vision was blackening, a sudden urge to sleep overcoming him. He yawned despite himself, struggling to keep his eyes open.

The shadow shifted, a long, straight blade gleaming in the light of another jagged bolt of lightning. He felt the weight on top of him roll off, exposing him to the falling rain.

Hunter stared upward, feeling oblivion coming for him. He tried to roll to the side, but a boot pressed into his belly, pinning him to the ground.

"Get off me!" he shouted, fighting to remain conscious. He bit his own tongue, using the pain to keep himself awake. But it was a losing battle. The shadow standing over him seemed to grow larger, until he saw a face staring at him, outlined by another flash of lightning. A pale face with large green eyes and prominent cheekbones, and short, light-brown hair.

Hunter's breath caught in his throat.

"Hey kiddo," a husky, feminine voice greeted.

And then sleep claimed him.

Chapter 20

Dominus stepped through the double-doors of the Acropolis, squinting in the bright sunlight shining down on him from directly above. The air was warm, a gentle breeze offering a pleasant contrast to the heat. He made his way to the carriage waiting for him a few meters ahead. Ornate beyond even his means, the carriage was wrought of gold and platinum, and encrusted with jewels that sparkled in the sunlight. Two massive horses stood at its front, a Royal guard sitting in the driver's seat…and many more guards standing around the carriage. The side-door was already open for him.

He walked toward it, his cane clicking on the stone path with every other step. He had no need of it anymore; his foot had almost completely healed. His hand, still covered in bandages, was healing nicely, his fingers regenerated to the second knuckle. He noticed he had more energy now, able to walk indefinitely without chest pain, and without that horrible gnawing pain in his calves. Indeed, he felt like a younger man, possessed of vitality he hadn't realized he'd lost.

Still, he felt a vague unease as he reached the carriage, though he knew it was unwarranted. He'd passed the Testing, after all…and Ratheburg was on board with his plan to deal with the Guild of Seekers. All was going according to plan.

But still he felt uneasy.

He hesitated before the open carriage door, looking inside. A man was sitting within. A man with long blond hair, striking blue eyes, and a full beard, neatly trimmed. He wore a plain white shirt and white pants, and nothing else…not even shoes. The man smiled at him…a genuine smile that lit up his face.

"Ah, Dominus!" the man greeted, patting the seat next to him. "Come, take a ride with me."

"As you wish, your Highness," Dominus replied, bowing deeply. But one of the guards blocked his way.

"Your cane," the guard stated sharply.

"Come now," King Tykus admonished. "Let him by."

"It's a cane-sword, your Highness," the guard protested. King Tykus gave a wry smile.

"Dominus would no sooner kill me than himself," he countered. "And if he does kill me, you can always make another one. Apparently I'm in infinite supply."

The guard bowed sharply, stepping out of Dominus's way. Dominus stepped up into the carriage, sitting down next to the king. It was strange seeing Tykus so young; the previous iteration of the king had been older than Dominus.

A guard closed Dominus's door, and the carriage began to move.

"A pleasure to meet you, Dominus," Tykus stated, putting a hand on Dominus's knee. Dominus stopped himself from jerking away from the man's touch, unaccustomed to allowing anyone to do so. The king of course had no fear of being overwhelmed by Dominus's will; he would simply cleanse by sleeping in his bed beneath the Ossae of Tykus, and be refreshed anew.

"Glad to have you back, my liege."

"I've heard a great deal about you," Tykus confessed. "Though I have vague memories of you from the boy who sacrificed himself to become me," he added. He grimaced then. "You know, in my…previous life, my original one, I inadvertently created a great many facsimiles of myself. A horrible thing to witness, let me tell you. To think I'm one of them now…"

He trailed off, staring out of his window at the passing scenery. They were traveling away from the entrance to the Acropolis, toward one of the many side-paths leading through the Royal Gardens. Tykus sighed, turning to face Dominus, and patting Dominus's knee.

"I heard about your son Conlan," he stated. "So many people have sacrificed themselves in the service of my immortality."

Dominus nodded, swallowing with some difficulty.

"You should have let him use my hammer on the Ossae, Dominus," Tykus admonished gently. Dominus blinked.

"But your Highness…"

"My bones hold their power whether they're broken or not," Tykus interjected, not unkindly. "There's nothing sacred about keeping them whole."

"I could not," Dominus protested, feeling himself choke up. "I…"

"You worship me," Tykus stated bluntly. Dominus nodded.

"Everyone does, sire."

Tykus withdrew his hand from Dominus's knee, leaning back in his seat and rubbing his chin thoughtfully. It was strange to see a man who appeared so young act so maturely. But of course Tykus had been ninety-seven when he'd died, during his original lifespan. He was an extraordinarily old man in a young man's body.

"Am I a god, Dominus?" Tykus inquired at last.

"No, sire."

"Then why do you treat me as one?"

"We worship humanity," Dominus explained. "And you were…*are*…the greatest man in our history."

Tykus burst out laughing, and Dominus flinched in surprise. At length the king stopped, shaking his head.

"How destitute our history must be, that I constituted the pinnacle!" he proclaimed. Then he sighed. "I suspect I would have been eclipsed if we'd allowed other wills to flourish instead of homogenizing the kingdom."

"But your Highness…"

"I was ninety-seven when I died," Tykus interrupted. "All of my friends were dead. My children were dead, my grandchildren in their fifties and sixties. Old men and women, their time coming to an end. Our generation had their time, their chance. We created wondrous things in that time."

"You did, sire."

"I wonder what other wondrous things the countless generations since would have created," Tykus mused. "…if it hadn't been for me?"

Dominus said nothing. *Could* say nothing. It was blasphemy, of course. Counter to everything he believed and cherished. But Tykus – and Tykus alone – had the right to speak it, to consider the forbidden.

"I'm making you uncomfortable," Tykus observed, his eyes twinkling mischievously. Dominus grimaced.

"Yes sire."

"Good!" Tykus declared. "I want you to be uncomfortable, Dominus. I've found that the greatest wisdom lies just beyond discomfort…beyond the things we forbid ourselves from contemplating."

"Yes sire."

"Now now," he admonished. "Rote answers won't do, Dominus. I hear you're a thoughtful man. I expect you to broaden your mind."

Dominus hesitated, then nodded.

"Hmm," Tykus murmured, eyeing Dominus critically. "You're going to be a tough nut to crack, I expect. Old men invariably are. Your ancestors certainly were." He smiled wistfully. "I remember the first Duke of Wexford," he mused. "I used to walk with him in these gardens," he added, gesturing at the scenery around them. "He was much like you, I suspect."

"By design," Dominus replied.

"Ah yes," Tykus murmured. "Everything by design. It's why I entrusted the first Duke of Wexford to create many of the systems you see around you. Your family always had a knack for organization."

"Thank you, sire."

"Always so rigid though," Tykus continued. "So serious! I rarely saw the first duke smile, and never saw him have fun. Not once, not in sixty years. What a bore!"

Tykus leaned forward suddenly, rapping his knuckles on the window in front of them. The carriage slowed, then stopped, and Tykus opened his door.

"Come, let's go for a walk," he stated, getting out of the carriage. "It's too beautiful a day to waste it away indoors."

Dominus complied, opening his own door and stepping down from the carriage. He walked to Tykus's side, glancing down at the man's bare feet. Tykus smiled at him.

"Shoes numb your feet," he explained. "There's nothing quite like the feeling of warm stone under your toes, or wet grass. Why deny myself such pleasures?"

"You are the king," Dominus replied. "You needn't deny yourself anything."

"Ha!" Tykus retorted. "Quite the opposite, actually. *Dictators* deny themselves nothing, Dominus. They take and take and take. They live lives of accumulation." He gestured at his feet. "By stripping away the things I think I need, I find that most of my needs aren't needs at all…and that having less is the secret to true happiness."

"I don't understand," Dominus admitted.

"What you own will own you," Tykus explained. "If you have only what you need, and a little of what you want, you'll learn to find great pleasure in small things, instead of little pleasure in great things."

"Like your bare feet," Dominus ventured. Tykus smiled, clapping Dominus on the back, then veering off the stone path onto the grass ahead.

"Precisely."

"I understand," Dominus stated. Tykus snorted.

"No you don't," he countered. "Your shoes are still on."

Dominus hesitated, feeling his guts squirm. His foot was nearly healed; if he exposed it to Tykus, it was possible that word would get back to Ratheburg, who had seen his foot earlier, when his toes had been amputated. They would naturally question how he'd manage to regrow his toes, and then…

"Relax," Tykus stated, breaking Dominus out of his morbid train of thought. "I won't order you to take off your shoes. I hardly expect a Duke of Wexford to be capable of enjoying himself!"

Dominus grimaced, realizing he'd stopped walking. He continued onward, side-by-side with the king.

"How is your hand?" Tykus inquired, glancing down at Dominus's bandaged right hand.

"Healing well, your Highness."

"I heard of the attack on Castle Wexford," Tykus revealed, his expression turning grim. "I've ordered a royal investigation, of course. And Ratheburg mentioned your concerns."

"Ah," Dominus mumbled. Ratheburg hadn't wasted any time, it appeared. And of course he would have gone directly to the king.

"I need to spend more time studying this guild," Tykus stated. "As you know, it didn't exist in my time. Consolidating so much power in an entity that collects artifacts – with so little oversight – was a mistake."

"I agree, your Highness."

"Of course you do," Tykus remarked. "You think they tried to murder you."

"Granted."

"I'm frankly surprised that my predecessors allowed such an organization to exist," Tykus continued. "The fact that they did gives me pause; there must have been something they knew that I do not. They *were* me, after all. I will of course spend a great deal of time meditating on this."

Tykus led them to a small brook winding through the gardens, and knelt down, dipping his fingers into the water.

"Why am I doing this?" he asked.

"I don't know, sire."

Tykus stood, smiling at him.

"I was a young man when I came to this world," he stated. "Nineteen, in fact. My grandfather founded a settlement after being exiled from his home, and raised my father there. Or rather, he had a servant raise my father. A man named Tyrker." He paused. "Have I told you this story?"

"No sire."

"I had two older brothers," Tykus continued. "Thorgils and Thorkell. Strong men, rather brutish in fact, especially Thorgils. He filled that role so completely that I had no choice but to become an intellectual to distinguish myself."

Dominus smirked.

"My father was quite the sailor," Tykus continued. "When a man called Bjarni Herjólfsson told my father he'd seen unfamiliar lands after being blown off course, my father sailed there. He found a land lush with grapevines and fields of wheat."

Tykus paused then, rising to his feet and continuing to walk. Dominus followed beside him.

"Over the years, my father made several trips to this new land," Tykus continued. "My father called it 'Vinland,' on account of all of the grapevines. Well, I never got to go, despite desperately wanting to. That is, until I badgered my uncle Thorvald into letting me tag along. He was a brute as well – with a vicious temper – but it was worth enduring to finally get a chance at adventure. We sailed, and came to Vinland. I was exploring the countryside with a few of my uncle's men when I came upon the portal to this world."

"I see," Dominus stated. He made a note to memorize what Tykus was saying; he'd never heard nor read of these stories before, and it was imperative that they be recorded.

"We found this kingdom," Tykus revealed. "Arriving before the foot of the hill. Beautiful buildings, marvelous architecture all around…and not a single soul. Not human, anyway."

"The Svartálfar," Dominus guessed. Tykus nodded.

"Yes, the dark elves," he agreed. "Or so we thought at the time. Now I suspect they were humans who had come before, and been transformed by this world. Vicious beasts, very clever. If they hadn't up and died, we would have been doomed."

"How did they die?"

"Who knows?" Tykus replied. "They were voracious eaters, that much I do know. Feasted on a few of my uncle's men," he added. "Lucky for us that more men came through the portal. Apparently they'd been sent by my uncle to find me. We managed to hold the Svartálfar off, gather supplies. We tried to find a way back to Vinland, but of course there was none."

"So you founded the kingdom," Dominus stated. Tykus smirked.

"Not without women we didn't," he countered. "You see, only men came through the portal. It was I who proposed that the natives of Vinland…beautiful people, really…must have come through the portal as well, and that we should send search parties for them. Eventually we did find settlements in the forest, and arranged for the natives to come to the kingdom with us. It took some convincing; they were terrified of the Svartálfar. In fact, some of them were survivors from the kingdom, having been driven out years before."

"So I've read," Dominus confessed. Tykus gave a conspiratorial smile.

"I imagine you have," he agreed. "But can you imagine what the natives looked like?"

Dominus shook his head.

"They had the most perfect golden skin," Tykus revealed. "And bodies to match. I daresay they looked more regal without clothes than we did dressed in our finest."

"I thought they were…"

"Like us?" Tykus interrupted. He shook his head. "No, not at first. You see, my powers hadn't reached their potential yet. I had no idea what I was, not until later." He sighed then. "The natives knew well before I did, of course. I suppose if they hadn't told me, I would've thought myself mad. Everyone around me began to change. Began to look more like me. To talk like me."

"You realized you were a Legend."

"I realized I was cursed," Tykus corrected. "Lucky that so many had been transformed by me," he added. "Otherwise those who remained themselves would have had me killed and thrown into the sea. I outnumbered them quite literally. And the longer I lived, the more of 'me' there was." He grimaced. "I had to seclude myself, Dominus. Just to save what remained of their wretched souls."

Tykus stopped suddenly, staring up into the sky, then turning to face Dominus. He put a hand on Dominus's shoulder.

"I spent my life staying away from people," he continued, "…secluding myself in the Acropolis so that my will would exert itself as narrowly as possible. My walks with your ancestor were few and far between…and we walked far apart, nearly having to shout at each other." He smiled. "And now, for the first time in this newest life, I can walk amongst my people, I can *touch* them. Without fear of transforming them, of losing them to my curse. I can dip my fingers into this stream without worrying about who might drink of the water downstream. Or of the fish and other creatures that might be transformed."

"I understand," Dominus stated.

"No one can understand what it's like to be a Legend," Tykus retorted gently. "Especially a Legend such as myself. Most Legends have powerful wills…but I'm Legendary in *all* aspects. My appearance, my mind, my memories…I transmit everything. Or at least my original body does."

"You are one of a kind, my liege," Dominus agreed. "That is why we worship you."

"Hmm," Tykus murmured, removing his hand. "I suspect if I were a horrible tyrant, you would not."

"Granted."

"I spent my life trying to minimize my influence on my people," Tykus admitted. "To give them an opportunity to live their own lives, to be themselves. Variety is critical, Dominus, particularly in a world like this. As is dissent."

"Your pardon?"

"Your son rejected his duty to become me," Tykus explained. "From what I hear, he wanted to rule as himself…to bring fresh ideas to bear. To modernize the kingdom."

"My son," Dominus replied stiffly, "…was a fool."

"Perhaps so," Tykus conceded. "You knew him, and I did not. But his sentiment was not incorrect. There is value in dissent, Dominus. Do you recall what I instructed you to do?"

Dominus stared at Tykus, his mind drawing a blank. Tykus smiled, patting Dominus's shoulder, then continuing their walk.

"The greatest wisdom lies just beyond the things we forbid ourselves from thinking about," he answered. "And you, Dominus, are afraid of change."

Chapter 21

Hunter groaned, opening his eyes…and immediately regretted it. Sunlight assaulted him, making his eyeballs ache. He squeezed them shut, raising his arm to shield himself.

Then realized that he could…that his arms weren't tied behind his back anymore.

He frowned, opening one eye and squinting. He saw blue sky far above, a few puffy white clouds floating there. The sun shone down on him, baking his dark skin with its warm rays.

What the…?

Hunter opened his other eye, gradually acclimating to the brightness. He realized he was lying on his back, on a bed of leaves and dirt. To his left was a sheer vertical rock wall, and to his right, a rocky shore, beyond which there was a large lake, its waters shimmering in the sunlight. And two islands in the center of that lake, with a very familiar house on the larger of the two.

He sat up, grimacing as his back complained bitterly. It was sore, and stiff, just like the rest of his body. His muscles ached with every movement…and his butt was on fire. He groaned, turning until he was on his hands and knees, getting the weight off his sore butt cheeks. Then he stood up, looking around. He was at the bottom of the canyon, that much was clear. Although how he'd gotten here…and how long he'd been out for…was beyond him. He closed his eyes, struggling to remember what had happened. Images of the Seekers coming for him, galloping toward him on their huge black steeds. Then the world spinning around him…

Something struck him on the left butt cheek. Hard.

Hunter howled, leaping forward, then spinning around, cupping his ass protectively. Someone was standing before him; a woman wearing a suit of dark brown leather armor, bones embedded in the fabric. The facial bones of a human skull were sewn into the leather at her chest, and on her wrists were ivory bracelets. A long, narrow sword was sheathed at her left hip, a mace on her right. Her hair was short, not quite long enough to be a pixie cut.

She stood there, arching one eyebrow.

"Not sure I wanna know why your ass is so sore," she said, looking him up and down. "God, you look like shit."

He just stared at her, his mouth agape.

"Missed me?" she inquired with a smirk.

"Vi?" he managed to blurt out. He could hardly believe his eyes. It *was* Vi, exactly as he remembered her. Other than her hair being a bit longer.

"Last time I checked," she replied.

"But you're dead!" Hunter protested. He backed away from her. He had to be dreaming…this couldn't possibly be real! He pinched himself on the forearm. The pain was immediate, and very real.

"I can slap your ass again if you want," she offered, striding toward him. He backpedaled quickly, covering his still-throbbing butt cheeks.

"Don't!"

"Spoilsport," she grumbled. "How come they get to play with your ass and I don't?"

"Nobody played with my ass," he retorted, feeling his cheeks flush. Then he remembered that first night with the Lady, and his face burned even hotter.

"Mmm hmm," she replied. "So where's my shit?"

"You can't be real," he protested. "You're dead…I saw it with my own eyes!"

"Yeah, well, about that," she replied, putting her hands on her hips. "I'm even harder to kill than I used to be. Turns out that client of mine was holding out on us."

"What?"

"My client," she explained. "There's a reason they wanted that glowing Ironclad's head…and my client didn't give a damn about killing their leader."

"Hold on," Hunter interjected, his heart pounding in his chest. "Your head was smashed in." He looked down at her arm…her left arm…and saw that it was completely intact. He pointed at it. "Your arm was cut off!"

She's an imposter, he realized. *Sent to fool me.*

"So I've been told."

"You're an imposter," he accused, backing away from her, and eyeing the weapons at her hips. If he could just manage to steal one of them…

"Still telegraphing everything, I see," she observed, shaking her head. "Didn't I teach you *anything*?"

"Who are you?" Hunter demanded.

"As I was saying," she replied, "…my client lied to us. He wanted the Ironclad head because of what it could do for him."

"And what was that?"

"The power to heal."

Hunter stared at her uncomprehendingly.

"That big Ironclad with the glowing mane?" she continued. "The one I decapitated? Turns out it has the power to regenerate…to heal from almost any wound. My client had to have known this."

"Dominus?"

She frowned, giving him a look.

"And how did you figure *that* one out?"

"From Traven," he answered. "He told me before I killed him," he added. "Right after he killed you."

"Aww, how sweet," she quipped. "I'd say you shouldn't have, but the prick had it coming. Too bad," she added wistfully. "Kinda wanted to kill him myself."

Hunter wavered, crossing his arms over his chest. She looked and sounded just like Vi…and acted like her too. It *could* be her…or someone who found her body. Someone weak-willed who spent enough time with her body to transform *into* her.

"You were saying?" he prompted.

"The Ironclad leader – what we thought was the leader – could regenerate," she explained. "And after I escaped from their cave, I got a whole mouthful of his glowing goo. Remember what happens when you swallow something with a powerful will?"

"You absorb it quickly," Hunter answered grudgingly.

"Right," she agreed. "So after I got my head smashed in, Traven – and you – left me for dead. Except I wasn't."

"You're saying you regenerated."

"Yup."

Hunter eyed her suspiciously.

"How do I know you didn't just find Vi's body and become her?"

She smirked at him.

"Now aren't *you* paranoid," she replied. Then she nodded approvingly. "Good thought. Except if that were true, I'd be weak-willed, and you'd change me pretty quickly. Not to mention I'd be a pale imitation," she added. "And I wouldn't have my memories."

He considered this, then nodded grudgingly.

"Granted."

"Trust me," she continued, gesturing at herself. "I'm the original."

"Thought I was the Original," Hunter countered, unable to keep himself from smiling.

"You're *an* Original," she retorted. Hunter stared at her, hardly believing what was happening.

"It really *is* you," he realized. His heart soared suddenly, making him feel almost giddy. He rushed up to her, throwing his arms around her and squeezing her tight. To his amazement, she allowed this…and even hugged him back.

"You *did* miss me," she said with a smirk. She pushed him away then, holding him at arms' length. "Kinda missed you too."

"Kinda?"

"Not gonna lie, you were a pain in the ass to keep alive," she admitted. "Never would've gotten stabbed by that big bitch if it hadn't been for you."

"*What?*"

"You distracted me," she explained. "Always having to make sure you weren't doing something stupid to get yourself killed."

"I saved *you*," he retorted. "She would've killed you if I hadn't blocked her."

"Only had to intervene because you caused the situation in the first place."

"Uh huh," he replied. "Keep telling yourself that."

She grinned at him, throwing an arm around his shoulders and steering him until they were walking together, toward Vi's house in the distance. *Her* house. Hunter shook his head again, still unable to believe what was happening. That Vi was alive, that she was *here*, talking to him. It was surreal, like a dream come true.

"Aren't *you* sentimental," she observed, eyeing him sidelong. "Stop, you're going to make me cry."

"Do you even know how to cry?"

"They say I did when I was a baby," she answered. "Bet you cried like one when you thought I was dead."

"You're an ass."

"You did, didn't you?" she pressed, ruffling his hair. "Aww, my poor little baby boy."

"Kinda regretting you're alive now."

"Mm hmm," she murmured. "Now, you never answered my question."

"What?"

"Where's my shit?" she asked. He frowned at her. "My sword," she clarified. "And my mace." He grimaced, slowing down.

"I uh," he mumbled. "I lost them."

Both eyebrows went up.

"It's a long story," he admitted.

"I got time," she replied. "You do realize they're saturated with my will, right?" He nodded. "Luckily I don't radiate skills much," she continued. "Still, I want them back."

"Well, I can tell you who has them," Hunter offered.

"Go on."

"Lady Camilla," he revealed.

Vi stopped in her tracks, turning to face him. She gripped his cheeks between her thumb and fingers, staring at him silently with those large green eyes, until he was forced to lower his gaze. She released him then, turning away.

"Well fuck," she muttered under her breath.

* * *

Hunter stared at Vi's back, his eyebrows furrowing. He was taken aback by just how strong she looked; she was impressively muscular, her arms well-defined, her legs thick and powerful. Whatever had happened to her in these last few weeks, she hadn't changed a bit.

"What's wrong?" he asked.

She sighed, turning to face him.

"That," she replied, "is a long story kiddo." She smirked then. "She and I didn't part on the best of terms."

"Yeah, same here."

"How'd *you* meet her?" Vi inquired.

"Got a letter from her," he replied. "Addressed to you."

"Pretty sure it didn't come with a map," she said, eyeing him critically. "Finally figured out you can absorb memories?"

Hunter's mouth fell open.

"How…"

"Back at the carriage," she interjected. "The one your buddy got disarmed at."

"His name was Kris," Hunter stated. "And you're an asshole." Kris had been disarmed quite literally; an Ironclad had torn his arm off.

"You picked up one of the Seeker's memories there," she continued, ignoring him. "You just didn't know it."

"Why didn't you tell me?"

"Had to teach you the difference between your elbow and your asshole first."

"Ha ha."

"So you met Camilla," Vi stated, giving him a look he couldn't read. "What happened?"

Hunter sighed, rubbing the back of his head.

"That's a long story."

"Like I said," she replied, "…I got time."

Hunter hesitated, then told her what had happened…how he'd found the Lady's mansion, his mission to the Crypt of Zagamar. He tripped over the name, hearing the voices in his head starting their awful chanting, and shoved them away, focusing on telling the rest of the story. He described waking up in the Lady's mansion, and then everything else that had happened. Almost everything, that is…he left out the part where they'd slept together voluntarily…and involuntarily. Vi'd given him plenty of flak about his problems with Trixie; he hardly wanted to give her yet another reason to talk shit about him. When he was done, Vi turned away from him, staring off into the distance for a long while.

"What?" he asked. She sighed.

"That's…a lot," she confessed. Then she turned to him. "You're in deep shit, Hunter."

"Tell me about it," he grumbled. "That bitch is crazy."

"Only about certain things," Vi replied. "You're lucky she didn't decide to fuck you."

Hunter grimaced, and Vi's eyebrow rose.

"Or did she?" she continued. She broke out into a grin, punching him in the shoulder…and knocking him back a few steps. "Hunter got laid!"

"I don't wanna talk about it," he grumbled, rubbing his shoulder.

"Bet she blew your goddamn mind," Vi ventured. Then her grin broadened. "And your…"

"I *don't* want to talk about it," he interrupted, blushing furiously.

"Now I know why your ass is so sore."

"Enough!" he blurted out angrily.

"Butt stuff can feel good you know," she continued. "No shame in that."

"That's not what I…" he began, then grit his teeth, throwing up his hands. "You know what? Forget about it."

"*Anyway*," Vi stated, "I wasn't talking about her. Camilla we can handle. But she screwed you over big time," she added. "She knew you'd do anything to avenge me, and took advantage of that. You're lucky you're an Original…and that you haven't been here that long."

"Why's that?"

"You're still made of matter from your world," she answered. "At least most of you is. If anyone else had drank from that skull, they would've already been turned into Zagamar himself."

Hunter grimaced at the name, hearing the voices chanting again.

Za-ga-mar!

"I'm surprised you weren't changed," Vi continued. "Camilla was hoping you would, I guarantee you that. She probably wanted to keep you to see if you'd start to change once more of your body converted to this world."

"Wait, what?"

"Zagamar's will is inside of you," she explained. "His very flesh is now incorporated into yours. It's fine when you eat the flesh of weak-willed animals and plants, but if you consume a Legend…"

"You're saying that when my…matter is converted to this world's matter, his will might start changing me?" Hunter asked, a chill running down his spine. Vi hesitated, then nodded.

"Afraid so, kiddo."

Hunter stared at her, swallowing in a suddenly dry throat. The thought of being corrupted from the inside, of having his soul taken from him bit by bit, until he was someone else entirely…

"The good news is," Vi stated, breaking his train of thought, "…you haven't seemed to change at all. It's possible that none of Zagamar's flesh was incorporated into yours…or that he wasn't a Legend at all, and his will is too weak to conquer yours."

Hunter grimaced.

"And what if I *have* changed?" he asked. Vi arched one eyebrow.

"Have you?"

He took a deep breath in, then let it out. Vi stepped forward, putting a hand on his shoulder.

"Tell me," she insisted.

"It's…hard to explain," he confessed. "After I drank from Za…from his skull, I had these flashbacks. Except they weren't my memories."

"They were his."

"Right," he agreed. He described the visions he'd seen, the armies chanting the Legend's name. Towns reduced to rubble.

"If that's all, then you'll gain more memories with time," Vi reasoned. "But nothing else…and you'll keep your own memories."

"Yeah, well," Hunter muttered. "About that."

"Go on."

He described everything he'd experienced in the crypt after drinking from the skull. The insatiable hunger, the slowing of time. The thoughts racing in his head, moving so quickly and precisely that it made his own thoughts seem vague and sluggish in comparison. Then he described how he'd escaped…how it'd happened to him again, allowing him to flee from the Lady's mansion with ease. When he was done, he felt drained…and felt as if a weight had been lifted from his shoulders.

Vi listened the whole time without interrupting, and when he was done, she dropped her hand from his shoulder. She looked troubled.

"What're you thinking?" Hunter asked. She shook her head, putting her hands on her hips.

"I need time to figure this out," she admitted. "*We* need time. You're saying this happened to you after you heard his name?"

"Yeah," he confirmed. "The second time anyway. The Lady kept saying his name, and then I started to hear the chanting."

"And then it was like you became him?"

"Sort of," Hunter answered. "Not completely. I mean, I wasn't exactly *me*, but I was aware of what was going on. It's hard to explain."

"Hmm," Vi murmured, rubbing her chin with one hand. "That might explain the seizures."

"How's that?"

"If Zagamar's will is only affecting parts of your brain – those that have been replaced by the matter of this world, or that are weak-willed enough to be changed – then it's no wonder your brain would malfunction."

"Causing the seizures," Hunter realized. She nodded.

"Right."

"But I didn't have any seizures after the second time," he countered. After he'd relaxed in the river by the mansion, he'd returned to his normal self. Starved and exhausted, but otherwise himself.

"So your two minds – his and yours – have learned to co-exist," she deduced. "Or maybe you just didn't push it as far this time."

"Maybe."

"The question is," she continued, "...what will happen as more of your Original matter is gradually replaced by this world's." She sighed. "If this guy's will is Legendary, then he's going to take over, day by day."

"I don't want to become anyone else," he protested. She sighed again.

"I know Hunter," she replied. "Believe me, I don't want you to be anyone but you either." She gave him a weak smile. "I'm probably the first person to tell you this, but I kinda like you the way you are."

"Can't I stop it?" Hunter pressed, ignoring her remark.

"That depends," she answered. "If this guy's a Legend, maybe not."

"There *has* to be a way," Hunter pressed, his heart pounding in his chest. Panic rose within him, the thought of slowly losing who he was...his very soul...terrifying him.

"Calm down," Vi stated, putting a hand on his shoulder. And despite himself, he *did* calm down, more from her influence than his own will. "We don't even know if this guy's really a Legend," she added. "Maybe he's not, and you'll be fine."

"But what if he is?" Hunter asked. Vi sighed.

"Then the only way you'll stop him from taking over," she replied, "...is if your will is Legendary, like your mother's."

CHAPTER 22

Hunter sat by the campfire near Vi's house, tearing into the bird Vi had shot down not a half-hour ago. It was a bit gamey, like duck, but after days of barely eating he was hardly going to complain. Hunger did indeed make the best spice. He glanced up, realizing that Vi was staring at him.

"Damn kid," she said, shaking her head. "When's the last time you ate something?"

"Couple days ago," Hunter answered. He glanced at the rest of the bird's roasted carcass, eyeing it greedily.

"Take the whole thing," Vi offered. "Can't have you bitching about how hungry you are during our trip."

Hunter obliged, chowing down until there was nothing left. Then he sighed contently, stifling a yawn. It was early afternoon, the sun still shining overhead, but he was exhausted. He hadn't slept much since escaping the Lady's mansion, after all. Then he frowned.

"Wait, what trip?" he asked.

"Through the Fringe," she answered. "Then into the deep forest."

"Why?" he pressed. "I just got here."

"Yeah, well," Vi replied, standing up. "Much as I'd like to relive old times, I've got a new job to do."

"A job?"

"Yep," Vi confirmed. "Got a new client now."

"Didn't you like, die a few weeks ago?" Hunter retorted. "How could you have gotten a new client?" She smirked.

"You got one," she reminded him. He grimaced.

"Touché."

"We should get going soon," she opined. "I'll get you some weapons and a bow. And some armor"

"Thanks," Hunter replied, standing up, then watching as she went into her house, then returned with a longsword and a bow. She handed these to him, then retrieved a quiver filled with arrows for him, and a pack. Then she went back inside, retrieving a metal breastplate. He took these, putting them on. "You got a helmet?" he asked.

"Probably," Vi answered. "Why?"

"Might protect me from absorbing memories," Hunter ventured. Vi shrugged, going back into her house, then returning with a simple metal helmet. He put it on. "How do I look?" he asked.

"Scrawny," she replied. "And ugly. You haven't changed a bit."

"So what's this job, anyway?" he asked, ignoring her. She pointed at him.

"You are."

Hunter stared at her.

"Excuse me?"

"You're the job," Vi repeated. When he continued to stare at her uncomprehendingly, she smirked. "My client wants you, so I'm going to bring you to them."

"Who wants me?"

"A Seeker doesn't reveal their clients," Vi reminded him. "Come on," she added, walking toward the long wooden bridge leading to the shore of the lake. Hunter hesitated, then followed behind her.

"What does this client want with me?"

"Can't say," she answered. Hunter fought down a surge of annoyance.

"Because you don't know, or won't say?" he pressed.

"Maybe I just like keeping you in suspense," she replied. And though he couldn't see her face – she was walking single-file ahead of him on the bridge – he *knew* she was smirking. And that she wasn't going to tell him, no matter how many times he asked.

"What about those Seekers?" he asked. "The Lady's Seekers. There could be more of them out there."

"Ooo, scary," she replied, her boots *thumping* on the wooden planks of the bridge. Hunter sighed, following her to the end of it, then starting up the long spiraling path along the canyon wall. He yawned, feeling utterly exhausted.

"I don't know how long I'll be able to hike for," he admitted. "I haven't slept much the last few days."

"Aww."

"You can carry me when I pass out then," he grumbled.

"Or I could leave you for the Lady's Seekers."

"Ha ha."

"We'll make camp soon enough," she promised.

After a few minutes, they reached the top of the canyon, the tree line of the Fringe ahead. Visions of the Seekers on their huge steeds came to him, of them battling the Ironclad that had attacked them. Hunter looked around for their corpses, but there were none.

"Where'd all the corpses go?"

"Hmm?"

"The Seekers," he explained. "And an Ironclad. Their corpses were right around here."

"Ironclad must have gotten them," Vi answered. "Either that or some more Seekers dragged the bodies away. They wouldn't want their bodies to fall into anyone else's hands."

"Why not?"

"Think about it," Vi replied. "The Lady's Seekers are highly-trained and strong-willed. The last thing she'd want is for some asshole from the Guild of Seekers to get ahold of the bodies and extract their abilities."

"Ah, right."

"Bodies are valuable," Vi continued. "Even the Ironclad take the bodies of their victims with them."

"But the Guild of Seekers didn't take *your* body," he countered. "You're the best fighter they've ever seen."

"I don't radiate skills well," she countered. "I absorb them, but don't transmit them much. Besides," she added, "…Traven and that other prick couldn't have gotten me up the ladder to the carriage. I'm sure the guild – and Dominus – sent people after my body, but by that time I was already gone."

"Oh," Hunter replied. Then he frowned. "Wait, say I kill someone with a weak will," he proposed. "If I stay near the body, will it start to look like me?"

"No," Vi answered. "Once something is dead, it acts like an inanimate object. So a dead body will still absorb and transmit traits. But like a rock, it won't change appearance."

"Gotcha."

They continued into the forest, Vi leading the way and Hunter trailing behind. She set a quick pace, as usual, but after weeks of daily hiking and training, Hunter found he didn't have quite as hard a time keeping up with her. It still wasn't easy – she was far more conditioned than him – but he was able to keep up with a little less effort. They fell into a comfortable silence, weaving around the densely-growing trees. Hunter found himself mulling over what Vi had said. That she'd gotten another client, and that *he* was her job.

She could be selling me out, he thought darkly. *There's got to be a bounty on my head. Maybe she's using me to get back into Dominus's good graces.*

He blinked, realizing that he was feeling a familiar irritation…one he'd felt the first time he'd gone into the Fringe, with Sukri and Gammon and Kris. The forest was affecting his mind, making him think bad thoughts. It hated humans after all…and made anyone who traveled through share that hatred.

He divorced himself from his feelings, stepping aside mentally, as if they were happening to someone else. It worked; although he still felt the anger, he did not have the urge to act on it, or to feed it. He thought back to Master Thorius then, his old teacher at the Guild of Seekers. About how the man had been able to hold the crystal sphere that had made Hunter practically homicidal. Not because Thorius hadn't felt the same emotion – he had – but because of his self-control.

I'm getting better, Hunter realized.

He found that he'd started to trail behind, and sped up, walking a few feet behind her.

"So," he stated, "…if someone managed to kill you and took your body, they wouldn't be able to get your skills?"

"You're awfully interested in me dying," she observed.

"Just a hypothetical."

"They'd get some," Vi admitted. "But it'd take a while. And they'd never be as good as me," she added. "My skills aren't just reflexes, remember?"

"I remember."

"We'll have to see how your skills are doing," she stated. "Probably gone to shit after you left me to die."

"We'll see about that."

"Ooo," Vi murmured. "Hunter didn't take the bait!" She glanced back at him. "I almost miss your little temper. It was so cute."

"You're the one who told me to reign it in," he retorted.

"Yeah, but you're *boring* now."

"Oh right," he shot back, panting a little. "I barely escape the Ironclad, have my best friend die on me, kill her murderer, kill a few more Seekers while I'm at it, then meet a psychopathic bitch who tricks me into being possessed by some asshole thousands of years old…" he stated, "…and *I'm* boring."

"It's not what you've done that's boring," she explained. "It's your personality."

"Not sure why I missed you so much when I thought you were dead."

"Because I'm not boring," she replied, slowing down until she was walking at his side. She grinned, throwing an arm around his shoulders and squeezing them. He smiled back grudgingly, putting an arm around her waist.

"I'll give you that one," he conceded. He hesitated, then gave her a squeeze. "I missed you," he admitted. "A lot."

"I missed you too kiddo," she replied. Then she held his gaze for a long moment without saying anything.

"What?" he asked.

"You aren't worthless, Hunter," she stated. He blinked.

"Huh?"

"You're not worthless," she repeated.

"I never said…"

"I've been feeling it around you," she interjected. "You're still beating the shit out of yourself for what happened to me…and to your mother."

Hunter said nothing, lowering his gaze to his feet.

"Just because you did something bad doesn't make you worthless," she continued. "Even if it was something *really* bad. No one is irredeemable, kiddo. The only way your life is worthless is if you decided that it is."

Hunter blinked away sudden tears, rubbing his eyes with the back of his sleeve. He felt her squeeze him.

"You nearly got yourself killed, Hunter," Vi continued. "You fell right into Camilla's trap because you stopped valuing your own life. Don't do it again."

He nodded silently.

She separated from him then, increasing her pace through the woods. He struggled to keep up, his legs starting to ache.

"Hey," he called after her. "Why'd you speed up?"

"Don't want you stealing all my memories," she answered, glancing back at him, flashing him a smirk. "Girl's gotta have her secrets you know."

"Ah," he muttered. "Forgot about that."

He followed after her, feeling disappointed. It was silly to take it personally, but he couldn't help but feel a little rejected. Still, she had a point. If he spent too much time close to her, he might very well absorb her memories. He already had a hard enough time sorting out which memories were his and which were not; absorbing more would only make things that much more confusing.

Perhaps this was for the best.

* * *

By the time they stopped to make camp in a small clearing in the forest, the sun was kissing the horizon, sending the last of its rays through the tree branches, casting long shadows over the thick tufts of grass on the forest floor. Hunter was utterly exhausted; Vi's suggestion that she might let him sleep earlier turned out to be lie, as she'd forced him in a veritable death march through the Fringe. They'd stopped only to eat and drink. Despite hours of hiking, Vi had shown no signs of slowing or tiring, as usual. Once again, Hunter felt inadequate. Not quite as inadequate as he had a few weeks ago, but emasculated nonetheless. She'd even been so cruel as to force him to gather wood for a fire, and to start that fire. By the time he'd done so, his eyelids were so heavy that he'd fallen asleep more than once while still sitting up.

"All right," Vi said at last, as she placed large rocks around the perimeter of the fire. A trick she'd taught him, so that the rocks would soak up the heat of the flames, then radiate heat for them long after the fire had gone out. "Go to bed."

"Mmm," Hunter mumbled, laying down on his side and resting his head on the pack she'd given him. He closed his eyes at last, feeling sleep tugging at him, inviting him into its comfy embrace. Still, he felt his mind churning, thoughts spilling over themselves in a rush to be considered. It was enough to hold sleep at bay, much to his irritation.

"I'll keep a lookout," Vi reassured. "You'll take over in a few hours."

"Can't wait," Hunter grumbled. He gave a heavy sigh, trying to get comfortable on the hard ground.

"What's wrong?" Vi asked. "Got used to Camilla's comfy bed?" Hunter opened his eyes, glaring at her…which only made her grin. "Bet she put you to sleep real good every night."

"Do you ever shut up?" Hunter groused.

"God, what I wouldn't give to have your power," she mused. "I *have* to know what she did to you."

"You're an evil bitch sometimes, you know that?"

"I just like seeing you in pain," Vi explained. "I wanna know how she hurt you so bad. Then I could do it to you myself."

"You wouldn't like what she did to me," Hunter mumbled.

"I liked what she did to *me*," Vi retorted. Hunter frowned, staring at her.

"Wait," he stated, perking up a little. "You guys…?"

"*Oh* yeah," Vi answered. Hunter stared at her.

"Wow," he muttered. He sat up then, and Vi smirked.

"Not so sleepy anymore, huh?"

"I thought she was your client," Hunter said. Vi shrugged.

"She was," she replied. "Still is. Camilla's a go-between for the Kingdom of the Deep…and less scrupulous clients in Tykus. The Kingdom of the Deep is the single largest exporter of wild artifacts in the known world. If you want to get to them, the best way is through her."

"Huh."

"They even provide her with Seekers," Vi continued. "The ones who tried murdering your ass."

"They weren't going to kill me," Hunter corrected. "Lady Camilla wants me alive."

"Bet she does," Vi agreed. "You're the greatest find she'll ever have. Seekers have been trying to get into the Crypt of Zagamar for thousands of years."

"Please don't say that name," Hunter pleaded.

"Why not?"

"It makes me start hearing the chanting," he explained. "If it gets too bad, I go into that…whatever it is. That state."

"Where he takes over?"

"Yeah," he confirmed. "And I hate it."

"Why?"

"Because it sucks," he answered. "I get hungry like you wouldn't believe, and I feel like shit afterward. And it's weird. I just don't like it."

"All right," she agreed. "I'll try not to say Zagamar anymore."

"I hate you."

"Anyway," she continued, "...people have been trying to get into his Crypt since forever. There's lots of crypts in the world, most of them for Legends...or people who fancied themselves Legends. Almost all of them have been looted, but not Zagamar's."

"Stop it," he pleaded. "Seriously."

"Only one person managed to go in the outer portion of the crypt and survive," Vi continued, ignoring him. "A guy named Jakar."

"The Lady told me about that," Hunter admitted.

"Yeah, well I bet she didn't tell you everything," Vi retorted. "Jakar was a Seeker before the Guild of Seekers even existed. He was an Original too. A lesser lord hired him to go into the crypt, promising him he'd be rich if he managed to find the Ossae they assumed was inside."

"And he didn't make it."

"No, he didn't," Vi agreed. "But he managed to steal an artifact – a medallion – from the crypt and bring it back to the kingdom. Something no one had ever done before. Everyone else who'd even gone close to the crypt had killed themselves."

"Not surprised," he said, recalling how he'd nearly sawed into his own skull with Vi's sword.

"Jakar brought it back," she continued, "...but the lord refused to pay him much for the medallion, because it wasn't the Ossae. He went nuts, became obsessed with the Deep."

"Heard that too."

"Eventually his son got the medallion," she stated, "...and founded the Guild of Seekers."

"Tell me something I don't know," he mumbled irritably.

"You know those medallions you were given when you started at the guild?" she asked. Hunter nodded. "They're all weaker versions of that medallion."

"Wait, what?" he blurted out, sitting up straighter.

"That's right," she replied. "You know what the guild calls Jakar?"

"What?"

"The Founder," she answered. "They think of Zagamar as the true founder of the guild, though. That his will transformed Jakar and Jakar's son through the medallion. That his will demanded the creation of the guild."

Hunter stared at her silently, a chill running through him.

"And you know who has Zagamar's medallion now?" she pressed.

He shook his head.

"High Seeker Zeno," she answered. "The leader of the Guild of Seekers."

CHAPTER 23

Sukri opened her eyes.

She was lying on her back on something soft yet firm, staring up at a ceiling high above. It was pure white, this ceiling, with blood-red wooden beams spanning it. She rubbed her eyes, feeling crust on her eyelids, then looked down at herself. She was lying on a large bed, a red sheet covering her body.

Her naked body, she realized.

She tried to sit up, and felt a sharp pain in her forearms. There were bandages wrapped around both of them, she found. She stared at them, utterly confused.

Where am I?

The room she was in was relatively large, with walls similar in design to the ceiling. It was quite ornate, and clean, with tasteful if sparse furnishings. She scanned the room, looking right, then left…and nearly jumped.

A woman was sitting in a chair beside her bed.

"Who the hell are you?" Sukri blurted out. The woman – Sukri's age, it appeared, and wearing a white dress – looked up from her knitting, nearly jumping out of her own skin.

"Oh!" she exclaimed, putting a hand to her chest. "You're awake!"

"No shit," Sukri grumbled. "Who are you?" she repeated. "And where the hell am I?"

"I'm Jenna," she answered. "Your nurse. And you're in the mansion of the Lady Camilla."

Sukri stared at Jenna, taking a moment to process what she'd said. Her brain was foggy, her thoughts sluggish.

The Lady!

She swore, bolting upright, ignoring the pain in her arms. The sheet fell from her chest, and she pulled it to her bosom quickly.

"Wait," Jenna exclaimed, rising from her chair and touching Sukri's shoulder. "You have to rest!"

"What the hell happened to me?" Sukri demanded. She couldn't remember how she'd gotten here…or what had happened after…

She swallowed past a sudden lump in her throat, remembering Gammon. Remembering what had happened to him.

Shit.

"It's the anesthesia," Jenna explained, gently pushing Sukri back down on the bed. Sukri let her, feeling suddenly exhausted. She stared at the ceiling, picturing the man with the mask. The one with the silver eyes. A chill ran through her.

The door on the opposite end of the room opened suddenly, an older-appearing man wearing red robes coming through. He was impressively portly, and had glasses with thick black rims magnifying his eyes like fishbowls. He waddled up to the front of Sukri's bed, his eyebrows rising in surprise.

"She's awake," he proclaimed. He gave Jenna a stern look. "You should have summoned me," he chided.

"She only just awoke, Dr. Phelbus," Jenna explained.

"Yes, well," Phelbus muttered, turning his attention to Sukri. He adjusted his glasses. "How has she recovered from the surgery? Any nausea or psychosis?"

"No doctor."

"Excellent," he exclaimed, clearly pleased. "An unfortunate side-effect of the extract, psychosis," he stated. "Of course we couldn't have restrained her wrists, as that would have endangered our surgical repairs. My dosage calculations were clearly correct."

"Just so, Dr. Phelbus," Jenna agreed.

Dr. Phelbus walked up to the side of Sukri's bed, leaning down to peer at her bandages. He reached out to grab her arm, and she yanked it away.

"Back off," she growled.

"She seems irritable," Dr. Phelbus observed. "Perhaps a late effect of the anesthesia," he proposed. "Or simply a matter of hunger."

"*She's* right here asshole," Sukri shot back.

"Hmm," Phelbus replied. "Yes, well, I need to assess your motor functions." He gestured at her hands. "Extend your fingers please."

Sukri frowned, then did as he asked, realizing that she *could* extend her fingers. She remembered the deep gashes in her forearms, how she couldn't open her hands to grab her sword.

"Excellent," the doctor exclaimed, clearly pleased. "The surgery was a success."

"What did you do?" Sukri asked.

"The sinews flexing your fingers were completely severed," Phelbus explained. "I reconnected them."

Sukri looked down at her hands, moving her fingers experimentally.

"Thanks," she mumbled.

"Her recovery should be uneventful," he explained to Jenna. "Barring infection, of course. Notify me immediately if you observe any redness or abnormal seeping of the incisions."

"Yes Doctor."

The door opened again, and this time a woman entered. A tall woman wearing a long, blood-red dress, her pale legs exposed by slits rising to her upper thighs. She wore a red corset studded with rubies, above which her considerable bosom practically spilled out of the deep V-cut in her bodice.

She was, in a word, gorgeous.

"Doctor Phelbus," she greeted, her eyes going from the plump doctor to Sukri. "I trust the operation was a success?"

"Yes, my Lady," he answered, bowing before her. Someone else strode into the room behind the Lady; a man in a red and black uniform, wearing an identically-colored mask. A man with silver eyes.

Sukri's blood went cold.

"How are you feeling?" the Lady asked her. Sukri ignored the question, glaring at the masked man. The Lady glanced back at the man, then returned her gaze to Sukri. "Ah, my apologies," she stated. "Leave us, Dio."

The masked man bowed sharply, leaving at once.

"I understand your anger," the Lady stated, stepping gracefully up to the foot of Sukri's bed. "I'm sorry for the loss of your friend."

"Go to hell," Sukri spat.

"What is your name?" the Lady asked.

"I said…"

"Don't forget that *you're* the one who attacked *me,*" the Lady reminded her. "Your guild struck without provocation, and I was well within my rights to defend myself."

"You kidnapped Hunter," Sukri retorted. "The guild sent us to save him."

"And I already told you they lied," the Lady retorted. She frowned then. "How do you know him?"

"We're friends," Sukri answered. "We were initiates of the guild together."

"I see," the Lady murmured. "And you're an apprentice?"

"Yeah."

"I thought so," the Lady replied. "Well, Hunter asked to work for me as an independent Seeker, and I agreed."

"Bullshit."

"In fact," the Lady continued, ignoring Sukri's comment, "…he came to me for help in avenging the death of his friend Vi."

Sukri's eyes widened in surprise. Vi had been Hunter's mentor, and a damn good Seeker.

"She's dead?"

"Tragically, yes," the Lady confirmed. She sighed. "Vi worked for me on occasion," she admitted. "And she was a good friend. More than a friend." Her expression darkened, and Sukri felt a sudden, smoldering anger come from her. "Your guild betrayed her…and Hunter. They killed her, and tried to kill Hunter, but he managed to escape."

Sukri took a moment to process this, then frowned, recalling how Hunter had been running when she'd first seen him during the raid on the mansion.

"So why was Hunter trying to escape this place?" she demanded.

"My dear," the Lady replied, "…he wasn't trying to escape *me*, he was trying to escape *you*."

"What?"

"Your guild sent you to kidnap him," she explained. "He knew the guild wanted him captured…or dead."

Sukri stared at the Lady mutely, replaying what had happened in her mind. She remembered how he'd ignored her when she'd called out to him, how he'd attacked her, shoving her out of the window. How he'd run from her and the other Seekers.

"But…"

"Why would the Guild of Seekers want Hunter?" the Lady asked. Sukri hesitated, then shrugged.

"I don't know," she confessed. He'd been disqualified from the guild, after all. They certainly hadn't wanted him as a Seeker. So why *did* they go after him?

"Because Hunter killed some of their Seekers," the Lady explained. "And he became an independent Seeker. The guild hates competition…which is why they killed Vi."

"They didn't order me to kill him," she protested.

"Naturally," the Lady replied. "They knew you were close to him. Of course they made sure to appeal to your desire to help him." She came to one side of the bed, opposite Dr. Phelbus. "Hunter came to me because he wanted to become powerful enough to get revenge on the guild," she revealed. "He didn't want to be an ordinary Seeker," she added. "He wanted to become a Seeker of Legends."

"Legends?"

"And he succeeded," the Lady continued. "He managed to recover the most powerful Ossae ever known. An Ossae the Guild of Seekers has been coveting ever since they were founded centuries ago." Her expression turned grim. "And now they will stop at nothing to find him…and to recover what he took."

"Okay," Sukri conceded. "I'm a Seeker…why keep me alive?"

The Lady smiled, gazing at Sukri…at her body, through the thin fabric of the sheet covering her.

"Dio knows I enjoy…beautiful things," she answered. "And you're a powerful Empath, which makes you valuable. And since you're a friend of Hunter's, that means we both want the same thing…to protect him."

"Oh yeah?" Sukri replied. "And why would *you* give a shit about him?"

"He's my Seeker," the Lady answered. "And he possesses the will of a Legend. A Legend I've spent my life studying."

"Who?"

"Zagamar."

"Never heard of him," Sukri stated. The Lady smirked.

"I wouldn't expect you to have," she replied. "He's old…older than the kingdom. In any case, Hunter consumed Zagamar's flesh, and now he carries the Legend's will within him. The guild wants him dead, as does the kingdom. And the Ironclad."

She reached down, putting a hand on Sukri's shoulder. Sukri allowed this, even though the woman's touch made her skin crawl. She sensed the Lady's trepidation, a sudden, urgent fear.

I'm an Empath, Sukri reminded herself. *I can use this woman's emotions against her.*

"Hunter is in grave danger," the Lady warned. "And right now, I'm the only one powerful enough to save him."

"So what do you want from me?" Sukri pressed.

"You'll see soon enough," she answered.

* * *

Dominus shifted his weight in his chair, leaning his elbows on a long table constructed entirely of human bones. The other five dukes were seated around the table, and at one end sat King Tykus. They'd convened here, in the Hall of Tykus. A small room located in the basement of the Acropolis, there was no other room quite like it. The floor was made of a thick block of polished, transparent crystal, within which countless human skulls – the skulls of their ancestors – had been suspended. Walls of unpolished gray stone surrounded them, yet more bones embedded within. Four stone pillars rose at each corner of the room, supporting the ceiling, which was identical to the floor. Hundreds of empty eye-sockets stared down at them from above, the noblest of their ancestors keeping watch on their progeny.

Dominus felt a familiar sense of comfort here, knowing that he was doing what countless generations had done before, meeting in this room. Knowing that he was faithfully continuing the rituals that had been created by the great men of the past, keeping this last bastion of humanity – of the greatest minds that had ever existed – alive. What they were doing now was sacred, a duty entrusted to them by the ancients.

"Duke Mezgar has been telling me about these creatures living past the Fringe," Tykus stated, his gaze sweeping over the assembled dukes. "The Ironclad, I believe you call them?"

"Yes sire," Mezgar confirmed. "They've attacked the kingdom and our military outpost in the Deadlands on several occasions," he added. "And we have reason to believe they attacked Duke Dominus's soldiers as well. They've also killed several Seekers."

"I see," Tykus replied. He steepled his hands in front of him. "Why?"

"Excuse me?" Mezgar asked, clearly taken aback.

"Why do they attack us?"

"They're beasts," Ratheburg offered. "Corrupted by the hatred of the Fringe."

"So I've heard," Tykus replied. He frowned then. "The forest did not hate humans in my time, you know."

"So I've read sire," Dominus stated. Tykus glanced at him.

"I'm sure you have," he agreed. "Yours was a family that always valued reading." Dominus nodded; it was true. He read every day that he could. But even he was nowhere near the voracious reader that Tykus was; the king was known to read several books a day, spending nearly half his waking hours immersed in literature. And in the ninety-seven years of his original life, he'd doubtless read more books than anyone at this table…indeed, more than any man alive. Books that didn't exist anymore, lost to the millennia.

King Tykus sighed.

"You've read a great deal," he stated, "…but I question how much of it you understand."

"Sire?"

"My father was a great man," Tykus continued. "A born leader. Thoughtful, considerate. He would always tell me to find the story behind the story."

"I don't understand," Dominus admitted.

"In every book," Tykus explained, "…there are the words on the page…the conversation the author is having with you. A conversation he can have well beyond the grave." He paused for a moment. "The words tell a story, but there is another story behind those words. The story of *why* the book was written. Of why each word was placed the way it was, the context in which it was written."

"I believe you mean subtext, sire," Dominus offered. Tykus smirked.

"A pithy word," he replied. "I've spent the last week devouring the histories of this kingdom," he continued. "I'm well aware of the nature of the Fringe, as you call it…and why it hates you so much."

"Nature is corrupt," Mezgar piped in. "It hates humanity itself."

"My father taught me another important lesson," Tykus replied, turning to Mezgar. "He'd tell me that whenever I felt the need to place blame for something, to first look in the mirror…and that more often than not, I would find the culprit I was looking for."

"Are you suggesting that *we* are to blame for the Fringe hating us sire?" Ratheburg inquired.

"But of course," the king answered.

"But…"

"For generations," Tykus interrupted, "…you've hunted its creatures, stripped its forest of trees for lumber, and expanded the kingdom at the expense of the creatures that lived there." He drummed his fingers on the tabletop. "The fear and hatred these creatures feel toward us is well-deserved, absorbed by the very earth itself over thousands of years."

"We cannot avoid…" another duke began, but Tykus cut him off with a gesture.

"You needn't be defensive," he interjected. "After all," he added with a wry smirk, "…I'm as complicit as you are in this."

This seemed to settle the duke. King Tykus waited, but no other dukes attempted to speak, quite aware that it was not their time to do so. King Tykus was back, with a vitality they'd all forgotten – or never realized – he'd had.

Tykus smiled, leaning back in his chair.

"This is simple cause and effect, gentlemen. You and your ancestors, and my predecessors, created this problem. And now it is *my* problem."

The dukes sat there wordlessly, all eyes on the king.

"The Ironclad may hate us because of the Fringe," Tykus continued. "Or they may hate us for another reason. Or they may not hate us at all. We cannot pretend that we understand their motives without getting to know them. No relationship can begin or survive without communication."

"Are you proposing we initiate a dialogue?" Ratheburg inquired incredulously. "The beasts cannot speak…and they attack us on sight!"

"I've heard that one of them does speak," Tykus corrected. Dominus grimaced, realizing that the king was correct. The new Ironclad…whose head still lay hidden in his most secret of vaults…had been reported to be capable of speech. He was surprised that, after only a week of being fully himself, Tykus already knew of this. The man did not waste any time…and he was a veritable sponge for information.

"An anomaly," Dominus declared. "And according to the Guild of Seekers, it is dead."

"Nevertheless," Tykus stated, "…it speaks to a level of intelligence. The organs of speech merely convey vibrations, after all; the capacity to speak begins in the mind. They are humanoid, are they not?"

"Barely," Ratheburg grumbled. Tykus turned to him, raising an eyebrow.

"You want to diminish them," he observed. "Why?"

Ratheburg hesitated, choosing his words carefully.

"They have killed our men," he answered at last.

"You hate your enemy," Tykus concluded. "A desirable emotion in a soldier – we need them to kill – but I daresay it's a poor one in a duke. Your role is to make decisions, not to make corpses." He glanced at the other dukes. "Who at this table has made good decisions under the power of negative emotions?"

No one spoke up.

"I was married for seventy years, which – considering I was a Legend – was quite a feat," Tykus stated, his eyes twinkling. "And I can tell you that nearly every bad decision I made in that relationship was under the influence of anger, or some other negative emotion." He smiled. "How much of my own suffering I could have avoided if I'd acted only when I was calm!"

"But about the Ironclad…" Ratheburg pressed.

"Yes, the Ironclad," Tykus stated. "Where do they come from?"

"Beyond the Fringe," Dominus answered. "They live in caves."

"I meant it in a more existential way," Tykus clarified. "How did they come to be?"

The room was silent.

"My predecessor suspected he knew the answer," Tykus revealed. Dominus frowned; each iteration of Tykus had kept a diary available only to each new incarnation of the king. Each king began his reign armed with only the memories of his original life. Thousands of years of Tykus's thoughts had been recorded, and each Tykus began their resurrection by reading these diaries.

It was troubling that the previous Tykus had kept such a realization from the dukes.

"You disapprove, Dominus," Tykus observed. Dominus grimaced. Tykus was ever observant.

"If your predecessor had knowledge of the Ironclad that could have helped us," Dominus stated carefully, "…I would have hoped he'd have shared it."

"Clearly I didn't for a reason," Tykus countered. "Just as I forbid a full-out war against them for a reason." He eyed Dominus with an expression Dominus couldn't read. "Do you understand why I entrusted you to have our great wall built around the city?"

"To keep out the Ironclad," Dominus answered. "And the remainder of the insurgents."

"And the Original," Tykus added. "Although I suspect they would have called themselves freedom fighters, or revolutionaries." He sighed then. "The Original fought against injustice, Dominus. She was an Original, like me. She was a Legend, like me."

"My liege…"

"She was," Tykus insisted. "We may fool the populace with our propaganda," he added, his tone deceptively mild. "But I will not tolerate self-deception in my dukes."

Dominus bowed his head.

"My apologies, your Highness."

"I can tell you from personal experience that those who come from my world cannot understand the true horror of this one," Tykus declared. "There is wisdom in what I have done here, in the kingdom I created…and that you maintain. What we have is at once terrible and great, a system borne of necessity. An imperfect solution to an unsolvable problem."

No one dared say anything.

"This Original," Tykus continued, "…did not have the time to acquire my wisdom. Her actions were just, in her eyes. She fought for the weak-willed, the oppressed. She fought for the right of her people to be different."

"As you say, my liege," Ratheburg mumbled.

"In my world," Tykus explained, "…these qualities would have made her a hero. We would have sung songs glorifying her for generations. But in this world," he added, "…it made her a fool."

"My apologies, your Grace," Mezgar interjected. "But why are we discussing the black bitch?"

"Hold your tongue!" Tykus snapped, his ice-blue eyes boring into Mezgar's. The duke's jaw snapped shut with a *click*, and he stared back at Tykus, his face turning deathly pale. Tykus held the stare, not so much as blinking. "Words have power," he stated icily. "Propaganda is a feast to be gobbled up by fools, not my dukes. Do not make me remind you again."

Mezgar's lower lip trembled, and he lowered his gaze to the tabletop.

"Yes my liege," he murmured, his voice barely audible.

Dominus glanced at Mezgar, then at Tykus. The old king had been quieter in his old age, more withdrawn. Dominus's father had mentioned that the iterations of Tykus often became this way after decades of rule. He couldn't imagine what it would be like to live for ninety-seven years, then to live again for another lifetime.

But it was clear that *this* Tykus…a fresh Tykus, one that no one in this room had ever witnessed, by virtue of the previous king's long reign…was far from complacent. He had all the wisdom of the old king, with the vigor of a young man.

"To answer your question Mezgar," Tykus stated, his tone mild once again, "…I speak of the Original because you all feel she was evil. Just as you feel the forest is evil, and the Ironclad are evil."

"I believe they hate humans," Dominus corrected. "And that they therefore represent a threat to our people."

"Intellectually, yes," Tykus conceded. "That is what you believe. But evil is not an intellectual term, Dominus. You cannot rationalize that something is evil. Nothing is evil when you consider cause and effect…it just *is*."

"But you said we think they *are* evil," Mezgar protested.

"I said you *feel* that they are evil," Tykus corrected. "And therein lies the problem. Evil cannot be reasoned with. Diplomacy is futile against it. There is only one thing for men who believe themselves to be good to do to evil…and that is to destroy it."

He leaned forward then, his gaze sweeping across the assembled dukes.

"You feel that the forest is evil, so you fight it, and it hates you for it. You feel the Ironclad are evil and you fight them, and they hate you for it. So they fight back, and you hate them more. And so on. Forever."

Dominus said nothing. Could say nothing. There was no denying it.

"With all due respect sire," Ratheburg stated, "…the Ironclad attacked us first."

Tykus turned to regard the duke.

"Why?" he inquired. Ratheburg frowned, clearly taken aback by the question.

"Because they are monsters, your Highness."

King Tykus smiled, his blue eyes twinkling. He leaned forward conspiratorially.

"So," he replied, "…are we."

CHAPTER 24

Thick clouds hung over the deep forest, a few miles past the Fringe. Vi led Hunter along the shore of a narrow, winding river, its waters a dull gray as it flowed in the opposite direction they were going. The dull rumble of thunder rolled through the forest, the aftershock of lightning that had flashed far in the distance nearly twenty seconds earlier. Hunter had been counting; the lightning was getting steadily closer, which meant that the storm would soon be upon them.

Cold rain, he grumbled to himself. *My favorite.*

He glanced at Vi, who was a few yards ahead. They hadn't said much to each other over the last day, for which Hunter was grateful. Over a day spent in the Fringe – and now the deep forest – had left him feeling irritable. The last thing he wanted to do was talk with a damn human.

Another flash of lightning, followed a while later by thunder.

Fifteen seconds.

Vi slowed suddenly, until she was walking beside him.

"How you holding up?" she asked.

"Just dandy," he muttered. She smirked.

"Damn kid, lighten up," she said, punching him in the shoulder. He glared at her. "You on your period?"

"I can't tell if it's the forest making me hate you," he replied, "…or if it's all you." Still, he felt his sour mood lighten, and knew it was because of Vi's closeness. She exuded calm, even more powerfully in person than she had through her sword back at the crypt. He couldn't help but smile.

"That's better," she opined.

"I don't know how you do it," he admitted. "Staying so calm all the time."

"Practice," she replied. "Emotions are manageable, you know. Most people let emotions run them all over the place. They get depressed and think it'll never end. Or hope that happiness will last forever. Emotions are temporary."

"Got that."

"I manage my emotions by not taking them too seriously," she continued. "Never take your thoughts or emotions too seriously," she added. "Otherwise they'll control you."

"So everything's a joke then?" Hunter asked. "That explains the sarcasm."

"You're one to talk," Vi shot back. "Take your reality seriously. Thoughts and emotions come and go. They're like lightning," she added, gesturing at the approaching storm. "Powerful, frightening…and gone in a flash." She stopped then, turning to face him, and he stopped as well.

"What are…?" he began.

"Unless you make them a secret," she interjected. He frowned.

"What?"

"What happened back there?" Vi asked. "At Camilla's place?"

Hunter stared at her silently. Then he turned forward again, continuing to walk. Vi barred his way with one arm, stepping in front of him. Her green eyes locked on his.

"Tell me."

"Nothing happened," he grumbled, trying to step around her. But she moved with him, continuing to block his way. "Come on," he complained, trying to push past her. Which was futile, of course.

"Hunter," she pleaded, gripping his shoulders tightly. "Talk to me."

He stared at her, then lowered his gaze, feeling warmth spread to his cheeks.

"I really don't want to talk about it."

Vi stared at him for a moment, then dropped her hands from his shoulders.

"You know what I think?" she asked. He looked up at her. "I think she hurt you. Hurt you bad. And the longer you keep what she did a secret, the bigger that hurt is gonna get."

Hunter said nothing.

"You want her to have that kind of power over you?" Vi pressed. "Go ahead. Don't talk. But if you want to be free of her, you need to let it out."

"Vi…"

"You wanna know how I stay calm all the time?" she interrupted. "I don't. But I'm calm a *lot* of the time, and it's because I don't keep shit inside. I get it out right away, before it can stick. Somebody fucks me over, I call 'em out. I screw up? I admit it and make amends. Right away, Hunter. Not days later, not years later. Holding that shit in will mess you up."

"It already happened," Hunter retorted. "Talking about it isn't going to change that."

"When bad shit happens it happens once," she countered. "You got a choice, Hunter. You either let it hurt you once, or let it hurt you over and over again until the day you die." She put a hand on his shoulder again. "You do that," she added, "…and you're giving that bitch power over you for the rest of your life. You want that?"

Hunter swallowed.

"No."

"So talk."

He sighed, feeling suddenly exhausted. He lowered himself to the forest floor, sitting there for a moment. Vi sat down next to him.

"It happened after I woke up from my seizures," he explained. "She came to see me, and we talked. That night, she…" he grimaced. "She ate dinner with me in my room, and we drank. She got me real drunk," he added ruefully.

"Let me guess," Vi ventured. "Red wine?"

"Yeah, actually."

"And then you got real horny," she guessed. He nodded.

"How'd you know?"

"Most people get horny when they're drunk," she replied with a smirk. "And have you seen Camilla? She's fucking gorgeous."

"Thought you wanted me to tell my story," he grumbled.

"That wine had a shit-ton of horniness absorbed into it," Vi explained. "Wineries design drinks for different purposes," she added. "Some are exposed to angry people, others to fearful people. Most are exposed to horny people…which is why the whorehouses in Tykus make so much money holding liquor for them."

"Oh," Hunter replied. It made perfect sense, of course. He'd definitely felt his body respond after that first drink…and the more he'd drank, the hornier he'd gotten. Now that he thought about it, he'd felt a stirring in his groin when he'd had that starfucker back in Lowtown…at the bar Sukri and Gammon had taken him to.

That's why it was called that, he realized. Had Sukri been trying to get him horny? She'd known that Gammon didn't drink…and she'd been the one to suggest they both get on the bed before Trixie came…

"Go on," Vi said, interrupting the thought. "You drank, got horny…"

"And then uh," he replied, blushing a little. "Well, you know."

"Damn right I do," Vi agreed, grinning and punching him in the shoulder. "I don't just go to her for the business, you know."

"Wait, you and her…?"

"*Oh* yeah," Vi confirmed. "I've had lots," she added, "…but I've never had anyone like her." She shook her head, still smiling. "You went from a lousy teenage prostitute to the best goddamn sex of your life in a few weeks. Trust me," she added, "…you'll never find better."

"Well that's depressing," he grumbled.

"Go on," she urged. "So you did it…then what?"

"I woke up the next morning and tried to leave," he replied. "And she wouldn't let me. Said I was too valuable, and she had to keep me a fucking prisoner to keep me safe." He grimaced. "She wanted to study me…and…"

Vi arched an eyebrow, waiting. He sighed.

"You know what?" he said, starting to stand up. "Forget…"

Vi pulled him right back down, wrapping an arm around his shoulders to stop him from trying again.

"Keep going," she prompted. Hunter sighed again, picking at his fingernails. He swallowed past a sudden lump in his throat.

"She wanted to get pregnant," he confessed. "So she could study the baby."

Vi kept silent, and he could feel her eyes on him. He stared at the ground, shame coming over him.

"She tied me down," he muttered, almost too quiet to hear. "Said she'd make me like it."

"Shit Hunter," Vi murmured. He shook his head, moisture blurring his vision.

"Don't make some glib remark," he muttered, trying to slip out of her arm. "I don't want to hear it." But she held him there, squeezing him gently.

"Hunter," she stated, using her free hand to force him to turn his head to look at her. Her expression was dead serious. He lowered his gaze. "You got raped."

Hunter felt his lower lip quivering, and hated it. Hated that she could see it. He pulled her hand from his cheek, turning away.

"Yeah, well," he muttered. "She said she'd make me like it…and she was right."

"Why?" Vi asked. "Because you came?"

His cheeks burned, and he grit his teeth.

"Nothing you can do about that," she said matter-of-factly. "That's gonna feel good no matter what."

"Yeah, well I shouldn't have gotten there in the first place," he shot back. Vi gave him a look.

"You're a teenager," she retorted. "A slight breeze'll get you hard. After that, it's just a matter of time. Your body doesn't give a shit if you want it or not. It does what it does."

"It didn't just feel *good*," he countered, feeling a fresh wave of shame come over him. "It felt *great*."

"Yeah, well," she replied. "Just because you enjoyed the destination doesn't mean you have to like the way you got there." She squeezed his shoulders. "A ninety-year-old one-eyed guy with a beer-belly coulda gotten you there too, you know."

"Yeah right."

"I could find one for you," she offered, giving him a sly grin. "And test it." He glared at her.

"You're just making me feel *so* much better."

"My point is," she stated, "…rape is rape. It doesn't matter if you came. You got raped, and that sucks. Believe me," she added. "I get it."

He frowned at her.

"You do?"

"Yep," she confirmed. "Remember how I said my parents never accepted me 'cause I liked girls?"

"Yeah."

"Well," she continued, "…I had an uncle who used to take care of me when my parents were at work. He figured he knew how to 'convert' me, if you know what I mean." She shook her head. "I was twelve at the time."

"Jesus."

"He was a typical guy," she continued, "…figuring the solution to every problem was his dick. So he forced me down and tried his solution on me."

Hunter lowered his gaze, shaking his head.

"Sorry Vi."

"Didn't work," she continued. "So he kept trying it, every time he got the chance. Till I realized he wasn't trying to solve my 'problem' at all." She took a deep breath in, then let it out. "And I was helpless," she confessed. "I didn't fight back. I just let it happen…and then I started to blame myself. I told myself I could've fought back. Could've told my parents. But I didn't, and that meant that, deep down inside, I must've wanted it."

Hunter felt a smoldering anger, and realized it wasn't his own…it was hers.

"It wasn't until I got into a good relationship – one I wanted – that I realized how full of shit I was," Vi continued. "But I'll tell you this…that helpless feeling my uncle gave me? I hated it so much that I promised myself I would never let anyone make me feel that way again."

"So you learned how to fight?"

"That's right kiddo," she agreed. "I vowed to become the best goddamn fighter in the world. Trained every day, long after everyone else quit. Made myself into what I am today."

"You're saying it was a good thing?"

"No," she retorted. "Just because I enjoy the destination doesn't mean I have to like the way I got there, remember?"

Hunter smiled ruefully, then nodded.

"Bad shit happens," Vi stated. "You can let it eat you up inside, or you can learn from it. Use it to make you stronger. You let it make you the victim, and you'll play the victim for the rest of your life." She slapped him on the back. "When she was doing it to you, did you want it?"

"No," he answered.

"Then that's that," she declared. "Everything else is mental masturbation."

"Wow," he muttered. "*Terrible* choice of words."

"Feel better?" she inquired, smiling at him. He smiled back.

"Yeah," he admitted. And he *did* feel better. A whole lot better. "Thanks Vi."

"Anytime," she replied, standing up and offering him a hand. He took it, and she hauled him to his feet. "Just remember," she added, "…holding something in is the exact opposite of letting it go."

"Didn't know you were a psychologist," he quipped.

"A what now?"

"Never mind," he mumbled. "So where we going?"

"So impatient," Vi scolded, resuming their walk. He walked beside her. "You'll see soon enough."

"Camilla's not your client, is she?" he pressed. Vi smirked.

"Of course she is," she retorted. "Not the client I'm working for now," she added.

"You're going to work for her even after what she did to me?" he asked incredulously. "Some friend *you* are."

"Business is business kiddo," Vi replied. "Believe me, I do business with my enemies all the time. And besides," she added with a wicked grin. "…I like what she does to me."

"You," Hunter muttered, "…are a horrible person."

* * *

The storm was nearly upon them by the time Vi led Hunter away from the stream they'd been following, taking them deeper into the forest. There was no path or trail of any kind, and Hunter wondered how Vi could possibly know where they were going. But he'd learned well enough not to question her. She'd never once failed him, after all. And she was as confident as she always was, which, by way of her proximity to him, made him feel a bit more confident as well. He was glad that his ability to absorb memories appeared to be inhibited by wearing the helmet she'd given him. Otherwise Vi might not have allowed him to be so close.

He wondered what it might be like to be so strong-willed that everyone around him would be fearful of him, and try to stay away. Then he remembered how the people in the Outskirts had reacted to him, and suddenly didn't feel so much animosity toward them. He'd thought they were dumb racists, but in reality they were just trying to protect themselves. He thought back to the Legendary tree, to the countless smaller trees around it. People who had been transformed against their will, suffering a fate worse than death. He turned to Vi, recounting the tale.

"Yep, seen it," she replied. "That reminds me…I've taught you how to feel emotions. It's about time we went over how to look at the world."

"What do you mean?"

"Everything influences everything else," Vi lectured. "Strong-willed plants and animals will make everything around them look like them."

"So look for clusters of things that look the same," Hunter guessed.

"Right," she agreed. "You have to assume they look alike because of their will, not because they happen to have grown together."

"So basically be paranoid."

"Wouldn't have it any other way," she replied with a grin. She stopped suddenly, grabbing his arm to stop him, then pointing at the ground ahead. "Check it out," she said. He frowned; she was pointing to some baby trees on the ground, barely taller than the blades of grass around them.

"The little trees?"

"Exactly," she confirmed. "What's up with them?"

He stared, but couldn't see what she was talking about. He shrugged.

"They're not trees," she explained. "Or at least they didn't start out as trees. They were blades of grass, like the ones around them."

"How can you tell?"

"Step back," she ordered. "Look at everything around them."

He did so, realizing that the tiny trees were all in a big circle…and that in the center of them was a larger sapling that looked identical to its smaller brethren.

"Well shit."

"Woulda walked right into that one," Vi declared, slapping him on the back and grinning at him. "Not that it would've done anything to you. Unless of course you happened to sleep next to it…"

She let the thought hang in the air, and Hunter felt a chill, remembering the man-tree he'd killed. Remembered the memories it had imparted on him, how it'd felt to *be* it.

"Best way to stay out of trouble," Vi advised, snapping him out of his morbid reverie, "…is to stick to streams and rivers. Running water is usually pretty clear of bad influences."

"Because it's always flowing and carrying them away?" Hunter guessed. Vi nodded.

"Just like the lake back home," she agreed. "And my storehouse." Hunter sighed, shaking his head.

"I have a lot of learning to do," he realized.

"That's what I'm here for kiddo."

They continued onward, and Vi pointed out the hierarchy of wills they encountered as they went, most of which Hunter didn't spot until she made note of them. Gradually he improved, and she quizzed him relentlessly, as was her way. After nearly an hour of this, he'd gotten much better at it. Nowhere near as good as she was, but serviceable. By that time, the forest had gotten considerably darker, the angry-looking clouds directly overhead. Whereas they'd gotten a break from the rain and lightning for a while, it returned with a vengeance, a drizzle turning quickly into an outright downpour.

What I wouldn't do for an umbrella, he thought wistfully.

"All right Hunter," Vi stated, stopping suddenly. He stopped as well. "Time for you to go on without me."

"Excuse me?"

"Go on," she prompted, gesturing further into the woods. Hunter just stared at her. "Keep walking," she urged.

"Why are…"

"Do you trust me?" she interrupted. He hesitated, then nodded.

"I do."

"Then go on," she repeated, waving him away. "Find a path up a hill. You'll know your destination when you see it."

He glanced at the forest ahead, peering into the darkness. It was getting hard to see, the storm clouds conspiring with the rapidly approaching nightfall to shroud the forest in shadow.

"You're not going to tell me what…" he began.

"Nope."

"What if I get lost?" he pressed.

"Taught you to track, didn't I?"

"Not in the dark," he retorted. "And in case you didn't notice, it's pouring rain." She smirked.

"Don't worry Hunter," she replied. "I'll find you."

He sighed.

"All right," he decided. "You'll be here?" She smiled.

"I won't give up on you," she promised. He smiled back, remembering how she'd promised that, days before her death. And how she'd kept that promise, cheating death itself to return to him.

"Thanks Vi."

She gestured for him to go, and he did so, taking one last look at her, then turning forward to walk through the forest.

Alright then, he thought.

Onward he went, weaving through the trees, trying to walk in a straight line. It was no use picking a far-away target – it was too dark to see very far, especially in the rain – so he did the best he could. He made sure to keep an eye out for telltale signs of strong-willed flora as he went, but so far there wasn't anything concerning. The downpour intensified as he went, lightning flashing in the low-hanging clouds, followed by rolling thunder. He shivered in the cold, grimacing at the heavy wetness of his thoroughly drenched clothes.

It wasn't long before the ground began to slope upward, the grass becoming sparser as he ascended. The slope gradually steepened, until it was at a 20-degree incline. His thighs began to burn, and he ignored the pain, focusing on setting one foot in front of the other.

If I keep doing this, he mused, *I'm gonna grow legs like Vi.*

After a few minutes, he spotted what Vi had been talking about…a wide dirt path climbing up the side of the slope to his right. He veered toward it, then followed the path upward. The going was rough, a stream of rainwater flowing down the path making it slippery.

He spotted something ahead…something on the path. A dark, wide shape, less than a foot tall. Water coursed around it.

He slowed, putting a hand on the hilt of his longsword. Striding forward, he stopped a few yards away from the thing. Lightning flashed, illuminating it for a split second, and Hunter's breath caught in his throat.

It was a body.

Hunter unsheathed his sword, holding it before him, and walked up to the body. It was human, that was certain, lying on its belly on the path. A young man dressed in a black and gold uniform.

A Seeker.

He kicked the body, but it didn't move. He kicked again – much harder, and still it didn't move.

Looks dead to me, he thought.

He hesitated, then lifted his sword up, plunging the tip down into the body's back. The blade slid through its flesh, stopping with a jolt as the tip buried itself into the ground beneath. He grimaced, withdrawing his sword.

Definitely dead.

Hunter knelt down, sheathing his sword and rolling the Seeker onto its back. Dead eyes stared up at the heavens, its flesh pale and bloated. A foul odor assaulted Hunter's nose, and he gagged, turning away for a moment.

Jesus.

He took a deep breath in, then held it, examining the body. Pressing on the Seeker's chest, he felt a sickening *crunch,* his fingers sinking into the flesh. He grimaced, withdrawing his hand. The Seeker's sternum and ribs had been crushed, that was clear. Blunt trauma to the chest. Maybe from a mace. Or a warhammer.

He hesitated, then took off his helmet, lowering his forehead to the Seeker's forehead, grimacing as his skin touched its rotting flesh. He closed his eyes…and felt himself laying on his belly on the dirt. A bolt of terror shot through him, and he screamed, rising to his hands and knees.

And then something struck his upper back, slamming his chest into the ground. Agony shot through his chest straight into his back, the breath exploding from his lungs. He tried to breathe, but no air came, an impossibly heavy weight pinning him to the dirt. He flailed his arms and legs, his vision blackening, his lungs on fire…

Hunter gasped, jerking away from the body and bolting to his feet. He backpedaled, his heart pounding in his chest, his breath coming in short gasps.

It's not real, he reminded himself, forcing himself to take slow, deep breaths. Still, the memory lingered. He stared down at the corpse, wondering what all these terrible memories were doing to him. The memory of Vi dying, of Traven dying. Of the two Seekers he'd killed. He'd experienced all of their deaths, the terror of the last moments of their lives.

Though it had never happened to him, he knew without a doubt what it felt like to die.

Focus, he chided himself.

Hunter put his helmet back on, then glanced about, searching the surrounding area. He saw nothing – only the path, with trees and shrubs on either side – but again, it was too dark to see very far. The corpse had been lying here for some time, that much was clear. So it was likely that whoever had killed it was long gone. The Seeker wore no medallion, so either it was stolen or the Seeker hadn't been wearing it. Likely the former; Seekers in their official uniform usually wore their medallions. He searched through his memories – the Seeker's memories – but had no recollection of what might have killed the man.

Probably Vi, he reasoned. She'd had to have been here earlier if she knew where he was supposed to go. Vi wouldn't have sent him right into the hands of the enemy, after all. Although he wouldn't put it past her. Could be some sort of test.

She would *do something like that*, he muttered to himself.

He sighed, continuing past the Seeker's body, his hand on the hilt of his sword. The slope became ever steeper, the going so slippery now that he was forced to walk on the grass to one side of it so his boots wouldn't slip constantly on the slick dirt and rocks. He kept his eyes on the path ahead; with the visibility decreasing as night descended upon him, he couldn't see much beyond a few yards.

A flash of lightning lit up the sky ahead, followed by a thunderous *boom.*

He froze.

In the brief moment of illumination, he'd spotted something ahead, standing on the path. The outline of a shadowy figure far in the distance.

He kept his hand on his sword, veering away from the path, crouching behind some bushes. He waited.

Another flash of lightning.

Hunter spotted the figure again…and a few dark shapes lying on the path. Shapes covered in black and gold uniforms.

More bodies.

He started to draw his sword from its scabbard, then stopped, sheathing it again. There was a good chance it would reflect light from another lightning bolt, giving his position away to whoever was standing on the path beyond the bodies. Sure enough, lightning lit up the sky, followed seconds later by an ear-splitting *boom.*

Again, he saw the figure standing there, some thirty yards away. A dark silhouette against the momentary flash of light.

He stayed low to the ground, moving forward from tree to tree, keeping out of the figure's line-of-sight. Moments later, the sky lit up again, the thunderbolt following almost immediately after. He froze in his tracks.

The figure was gone.

Shit.

Hunter crouched behind a tree, weighing his options. There was no way for him to know where the person was. They might have walked further up the path, or veered off the path into the trees. If they'd seen him, they could be hiding, waiting for him to get close. He hesitated, glancing back the way he'd come.

Maybe I should go back.

Then a thought came to him, and he grimaced.

If this is Vi fucking with me...

He waited for another flash of lightning to get a quick glimpse of the hill ahead, then moved forward and upward, stopping behind another tree. The downpour drowned out any sounds of his movement, thank goodness. He continued forward, bit-by-bit, until he'd reached the general area the shadowy figure had been minutes before. There was a large boulder by the path ahead, and another body splayed on the path itself. He waited for more lightning, surveying the area. The coast was clear.

Hunter hesitated, then moved toward the boulder, hiding behind it. He glanced at the body – another Seeker, a woman this time – then peered out from beyond the boulder.

Until it moved.

Hunter jumped to the side before the thing could roll over him...then froze. For the boulder was growing. No...it was *unfolding.* Rising up until it towered over him in a massive silhouette, a pair of huge arms seeming to sprout from its sides. And below that, a second set of arms...and two huge legs.

Shit!

Hunter backpedaled rapidly, his sword already in his hands. Lightning shot down from the heavens, the instantaneous flash revealing a black monstrosity before him. A humanoid creature nearly eight feet tall, covering in thick black plated armor. A ghastly face with two black eyes staring down at him. Massive hands balled into fists, each as big as his head.

The creature emitted a low growl, the sound making the hair on the nape of Hunter's neck stand on end. He stared at the thing, flipping his sword around so he was holding by the blade, shivering as a cold breeze whipped through his soaked clothes. He waited for it to lunge at him, to attack.

But it just stood there.

"What do you want?" he demanded. As if the beast could understand him.

The Ironclad extended one arm, then gestured for him to come closer. Or rather, to follow; the beast turned around, stomping up the path. Not even bothering to look back.

The hell?

He stared at the thing's back, weighing his options. Going back down the hill was the obvious choice. The path wasn't safe, and he wasn't sure how many Ironclad he could take on…assuming he could beat even one of them. But the beast hadn't attacked him. It could be luring him into a trap, waiting to have superior numbers. Waiting to exact revenge for the murder of its queen.

Hunter hesitated; the beast was nearly out of sight now, so far ahead that the darkness threatened to swallow it whole.

Yeah, nope.

He turned to walk back down the path, then stopped in his tracks. Another Ironclad stood on the path, blocking his way. He swore under his breath, backing up quickly. But the Ironclad did not attack. It gestured for him to walk up the path.

Guess I don't have a choice.

He turned forward, making his way quickly up the path after the first Ironclad, who had vanished into the darkness ahead. Eventually he caught up to it enough to see it, walking leisurely up the hill, its feet *thumping* on the packed dirt. Still, the Ironclad walked far quicker than he could, as if there was no rain at all. For his part, Hunter focused on not slipping all the way down the path. Or slipping into the Ironclad that he realized was following behind him.

At length, he reached the top of the hill, the path leveling off and taking a more serpentine route through the trees. Minutes passed, the Ironclad ahead of him and behind him maintaining a steady pace. A flash of lightning revealed a small lake ahead, a large stream feeding it from the left.

And dozens of dark shapes lining the shore of that lake. Moving shapes.

Christ.

He glanced back at the Ironclad behind him, remembering how fast they could run. How they'd caught up to him and Vi easily in the Deadlands, when they'd been running back to Tykus. There was no way he would be able to escape, he knew. He was going to have to see this through.

He realized he'd stopped walking, and swallowed in a dry throat, returning his gaze to the Ironclad ahead of him. The path ended, and the Ironclad continued past it, walking toward the shoreline ahead.

Hunter took a deep breath in, then strode forward, matching the Ironclad's pace, unable to help himself from glancing back at the Ironclad following him.

What do they want?

As he got closer to the shore, he got a better look at the figures lining it. Dozens and dozens of Ironclad, standing there densely packed in the rain, forming a long line stretching over a hundred feet across and several rows deep. A veritable wall of armored flesh. The Ironclad who'd led him reached his fellows, joining them.

Hunter slowed, then stopped, staring at the assembled Ironclad. And, to a one, they all stared back at him.

I'm going to die, he realized. *They're all going to charge me and tear me apart.*

Revenge for killing their queen. For murdering his own mother.

And there wasn't a damn thing he could do about it.

"So this is how I die," he muttered under his breath. He hesitated, then sheathed his sword. "Alright then," he decided. He'd experienced death many times before, in the memories of the people he'd killed. Taking a deep breath in, he stepped forward toward the line.

Might as well get on with it.

He continued forward, head held high as rain poured from the heavens in heavy sheets, a sudden gust of wind whipping through his hair. He squinted, barely able to see more than twenty feet ahead. As he drew near, the Ironclad parted before him slowly, forming a path through the darkness. Hunter hesitated, then continued forward, passing row after row of Ironclad. Their heads turned as he passed by, countless eyes following him. He turned his focus inward, hoping to sense their emotional state, but all he felt was a jumble of emotions…far too many to make sense of them.

The final row of Ironclad ahead parted, revealing the edge of the lake beyond…and something else.

A light shining through the darkness.

He glanced back, seeing Ironclad spill inward to fill the gap they'd made to let him pass, the wall once again unbroken. Then he turned forward, walking toward the light…and the shore. He stopped at the edge, looking down at the water. It was surprisingly shallow, only a few inches deep.

He glanced back at the Ironclad again, but they only stared at him.

Hunter stepped into the lake, his boots splashing in the shallow water. Onward he went, toward the light ahead. It grew larger and brighter as he continued forward, and he realized it was floating high above the ground. At least a few feet higher than his head.

Suddenly the light moved…right toward him.

Hunter froze, watching as it approached. A narrow glowing band piercing through the darkness, casting the ground in a pale blue hue.

There was another flash of lightning, following by the deafening *crack* of thunder that echoed across the lake.

His breath caught in his throat.

For there, standing not ten feet before him, was a monster. Easily eight feet tall, if not nine, with jet-black armor and twin pairs of massive arms. A blue, glowing mane extending from the top of its head like a mohawk, but made of a thick membrane filled with luminescent gel.

Hunter's jaw dropped.

"HUNTER," the beast greeted, its deep, raspy voice sending a chill down Hunter's spine. He took a step back involuntarily, staring in disbelief.

"No," he blurted out. "How…?"

The Ironclad strode forward, stopping inches from Hunter, then putting one huge hand on his shoulder. A hand so large it could've wrapped around Hunter's skull and crushed it like an egg. He didn't even bother to shrink away from the thing's touch.

"MY NAME…XERXES," it stated, each word spoken as if it was painful to do so, a deep, raspy sound that he had to concentrate to understand.

"I'm Hunter," Hunter replied automatically. A corner of the beast's black lips curled upward. "What are…" He swallowed in a dry throat. "What are you doing here?"

"HERE FOR…YOU," it answered in that awful voice.

"Me?"

It nodded.

"WELCOME…HOME," it growled, staring down at him with those beady black eyes, its angular features cast in an unholy blue glow. "MY…BROTHER."

CHAPTER 25

Hunter stared up at the massive Ironclad standing before him, hardly noticing the rain pelting him, or the freezing wind whipping through his soaked clothes. Stared into those black eyes, into that armored face, cast in a faint blue light from its glowing mane. It smiled, the beast, and Hunter felt a sudden elation, so powerful that he wanted to weep. It was not his emotion, he knew. It was this creature's.

Xerxes'.

"I shot you," Hunter said at last, shaking his head. "I shot you in the face. I watched men crush your skull!" A vision of Alasar – the sergeant who'd "saved" Hunter from the Ironclad when he'd first come through the Gate – came to him, of Alasar slamming his warhammer into Xerxes' head. Of Xerxes' face caving in, his head crumpling under the blow, chunky yellow stuff oozy out of either side of Alasar's hammer.

Xerxes flashed a horrible grin, lowering his hand from Hunter's shoulder and stepping back.

"GOT…BETTER."

"It was you in the caves?" Hunter asked, hardly believing it. He'd assumed there'd been more than one Ironclad with a blue glowing mane. Xerxes nodded. "But Vi…she cut your head off!"

"GOT…BETTER," Xerxes repeated.

"But *how*?" Hunter pressed. "You can't just grow another head!"

Xerxes grunted, raising one hand and making a series of rapid hand signals at the Ironclad all around them. The Ironclad turned at once, stomping away from the shore of the pond, vanishing into the darkness beyond. Hunter watched them go, then turned back to Xerxes, who was still grinning at him. He stared at Xerxes for a long moment, then shook his head.

"I don't believe it."

Xerxes grunted again, but said nothing.

"So you were trying to save me, at the Gate," Hunter stated. "From Tykus."

Xerxes nodded.

"And when you guys attacked us at Vi's place before?" Hunter pressed. Ironclad had descended upon the canyon weeks ago, smashing through Vi's front door. He and Vi had barely escaped with their lives…or so they'd thought.

"BRING…HOME," Xerxes grumbled.

"You were just trying to bring me home?" Hunter clarified. Xerxes nodded. Hunter considered this, feeling numb. "Shit."

Xerxes chuckled, a low, raspy sound that rumbled in his chest. Which Hunter's head didn't even get close to reaching.

"Why didn't you tell me?" Hunter asked. Xerxes lifted one hand, pointing to his own throat.

"TALK…HARD."

"But you could've said *something*," Hunter retorted.

"HARDER WHEN…WITH THEM," Xerxes said, gesturing at the retreating Ironclad.

"Because they can't talk?"

Xerxes nodded.

"You're saying that if you stay with them too long, *you* can't talk?" Hunter pressed. Another nod. He frowned, mulling it over. If Xerxes absorbed physical traits at all, then staying near other Ironclad *would* change his anatomy, at least eventually.

Hunter took a step back from Xerxes, who chuckled again.

"Why are you here?" he demanded. Xerxes pointed at him.

"WAIT LONG…TIME…FOR YOU."

Hunter just stared at him.

"FAMILY," Xerxes explained, putting a fist to his own chest and thumping it. He tapped Hunter's chest then. Gently, thank goodness.

Hunter lowered his gaze, a vision of his mother laying on the ground coming to him, Vi's sword plunged into her chest. Of her gasping for air, trying desperately to tell him something. And then, her last breath. Her eyes staring vacantly upward as death claimed her.

"I'm sorry," he mumbled, moisture blurring his vision. He was suddenly glad for the rain. "I didn't know."

He felt Xerxes' hand on his shoulder again, surprisingly gentle. He looked up, seeing Xerxes staring down at him. The beast – his brother – shook his head.

"NO…SORRY."

Hunter swallowed, feeling nauseous. Of course Xerxes hadn't seen him kill their mother. He'd been decapitated at the time. But the other Ironclad had to have told him what had happened. They'd seen it all, the Ironclad. Watched as it'd happened, doing nothing.

If only they'd stopped me, he thought bitterly. *If only they'd killed me before I…*

"NO…SORRY," Xerxes repeated. Hunter shook his head.

"But I killed her," he retorted. "I killed Mom!"

Xerxes grunted.

"I did," he insisted. He lowered his gaze, shaking his head. An all-too-familiar shame came over him. "I'm sorry," he repeated.

"COME," Xerxes commanded, gesturing back the way he'd come, at the wall of Ironclad. They parted immediately, creating a gap for Hunter to pass through.

"Where are you taking me?" Hunter asked. Xerxes strode forward, passing through that gap, not even bothering to glance back at him.

"SHOW."

Hunter swallowed past a lump in his throat, then took a deep breath in, and followed behind the Ironclad…behind Xerxes.

Behind his brother.

* * *

The way back down the path was harder than the way up, the rain making the going treacherous. Hunter had slipped more than once, nearly sliding right into Xerxes, who was walking ahead of him. Xerxes seemed to have no trouble with the terrain at all, his big feet sinking into the dirt with each step. The behemoth had to be well over six hundred pounds, if not heavier. Eventually they reached the bottom of the hill, continuing onward through the forest. Xerxes led them all the way back to where Hunter had started…and Hunter found someone familiar waiting for them.

"Vi!" he exclaimed, rushing up to her. She was on her feet, leaning against a tree. She smiled at him.

"Hey Hunter," she greeted. She glanced at Xerxes. "Hey Blue."

Hunter frowned, glancing at Xerxes, then at Vi.

"Wait, you know each other?" he asked.

"Of course," she answered. "I cut his head off, remember?"

Xerxes grunted, glaring at her.

"He's definitely your brother," Vi continued, smirking at Xerxes. "Always getting mad and losing his head. Except *he* loses his literally."

Xerxes shoved Vi with one hand, or at least he tried to. She dodged easily, slapping his big hand away.

"You knew he was up there?" Hunter pressed. "And the rest of the Ironclad?"

"Duh."

"Are you saying *he's* your client?"

"I'm not saying anything," Vi retorted. "Client-Seeker privilege, kiddo."

Xerxes grunted again, ignoring them both and turning to the left, stomping off through the forest. Vi grinned at the Ironclad, then went on after him, leaving Hunter standing there. He stared at them for a moment, then sprinted after them, slowing down to walk at Vi's side.

"What's going on, Vi?" he asked.

"You'll see."

"Come on," he pleaded. "Tell me *something.*" He glanced at Xerxes' broad back. "How do you two know each other?"

"I cut off his head," she answered. "Swallowed his blue glowing shit, and healed up. Blue dragged me to a safe location, and I woke up."

"How?" Hunter asked.

"How what?"

"How did he drag you to safety if his damn head was cut off?" he demanded.

"Same way I grew my arm back," she explained. "He regenerated it."

"His whole *head*?"

"Yep."

"Does he…remember everything?" Hunter asked. Xerxes grunted, clearly able to hear everything they were saying.

"YES," he growled.

"He's still being a little bitch about it," Vi said, grinning at Xerxes' back. "Being beaten by a woman and all."

"NOT…BEATEN."

"Uh huh," Vi teased. "Keep telling yourself that."

"So uh, did his body grow his head back, or did his head grow his body back?" Hunter asked.

"The former," Vi answered. "The Seekers probably have his head by now." Hunter frowned.

"No, Camilla said Dominus took it from them," he corrected. Vi's eyebrows rose.

"Oh really," she murmured. "Seekers'll be pissed about that."

"Doesn't that mean Dominus will get his ability to regenerate?" Hunter pressed.

"Slowly," Vi answered. "And not very well. The glowing shit is what transmits regeneration the best, and most of it spilled onto me before the Seekers got ahold of it."

Xerxes grunted, clearly irritated by their conversation. He guided them through the forest, walking parallel to the base of the hill, his glowing blue mane – extending from his head all the way to his short, broad-based tail – lighting the way.

"Where are we going?" Hunter asked.

"Ask him," Vi replied.

Hunter repeated the question, louder this time. But Xerxes just grunted again.

"Yeah, Blue doesn't say much," Vi explained. "It's his one redeeming quality."

One of Xerxes' massive fists shot out, striking a small tree he was passing. Its trunk split with a loud *crack*, the sound echoing through the forest like a gunshot. He glanced back at Vi, giving her a murderous glare.

"And his temper," Vi added with a grin. "God I love his temper."

"So you cut his head off," Hunter stated, "...and then he drags you to safety?" He shook his head. "I don't get it."

"You will," Vi promised.

"But..."

"Not gonna tell you," she interrupted. He sighed, glaring at her. "All in good time," she added. "Be patient for once."

Hunter didn't bother pushing the issue, knowing that Vi wasn't going to tell him anything he wanted to know. Hell, she was probably enjoying keeping him in the dark, sadist that she was. He sighed again, following alongside her, Xerxes leading them wordlessly through the forest. His boots began to make a crunching sound on the grass, and he looked down, realizing that each blade was black and stiff, no doubt influenced by decades of Ironclad walking over it. Which meant they had to be reaching Ironclad territory.

The hillside to their left grew steeper as they went, until it shot nearly straight up from the earth. The path veered toward it suddenly...and toward a few dozen Ironclad blocking the path, their massive bodies barely visible in the darkness. Xerxes grunted as he approached them, and they made way for him, parting to reveal what lay beyond: the entrance to a cave.

Hunter followed Vi and Xerxes up to the mouth of the cave, and Vi stopped suddenly, turning to face Hunter.

"Stay here," she ordered. "I'll be back."

She left then, walking through the mouth of the cave, vanishing into the darkness beyond. Hunter watched her go, then glanced at Xerxes.

"What's she doing?" he asked. Xerxes ignored the question, folding one pair of arms over his massive chest. Hunter stared at his brother, then sighed, kicking a stray rock on the ground. "So nice to have an Ironclad as my little brother," he grumbled. "Think of all the great conversations we'll never have."

Still Xerxes said nothing.

Hunter sighed, crossing his arms and staring at the mouth of the cave. Minutes passed, and he shifted his weight from foot to foot uneasily. He wondered what Vi was up to...and when she'd be back. He didn't bother asking Xerxes, knowing that the big guy was unlikely to answer, even if he knew what was going on.

More time passed, and his mind began to wander.

Eventually he saw a figure emerging from the mouth of the cave, and saw that it was Vi. She strode up to Hunter and Xerxes, grinning at them both.

"Miss me?" she asked.

"Little bit," Hunter admitted. "Where'd you go?"

"Same place you're going," she answered. "Go on," she added, gesturing at the cave entrance. "I'll stay here. Blue will take you inside."

"What?" Hunter replied, glancing at Xerxes.

"You'll be fine," she reassured. "And I'll be here when you get back. Promise."

Hunter nodded, and Xerxes continued forward into the cave. Hunter followed him reluctantly, finding himself in a large tunnel some ten feet high. It was clearly man-made, or at least Ironclad-made, constructed of large gray bricks mortared together. The light of lanterns bolted to the walls on either side bathed the tunnel in a soft orange hue, their heat warming the chilly air. The *thump, thump* of Xerxes' huge feet punctured the silence, the sound echoing off the walls.

The tunnel led to a small, natural cavern, and Xerxes led him leftward through it to another man-made tunnel. They reached stairs leading upward, which were fit for a human, but not for Xerxes, who took them six at a time. The tunnel forked to the left and right beyond, and Xerxes went rightward, leading Hunter to a huge room. It was man-made, with stone pillars supporting the ceiling twelve feet above. A long rectangular table – as long as an aisle at a grocery store – sat in the center of the room, with countless Ironclad seated on chairs around it. Some Ironclad were eating, while others were signing at each other. It was eerily quiet, the only sound the smacking of lips. The Ironclad stopped as Xerxes entered the room, bowing their heads immediately.

Xerxes grunted, waving one hand at them, and the Ironclad resumed eating and signing. He led Hunter across the large room, bringing him to yet another tunnel.

"Who're they?" Hunter asked after they'd passed.

"OUR…PEOPLE."

Onward they went, passing through more large rooms and many more Ironclad. It was like a sprawling, subterranean city, but eerily silent. As they went, Hunter noticed something different about the walls; there were bones embedded in the bricks. And a thick layer of white dust covered the floor, one that was kicked up by their passage. Hunter sneezed.

"Why the dust?" he asked. "What is this stuff?"

"BONES."

Hunter frowned, staring at the floor. There *were* bones at the edges of the floor, near the walls. Or at least pieces of bones. Most had been crushed, undoubtedly by countless Ironclad stepping on them over the years. He glanced at the bones embedded in the walls, seeing a skull there. It looked human.

"Are these *people*?" he pressed. Xerxes grunted, but said nothing more, leading Hunter deeper into the underground city. They walked silently for what seemed like an eternity, weaving through the maze-like tunnels until Hunter was sure that he would never be able to find his way out on his own.

Eventually they came to a larger tunnel, one well over twenty feet tall, its rough-hewn walls making it clear that it wasn't man-made. Hunter heard rushing water in the distance, and felt a cool breeze on his skin. Ironclad lined the walls of the huge tunnel, facing inward. Each was armed, unlike most of the Ironclad they'd passed by. Some carried huge shields, while others wielded swords or warhammers. None of them moved when Xerxes and Hunter passed by, but Hunter could feel their black eyes staring down at him. Bones littered the floor ahead, so thickly that Hunter had to be careful not to roll his ankle stepping over them. Again, they were all obviously human. Hundreds, if not thousands, of skeletons.

Hunter felt a chill run down his spine. Who were these people the Ironclad had killed? And what horrible influence might they have over him? After all, there was no way to tell how strong-willed some of them may have been. To walk among them so carelessly…

He glanced up at Xerxes' broad back, but if the beast was at all concerned about the corpses, he didn't show it. Which meant that he had to be strong-willed, like Hunter.

Or maybe even stronger, Hunter thought darkly. He slowed down, creating more space between them as they walked.

The tunnel curved gently to the left, the sound of rushing water growing louder as they went. The two lines of Ironclad extended all the way down the tunnel, hundreds of armed warriors standing at attention. Xerxes payed them no mind, leading Hunter down the tunnel. The sound of water grew ever louder, until it was a dull roar that echoed through the tunnel.

Suddenly, the tunnel ended, opening up into a massive chamber.

Rough stone walls rose upward from the rocky floor, curving inward to form a domed ceiling over fifty feet above Hunter's head. In the center of that ceiling was a large hole, faint starlight shining through it. A glowing blue waterfall cascaded downward from this hole, forming a hollow cylinder of water that fell to a large, shallow circular pool in the center of the cavern. The waterfall obscured a rocky island in the center of the pool, the roar of its water almost deafening now.

Hunter stared at that waterfall, goosebumps rising on his arms.

Xerxes strode forward, countless bones crunching under his feet. Skeletons were piled up along the walls of the huge chamber, and many more had been strewn across the floor. But there were no bones near the shore of the pool. The gaping maws of other tunnels lined the walls of the cavern at irregular intervals, all guarded by Ironclad. Countless more Ironclad stood at the periphery of the chamber, all facing the pool at the center, their black eyes glittering in the faint starlight and the light of the lanterns bolted on the walls.

Xerxes stopped at the edge of the pool, turning to face Hunter, who was still standing near the tunnel they'd entered through. His brother's black eyes locked on his, and Xerxes gestured at the pool with one big hand.

"COME," he growled.

Hunter hesitated, then walked forward, bones crunching under the soles of his boots as he made his way to the edge of the pool to stand beside Xerxes. His brother put a huge hand on Hunter's upper back, resting it there gently. Xerxes gestured again at the waterfall.

"What?" Hunter asked.

"GO."

Hunter turned to look at the waterfall, at the island obscured beyond. He swallowed past a sudden lump in his throat, a vision of his mother lying on the ground there, eyes staring vacantly upward, a gash in her chest where Vi's sword had impaled her. Where Hunter had finished the job, killing her. He shook his head.

"I can't."

Xerxes grunted, pushing him toward the very edge of the pool. Hunter tried to resist, but his brother was far too strong, and soon he found himself teetering at the edge of the water.

"No," Hunter protested. "Xerxes, stop!"

Xerxes shoved him into the pool.

Hunter gasped as he fell face-first into the pool, chilly water enveloping him instantly, soaking him to the bone. A powerful current threatened to pull him to the left, and he resisted it, planting his feet on the pool bottom. The water rose up to his thighs, tugging at them, but he managed to keep his balance. He turned to glare at Xerxes, who simply gestured at the waterfall again.

Hunter took a deep breath in, then turned forward, wading through the shallow water toward the waterfall. He stopped before it, water splashing his face and chest. He glanced back at Xerxes, who just stood there staring at him. There was no way the big lout was going to allow him to leave the pool. There was only one way out of this…and that was to go forward.

He took another breath in, steeling himself, then stepped forward, the waterfall crashing onto his head and shoulders. He pressed onward, reaching out blindly and finding the slippery ledge of the island beyond. Hunter pulled himself up onto the ledge, water blurring his vision. He wiped the moisture from his face, squinting against a sudden bright, blue light that assaulted his eyes.

Slowly, his vision acclimated.

The bare rock of the circular island lay before him, surrounded on all sides by the cylindrical wall of water formed by the waterfall. These walls were bathed in a soft blue glow, as was the island itself. But the light did not come from the stars twinkling high above the hole in the ceiling. No, it came from something in the center of the island.

Hunter's breath caught in his throat, the hairs on the nape of his neck rising.

For there, sitting cross-legged in the center of the island, was a tall figure. A creature much like the Ironclad he'd seen earlier. Only this one was taller – much taller – and more slender, wide hips leading to a narrow waist. This led to an armored chest, the twin swell of large breasts betraying its femininity. Two pairs of slender arms, four hands resting in its lap. A black-armored face, with full black lips and high cheekbones, eyes closed. And innumerable long antennae rising from its scalp like strands of hair, some black like its flesh, others glowing bright blue like Xerxes' mane, cascading down to drape over its breasts, casting its body in blue light. More tendrils of blue ran down its scalp and neck like glowing veins, extending down its arms and legs.

Hunter stared at this creature, unable to talk. Unable to breathe.

Its eyelids opened, revealed black eyes that focused on him. It stirred then, rising to its feet in one graceful motion, standing well over ten feet tall. It stayed where it was, staring down at him.

Hunter stared back, his lower lips trembling, his legs feeling like jelly. He shook his head, staring at this creature, unable to believe his eyes.

"Hello Hunter," it greeted. Its voice was smooth and a little deep, but feminine. A voice plucked from his past, one he remembered only from the videos he'd watched a thousand times as a child. Memories of a better time.

Hunter swallowed past a lump in his throat, tears blurring his vision. His legs wobbled, and he fell to his knees, barely feeling the pain as his kneecaps struck stone.

"Mom?" he blurted out. The creature's lips curled into a smile.

"Welcome home, Hunter," she replied.

CHAPTER 26

The morning sun greeted Dominus through the blinds hanging before the large windows of his bedroom in the Acropolis, casting its light across his stark white bedsheets. He yawned, stretching his arms to the sides, then glancing at his right hand. It was covered in bandages, as was his right foot. One the victim of time, the other of violence. He stared at the bandages covering his hand, then unwrapped them, revealing his wrist, then his palm. Still he unwrapped, seeing four fingers and a thumb.

Whole fingers, complete with fingernails.

His jaw fell open, and he turned his hand around, staring at the back of it. It was completely intact, as if it'd never been severed.

He glanced down at his right foot then, tearing the bandages from it. It too was whole – completely, fully intact – the skin pink. He ran his fingers over it, feeling not a trace of numbness there.

My god!

He felt something that he hadn't felt in a long time then, a sensation so foreign to him that it took a moment to recognize what it was.

Joy.

Dominus stifled the urge to cry out, leaping out of bed and running to the bathroom. He stared in the bathroom mirror, then froze.

His reflection stared back at him, but there was something wrong. Something terribly wrong. His face was too smooth, a few of the many wrinkles that had crisscrossed it having faded away. His eyes looked brighter than usual, not as sunken as they'd appeared only days ago. His hair – usually a stark white – had a few blond strands in it. Even his teeth were different, not as yellow as before. He'd chipped his upper front tooth a long time ago, but it'd somehow filled in, whole once again.

He stared at himself in the mirror, horror gripping him.

No!

Dominus ran his fingers down the sides of his face, feeling the unfamiliar softness of his skin. More supple than before. It was as if he was looking at himself five years ago, maybe even ten. He felt panic grip him, and steeled himself against it, gripping the edges of the granite countertop so tightly his fingertips turned white.

No no no!

He'd cleansed himself of impurities at the shrine of his ancestors, trying to remove any traces of the Ironclad's foul influence. But this…this was not an impurity. This was his youth returning to him. He'd escaped death, regenerating his diseased and severed limbs, all while managing to maintain his self. His identity.

But this…he never could have imagined *this.*

He stared at his reflection in disbelief, shaking his head slowly. There was no way to cleanse this. To remove it.

Dominus turned away from the mirror, his heart pounding in his chest.

I have to meet the king today, he realized.

King Tykus had requested that Dominus accompany him on another walk through the royal gardens this morning. There was no way to decline the invitation…he had to go.

Maybe he won't notice, Dominus reasoned. Tykus had only met him twice, after all. The changes he was seeing weren't subtle to him, but most people paid little attention to such details. King Tykus, however, was not most people. The man was frighteningly observant. Still, Dominus could very likely get away with it…unless of course this wasn't the end of his transformation.

He stood there, staring at nothing in particular, a chill running down his spine.

If this terrible power – his ability to regenerate – continued to work its influence on him, he might continue to grow younger. There was no telling when it might stop…or whether it would stop at all.

I have to get out of here!

His only chance was to flee the Acropolis, to return to Wexford and never return. He could claim that he was too sick to travel…that his disease had reared its ugly head again. It was a believable excuse, one that would most certainly work.

Until it didn't.

He cast the thought out of his mind, focusing on what he needed to do. If he didn't leave his suite soon, guards would be sent to him for a wellness check. He needed to get dressed and face the king.

After that, he would find a way to return to Wexford…and then he could focus on a plan for his future.

* * *

Dominus walked alongside King Tykus on a wide cobblestone pathway through the gardens in the courtyard outside of the Acropolis, his cane clicking on the stones underfoot. He held the cane in his right hand, freed from its bandages. Walking with a limp had proven difficult to do consistently, and he'd been forced to put a small pebble in his right shoe to remind him.

"You're troubled," Tykus noted, glancing sidelong at Dominus. The king wore simple robes, his feet bare as usual. Unlike Dominus, Tykus appeared utterly relaxed.

"I am," Dominus confessed.

"Go on," Tykus prompted. Dominus hesitated, then sighed.

"This issue with the Seekers troubles me," he admitted. Which was true, if evasive. "As you said, they have great power in the kingdom. What if they were to make the attempt again?"

"You don't strike me as a man overly concerned with dying," Tykus countered. Dominus suppressed a grimace.

"I do not yet have a suitable heir to the Duchy," he replied. Again, it was technically true. Tykus smirked.

"If you were to die today, I myself would find a suitable heir for you."

Dominus said nothing, knowing that Tykus was right.

"You wouldn't appreciate that, of course," the king conceded. "You're too much like the Duke of Wexford I knew. Never trusting others with the details, always needing to be in control." He smiled, putting a hand on Dominus's shoulder. "Tell me…do you suppose the kingdom would fall into ruin if you and your heirs ceased to exist?"

Dominus stared at him, unable to answer the question. To do so honestly would be to insult the king.

"That," Tykus stated, giving Dominus a sly wink, "…is why I gave your progenitor the Duchy."

"I don't understand, sire."

"You don't need to," Tykus retorted. But his tone was not unkind. "A man's nature is far more important than his education. My father was a great leader because he understood this."

"I understand, my liege."

"When I was a boy," Tykus stated, "…my father gave me a pig, and told me to train it to kill mice." He chuckled. "I had a devil of a time at it, but I was a stubborn child. After a few months, damned if I didn't succeed." He gazed up at the sky, his eyes twinkling. "I brought the pig back to my father, and showed him what I had accomplished. I thought he'd be so proud!" He sighed then, lowering his gaze to Dominus. "And do you know what he did?"

"No sire."

"He had a servant fetch a stray cat," Tykus replied, "…and it killed a mouse in a fraction of the time it took my pig to do it."

"Ah."

"Give men roles in harmony with their natures, my father told me," Tykus stated, "…and you will enjoy great success."

"I see, sire."

"Of course you do," Tykus agreed. He sighed then. "A gift…and a curse…that our natures can be twisted."

Dominus stopped in his tracks, staring at Tykus, who stopped as well, turning to face him. He felt a chill course through him, and forced himself to keep his expression – and body language – neutral.

"My liege?"

"I have reviewed my predecessors' notes on the Guild of Seekers," Tykus stated, clasping his hands behind his back. "And on these 'Ironclad.' I will task Duke Ratheburg with our strategy against the guild," he declared.

Dominus frowned at Tykus, his brow furrowing.

"But my liege," he began, but Tykus stopped him with one hand.

"You expected to head the campaign against the Seekers," he guessed. Dominus nodded.

"Yes my liege."

"Do you trust me, Dominus?" Tykus pressed.

"Implicitly," Dominus replied immediately. And it was true. He trusted few men, and being well into his seventh decade of life, held remarkably few in high esteem. He'd always been told of the king's virtues, but the old king had not spoken to Dominus much, mostly staying to himself in his later years. This was the first time Dominus had actually spoken to the man at any appreciable length.

Tykus smiled.

"Then trust that I have chosen wisely."

"Yes sire."

"I've spent the last few days reading about the civil war," Tykus stated. "My predecessor viewed it as a necessary evil, to quash the uprising." He reached down, plucking a flower and sniffing it. "You see these flowers?" he asked, gesturing at a long row of daisies. "All the same. Boring, isn't it?"

Dominus nodded; his gardens at Wexford were far more complex.

"This is our philosophy, is it not?" Tykus mused. "Everything of a type together, separate from the rest. The only way to maintain our species in this terrible world."

"It is," Dominus agreed.

"Those who understand they have power are destined to rule over those who don't," Tykus replied. "That is the same everywhere. But in my world, even the weak were allowed the dignity of their souls."

"Yet here, the weak have the opportunity to elevate their souls," Dominus countered. Tykus arched an eyebrow.

"Ah, there we go," he replied, breaking out into a grin. "Finally you decide to contribute to our conversations!" He nodded. "Yes, but only by becoming someone else," he added. "There is value in diversity, Dominus."

"And in commonality."

"In proper proportion," Tykus conceded. "Yet in this world, diversity may only flourish when the strong-willed are scattered," he continued. "Tell me…do you understand the *real* reason my predecessor allowed you to destroy a third of the city, then build a wall around the remainder?"

"To protect the kingdom from the rest of the world," Dominus answered. Tykus chuckled, shaking his head.

"No Dominus," he replied. "It was to protect the rest of the world from *us*."

CHAPTER 27

The roar of the waterfall surrounding the rocky island assaulted Hunter's ears, a frigid breeze whipping through his hair. He stood there, his clothes soaked, shivering in the cold. Staring at the creature standing before him, in the center of the island.

"Mom?" he managed at last. "You're…"

"Alive, yes," she replied. She smiled at him, and in that moment he saw his mother, saw past the terrible transformation she had undergone. "I always hoped you would come for me," she added. "But I never thought…" She trailed off then, her eyes moist.

"It's really you," he realized. He felt numb, unreal. Like this was all just a dream.

"I missed you baby," she murmured, his voice breaking. Tears trickled down her inky black cheeks. Hunter felt tears of his own well up in his eyes.

"Mom!" he cried, rushing toward her. But she jerked backward, a look of horror on her face.

"Stop!" she shouted.

Hunter froze, staring at her silently. Her expression softened.

"I'm sorry," she apologized. "I didn't mean to yell at you. It's just…you can't go near me, Hunter."

"But why?"

"I'm a Legend, honey." she answered. She stared at him then, shaking her head slowly. "How many nights I dreamed of a day when you and your father would come after me!" she exclaimed. "Your brother sent patrols out to the Gate every day. I told him it was pointless, but he never gave up on you."

"But I killed you," Hunter protested. "I watched you die!"

"No honey," she retorted gently. "I can't die."

Hunter stared at her, at the glowing, blue strands of hair-like appendages extending from her scalp.

"You can regenerate?" he asked. "Like Xerxes?" She gave a rueful smile.

"Even faster than your brother," she answered. "As I recall, you shot me in the eye with an arrow. Did you realize I'd healed?"

Hunter stared at her, remembering how Vi had been impaled by his mother's sword. How he'd shot an arrow right into her eye, piercing it just before his mother had finished Vi off. And how he'd stared into her eyes afterward, as she'd laid on the ground, gasping for air. Of course her eyes had been whole, but he hadn't noticed at the time.

"Shit," he mumbled.

"Just like your father," she mused, shaking her head. "Can't see what's right in front of you."

"But…" Hunter protested. "…you weren't breathing," he protested. "Vi's sword was through your heart!"

"And once you removed it," she replied, "…I healed."

"But…"

"You ran before I could stop you," she continued. "My people tried to corral you, but you gave them the slip."

Hunter grimaced, realizing that she was right. He'd left as quickly as he could. If he'd only waited a few minutes…

"Why didn't you tell me?" he asked.

"Honey, I'm sorry," she apologized. "I didn't have time. You stabbed me through the heart before I could tell you."

Hunter had to smile at that.

"So you're apologizing for me stabbing you?" he quipped.

"I was being sarcastic," she retorted.

"Ah."

"*Any*way," she continued, "…I didn't even recognize you until you got closer. And by then, it was too late. You wouldn't listen to me."

"You killed my friend," he reminded her, rather defensively.

"Maimed," she corrected. "You should get in the water," she added.

"Why?"

"I'm a Legend," she answered. "Do you know what that is?"

"I do."

"If you stay here," she stated, "…you'll become like me. You'll turn *into* me." She shook her head. "I can't lose you like that." She gestured at him. "Go, wade in the pool. The water is cleansing…it'll protect you."

He hesitated, then did as he was told, passing through the cold waterfall and lowering himself into the pool beyond. He took a few steps, then turned to face the waterfall. Moments later, his mother came through the wall of water, stepping down into the pool. She was so tall that the water barely reached her mid-shin, and it glowed blue under the light of her luminescence.

"You must have a lot of questions," she ventured.

"Well yeah," he admitted, gesturing at her. "I mean, how did you…?"

"End up like this?" she finished, gesturing at herself. He nodded. "What have you heard about me?" she asked.

"That you came to this world through the Gate," Hunter answered. "And started a war with Tykus."

"I did," she agreed.

"You fought for the people in the Outskirts," he added. She sighed.

"I tried to," she replied.

"What happened?"

"I failed," she answered. He just stared at her, and she shook her head. "I didn't know what I was. I didn't realize that I was more of a threat to the people in the Outskirts than the kingdom was," she added, "…until it was almost too late."

"You changed them?"

"Started to," she confirmed. "When I realized what I was, I fled the kingdom," she continued. "I went past the Fringe into the deep forest. My people – the survivors – came with me, even when I ordered them not to. We hid in these caves while Tykus's soldiers searched for us."

"But how did you end up like this?" Hunter pressed.

"These caves are home to beetles," she answered. "Black beetles with an incredibly strong outer shell. Some of them must have had powerful wills, and began to change my people. We couldn't leave the caves, not without the kingdom finding us. We had a choice…die, or become what you call the Ironclad."

"But you're a Legend," he protested. "How could the beetles change you?"

"They didn't," she replied. "Not at first. I could have changed my people back to being human, but they would've become *me.* The only way to preserve some part of who they were was to allow them to change." She gestured to Xerxes then, still standing at the edge of the pool. "Including your brother."

Xerxes stared at them silently, his mane glowing in the darkness.

"So how *did* you change?" Hunter pressed.

"When Xerxes began to change," she replied, "…I was terrified I would lose him completely. I left the caves, risked being caught by Tykus's soldiers and killed, to find a way to help him. A noble family specializing in knowledge of the Deep had fled the Acropolis during the civil war; I went to get their help."

Hunter's guts squirmed.

"You mean Lady Camilla," he guessed.

"You know her?"

"We've met," he grumbled.

"Her father helped me," she stated. "Told me that there was a chance I could stop Xerxes from changing…maybe even stop *all* of my people from changing…if I went to the Kingdom of the Deep."

"Why go there?"

"The Kingdom of the Deep is the gateway to the Deep itself," she answered. "Do you know what that is?"

"Isn't that the place where the rules of the world go haywire?"

"In a way," she conceded. "The Deep is…" She hesitated, choosing her words carefully. "It does different things depending on how far you go. At the outer edges, it locks in the nature of things."

"I don't get it."

"I went to the Deep to stop him from changing," she explained. "The Lesser Deep had the ability to lock in his nature, so that nothing could change it."

"Ah," he replied. He glanced at Xerxes. "I'm guessing it didn't work."

"Not in the way I expected," she agreed. "My plan was to bring back water from a stream at the Lesser Deep, so that he could drink it. As a Legend, I thought I had nothing to fear…that nothing could change me."

"What happened?" he asked.

She hesitated, then stepped forward, only a couple of feet from him now.

"Vi told me you can absorb memories," she stated. "Is this true?"

"I can."

"How well?" she pressed.

"Pretty damn well," he admitted. "They feel like my own memories," he added. She nodded.

"Your brother has the same gift," she revealed. "But much weaker than yours. That's how he knew that you'd been taken by Vi after she killed one of my Ironclad in the Fringe."

"The one that attacked me and my friends?"

"The one that tried to rescue you," she corrected.

"Yeah, well it murdered my friend," Hunter retorted. "Tore his damn arm off!"

"He didn't know who you were at first," she explained.

"Right," he grumbled.

"The point is," she continued, "…you can absorb memories. It'll be easier for me to show you what happened to me if you experience it for yourself." She gestured at him. "Take off your helmet."

He did so, and she took another step forward, then leaned down until her forehead touched his.

***

The sun hung low over the horizon, its rays casting the scattered clouds overhead in a reddish-purple glow. Stars were already starting to peek through the sun's dying light, barely visible in the heavens. The air was warm and uncomfortably moist, a slight breeze feeling marvelous against Neesha's sweat-slicked skin as she hiked up a steep, rocky slope. Twisted trees dotted the landscape, a far cry from the dense forest behind her. A forest she'd been traveling through for days now, ever since passing the Kingdom of the Deep.

She stopped to catch her breath, bushing a few gray curls from her face. She leaned forward, hands on her knees, waiting for her breathing to slow.

Too old for this shit, she grumbled to herself.

She stood up straight, her backpack weighing heavily on her trapezius muscles. She tightened the strap around her waist, shifting the bulk of the weight to her hips. Glancing back the way she'd come, she saw the ground sloping downward to a rocky field extending for a good mile or two, merging with a vast forest beyond. And far, far in the distance, obscured by traces of dense fog, the black spires of the Kingdom of the Deep.

She sighed, facing forward and continuing her trek up the steep incline. Not so steep that she had to use her hands to climb it, but steep enough to make her ass and hammies ache. And her knees. She was in good shape – especially for a woman in her sixties – but not nearly as strong as she'd been before she'd come to this god-forsaken world. Time had not been kind to her…or to her son.

Neesha felt a familiar hopelessness come over her, and shoved it aside. There was no time for it; she'd mourned for Xerxes enough. A good son, with a nasty temper but loyal beyond measure.

And now he was changing. Changing like the rest of them.

Focus, she scolded herself.

She couldn't change what had happened, but she *could* stop Xerxes from changing any further. He could still speak, thank god…not like most of the others. She'd had to teach them sign language, a skill she'd learned from having a deaf brother.

If she could make it to the Lesser Deep, she could save her son. He was changing more slowly, on account of his powerful will. But if she didn't get back soon…

Neesha grimaced, moving faster up the rocky slope.

To her relief, the terrain leveled out a bit ahead. Bones littered the ground, some tiny, some quite large. None were recognizable. Trees – or what might have once been trees – grew in dense clusters amid the rocks. They were all wrong…some had trunks covered in scales instead of bark, while others had massive fleshy tumors sprouting from them. One tree – clearly quite dead – had a thick blanket of matted-down feathers all around it. Another had eyeballs winding up its trunk and branches.

She was getting close.

Neesha felt a tickling sensation on her neck and swatted at it. The bugs here were bizarre as well, and one of them had been particularly persistent, annoying her for the last few hours.

Better not be a god-damn spider, she thought darkly. She *hated* spiders.

The landscape ahead rose in a slight incline, a layer of dense fog hanging low over the ground, the ghostly shadows of deformed trees piercing through it.

She continued onward, the backpack's straps chafing her shoulders after so many days of traveling. The bulk of its weight was in the flasks of water she'd brought. She'd saved one of them to take water from the Lesser Deep back to Xerxes. According to the researcher she'd spoken with weeks ago, the Lesser Deep – the shallows, as the locals called it – had the ability to stop Xerxes from changing any further. It could never change him back, but it might preserve what humanity her son still possessed. Thank god that his mind was strong; when she'd left him, he'd still been himself. A human mind trapped in the body of a beast. But it was only a matter of time before that too was lost.

Neesha walked through the fog, peering through it, what little of the landscape she could make out dull and gray. After a few minutes, the fog was less dense, allowing her to see a few dozen yards or so. Tall structures rose from the ground ahead and to her left, what appeared to be the ruins of an ancient stone building. A few columns standing some twenty feet high, and a partially preserved archway. Nature had overtaken the ruins, vines winding their way up the columns, and strange clumps of brownish flesh sticking to their bases.

Neesha stared at the ruins, the archaeologist in her tempted to veer off to study them. She resisted the urge, knowing that time was of the essence…and that her rations would only get her so far. Nothing here looked safe enough to forage, after all.

She passed the ruins, studying them as she did so. They could be religious structures, a temple of some kind. The denizens of Kingdom of the Deep worshipped the Deep as much as they feared it. To them, it was the source of life itself, the wellspring from which all creatures – except humans, of course – came. There were tales of people who had gone to the Deep, legends of strange and miraculous things that had befallen these travelers over the last few millennia. Most of course were utter nonsense, or changed beyond recognition by generations of re-tellings. But many tales had at least a kernel of truth to them.

Only the mad dared travel to the Deep, of course. And Legends. For only a Legend could enter the Deep without fear of being transformed by the powerful wills that lived within it.

Neesha continued onward, the ground sloping upward again, this time at a less steep incline. The soles of her boots made a *crunch, crunch* sound on the rocky debris underfoot, the fog rising to chest-level around her. The terrain leveled off, and she spotted more structures ahead, this time to her right. Huge, curved structures made of white stone, piercing through the low-lying fog. The closest ones were at least fifteen to twenty feet tall, lined up one after the other in a perfect row. The structures became gradually smaller, the last ones appearing to be as tall as Neesha herself.

Strange, she thought.

She kept walking, studying the huge structures as she went. After a few minutes, she passed the row of structures completely, and glanced back at them curiously.

I wonder what…

Then she saw it.

From this angle, it was suddenly all-too-clear what the structures were: bones. Massive vertebrae stacked in a long column, the backbone of a creature of unimaginable proportions. Larger than any dinosaur…larger than any creature could possibly be.

Neesha stared at that spinal column, a chill running through her. She found herself touching the hilt of the sword sheathed at her waist, and forced herself to relax. If there were creatures like this one, living ones, then she would have no chance at protecting herself against them.

She peered through the fog around her, wondering what other creatures might live in this ungodly place.

Keep moving.

After a few minutes, Neesha reached the base of a large hill. She started up it, then stopped as her foot sank into the hill itself, her boot plunging into the moss-covered rock with a muffled crunching sound. She withdrew her foot, then stared at the hole it'd made. At the ivory-colored bones laying exposed, piled on top of each other in a dense jumble.

This wasn't a hill…it was a mass grave.

She hesitated, lifting her gaze to the top of the giant pile of bones. There had to be hundreds of thousands of dead bodies here, if not millions. The question was, what had killed them?

The Deep, she guessed. *I must be close.*

Or maybe she'd already arrived.

Neesha took a deep, steadying breath, then resumed walking up the hillside, her boots sinking all the way to her ankles with each step. She grimaced, making her way forward carefully, rising above the fog blanketing the base of the hill. Slowly, testing each next step as she went, she finally reached the top, the pile of bones giving way to a narrow, rocky ledge, a thick carpet of moss-like flora growing on it.

She froze.

Ahead of her, the earth gave way to a truly massive pit in the earth, easily several miles in diameter, extending thousands of feet downward. So far downward that the waning sunlight couldn't reach the bottom.

Neesha stared into that massive abyss, feeling suddenly dizzy.

The ledge ahead of her dropped almost straight down, leading to another broad ledge some twenty feet below. More ledges protruded from the pit walls further down in a terraced fashion, a little like a rice field. These extended downward as far as she could see; some of them contained small pools of water, a few of which glowed a faint blue in the dying light. Others hosted trees and shrubs, or large vines that wound their way up the side of the pit, green tendrils clinging to the rocky walls. Small waterfalls flowed from holes in the side of the pit, cascading down into the pools below. They had to be underground aquifers draining into the pit, Neesha realized.

Now all she had to do was get to the water, fill up a flask, and get out.

She stepped up to the very edge of the pit, studying the terrain. The nearest ledge was twenty feet down…too far a drop for an old woman. If she broke a hip, she was screwed. She glanced to the right, spotting a large green vine – wider than her waist – climbing all the way up the pit wall, then draping over the ledge she was standing on, only a few yards away. A single blue stripe wound around the huge vine, glowing faintly in the darkness.

She followed the vine's length downward with her eyes, spotting a terraced ledge some sixty feet below. It appeared to come from that ledge, roots embedded into the rock there and dipping into a glowing pool of water no bigger than a modest swimming pool.

If I can climb down that vine, she thought, *I can get the water from the pool and go.*

Neesha hesitated, scanning the pit for alternative routes. She would only get one chance to get this right after all…and the consequences for failure were far worse than her own death. After everything she'd gone through – after what she'd become – death was hardly something to be feared. At least if she died here, she'd never have to worry about what her body would do to anyone else. Too many had suffered from her horrifying power already.

There were no other routes she could see; the vine it was then.

She walked up to the vine, being careful to keep a few feet away from the edge of the pit. She reached the base of it, ducking below the branches spreading outward from it, then climbing onto it. The vine's rough bark offered plenty of handholds and footholds, and she lowered herself into the pit carefully. Then she swore under her breath – she was still carrying her backpack. She climbed back up, taking her backpack off and retrieving an empty water flask from it, shoving it in her pants pocket. Then she returned to the vine, climbing downward.

Neesha lowered herself slowly, carefully testing each foothold and handhold, taking her time. She felt something crawling on the back of her neck – another damn bug – and swatted at it.

Better not be a goddamn spider, she thought darkly. *Or I swear I'll jump off this damn vine just to kill it.*

A sudden breeze whipped around her, and she stopped, gripping the vine tightly, waiting for it to pass. Then she continued downward, eventually reaching the bottom. She let go of the vine, surveying her surroundings. She was standing on a small, moss-covered ledge twenty feet above a glowing blue pool. The narrow ledge sloped downward to her left, leading to a carpet of moss-covered rock at the edges of the pool. The moss closest to the pool glowed blue, just like the water and the glowing stripe on the vine.

It was a straight drop to the pool ahead; too steep to climb down. It was hard to guess how deep the pool was…but might not be safe enough to just jump into. Besides, she needed to have a way back up to the ledge she was standing on after she got a sample of that water.

That meant the only way down was to follow the narrow ledge sloping down to the left. But it looked awfully slippery.

"I am too damn old for this *shit*," she grumbled.

She sighed, steadying herself with one hand on the pit wall, then stepping down the steep slope. Her foot didn't slip…so far, so good. She took another step down, then another. Then her foot slipped; she cursed, catching herself before she fell.

Gonna be real fun getting back up.

Neesha steadied herself, then took another step…and her foot slipped again, sliding to the right. She lurched to the left, slamming her temple on the rock wall, then falling onto her left hip.

A loud *snap* echoed through the pit.

She screamed, feeling herself sliding off the narrow ledge, agony shooting through her shattered hip. Her legs dangled off the edge, hanging over the pond some fifteen feet below…and threatening to pull her over the edge. Neesha dug her fingers into the slick rock, trying to stop herself from sliding off, but it was too slippery.

She felt herself slide off, felt herself falling. There was a bright blue light, and then warm water engulfed her.

Neesha's breath locked in her throat as she plunged deeper into the water. She reached her arms up, raking downward with her hands, trying to claw her way up through the water. But without her legs – and with her clothes weighing her down – she continued to sink. She felt her right foot hit something hard, and realized she'd hit the bottom of the pool. She pushed off it, using the momentum to swim up toward the surface, ignoring the pain in her left hip as she did so.

Neesha's head burst through the surface of the pool, and she gasped for air, swimming toward the nearest edge of the pool. Her left leg dangled uselessly beneath her, every stroke bringing a new wave of pain. She was only a few feet away now, but her clothes weighed heavily on her, her boots threatening to pull her under.

Come on…

She lunged at the shore, reaching out with one hand and grabbing the mossy stone ledge. Her fingers slipped off the slick glowing moss, and she gasped, her head plunging beneath the water. She gathered herself again, lunging outward, and this time she managed to grip the ledge, pulling herself to it and resting her arms atop it.

Neesha stayed there, floating in the water, her breath coming in short gasps, her hip on fire.

Okay.

She closed her eyes, forcing herself to slow her breathing.

Focus.

And then her arms began to burn.

Her eyes snapped open, and she jerked her arms from the ledge, sinking immediately into the water. She reached out, clutching the ledge with both hands, feeling burning in her forearms…and her fingertips. She pulled her head out of the water, staring at her arms.

The skin on the front of her forearms was rising up, as if new veins were growing there, engorged with blood.

The pain intensified, and she cried out, clinging to the ledge even as her hands felt as if they were on fire. It took every bit of willpower for her to hold on; she saw the vein-like bulges extend down her arms, all the way to her hands. They looked blue in the light from the glowing pool.

No, *they* were glowing blue.

She stared at her arms incredulously, feeling the burning intensify. It crawled up her shoulders to the sides of her neck, then to her scalp.

Oh god oh god…

She gasped, gritting her teeth against the pain. It shot down her spine then, spreading to her legs, then her feet. Pain far worse than her shattered hip. Pain beyond anything she had ever suffered.

Neesha felt her grip on the ledge slipping, and lunged forward, resting her arms on the rocky ledge, holding on for dear life. She watched as the vein-like structures on her hands and arms glowed brighter blue, as bright now as the water itself, and the moss on the ledge.

And as she watched, the wrinkles on her hands began to disappear, her skin smoothing out and thickening before her very eyes. The pain in her hip vanished, the burning throughout her body slowly fading away.

She stared at her hands, unable to believe her eyes.

There was a tickling sensation under her right sleeve, and she turned to look at it, seeing something come out from underneath it. A small bug.

A black beetle.

She stared at it, watching as it crawled across her arm. It made it halfway…then melted, forming a small black puddle on her skin there.

What…

Then the blackness began to spread…and with it came sheer agony.

The blackness spread across her forearm, engulfing her hand, then moving up her upper arm to her shoulder. Wherever it touched came indescribable pain; she felt it expand across her chest, her neck, even her face. Watched it spread down her other arm, covering her entire body.

She screamed.

Her jet-black skin rose upward, forming thick plates on her arms. She felt a horrible *pulling* sensation in her wrists, then heard an awful cracking sound. Pain lanced through her wrists, and as she watched, her forearms began to elongate, growing thicker as they grew longer. Her hands began to grow as well, the bones of her fingers cracking, then elongating before her very eyes.

Then *all* of her joints shattered, bones breaking, then growing and reforming. Pain shot down her spine, her vertebrae popping one after the other. She howled, her screams echoing off the walls of the massive pit.

And then the pain stopped.

Neesha clung to the rocky ledge, her breath coming in ragged gasps, her heart pounding in her chest. She waited for another wave of pain, steeled herself against it, but none came.

She closed her eyes, forcing her breathing to slow, and focused internally.

I'm alive.

She realized her feet were resting on something hard, and looked down. Her feet were touching the bottom of the pool…she could stand in it without clinging to the ledge. She let go, gazing down at herself.

Black, armored plates covered her breasts, her belly. Her legs. Every inch of her body. Glowing blue vein-like structures ran down her limbs, with more cascading down her chest like thick strands of hair, mixed with thick black strands. Her clothes hung from her body, torn to shreds, as were her boots. Her limbs were freakishly long, though in proportion to her body.

Neesha tested her right hip, flexing it gingerly.

No pain.

She pulled herself out of the water then, rising to her feet on the narrow ledge. Beyond, the massive gaping hole of the Deep stared back at her. She stood there for a long moment, then turned, kneeling before the pond, lowering her face until it was only a few feet from the gently rippling surface. She gazed into the water, waiting for the rippling to stop, then stared at her reflection.

And screamed.

CHAPTER 28

Hunter jerked away from his mother's forehead, stumbling backward. He lost his balance, falling into the shallow pool surrounding him. The current pulled him leftward, and he gasped, struggling to get to his feet. There was a loud *splash* behind him, and powerful hands grabbed him from behind, pulling him to his feet and holding him fast against the current. It was Xerxes, he realized; his brother had waded into the pool to save him.

"Jesus," he breathed, staring up at his mother. At the enormous creature she had become. He looked down at his own hands, remembering that horrible burning sensation, but they were normal. Unchanged.

Still, the memory felt like it was his, indistinguishable from any other memory. Like it had happened to *him*.

Neesha took a few steps back, her long legs bringing her to the edge of the island, the waterfall pouring down her back. If the cool water bothered her, she certainly didn't show it.

"You saw?" she inquired. He nodded.

"I saw."

"Then you understand what happened to me," she stated. He hesitated, then shook his head.

"No," he admitted. "I mean, I get that you changed, but how?" he asked. "And how…"

"One question at a time," she interjected. "Never ask more than one at a time."

He grimaced, then gave her a sheepish grin. She'd told him that countless times when he was younger. Before she'd left him and Dad.

"How did you change?" he asked.

"The Deep changed me," she answered. "From what I've gathered, the Lesser Deep does lock in traits, as I was told. But it can also fuse living things together into one being."

"Like the beetle?"

"And the blue substance," she added.

"From the moss?"

"From the pool," she corrected. "The moss was changed by tiny organisms – something like planarians – that lived in the pool."

"Planarians?"

"Like tiny worms," she clarified. "They have the power to regenerate."

"How do you know that?"

"I brought a flask of the water back to your brother," she answered. "I gave him some, and studied the rest."

"And he grew that...mane," Hunter guessed, glancing at Xerxes, who was still standing in the water next to him. Mom nodded.

"But his traits weren't locked in," she stated. "Turns out the water isn't what changed me. It was the Deep itself, fusing my body with the planarians in the pool...and the beetle." She sighed then. "And locking me in this body forever."

"But you're a Legend," Hunter countered. "You can't be changed."

"My mind is Legendary," she corrected. "But my body was only near-Legendary. Anything less than Legendary can be changed by the Deep. The beetle must have been near-Legendary itself, to not be changed by me during my trip."

"So why not go back to the Deep?" he asked. "Bring a human along so you change back?" She gave him a sad smile.

"The Deep locked me in," she answered, gesturing at herself. "I can't change anymore. I don't age. And I can't die."

Hunter stared at her for a long, silent moment, then gestured at the pool...and the island.

"So why all of...this?"

"I'm a Legend," she replied. "Everything I touch...everything close to me...changes *into* me. Their minds are transformed into *my* mind. If I were to walk among my people, they would lose who they were. If I stay near you or Xerxes for too long..." She shrugged.

Hunter swallowed in a dry throat, taking an involuntary step backward. His mother sighed.

"Even if I die, my body will continue to change others," she stated. "The only way for me to minimize my influence on others is to stay here," she added, gesturing at the island.

"So you just...live here?" Hunter asked. "On the island?"

"Yes."

"But..."

"My people need me," she interrupted. "Their minds have been changed by their transformation. They're loyal to me without question, but not to each other. Without Xerxes and I, they would be easy prey for Tykus." She paused for a moment. "I did this to their parents," she confessed. "It's my responsibility to protect them."

"Their parents?"

"It's been half a century since I came through the Gate," she explained. "Most of the people in the Resistance are dead now. These," she added, gesturing at the Ironclad stationed at the periphery of the huge cavern, "…are their children."

Xerxes grunted, walking back to the edge of the pool and getting out. He stood there, water dripping from his legs, staring at them. Hunter watched him go, then turned back to his mother.

"So what now?"

"According to the Seekers we captured and…interrogated, Tykus is planning to declare war on us," she answered. "I hired Vi to bring you back to me. The Seekers want you dead, and so does Duke Dominus. You'll be safest with Xerxes and I protecting you. And Vi."

"You're Vi's client," he realized.

"Correct."

"Why did you save her?" he asked. "She tried to kill you."

"A misunderstanding," she explained. "Had she known who I was, she never would have attacked me. And," she added, "…you love her."

Hunter lowered his gaze. It was true, but he'd never told Vi how he felt. He loved her as a sister…and as his best friend. But it could never be more than that.

"Did she tell you that?"

"Yes."

"Great," he muttered.

"She's quite extraordinary," Neesha mused. "I've never seen anyone fight like she does. If I hadn't surprised her, I'm sure she would have defeated me, at least temporarily. And many of my people."

"Yeah, she's pretty fucking awesome."

"Aw, thanks kiddo," he heard a voice from behind say. He spun around, seeing Vi walking toward them. She stopped next to Xerxes, elbowing him in the hip. "How's the family reunion going, Blue?"

Xerxes grunted.

"All caught up?" Vi asked Neesha.

"Mostly," Neesha replied. "The rest can wait. You look exhausted, Hunter."

"I'm alright," he protested.

"Get some sleep," she insisted. "You'll need your rest for tomorrow."

"There is *one* more thing," Vi interjected. All eyes went to her. "We need to talk about Zagamar."

"Zagamar?" Neesha asked. Hunter grimaced, the name echoing through his mind. He grit his teeth.

"Don't…" he said. "Don't say his name. Please."

"What's going on?" Neesha pressed.

Vi recounted the tale, starting with Hunter meeting Lady Camilla, then his visit to the Crypt. She was quick and to the point, and thankfully she avoided saying the 'Z' word…and skipped the things that Camilla had done to him after he'd returned. When she was done, Neesha turned to Hunter, clearly troubled.

"This is bad," she stated bluntly. She stared to pace. "This is very bad."

"Tell me about it," Vi agreed.

"Thank god you're an Original," Neesha continued. "If you hadn't been, I would've already lost you." She stopped pacing, looking shaken. "As it is, we *will* lose you unless we do something to stop him from taking over."

"Like what?" Hunter asked. He'd managed to avoid thinking about that with everything else that'd happened recently, but hearing Mom bring it up send a fresh burst of anxiety through him. "You really think he'll take over?"

Neesha sighed.

"I learned a great deal from Camilla's father," she explained. "His knowledge was extraordinary. Camilla wasn't being entirely honest with you."

"No surprise there," he grumbled.

"Her father and I talked for some time," Neesha continued. "His interest was in cannibalistic cultures of the pre-Tykus era. Tykus was an Original…he came to Varta about six millennia ago. At that time, there was a city on the hill where the kingdom is now."

"So the Lady told me."

"Well she didn't happen to be an archaeologist," Neesha countered with a smirk. "I was. And I can tell you that the kingdom is a hodgepodge of influences, from Roman to Nordic to the English Renaissance."

"Makes sense," Hunter replied. "People came through the Gate throughout history."

"Exactly," Neesha agreed. "Six millennia here would be about a thousand years on Earth. The only known Europeans in America at that time were the Nords."

"So you're saying Tykus was a Viking?"

"He named this world Varta, after Svartálfaheimr," she answered. "That's from old Norse mythology. He called Earth Miogaror. It all fits."

"Huh."

"But the pre-Tykus architecture shows Roman influences," she continued. "…and when I left Earth, archaeologists were starting to understand that the Americas might have been inhabited by ancient Romans millennia ago."

"Huh," Hunter murmured. Then he frowned. "What about the Native Americans?"

"They populated the forests to the south," Neesha answered. "Including the Kingdom of the Deep."

Hunter's eyebrows rose.

"They're Natives?"

"They were," she corrected. "Natives were much more in touch with nature," she continued. "When they came here, they were far more accepting of nature's ability to change them. They've evolved far beyond their human origins."

"Okay," Hunter stated. "But what does any of this have to do with Zag…with *him* taking him over?"

"The Iroquois were natives that practiced cannibalism," Neesha explained. "They also believed that everything – rocks, plants, people – had a spirit…and that to eat something was to gain its power. So when they came here…"

"They ate people?"

"Yes," she confirmed. "And animals. But early natives wouldn't have known to test the wills of the animals they killed before eating them. And by eating them, they would have acquired some of their traits."

"They ate humans to gain *their* strengths?"

"Exactly."

"So you think Zagamar was a native?"

"Probably not," she replied. "Not based on Vi's description of his tomb. He might've been Roman. Either way, he had to have known the power of cannibalism…especially for a Legend."

"And what's that?"

"When you eat the flesh of a Legend," she replied, "…or anything stronger-willed than you, its will is incorporated into your flesh, a small part of your body *becoming* it. So, by consuming a small part of Zagamar's brain…"

"Part of him is inside of me?"

"Permanently," Neesha confirmed. "And his Legendary will is going to act on you from the inside, turning you into him more completely than merely exposing yourself to his bones."

"Jesus," he breathed. He swallowed in suddenly dry throat.

"And the more you consume," she continued, "…the closer to the original Zagamar you'll become."

Hunter said nothing, feeling suddenly sick to his stomach. The thought of someone destroying him from the inside, changing him…

"Zagamar *wanted* you to drink his flesh," she stated. "His tomb was designed for it…for someone of a powerful enough will to get past his defenses to consume his brain."

"But why?" Hunter pressed.

"Immortality," she answered.

He just stared at her.

"King Tykus comes back generation after generation," Neesha explained. "…by exposing a man to his Ossae. The result is that Tykus returns, but he's a shadow of the original, having his memories and looks and mind, but he's no longer a Legend…only the Ossae retain this power. And he's a new person…the original Tykus is still dead."

"Okay…"

"But ancient cultures – and those in the Kingdom of the Deep – believe that by consuming a Legend slowly, more and more of its original flesh will replace the person consuming it. They'll gain much of the power of the original…and the original Legend will awaken in this new body."

"Is that true?" Vi asked.

"Maybe," Neesha conceded. "In any case, scholars at the Kingdom of the Deep realized that with each subsequent generation, less and less of the consumed Legend would exist in the ones consuming it. So a Legend can gain multiple reanimations, but will eventually be destroyed in the process."

"Unlike Tykus," Vi stated.

"Right," Neesha agreed. "By not consuming him, he may exist forever."

"You're saying Zagamar…" – he tripped over the word, grimacing as he did so – "…you're saying he wanted to be reborn in *me*?"

Neesha nodded.

"I'm afraid so."

"We have to stop him!" Hunter proclaimed, his voice rising in panic. "How do we stop him?" Neesha took a deep breath in, letting it out slowly.

"The same way I tried to stop Xerxes from changing," she answered. "You need to travel to the Deep."

* * *

Hunter emerged from the mouth of the cave, Vi walking at his side. His head was still swimming from the revelations of the last hour. He still couldn't believe that his mother was alive…that he had a brother.

And that if he didn't do something to stop it, this cancer within him…the mind of a Legend…would consume his very being, would grow inside of him until it replaced him.

That with every second that passed, a part of him might be dying.

"Sorry kiddo," Vi stated, putting a hand on his shoulder and giving it a gentle squeeze. He swallowed, unable to say anything. "That's a lot of shit to eat in one sitting," she added.

He nodded silently.

"Not even gonna ask if you're okay," she continued.

"Take me to the Deep," he blurted out. She stopped, and he stopped beside her.

"Hunter…"

"I have to stop him," he insisted. "You have to take me there!"

"No."

"What? What do you mean 'no?'"

"I can't do it."

"Why not?" he retorted.

"Because I can't," she repeated. He was about to argue with her when she stopped him with one hand. "Shut up and listen." He grimaced, clenching his teeth.

"Fine."

"The Deep merges creatures," she explained. "If I go with you, *we* might be merged." She smirked then. "And as much as I like you, I would never want you inside of me."

"That's a shame," he muttered. But he couldn't help but smile back. She arched one eyebrow.

"You pining after me, Hunter?"

"Nah," he replied. "Not gonna lie, if you were interested in guys, I'd be intrigued."

"I'd break you," she shot back.

"Would it be worth it?"

"Probably," she answered with a grin. Then her expression grew serious. "If you're going to the Deep, I can help you get close, but the rest is up to you."

He nodded.

"Keep in mind that you're not a Legend," she continued. "Your mother was…and look what happened to her. If you go to the Deep, you might stop Zagamar…but you could also die, or become something inhuman."

"How could I die?"

"Your mother told me that most of the things she saw in the Deep…the corpses…were of things that combined, but didn't survive the process. She thinks the only reason *she* survived was because she merged with the regenerating shit first."

"Makes sense," he conceded.

"If you're not careful," she continued, "…you could merge with something and not survive."

"Better than being replaced," he countered.

"Granted."

"Let's go then," he stated. "I'm ready."

"Hold on," she retorted. "Not so fast. We can't go there yet." He frowned.

"Why not?"

"Your mother hired me to help her," Vi replied. "I have to do that first."

"Help her do what?"

"There's a war coming," she answered. "Tykus knows where your mother lives now. Dominus hired me to kill your brother, not just to get his head, but to weaken the Ironclad. He wants them all dead. Every single one of them."

"So why don't we kill him?" Hunter pressed. "That was my plan all along: get the head, get stronger, kill Dominus and the Seekers."

"Those aren't plans," Vi retorted. "Those are goals. Besides, even if we did manage to kill Dominus, we'd still be up against the rest of the kingdom…and they know where your mother lives."

"Can't we just move?"

"We run now," she replied, "…we run forever. If we don't take a stand, we're screwed."

"We?" he asked. "You're acting like you're one of them."

"I am," she stated. "And so are you. We're all outcasts from the kingdom. Cast out for being different." She shoved him to the side, making him stumble. "And they're *your* family, in case you forgot."

"I didn't," he retorted. "I just…I'm surprised you agreed to get caught up in all this."

"Why, 'cause I'm a self-centered bitch?" she retorted.

"Well yeah."

"Granted," she replied with a grin. "But I promised you I wouldn't leave you, remember?"

"True," he conceded, smiling at her.

"You're stuck with me," she stated. "And I'm stuck with you…and your family. Your mother saved me even though I tried to kill her and your brother. I owe her my life…and I don't take that lightly."

Hunter slung an arm around Vi's shoulders, and she did the same to him.

"Thanks, Vi."

"You're welcome," she replied. She ruffled his hair then. "Don't worry kiddo. We'll get you to the Deep."

"Soon?"

"Soon," she agreed. "You've got time, believe me. It can take a couple years for your body to convert completely to this world's matter."

"Yeah, well," he grumbled. "I'd prefer not to let this fucker take any more of me than he already has."

"About that," Vi replied. Hunter raised an eyebrow.

"Hmm?"

"We need to figure out what you can do now," she stated. "How we can trigger Zagamar to lend you his power…and what that power is."

"I really wish you wouldn't say his name," Hunter grumbled.

"Well, you better get used to it," she retorted.

"Oh yeah?"

"Yep," she replied. "Because if I'm right – and I usually am – that's exactly how we're going to unleash him."

Chapter 29

High Seeker Zeno walked down a wide hallway on the fourth floor of the Guild of Seekers, making his way past a long row of windows lining the rightmost wall. He glanced out of them as he passed, seeing the skyline of Tykus backlit by the three moons, which were nearly full. He only barely registered the scenery, mentally reviewing the tasks he'd given himself before going to bed.

First, the library. Then an hour in his office to prepare for the next day's events.

He spotted movement in his peripheral vision, and stopped, glancing out of the nearest window. The hill leading from Lowtown to Hightown was barely visible, the roads snaking between the buildings shrouded in darkness. Zeno frowned; the streets should have been lit by lanterns, one of the nightly duties of the kingdom's guards.

That's strange, he thought.

He looked straight down, spotting movement in the courtyard below, just in front of the guild. Inky shadows streaming toward the guild.

Dozens of them. No…*hundreds* of them.

Zeno spotted a glint of silver starlight on a naked blade, and cursed. He turned away from the window, sprinting down the hallway toward the double-doors of the library, shoving them open. The two Seekers guarding the other end backpedaled, drawing their longswords…that is, until they saw who it was. Then they lowered their weapons, bowing deeply.

"High Seeker!" one exclaimed.

"Soldiers are storming the guild," Zeno snapped. "Get me Grand Councilor Nova, now!"

They both burst into action, sprinting out of the library. Zeno watched them go, then heard shouting, followed by a dull *thump* from outside the guild. There was another *thump*, and he heard a loud cracking sound.

They've forced entry!

Zeno swore, feeling his heart hammer in his chest. He closed his eyes, forcing himself to take slow, deep breaths.

I've planned for this, he told himself. Planning was the antidote to panic, action the cure for hopelessness. Panic was chaos, the opposite of organization. And right now, the guild needed to be organized. They were unprepared for a raid by the government; their stores of illegal artifacts were safely hidden within vaults, but it was possible the kingdom would discover these. This would be no ordinary audit, he knew. The failed attack on Dominus was having its expected repercussions. He had to assume the soldiers would gut the guild, break down every wall.

So be it.

Zeno opened his eyes, tranquility returning to him.

There was more shouting, and he spotted a woman running down the hallway toward him. It was Nova; her face was flushed, sweat dripping from her forehead. She entered the library, skidding to a stop before him and bowing sharply.

"High…Seeker," she gasped.

"We're under attack," he stated calmly. He felt a sudden burst of fear, and ignored it, knowing it was coming from her. He forced himself to smile. "Relax, Nova," he soothed. "You should be rejoicing, not panicking."

"High Seeker?"

"The time has come," he declared, putting a hand on her shoulder, "…for the Ascension."

Nova's eyes widened, her mouth falling open. The blood drained from her face, and she swallowed visibly. But to her credit, she bowed again, more deeply this time.

"Yes High Seeker."

"You know what to do," he stated. Then he gripped her shoulder tightly, staring intently at her. "The fate of the guild is in your hands now."

She bowed again, then glanced up at him, her lower lip trembling.

"It's been an honor working for you, High Seeker," she declared, her voice breaking. He nodded, smiling at her again. He felt no emotion – *could* feel nothing, not for her – but he knew the gesture would mean everything to her. Would make her move worlds for him, make her give her life for him, and the guild.

"The honor is mine," he replied. Then he lifted his hand from her shoulder. "Go now," he stated. "Secure the vaults. Prepare the tunnels with our best Seekers."

"And you, High Seeker?"

"They will take me," he answered. "Let them."

She nodded, not questioning him. Then she spun about, running out of the library and into the hallway beyond.

Moments later, he heard a bell ringing, a loud, deep sound that echoed through the air, permeating every inch of the guild. A bell that had never been rung before…but one that all high-level Seekers had been trained to understand.

For when the great bell tolls, he recited, *the Ascension shall begin.*

The bell continued to toll for nearly a minute, the sound reverberating through the library. At length, it stopped, and he heard muted shouting from the floor below. He looked around, spotting a table with chairs surrounding it. He sat down on one of them, folding his arms in front of him. Waiting.

Our grand plan, he mused. *Centuries in the making.* He felt a chill run through him, and smiled. *Here at last.*

To think that *he* had been the one to see it come to pass!

Zeno heard a blood-curdling scream from below, muted by the floorboards. His Seekers were fighting back, resisting the inevitable advance of the soldiers. His men were outnumbered, that was certain. He suspected that, if he'd ordered it, they could have defeated the small army anyway. But that was not the plan…his Seekers fought not to stop the soldiers, but to delay them.

More shouting. The voices were getting louder. Closer. The soldiers must have made their way to the third floor.

He felt his shoulders tensing up, and forced them to relax. What happened to him now was irrelevant. The Ascension had begun, and would proceed with or without him. If he was to die, this was a fitting final act. A greater honor than any High Seeker before him had been bestowed. He would be immortalized by future generations of Seekers, and eventually by the entire kingdom. A figure as revered as Tykus himself.

He heard footsteps rushing down the hallway toward the library, and looked down at the books strewn across the table. He reached for a familiar one, the guild's apprentice training manual, opening it up and skimming a page.

The infant mind is ever-present. A primitive construct ignorant of the forces that compel it. The adult brain grows over it in layers of erroneous rationalization, believing itself capable of understanding these compelling forces.

But without the understanding that we are forever an infant, we will never understand our own emotions, which rule our behavior. Hunger and fatigue poison the mind. Sloth dulls it. Activity energizes it. All are internal forces. External forces have less effect, though they are the first to be blamed.

The infant mind knows nothing of the passage of time. All emotions are, in the moment, all-encompassing, and seemingly eternal. Yet experience proves otherwise, and gives rise to the First Principle of the Seekers:

Emotion is temporary, action is forever.

Soldiers burst into the library, and Zeno glanced up from his book. There were five of them, all with longswords drawn. They spotted him immediately, rushing in to surround his table.

He watched them impassively, knowing that, should he choose, he could kill them all without so much as breaking a sweat. But he stayed seated, steepling his hands before him.

For the Ascension, he thought.

"Good evening, gentlemen," he greeted, his voice utterly calm. The soldiers scowled back at him, and he felt the presence of one of them standing behind him.

"Stand up," one of them ordered. "Hands in the air. Now!"

He pushed his chair back, then stood slowly, obeying their commands.

"I would advise you not to attack me," he warned. "My reflexes are considerable, and beyond my control. I have no desire to harm you."

"Shut up," a guard snapped. But the soldiers kept their distance. They all knew who he was…and knew damn well that the leader of the Guild of Seekers was no one to be trifled with. An armed Seeker could kill most guards with ease; Zeno could kill these men – all of them – with his bare hands.

A sixth man entered the room, his eyes falling on Zeno. The man was not a guard; he wore bright white armor, a blue cape draped over his shoulders. The uniform of an Assessor, a lower Lord with the ability to cast Judgement.

Zeno watched the Assessor calmly, following him as he strode up to Zeno, stopping a meter before him. The Assessor put a hand on the hilt of his silver sword. An instrument of justice, the sword was only partly ceremonial. If deemed guilty, it would be used to kill Zeno on the spot.

"High Seeker Zeno," the Assessor stated, his tone hard, his blue eyes boring into Zeno's. "You are accused of high crimes against the kingdom."

"My accuser?" Zeno inquired, knowing that he had a legal right to the information.

"Duke Dominus of Wexford," the man answered. "And Lady Camilla."

Zeno took this in, hiding his surprise at hearing Camilla's name. A gamble on her part, to move against the guild. She was powerful, and protected by the Kingdom of the Deep's bizarre monstrosities. A fact that he wished he'd known before going after the Original. But he was still an enormous threat to her.

"Take his possessions," The Assessor ordered the guards. "Leave nothing but his clothes."

The guards swarmed in around him, tearing the sword and its sheath from his hip, then removing his medallion. He felt a burst of anger as they took the latter, and immediately suppressed it.

Emotion is temporary.

The medallion would be the guild's again soon enough. Nova would see to it. But he dreaded the thought of these imbeciles handling the precious artifact. They didn't deserve to stand in the same room as it, much less touch it. He felt his arms being pulled behind his back, felt them being bound at the wrists.

"And my alleged crimes?" he inquired, his voice still icy calm.

"You are accused of attempted murder of the Duke of Wexford," the Assessor declared. "And conspiracy against the kingdom, and possession of illegal artifacts."

"Conspiracy against the kingdom?" Zeno pressed. The Assessor nodded.

"Correct," he replied. "How do you plead?"

Zeno lowered his gaze to the Assessor's hand, still resting on the hilt of his silver sword. If Zeno admitted to his crimes, he would be beheaded on the spot. If not, he would face the High Court of the Acropolis.

"How do you *plead*?" the Assessor pressed, gripping the hilt tightly and pulling the blade out of its sheath a few centimeters. Zeno looked directly into the Assessor's eyes.

"Not guilty," Zeno replied. Then he smiled ever-so-slightly. "Not yet."

* * *

Sukri stood in the great library of Lady Camilla's mansion, gazing at the enormous variety of artifacts and books on the shelves lining the walls. Each artifact was held within a multi-layered glass or crystal display case…and many appeared to be highly illegal. For wild artifacts – those from nature – were forbidden in Tykus.

"You like my collection?" Lady Camilla inquired. Sukri turned to face the Lady; she was wearing a simple black shirt and pants, the top few buttons of her shirt left unbuttoned. Obviously on purpose, to give her guards – mostly men – a glimpse of her goods.

Damn hussy.

Still, Sukri had to admire the Lady. She held herself with utmost confidence, graceful and well-mannered, a woman commanding the men around her. Such a thing would never be allowed in Tykus.

"It's all right," Sukri replied at last, almost forgetting the Lady's question. "The guild's is bigger."

"Bigger isn't always better," Camilla countered. Sukri smirked.

"That what you tell the guys?"

"Quality matters," the Lady stated, ignoring Sukri's comment. "In artifacts, as in people. I surround myself with quality, Sukri."

Sukri raised her eyebrows, surprised that the woman remembered her name.

"How are your wounds?" the Lady inquired. Sukri glanced down at her forearms, still bandaged. She'd taken a look under the bandages that morning, seeing the angry-looking wounds on her forearms, the stitches holding the skin edges together. She could use her hands, for which she was grateful. Doctor Phelbus, for all his faults, was an accomplished surgeon.

"Healing," Sukri answered. She paused then. "Thanks," she added grudgingly.

"You're welcome," Camilla replied. "Sukri, why do you think I brought you here?"

"Hell if I know," Sukri answered. "Why *did* you bring me here?"

"Because I want to show you who I am," the Lady explained, gesturing at the artifacts around them. "I'm an academic…a researcher. I specialize in the study of wills, and the artifacts and Ossae that contain them. My family is a very old one," she added. "We were once part of the kingdom."

"Before the Civil War," Sukri guessed. The Lady nodded.

"Correct. The Guild of Seekers waged a centuries-long campaign against my family, as we were their only real competition. The guild wanted a monopoly, and eventually they got it."

"So?"

"Monopolies are bad for the market," she explained. "They increase prices and inhibit progress. The guild uses their dominance as leverage against the kingdom…and against independent contractors and smaller employers such as myself."

"Gonna be honest," Sukri replied. "I don't give a shit."

"Yes," the Lady murmured, eyeing Sukri with a look she couldn't read. "I find your honesty refreshing," she added. "It reminds me of…someone."

"What do you want with me?" Sukri stated bluntly.

"You're an Empath," Camilla replied, "…and strong-willed."

"How…?"

"You give off absolutely no emotion," the Lady explained. "That's how Dio knew what you were…and why he didn't kill you. You were terrified and grieving for your friend, but he felt nothing coming from you."

Sukri swallowed visibly, saying nothing.

"You're also still mostly yourself, despite the guild's efforts to indoctrinate you with those medallions," the Lady added.

Sukri frowned, her hand going automatically to her chest, where her Seeker medallion used to be.

"They can't risk new Seekers going out into the world with their medallions," the Lady stated. "The guild doesn't want their enemies acquiring their artifacts."

"So what do you want from me?" Sukri demanded.

"You have the qualities of a Seeker," the Lady answered. "And you're a powerful Empath. It's clear you've trained in separating your own emotions from those of others. That makes you extraordinarily useful."

"Oh yeah?" Sukri replied. "Useful for what?"

"For me, of course."

"Great," Sukri muttered. "Used by the Seekers, used by you."

The Lady chuckled, then stepped forward, putting a hand on Sukri's shoulder. Sukri felt a sudden affection for the woman. And not just affection; she found herself gazing at the woman's impressive physique, so tastefully clad in those tight clothes. Wondering what it would be like to…

Sukri blinked, forcing herself to look up into the Lady's eyes…and caught the Lady gazing at *her* body. It was the Lady's emotion she was feeling, she realized.

She's attracted to me.

It was a familiar feeling…and there was a longing to it. The woman missed someone…someone that Sukri reminded her of.

Use it, Sukri told herself.

"It isn't so bad to be used, you know," the Lady murmured, squeezing Sukri's shoulder. Sukri forced herself to smile.

"Depends on how I'm being used," she replied. The Lady arched an eyebrow at that. Sukri resisted the urge to pull away from the Lady's touch. It was clear the woman liked her…and it could be useful to nurture that. Sukri thought back to Seeker Hanlen's lectures; as an Empath, she could sense the Lady's emotions, while the Lady could not sense Sukri's. That gave her an advantage…one that she could use to get the upper hand on the woman.

"I assure you," the Lady replied with a twinkle in her eyes, "…that you would find it most rewarding."

"Mmm," Sukri murmured. She felt her attraction grow stronger, and hesitated. She could give into it, if only for a while. Make it believable. She dropped her gaze to the woman's body, lowering her guard. Imagining what it would be like to touch Camilla, to be touched by her. It wouldn't be the first time Sukri had fooled around with a woman…and she had to admit, the Lady was fucking gorgeous.

Could be worse, she thought.

Lady Camilla let go of Sukri's shoulder, backing up a step.

"I employ many Seekers," she stated. "But I'm missing a strong Empath."

"You want me to be your Seeker?"

"Yes," Camilla confirmed.

"Like that asshole with the silver eyes?"

"You mean Dio," the Lady stated. "Not at all. He started as a Seeker, but he's my bodyguard now. You would be a Seeker, just like you were in the guild."

"No thanks," Sukri grumbled. "I've had enough of people fucking with my brain." The Lady gave Sukri a sour look.

"The guild uses their medallions to brainwash their Seekers," she stated dismissively. "Forcing them to become good little boys and girls. They're a cult, dear. I don't work like they do."

"So how *do* you work?"

"I operate by the rules of the Seekers of the Deep," she explained. "Seekers there aren't part of a guild. They work under a patron, or do freelance work."

"Go on."

"They're allowed to expose themselves to the artifacts and Ossae they acquire," the Lady continued. "Unless explicitly prohibited by their clients. They guide their own…metamorphosis, exposing themselves to wills that give them an edge. Make them better."

"And you want to be my patron?"

"Correct."

"And you're really not gonna fuck with me?" Sukri pressed.

"Not at all," the Lady answered. "I have no medallion to brainwash you. You'll wear a uniform, yes, but it will be neutral until you wear it."

"Do I get paid?"

"I'll give you free room and board here in the mansion," the Lady answered. "You'll get a base stipend plus fifty percent of the value of any Ossae and artifacts you recover."

"Who determines the value?" Sukri asked. "You?"

"An independent appraiser," Camilla corrected. "I resell what you find, or keep it for my collection."

"All right," Sukri stated, putting her hands on her hips. "So what if I refuse?" The Lady smiled.

"Then you're free to go."

Sukri gave her a look.

"Bullshit," she shot back. "You know damn well I can't go back to the kingdom. The guild told me to off myself if I failed, and they'll hunt me down and kill my ass if I try going back."

"Granted."

"So I don't have a choice," Sukri concluded, crossing her arms over her chest. The Lady shrugged.

"Then my offer is even more valuable," she replied. "You get employment, a place to live, free meals…and maybe more," she added, her gaze dropping to linger on Sukri's body. Sukri felt the Lady's lust, and hesitated, loathe to give in to the emotion.

Do it.

She let herself go, allowing the lust to wash over her, and smiled at the Camilla, allowing her own gaze to drop to the Lady's deep cleavage.

"Gotta admit," she replied. "I'm intrigued."

The Lady smiled back, putting a hand on Sukri's cheek, then sliding her fingers down Sukri's neck. Her touch sent goosebumps rising on her arms, and she shivered. The Lady's hand continued downward, stopping just above Sukri's left breast. Sukri felt the heat of her palm, and suddenly wanted very much for it to continue downward. For the Lady to cup her breast, to lean in and kiss her.

"Do we have a deal?" the Lady murmured. Sukri swallowed in a dry throat, looking up into the Lady's green eyes.

"Deal."

Camilla leaned in, her lips centimeters from the side of Sukri's neck. Sukri's felt hot breath on her skin, and suppressed another shiver.

Then the Lady drew back, smiling down at Sukri.

"Good," she replied. She reached out, brushing a strand of hair from Sukri's face. "One more thing," she added.

"Yeah?"

"You'll need a teacher," she stated. "Someone to mentor you." She tapped her chin, thinking it over. "I'll give you the best Seeker I have."

"Who's that?"

"That," the Lady replied, "…is Dio."

CHAPTER 30

The bright rays of the morning sun pierced through the leaves above Hunter's head, lighting upon the patches of blackened grass on the forest floor. Each blade of grass was covered in a thick black shell, a warning to anyone traveling in this region that they were in Ironclad territory.

Vi stood before Hunter, dressed as usual in her leather uniform, the ever-grinning skull on her chest staring back at him. She crossed her arms, blocking his view, and smirked at him.

"All right," she declared. "Time to see what you've got swimming around in that fucked up brain of yours."

"I still don't understand why we're doing this," Hunter grumbled. They'd slept in a fairly neutral room in the Ironclad caves – one the Ironclad never entered – and Vi had taken him out here right after breakfast. A very meager breakfast, which was probably why he was in such a bad mood. Of course, the prospect of Vi unleashing the Legend within him wasn't doing much to improve his state of mind.

"So I can meet the guy who forced himself inside of you," Vi replied with a lopsided grin.

"You sure have a way with words," he groused.

"Zagamar's a part of you now," she countered. "You can piss and moan about it like a little bitch, or you can figure out how to take advantage of it. Your choice."

"Is it really?"

"Nah," she answered. "I'm gonna force it on you. Hell, you should be getting used to that."

"Anyone ever tell you you're a terrible person?" he grumbled.

"Only people that really know me."

Hunter sighed, crossing his own arms in front of him.

"All right," he muttered. "Let's get this over with. But you better have something for me to eat," he added. "I get fucking *starving* afterward."

"Guess I'd better do the hunting then," she replied. "If I leave it to you, you *will* starve."

"Ha ha."

"So," she stated, "…tell me about this Zagamar."

Hunter grimaced at the name, taking a deep breath in, then letting it out.

"He's like you," he replied. "He likes girls."

"Oh yeah?" she stated. "How do you know that?"

"Because I absorbed memories of him being…serviced by a few of them."

"Ooo," she replied. "All at once?"

"Guess he was popular."

"Maybe having Zagamar in there will do you some good," she ventured. "Sounds like he was quite the ladies' man."

"Yeah, well whatever he was, he was smart,"

"In that case, maybe we *shouldn't* go to the Deep," Vi ventured. "Sounds like Zagamar might be worth keeping around."

"And I'm not?"

Vi grinned at him, shoving him playfully with one hand. Hunter twisted to the side, dodging the blow. Or at least he tried to; she corrected for his dodge, moving with him and shoving his shoulder. He stumbled backward.

"Feel Zagamar coming out yet?" she asked. Hunter grit his teeth, hearing a faint echo of the name in his head. But it was far away. Annoying, but tolerable.

"Not really."

"Funny," she stated. "You usually get all whiny when I say Zagamar."

"Well, it's not working now," he grumbled. A part of him was relieved; he hardly treasured the thought of being taken over by the powerful will inside of him. But he was also a little disappointed. Hearing Zagamar's name – or even thinking about him – had worked before. Why wasn't it working now?

"You're disappointed," Vi noted. "I can smell it all over you. Don't worry kiddo…if I'm right, I just have to make you even *more* uncomfortable."

"Your specialty," he shot back. She winked at him. "So how are we gonna do this?" he asked.

"Tell me about Zagamar's tomb," she requested. "What did it look like?"

"You mean the room with the statue and the skull?"

"Duh."

Hunter frowned, picturing the pitch-black room inside the massive dome. He saw himself wading through the pool of water, felt that water rise up to his belly button. Light from his torch illuminated the large circular platform in the distance, life-size statues of gaunt, kneeling and bowing creatures arranged in a huge circle. All of them facing the center of the platform.

He closed his eyes, picturing the huge statue standing before him, a skull with the dome of its head missing, and from that cranium, another statue. One rising thirty feet into the air, arms raised into a "V" above its head, its face twisted in eternal agony. And set in front of it, a large stone bowl with a skull resting within.

Hunter described this to Vi, including every detail he could remember.

"Sounds like a cheerful guy," she quipped. "So you're saying he had a big penis hanging right above the bowl with the skull?"

"Yeah," Hunter replied.

"Men," she opined with a smirk. "Always trying to put their dicks into everything." She rubbed her chin. "Probably meant that the skull contained his fluids, which would give birth to himself. Rebirth, if you will."

"Yeah, well," Hunter grumbled, suddenly feeling queasy. "It'd better have been his brains I drank." She grinned.

"Thought you said it was salty…"

"Kinda wished you'd died back there," he muttered. "Not missing you at all right now."

"Just teasing, kiddo," she reassured. "It was brains, trust me. Keep going…what happened next?"

He sighed, closing his eyes again and focusing inward. He ascended the stairs, then stood before the bowl, staring down at the skull. It was embedded in a block of transparent crystal, the dome of the skull emerging from that crystal. He felt a slight pain in his belly, heard chanting echoing through the tomb.

Za-ga-mar!

The pain grew, a sharp, cramping sensation that demanded to be acknowledged. It intensified quickly, so powerful that it made him double over. He grit his teeth, feeling something else accompany that pain. A sensation so overwhelming it took his breath away.

Hunger.

Hunter's eyes snapped open, and he gasped, clutching at his belly. The pain faded quickly, only a memory now.

"Hunger!" he exclaimed.

"What?"

"Hunger," he repeated. "That's what I felt right before I drank. And right before he took over. Hell, *every* time he took over. I was always hungry!"

Vi grinned, uncrossing her arms and patting Hunter on the shoulder.

"Good job kiddo," she replied. "Damn…too bad I fed you breakfast."

"Yeah," Hunter agreed, wiping sweaty palms on his pants. "Alright…what now?"

"Now," she replied, "...you starve."

* * *

Hunter lowered his bow, watching as the arrow he'd shot sailed through the air. It struck a large bird perched on a branch over a hundred feet away, sending it tumbling to the forest floor. He grinned with no small amount of satisfaction at Vi, who was standing beside him. She clapped him on the back.

"Not bad Hunter," she stated. "You're finally living up to your name."

"Told you I've been practicing."

"Must've had a damn good teacher," she said with a grin. "Come on, grab that shit and throw it in with the others."

He did just that, retrieving the body and tossing it into a pile of other birds. They'd been hunting for the last few hours, preparing a veritable feast. Hunter preferred to eat plants, on account of the fact that they usually didn't have any absorbed memories, but Vi had insisted on a more varied diet. It was all in preparation for his insatiable hunger after letting the Legend within him loose.

If their plan worked, that was.

"All right," Vi declared when he was done. "Zagamar ready to come out and play?"

Hunter sighed, standing before. His belly growled angrily, so loud that he was sure she could hear it.

"Yeah yeah," he grumbled. "Let's just get this over with."

"Aww, no foreplay?" she quipped.

"Not in the mood," he shot back.

"That's okay," she replied with a wicked grin. "I'll just take it from you anyway. You seem to really enjoy that." He glared at her.

"You know, it really reflects well on you as a person when you keep making fun of me for getting sexually assaulted."

"Don't worry," she stated, still grinning. "Zagamar's the one who's going to be coming this time, not you."

Hunter rolled his eyes, waiting for her stupid grin to fade.

"You hearing Zagamar's name in your head yet?" she asked. He shook his head. "So saying Zagamar isn't working?"

He paused, realizing that it wasn't. He'd been too distracted by her antics to be bothered much.

"Maybe I have to be in a certain state of mind," he offered.

"And what state of mind is that?"

"The first time I was all stressed out in the tomb," he answered. He paused then, thinking it over. "The second time, I was trying to escape from the Lady's mansion. I'd just hit my head, and then she said his name."

"Ah," Vi replied. "You need to be stressed for it to work. Hungry and stressed…or maybe hunger was *part* of the stress?"

"I don't know," Hunter admitted. "Doesn't seem to be enough right now though."

"Oh well," she replied. "Guess I'll have to beat the shit out of you then."

"Wha-?"

She lunged forward before he could finish, and before he knew it, he was lying on the ground, the heel of her boot grinding into his breastbone.

"How's that?" she quipped, smirking down at him. He grabbed her foot, trying to pull it off, but it was no use. She was far stronger than he was.

"Get…off," he gasped, struggling to breath. She ignored him, pressing down harder…so hard he couldn't breathe.

"Still suck at fighting I see," she observed. "How does it feel to know I could kill you right now, and there'd be absolutely shit all you could do about it?"

Hunter gasped for air, his lungs burning, his head starting to swim sickeningly. He gripped her boot with both hands, trying to lift it straight up. But she leaned in harder, sending an awful pain through his chest. He felt his arms weaken, his vision starting to blacken.

"Bet Zagamar wasn't such a little bitch," she quipped.

He struggled to take a breath in, his chest on fire. Her words echoed through his mind, the chant of men long dead, voices spanning the millennia.

Za-ga-mar!

Images of a buildings all around him, reduced to rubble. Streets covered in white and black ash, the air thick with the scent of burning flesh. An entire city destroyed, kilometer after kilometer laid to waste. All by his hand.

Za-ga-mar!

He saw himself standing at the brink of a massive gaping pit in the earth, a mountain of corpses strewn at the edge, wave after wave of unworthy souls crawling on top of the dead, joining them. All in a doomed pilgrimage to the greatest power of all.

Za-ga-MAR!

He stared at the woman standing on his chest, time slowing to a crawl. It was pointless to resist her, he knew. The woman was physically superior, and he was steadily weakening. He couldn't talk either; debate was pointless.

He relaxed, and waited.

The boot on his chest lifted, and he heard the woman talking to him.

* * *

"There you are," Vi said, lifting her boot off Hunter's chest. The change had been sudden and subtle, but to her it'd been obvious. The great vessels at his neck had started to pulse far more quickly, his pupils dilating. A sudden flattening of his expression. And the way he looked at her…as if studying her. The way someone would study an insect.

"You still in there Hunter?" she asked, knowing the answer. It was a test, of course.

"Yes," came his reply. But he spoke far too quickly, answering almost before she'd finished speaking. And his tone was different. Impatient.

"Uh huh," she replied with a smirk. "You're as bad a liar as he is."

"Lying is for the weak," he retorted, speaking more slowly now. "He's still here," he added. "For now."

A provocation…either Zagamar was an asshole, or *he* was testing *her*.

"Tell me about yourself," she requested.

"What do you know of me?" he asked, again barely waiting for her to finish speaking before replying. His accent was strange, one she'd never heard before.

"Not a damn thing," she admitted. "Other than you're a Legend."

"My memories are incomplete," he observed. "I'm not fully me. This body must be a new Original."

"Good g-"

"All of my guesses are," he interrupted.

"Nice to see you have a high opinion of yourself."

"Well deserved," he shot back.

"We'll…"

"See about that," he finished for her. "I know what you're going to say before you say it. You're predictable," he stated dismissively. "All of you are. Your minds are inferior. Slow."

"Kinda want to stomp you in the chest again."

He smirked, rising to his feet. He moved too quickly; it was just as Hunter had described…time must be moving more slowly for him, his movements faster as a result. He stood there, staring at her, his pupils like saucers, his chest rising and falling quickly with each breath.

"So you're the mighty Zagamar," she mused. "Nice crypt, by the way. Took a few thousand years for someone to crack it."

"Obviously," he replied dismissively. "What year is it?"

"That won't help you," she answered. "Calendar reset when Tykus came here. That was six-thousand one-hundred and four years ago."

"Tell me about Tykus," he ordered, barely waiting for her to stop talking. She didn't like his tone, but she decided to humor him.

"A L-"

"I know that," he snapped. "I know some of what this body knows, but it's fragmented."

"Then lead with that next time, asshole," she retorted. He smirked.

"You hate Tykus."

"I don't give a shit about Tykus," she corrected. "Never met the guy and never will."

"His kingdom discarded you," he pointed out. "He had no place for you. But I do."

"Yeah, sorry, but you're not sticking around long enough to play warlord," she replied.

"My will is all powerful," he retorted. "This body is weak. It's only a matter of time."

"Uh huh."

"You don't know who I am," he stated calmly. "Or what I'm capable of. But you will. Everyone will." He gestured around himself. "I ruled the kingdom Tykus took for his own. I laid waste to the world and rebuilt it in my image…and I will do it again."

"Ooo," she replied.

"I'll forgive your ignorance," he stated calmly. She smirked.

"So magnanimous. Too bad your 'body' sucks at fighting," she replied, putting a hand on the hilt of her sword and arching an eyebrow at him. "I could stop all those grand plans right now."

"You won't kill your friend," he pointed out. "And I will rule again," he added. "With this body or the next."

"Yeah, well you'll have to wait a few more millennia," she grumbled. "Time to come back, Hunter."

"Don't…" he began, but she burst forward, tripping him. Or at least she tried to; he moved out of the way with uncanny speed. She smirked at him.

"Zaggie wants to play," she murmured. "Oh but I do love me a challenge."

She lunged forward again, trying to trip him…and punched out where he'd dodged to before. He didn't fall for it, dodging in the opposite direction…and right into the path of her left boot. She struck his upper thigh, but he'd already shifted his weight to the other foot, the blow knocking his leg back, but not making him lose his balance. He smirked at her.

"You're slow," he stated. Vi smirked back.

"Oh honey," she countered. "I'm just getting started."

He was fast, or at least he seemed to be. His muscles were no different than Hunter's, and she could almost certainly move faster. But time was moving slower to him, so he could see her attacks coming from a mile away. Of course, she had superior skill, and strength…and strategy.

She burst forward again, punching at his chest. He could dodge left or right or back, or block.

He blocked and dodged to the left, toward her back, planting his feet on the ground. Vi didn't even wait, kicking at his shins. He lifted his leg out of the way of her kick – as expected – and she kicked again, this time at his chest. With one leg up, he couldn't dodge out of the way…he had to block, which he did, knocking her leg to the side with one hand.

Now who's predictable, she thought.

Vi leapt into the air, using the momentum from his block to rotate in mid-air, kicking him in the shoulder. She moved fast, far faster than before, but pulled the kick at the last second. At full force, it would've dislocated his shoulder…or shattered it.

The blow connected, sending him flying to the ground.

He tried to get up, but she leapt on top of him, forcing him into an arm-bar. He cried out in pain, and she smirked at him, watching as he squirmed in her grasp, trying to break free. It was futile, of course; he was nowhere near as strong as she was, and had no skill in grappling. After a second or two, he relaxed.

"You're good," he admitted.

"Damn right," she agreed. "Nighty night," she added, transitioning to a chokehold. He struggled again – futilely – until his eyes fluttered, and he went limp. Still she choked him, knowing that he was clever enough to fake passing out.

At length she let him go, rising to her feet and staring down at Hunter's limp body.

"Well then," she muttered. "This is going to be interesting."

Chapter 31

The sun beat down on Dominus's scalp and shoulders as he strolled through the Royal Gardens, his boots crushing the short grass underfoot with each step. The sun shone overhead, but in the distance, thick clouds were forming, ominous-looking giants with dark underbellies. The clouds were moving slowly, but it was only a matter of time before the storm would be upon them. A boon for the gardens, he supposed, but unpleasant for Man. Yet another example of Man's displacement from the natural order, his vulnerability to the elements. Only by staving off nature could he hope to survive.

King Tykus walked at Dominus's side, uncharacteristically silent. The young man was staring off into space, his blue eyes cast downward. Dominus did not interrupt the king's train of thought; when it was time for the great man to speak, he would do so.

At length, Tykus blinked, then glanced sidelong at Dominus.

"What are you thinking, Dominus?" he inquired. His tone was utterly genuine, and from their many conversations since Tykus's return, Dominus knew that the question was no idle conversation-starter. The king did everything for a reason – and everything he did was a lesson.

"I was contemplating the coming storm," Dominus answered. Tykus glanced upward at the approaching storm, then nodded.

"Where I come from," he stated, "…men believed that the gods controlled the weather. Njord was the god of the sea, and sent the winds. Odin controlled the weather. We would pray to them to keep the seas calm."

"I see," Dominus replied. He had no belief in such gods, of course. Tykus raised an eyebrow.

"Do you?"

"Your highness?" Dominus inquired.

"Nature is the gods," Tykus explained. "And the gods are nature. But a god is a man, while nature is not. Why do you suppose that is?"

Dominus considered this, then shook his head.

"A man can be reasoned with," Tykus answered. "Can be bartered with in our prayers. Nature is a force, not a being; it does what it does, and cannot be persuaded to do otherwise."

"So men created the gods to try to barter with nature," Dominus reasoned. Tykus smiled.

"With obvious results," he agreed. "Strange that we humanize what we want to control."

"How do you mean?"

"We do this because we control each other," Tykus explained. "Man will always control Man. And most men secretly desire to be controlled." He gestured at the gardens, and at the high walls of the Acropolis in the distance. "Is that not what all of this is?"

"It makes us strong," Dominus argued. "Hierarchy is necessary for organization."

"Regrettably," Tykus agreed. Dominus frowned.

"Why should this be regrettable?"

"The nature of the hierarchy is foolish. The strongest-willed lead," he explained. "Not the wisest. Men will kneel for a fool as readily as they kneel for a philosopher."

"But you are no fool," Dominus protested. Tykus chuckled.

"What luck!" he proclaimed. "The king is not a fool. Or perhaps I am," he added. "I chose this, after all," he said, gesturing at himself.

"Immortality?"

"Yes," Tykus confirmed. He gave a wistful sigh. "What great luck that my old bones can turn a fool into a wise man. Perhaps that is my greatest power."

"Your wisdom is, your Highness."

"And that," Tykus replied, "…is precisely why I allow this kingdom to exist." Then he grimaced, gesturing at everything around them. "And it," he added, "…has become a greater power even than me."

Dominus frowned, but said nothing, knowing that Tykus would explain.

"Do you know why I speak of gods and nature, Dominus?" Tykus inquired.

"To explain human nature."

"To explain *nature*," Tykus corrected. "Humans are not separate from nature any more than the weather is separate from the oceans. Everything is nature…and nature is a system of systems." He gestured at the Acropolis. "This system – this grand system that I have constructed and that we maintain – is a part of nature. It has its rules, it is alive and self-sustaining in its own way."

Dominus grimaced, and Tykus must have noticed it.

"You believe nature is the enemy," he stated. "That everything beyond these walls aims to corrupt our humanity, to change us."

"It does."

"Yes," Tykus agreed. "Tell me…why is that bad?"

"Because we'll lose our identity," Dominus answered. "Our way of life…everything we hold dear. We'll become…beasts."

Tykus chuckled, stopping suddenly and putting a hand on Dominus's shoulder.

"You're already on your way, aren't you?" he countered.

Dominus froze, his breath catching in his throat. His whole body suddenly felt cold, as if freezing water had been poured over him. He stared at Tykus, his heart hammering in his chest.

"I don't…" he began, his voice cracking. Tykus raised one hand.

"Relax Dominus," he soothed. "And take off your boots."

Dominus stood there, unmoving. He had the sudden urge to flee, to bolt across the gardens and take a carriage back to his castle. But it would be pointless; the king knew. Somehow, he *knew.*

A brief image of himself slashing at Tykus's throat came to him.

I could blame it on one of the guards, he thought. *Or a lesser noble.*

He recoiled from the thought instantly, horrified by it.

"Dominus," Tykus stated, his voice still calm. He gestured at Dominus's feet. "Take off your boots."

Dominus swallowed in a dry throat, glancing down at his feet. There was no way to avoid this. It'd been voiced as a request, but he knew very well that it was an order. He obeyed, leaning over and pulling off each boot.

"And your socks," Tykus requested.

Dominus obeyed, removing these…and exposing his perfectly whole feet. For his part, Tykus didn't even look at them; he smiled at Dominus, his eyes twinkling.

"Now," he stated, continuing forward, and pulling Dominus with him. "Doesn't that feel better?"

Dominus paused, realizing it did. The grass tickled his feet, a novel sensation. One he hadn't felt since he was a child. It was cool, and a little wet.

"We're taught when we're very young to separate ourselves from nature," Tykus lectured. "Our very connection to this world – through our feet – is encased, protected from ever having to experience the natural world. We feel we are not nature at all. That there is nature, and there is us."

Dominus said nothing, having no idea how to feel. All he felt was numb.

"Tell me Dominus," Tykus said, raising one eyebrow. "Am I what you expected me to be?"

"No sire."

"What did you expect?" he pressed. Dominus hesitated.

"That you would be more…dominant," he answered. "More formal."

"Ah yes," Tykus replied. "I was, in my youth," he admitted. "But great age taught me to take off my boots, so to speak. To do so emotionally as well as physically."

"To…connect?"

"Aha!" Tykus exclaimed. "Correct!" He clapped Dominus on the back. "Life is so much grander when you stop protecting yourself from it. You can experience its mysteries, allow it to change you, and for you to change it." He sighed then. "Dominus, the walls protecting you from your fears are taller and thicker than the ones we built around this kingdom."

"I…" Dominus began, but Tykus stopped him with a look.

"And yet, nature has found its way into your heart. Has climbed those walls and claimed you nonetheless."

Dominus stopped, and Tykus did as well, turning to face him head-on.

"What do you know?" Dominus stated bluntly. Terror gripped him, and it was all he could do to keep his expression neutral.

"I know that you learned of a novel Ironclad from the Seekers," Tykus answered. "And that it possessed an incredible capacity to heal. I know that you conspired to take it from the guild, and that you now possess it. And I know that you've gained its power, and have healed from your wounds…and that it is healing much more than that."

Dominus took this in, his heart sinking.

It's over.

"How?" he managed. Tykus sighed.

"High Seeker Zeno accused you after his arrest," he confessed. Dominus was about to protest when Tykus gestured at Dominus's bare feet. "And my own eyes have confirmed it."

Dominus swallowed past a lump in his throat, blinking away moisture blurring his vision. He looked up at the sky, at the sun shining from above…and at the dark clouds heading their way.

"What I know doesn't matter," Tykus stated quietly. Dominus lowered his gaze to the king.

"It doesn't?"

"No," Tykus confirmed. He sighed again. "Your family is an unbroken chain, generation after generation of…you," he added, "…for six thousand years." He smiled. "A chain that has bound you so tightly I feared you'd never break free."

"You…*approve*?"

"As much as that matters," Tykus replied wearily. "I'm afraid the opinion of your fellow dukes carries far more weight."

Dominus's eyes widened with shock.

"They know?" he blurted out, a fresh bolt of fear piercing his guts.

"They do."

Dominus's shoulders slumped.

"Then I'm a dead man," he muttered.

"Duke Ratheburg has already demanded a test," Tykus informed. "You will be detained, and placed under constant observation. You will be wounded, after which your ability to heal will manifest itself."

"And then I'll hang," Dominus muttered.

Tykus turned away, gazing at the massive walls of the Acropolis.

"In my world, we created gods to barter with nature. And as I said, this kingdom is a part of nature. It has its rules, and its gods," he added, gesturing at himself. "But in the end, it cannot be bartered with…not without killing it."

Dominus stared at Tykus, a part of him wanting to beg the king to save him, to intervene on his behalf. But he knew it was impossible. Tykus was right…the kingdom was a system, self-perpetuating. Every system had rules. Rules more powerful even than a king. For if Tykus intervened, he would usurp the rule of law, upsetting the mechanism of the kingdom and becoming a dictator. And the dukes – and the rest of the Acropolis – would lose faith in their king, that he would allow corruption in his kingdom.

Everything Dominus had worked so hard to preserve might be destroyed.

Dominus stood up straighter, squaring his shoulders and facing Tykus.

"Then I'll die as I lived," he decided. "For the kingdom."

* * *

Hunter leaned against a tree trunk, rubbing his aching left shoulder and glaring at Vi. She smirked at him, her hands on her hips.

"You know, that Zagamar's an even bigger ass than you are," she opined. "Not gonna lie…I enjoyed the shit outta taking him out."

"Yeah, well, you took *me* out too," Hunter grumbled.

"So you remember everything?"

"Yeah," he answered. It'd been him all along, or at least sort of. Like he'd been thinking with a different brain. Not like there was another person battling for control inside of him, but like he *was* Zagamar. And Hunter. It was…weird. Similar to how he sometimes forgot that the memories he'd absorbed from others weren't his.

"What was it like?" Vi asked. Hunter sighed; he was irritable, he knew, and not just because of his shoulder. He was starving too, as he always was after turning into…*him.*

"It was like I was him," he explained. "But my own memories didn't feel like my own…they were like I – like *he* – said. Fragmented."

"Go on."

"Time went slow," he continued. "You were moving in slow motion, speaking in slow motion. My mind was moving fast…even for how slow time was moving." He smirked. "I thought you were stupid," he confessed.

"I knew what you were going to say before you said it. And I…*he*…planned out the conversation a dozen points and counterpoints in advance. Plotting everything."

"Didn't help him when he was fighting."

"I think he was frustrated," Hunter stated. "Like he was used to being stronger and faster. My body wouldn't do what he wanted."

"Unlike with Camilla," Vi quipped. Hunter blushed, then shot her a baleful glare.

"You just won't let that go, will you?"

"If you can make fun of something bad," she replied evenly, "…it'll lose its power over you."

"Maybe I should make fun of *you* then."

"Seriously," Vi insisted. "Camilla only has power over you if you give it to her. You need to find a way to take your power back."

Hunter didn't reply, and Vi sighed.

"So anyway," she continued, "…Zagamar's smart, and he's strategic. And he can slow down time. We need to find a way to use his abilities while keeping you…you."

"That'd be nice."

"If we can't, I'll have to figure out a way to convince Zagamar it's in his best interests to cooperate with us," she continued. Hunter gave a sour look.

"Good luck," he muttered. "You may be a better fighter, but good luck trying to manipulate him. He's fucking brilliant…he'll see right through you."

"Probably."

"Let's go with keeping me 'me,'" he stated. "I don't want that guy taking over again." He glanced at the carcasses Vi had assembled during her hunting spree. "All I'd have to do is make sure I never get hungry."

"Not the way *you* hunt," Vi quipped.

"Ha ha."

"Well, you'll have to stay hungry for a bit longer," she stated. "Time to try again. This time, you need to try to take control. Try to pull up memories of your past, good ones. Bad ones. Anything that might ground you. Remind you who you are."

"How's that gonna help?"

"Memories help make us who we are," she explained. "And you're full of other people's memories. Focus on the ones that are yours and you'll feel like you." She folded her arms across her chest. "Ready?"

"Not really."

"Too bad," she shot back. "You don't eat until you've got this."

"I hope Zagamar beats the shit out of you this time," he grumbled. "But try not to hurt me again," he added hastily. Vi smirked.

"No promises."

He sighed, taking a deep breath in, then letting it out.

"Ready," he grumbled.

"Come on out, Zagamar," Vi prompted. Hunter focused on the name, letting it echo in his mind. He drew up the memories he'd absorbed…Zagamar's memories…and let them fill his mind's eye. A vision of his men standing in a huge courtyard below came to him, thousands of soldiers chanting his name, their fists in the air.

Za-ga-mar!

"He's coming," Hunter warned, grabbing onto the tree trunk behind him with one hand.

"Find a memory of yours and hold on to it," Vi instructed.

He closed his eyes, seeing the bodies of babies and children strewn across an ash-covered street, their skulls dashed across the cobblestones. Angelic faces staring outward at oblivion. Children of lesser men, men who blindly followed false leaders. Leaders who feared him and sought to destroy him. But he would do better than they had. Better than the Legends who had come before. He would create a legacy far greater than that of his bones.

A new world would be born from him. He was the source, the beginning of a new race. A race of men elevated beyond their humble origins.

Za-ga-mar!

He smelled burning flesh, saw buildings on fire, black smoke filling the sky.

Za-ga-MAR!

"Find a memory, Hunter," he heard the woman say.

He ignored her, feeling the hunger growing within him, his heart beating faster. There was a *shift* as time slowed, his eyelids opening slowly, every movement of his eyes seeming to take seconds. He focused on the woman – he couldn't remember her name – and smirked.

* * *

Hunter groaned, rolling onto his back on the forest floor. He opened his eyes, seeing Vi standing over him. She was smirking down at him, her arms crossed over her chest.

"Nice try," she stated.

He grimaced, sitting up with some difficulty. His other shoulder hurt now, and his lower back was aching.

"Well that didn't work," he grumbled.

"Speak for yourself," she retorted with a grin. "I enjoyed the shit outta that."

"Asshole."

"Get up sweet cheeks," she ordered, reaching down and grabbing one of his arms. She hauled him upward easily. "Time for another round."

He sighed, brushing the dirt off his clothes, then facing her. He closed his eyes, focusing inward, trying to conjure up Zagamar's memories. This time they came a little easier, images flashing before his mind's eye. A parade of battles, a procession of the dead. He saw himself lying on his back, a woman straddling him. Felt himself inside of her, his pleasure mounting as she rode him.

Za-ga-mar!

He moaned as she brought him closer to the finish, saw the glint of light from the fireplace to his right as it reflected off of two of his soldiers' swords, pointed at the woman's back. They watched as the woman brought their master closer to the edge of ecstasy, as she was forced to coax out his seed and accept it inside of her.

Za-ga-mar!

He saw himself standing at the edge of a cliff that dropped off into an endless pit, utterly naked. Looked down to see a long, chiseled torso, his skin as black as night.

Za-ga-MAR!

And then he remembered his mother. How she'd stood in the glowing blue pool, her transformation complete. How she'd looked down at her hands, seeing long, black fingers.

I'm Hunter.

He saw himself standing before a large hole in the side of a cliff, a long line of men and women on a dirt path leading to it. Their hands and feet were bound, their clothes ragged and soiled. They screamed at him, their eyes wild. A procession of the mad, nearly Legends in their own right. Aimless in life, he would give them purpose in death.

Za-ga-MAR!

Hunter shoved the image aside, picturing his father, sitting on the couch in front of the TV, a drink in his hand. His eyes as dull as his soul had become, destroyed by the loss of his greatest love.

Za-ga-MAR!

He grit his teeth, feeling the Legend within him growing stronger, demanding to be set free. But it was no use resisting; Zagamar was too strong.

Unless…

He relaxed, pulling himself out of the stream of his emotions, standing at the shore. He watched himself, observed himself. Observed Zagamar, this thing inside of him. Watched as time began to slow, as the Legend's heart began to hammer in his chest.

He's not me, he realized, feeling utter calm come over him. Hunter observed as Zagamar opened his eyes, staring at Vi.

"You in there Hunter?" she asked.

Hunter felt Zagamar's mind begin to race, calculating a dozen possible conversations. Each statement led to a response, which led to another statement. The potential futures branched out before him, like trees in a small forest.

Hunter dipped his toes into the stream, feeling what Zagamar felt, but without being carried away.

"I am," he replied. He saw Vi smile.

"Good job kiddo," she congratulated. He smiled back.

And then he felt himself being pulled into the stream, and tried to extricate himself. But the harder he tried, the stronger the current became.

"Take me out," he said, right before he was swept away entirely. "And be gentle."

* * *

By the time Vi let Hunter rest, the sun was descending toward the horizon, sending long shadows of the trees around them splashing across the forest floor. After far too many attempts, Hunter had finally managed to wrestle control back from Zagamar without having to be taken down, which was just as well. He was sore as hell, and hardly relished getting his ass kicked again.

"Not bad," Vi stated, nodding at him in approval. "You done good, kid."

"Yeah, well," he replied, "…I still didn't have complete control. And I knocked him out of my mind completely," he added. "Instead of keeping him in check and using his power."

"Quit beating yourself up," Vi retorted, punching him in the shoulder. He winced, and she gave him a wicked grin. "That's my job."

"And you enjoy it."

"You're doing great," she insisted. "With practice, you'll do even better. The take-away is that you *can* control him. That's huge, Hunter."

He smiled grudgingly.

"Thanks," he replied. Then he grimaced. "But he's just gonna get stronger the longer we put off going to the Deep."

"Soon," Vi promised. "We got a job to do first."

"A job?" he asked. "What kind of job?"

"For your mother," she answered. "I'll let her tell you. Come on," she added, grabbing his arm and pulling him to her. She wrapped an arm around his waist, giving him a squeeze. "You've earned your dinner. Let's haul this meat back to the caves."

"Yes your highness."

"You got that right," she agreed. "My loyal subject."

"I'd rather be the royal concubine," he retorted with a sly grin. She snorted, shoving him away.

"You're *used*," she retorted, wrinkling her nose in disgust. "And not gently, either."

"Can't imagine you like it gentle," he countered. She gave him a lopsided grin.

"Depends on my mood."

"I can't imagine you'd be much better than Camilla," he ventured. She helped him gather up the carcasses of the birds she'd shot down, and then they made their way through the forest toward the Ironclad caves.

"Oh Hunter," she replied, giving him a pitying look. "You'll never know."

Chapter 32

High Seeker Zeno sat cross-legged on the cold gray stone floor of his prison cell, gazing past tall steel bars to the wall of the hallway beyond. His stomach growled, empty after days of being filled with nothing but water. An attempt to weaken him, to make him more pliable. More likely to confess to his crimes. As was the fact that his guards would run the hilts of their swords against his prison bars every hour, day and night, waking him from his sleep.

Standard procedure, he knew. And utterly pointless. His mind had absorbed the will of an ancient being, a will so powerful that nothing could break it. Even the sliver of Zagamar's will within him was enough to elevate him beyond anything his captors could fathom.

He would not break. He would not even bend. The will within him was indomitable. And it would know life again. It would rise from the ashes of history. But this time…*this* time…it would be eternal.

Zeno felt a chill run through him, and smiled grimly.

The great one's plan, millennia in the making…and soon it would be executed.

He sighed then, closing his eyes.

If only I could be there to witness it.

It was too much to ask, of course. It was enough that he had been the one to initiate the Ascension. An honor his predecessors would have done anything to have earned.

Zeno heard footsteps approaching, and opened his eyes, seeing a guard walk up to his cell, peering at him through the bars. Another man appeared beside the guard; a man in a crisp white uniform. He was perhaps fifty, with long salt-and-pepper hair and a long, but carefully groomed beard.

"High Seeker Zeno," the man greeted. His tone was crisp, no-nonsense. "I'm Orlan, your lawyer."

Zeno gazed at him impassively.

"You're familiar with the allegations against you?" Orlan inquired.

"Intimately," Zeno answered. Orlan blinked, then cleared his throat.

"Your trial is scheduled to begin four weeks from now," he informed. He gave Zeno an apologetic look. "The court has decided to accelerate the process given your…position."

Zeno was hardly surprised by that. The longer he stayed in prison, the more likely it was that his Seekers might attempt to free him. Frankly, he was surprised that he was being given as much time as he was. Commendable that the court, like the rest of the kingdom, was run with such adherence to principles and due process.

A good foundation, he thought. *For the world we will create.*

"I see you've plead 'not guilty,'" Orlan stated. "I assume that will be your plea in court?"

"Yes," Zeno answered.

"Very well," Orlan replied. "Well, as your lawyer, I have to advise you that doing so will prevent you from being able to negotiate with the prosecution for leniency," he warned. "And I'm sorry to tell you this, but the chances of you winning this case are…miniscule. Regarding the first allegation – that you conspired to kill Duke Dominus – it's his word, and Lady Camilla's, against yours. The Duke has a stellar reputation, even if Lady Camilla does not."

Zeno remained silent.

"Regarding the second allegation," Orlan continued, "…that you harbored illegal artifacts in your guild, I'm happy to say the kingdom's soldiers found no evidence of this." He grimaced then. "However, there is the unfortunate fact that they seized the medallion on your person."

Zeno suppressed a grimace of his own. The idea that anyone but him was handling the precious artifact was unthinkable. But it could not be helped…and soon the medallion would mean nothing.

"The medallion was Tested," Orlan explained. "And was found to be illegal." He sighed, scratching his head. "Which makes it indisputable that you were, in fact, personally in possession of an illegal artifact. Which, you must know," he added, "…is a felony for which the prosecution can request the death penalty."

Zeno waited for the lawyer to continue, but he was clearly finished.

"Is that all?" he inquired calmly. Orlan frowned.

"Isn't that enough?"

Zeno smiled ever-so-slightly. It was his right to know all of the formal accusations against him. If this was the prosecution's entire case, then that meant the kingdom hadn't discovered the tunnels far beneath the guild. Tunnels that led all over the kingdom…and even beyond it, past the wall.

"You may leave me," Zeno stated dismissively. Orlan blinked.

"Excuse me?"

"Leave," Zeno repeated. "You're not longer of use to me."

"No longer of…?" Orlan blurted out incredulously. "Do you understand what's going to happen to you?"

"I do."

"If you don't negotiate a plea deal," Olan warned, "…they're going to make an example out of you. Do you understand what that entails?"

"I can imagine."

"They'll kill you," Orlan stated bluntly. "And it won't be pleasant. Have you ever seen a man drawn and quartered?"

"I have."

"*That's* your future," Orlan said, jabbing a finger at Zeno. "So if you don't want to be systematically tortured, I *am* of use to you."

"I see," Zeno replied. He gazed at Orlan impassively. "I believe I asked you to leave."

Orlan stared back at Zeno in disbelief, standing there silently for a long moment. Then he stood taller, smoothing out the wrinkles in his uniform.

"Fine then," he muttered.

He turned crisply, walking out of view, his footsteps *clopping* on the stone floor, echoing through the barren hallway. Zeno sighed, lowering his gaze to the floor of his cell, relief coursing through him.

They don't know.

Everything was going according to plan, then. Nova hadn't been captured, that much was clear. And even if she had been, the process of the Ascension had already been initiated. There was no stopping it now; the process had been designed to be decentralized. There was no one man responsible for its execution. No head of the snake to cut off.

He heard the footsteps stop, then heard them again, faster now, getting louder. The lawyer was returning, and he was angry.

"You realize you're going to die, don't you?" he blurted out, glaring at Zeno. "If you don't let me help you, you're going to die…and badly."

"We're all going to die," Zeno replied. "It doesn't matter how. But what I leave behind," he added with a grim smile, "…will never be forgotten."

* * *

A cool breeze blew across Hunter's skin, the air passing through the hole in the domed ceiling of the cavern far above his head cool and damp. The roar of the cylindrical waterfall surrounding the island in the center of the cavern was ever-present, growing louder as he and Vi approached the edge of the pool. Xerxes stood by them, his huge frame dwarfing them all, the light from his mane and short, broad tail casting them in a blue hue. Hunter glanced at the tail, seeing it twitching side-to-side. Xerxes was clearly impatient, or at least irritated; an emotion he seemed to feel often.

Xerxes emitted a low howl, the mournful sound echoing through the cavern, piercing through the din of the waterfall. Moments later, a portion of the waterfall glowed a steadily brighter blue, until a familiar figure emerged from it.

"Good evening," Neesha greeted, stepping down into the pool beyond the waterfall, nodding at the three.

"Evening," Vi replied, elbowing Hunter in the side. Hunter grunted.

"Evening," he grumbled.

"How did your training go?" Mom asked, turning her gaze to Hunter.

"Painful," he answered. "But good. I'm learning to control him." It was more managing than controlling, but still.

"Good," Mom replied, clearly relieved. She glanced at Vi. "What have you found?"

"Zagamar's a megalomaniac," she replied. "But he's got a reason to be. He's fucking brilliant…and he definitely experiences time differently than we do."

"How did you unleash him?" Mom asked.

"Hunger," Vi answered. She grinned at Hunter. "You always were a little bitch when you were hungry," she added. "Now you're insufferable."

"He gets that from me," Neesha stated, giving a rueful smile. "Your poor father," she added. "I think that's why he cooked so much."

Hunter smiled, remembering the good old days, before Mom had vanished through the Gate. Dad *had* cooked a lot back then. He'd done a lot of things then, before he'd turned to the bottle. With every ounce of liquor he'd consumed, it in turn had consumed him.

"Do you think he'll come after you?" Mom inquired, her tone hopeful. Hunter hesitated; he'd often wondered the same thing. A vision of the revolver in Dad's glove compartment came to him, the single bullet in its chamber. He swallowed past a sudden lump in his throat, lowering his gaze.

"I don't know," he confessed. "Dad…" he added, "…he's…broken."

Neesha nodded, but she didn't seem dismayed.

"Your father stayed on Earth for you," she reasoned. "With you here, he doesn't have a reason to stay there anymore."

Hunter shrugged noncommittally. She only remembered the man who'd been strong, both physically and emotionally. Not the burnt-out husk of a man he'd become. Hunter wouldn't spoil her memory of Dad. It was better that she remember the man she'd loved, not the man she would've despised.

"I wanted you to come here to discuss the mission," Neesha stated. "I believe the kingdom is organizing for an all-out attack. The Seekers have left our lands, and our scouts say the military base in the Outlands is preparing for war." Her expression darkened. "Tykus has betrayed us. I need to organize our defenses while you complete your mission."

"You mean the mission to get Xerxes' head back?" Hunter asked. Neesha nodded.

"That's right," she confirmed.

"Have you tried looking up his ass?" Vi asked, slapping Xerxes on one massive butt cheek. Which was nearly at eye-level for her. Xerxes glared down at her. "I nominate Hunter to go fishing for it." She flashed Xerxes a wicked grin. "Try not to enjoy it too much, Blue."

Xerxes grunted, and Hunter felt the irritation radiating from his brother. Which was the emotion he usually felt from his brother. And he thought *he'd* had a bad temper.

"We need to prepare our defenses for the upcoming battle," Neesha said, ignoring them. "But we also need to ensure that the power of regeneration doesn't get into the hands of the kingdom. The aristocracy will never allow their soldiers to be exposed to Xerxes' head, but if Vi is right, Dominus will."

"He's pretty damn corrupted," Vi agreed. "Last thing we want him to have is an immortal army."

"They can never have the degree of regeneration that we have," Neesha countered, "...but it will still make them far more effective against our Ironclad."

"So my original plan was the right one," Hunter observed. "Get the head, get stronger, kill them all."

"Those aren't *plans*, Hunter," Vi retorted. She turned to Neesha. "So what *is* the plan?"

"You and Xerxes will travel to Castle Wexford tomorrow," Neesha answered. "Together, the two of you should be able to handle the castle's defenses and retrieve the head."

"Wait, that's it?" Hunter asked, glancing at Vi. "Won't there be like, hundreds of soldiers there?"

"Perhaps more," Neesha admitted. "But with Xerxes' power, and Vi's skill – and her new ability to heal – it should be enough."

"Yeah, well," Hunter replied, "...sorry if I find that hard to believe."

Xerxes grunted, slamming one huge fist into his own chest.

"WE...WIN."

"I seem to remember you getting your face smashed in," Hunter countered. "And that was only with a handful of soldiers."

"YOU...SHOT ME," Xerxes pointed out. Hunter grimaced.

"I did do that," he admitted, giving Xerxes an apologetic look. "Sorry, by the way."

Xerxes smirked, slapping Hunter in the back with one big hand. He stumbled, nearly falling into the pool. Vi saved him, grabbing his shirt from behind and hauling him backward.

"Ow," Hunter complained, rubbing his back. "Jesus dude, be gentle. I don't heal like you, remember?"

Xerxes chuckled, a low, rasping sound that seemed to come from deep within his massive chest.

"Why not send a bunch of Ironclad too?" Hunter asked Mom.

"We can't risk using a large contingent," Neesha explained. "We need as many men here to defend our territory as possible. And a small force will be able to infiltrate the castle grounds without attracting a lot of attention," she reasoned. "The element of surprise will work in our favor, and prevent the enemy from organizing."

"I don't know," Hunter grumbled. "Excuse me if I don't like the thought of having hundreds of soldiers coming after me."

"You don't have to worry about that," Neesha replied. He frowned.

"Why not?"

"You're not going," she answered. Hunter stared at her.

"Excuse me?"

"You're going to stay here, where you'll be safe," she explained. "I won't risk anything happening to you."

"Now wait a minute," he retorted. "That's not fair!"

"Not fair?"

"I spent the last few weeks risking my life to get my revenge against Dominus," he explained. "That bastard got my friend killed, and tried to kill me. He used Vi and I to get the head, then got the Seekers to double-cross us." He shook his head. "I'm not giving up on my only chance to get back at that bastard."

"Hunter…" Mom began. But Hunter cut her off.

"The only reason I went to that bitch's mansion was to get her help so I could get that head back," he stated angrily. "I went into the Crypt of goddamn Zagamar," he added. "And now that asshole is stuck in my head, eating me up from the inside, and you won't let me go?"

"Hunter…"

"Bullshit," he interjected. "I drank some dead guy's brains for a chance at this. I got fucking *raped.* I'm not staying here while these guys go out!"

Neesha stared at Hunter, her mouth opening, then closing.

"Raped?" she asked at last.

"Camilla tied him down and took him," Vi explained. "She hoped Zagamar's will was inside his…juices," she added. Neesha's eyes hardened.

"I'll take care of that," she promised.

"No," Hunter shot back. "*I'm* going to take care of it. You're not fighting my battles for me, Mom." He held up both hands. "I appreciate the offer, I do," he added. "But I need to take care of my own problems."

"You may not be able to," Mom countered.

"I have to try."

"In any case," she stated, "…it's too dangerous to go with Vi and your brother."

"I'll protect him," Vi piped in, wrapping an arm around Hunter's shoulders. "You can trust me." Neesha turned to face her.

"I know I can," she conceded. "But you'll need to focus on getting the Ossae."

"I can do two things at a time," Vi reassured her. "Besides, Hunter can channel Zagamar. He's actually not half-bad at fighting when that asshole is around."

"I don't know," Neesha grumbled. Xerxes grunted, putting a huge hand on Hunter's shoulder. He flashed a few rapid hand signals, then thumped himself in the chest. Neesha sighed.

"What did he say?" Hunter asked.

"That he would be honored to go into battle with his brother," she answered. "And that you will have your revenge."

Hunter smiled at his brother, feeling a sudden burst of affection for the big guy. He patted him on the back…or tried to. His hand went right on Xerxes' butt, which was at Hunter's eye-level. Hunter blushed, standing on his tip-toes and reaching up to pat the guy on the lower back. He caught Vi smirking at him.

"Thanks bro," he mumbled, his cheeks burning. Xerxes gave him what was probably supposed to be a smile.

"I'll think about it," Neesha decided. Hunter felt a burst of irritation, and opened his mouth to protest, but Vi gave him a look. He swallowed his anger, stepping back from it. After so much practice, it was almost effortless. He'd come a long way, he realized.

Emotion is temporary, he recited. And knowing that made it far easier to manage. Knowing that it would fade quickly, like a flash in a pan. He thought back to his early lessons with Thorius, his trainer at the Guild of Seekers. The guy probably would've been proud of him.

Double-crossing bastard that he was, he thought darkly.

"In any case," Vi stated, "…the Ossae will most likely be in a vault below the castle. Most of the important artifacts and Ossae the aristocracy hoards are," she explained. Hunter could hardly argue with Vi's experience; she' made a living plundering vaults for her clients. "It might be difficult to find," she warned. "For a guy as paranoid as Dominus, it might be downright impossible."

"I see," Neesha replied, clearly taken aback by this.

"Maybe not," Hunter offered. They both turned to look at him. "I can absorb memories, remember?" he added. "If you let me go, I can get Dominus's memories from his stuff, or from the bastard himself if I have to."

"He's got a point," Vi said, nodding at him approvingly. "Good thinking, Hunter."

"Xerxes has the same ability," Neesha stated. "But it's far too weak to be of much use." She paused, then sighed. "I suppose we have no choice then."

"I can go?" Hunter pressed.

"You can go," she agreed. She turned to Vi then. "I expect you to bring him back alive and well," she added. "If anything happens to him…"

"I'll keep him safe," Vi promised. "And so will Xerxes." Xerxes nodded, thumping himself on the chest again, then putting a hand on Hunter's upper back.

"You'd better," Neesha warned. "I lost my son once," she added. "I won't do it again."

CHAPTER 33

The waters of the River Ormr were dull gray in the distance, mirroring the somber-looking clouds that crowded out the sun overhead. Not ten meters from the river's shore, the Lady's mansion stood, with Sukri and Dio just outside of it. The Lady's creepy-ass bodyguard had led her here for her first training session.

Sukri glanced at the silver-eyed Seeker, staying as far away from him as possible. She could feel his emotions if she got too close…or at least the one emotion he always seemed to feel. That cold, inhuman calm.

Figures that bitch would do this to me, she thought darkly.

The Lady knew full well how Sukri felt about Dio. What Dio had done to Gammon. It *had* to be intentional, having this bastard be the one to train her.

Sadistic bitch.

The backyard of the mansion was mostly grass until it reached the sandy shore of the river. Dio led Sukri wordlessly toward a long line of wooden weapons lying on the ground ahead. He stepped up to the first weapon – a short sword – and gestured for Sukri to pick it up. She did so reluctantly, and Dio picked up one as well. He faced her then, staring at her with those eerie silver eyes.

"What now?" she asked.

He shifted into a fighting stance, and she immediately took a step back, her heart leaping into her throat. A vision of Dio slashing at Gammon's neck came to her, the flesh gaping…

Dio lunged at her, slashing at her shoulder!

Sukri moved frantically to intercept the blow, barely doing so in time. The *clack* of their wooden swords striking echoed through the air.

Dio relaxed, nodding at her. Then he lunged at her again – with the same attack – and this time Sukri blocked it a little easier. But Dio immediately followed up with a slash to her other shoulder, and struck her hard enough for it to smart. She stumbled to the side, barely able to keep her balance.

"Damn," she swore, rubbing her shoulder. She glared at Dio. "Take it easy, asshole."

Dio returned to his beginning position, then lunged at her again.

He repeated the first two attacks, and this time Sukri managed to block both of them. Dio stopped then, nodding at her…and immediately attacked again.

Son of a…

Dio repeated the first two attacks, then followed up with a quick thrust into Sukri's belly. She tried to twist out of the way, but was too slow; he struck her in the flank. Hard.

"God damn it!" Sukri swore, backing away and rubbing her throbbing flank.

Dio returned to his starting position…then went at her again. Same three attacks, and this time Sukri blocked all three…and got hit by a follow-up slash at her thigh. Again and again Dio went, and every time Sukri successfully blocked all of his attacks, he added another one. When she failed, they did it all over again.

After nearly a half-hour of this – and a string of ten attacks successfully blocked – Dio set his wooden sword on the ground where he'd gotten it, gesturing for Sukri to do the same. She did so, and he picked up the next weapon on the ground: a longsword. He handed it to her, then grabbed a longsword for himself.

And they went at it again. Same strikes, same rules.

This time, Sukri did much better. Not just because she'd memorized his attacks, but because she'd used a longsword before…and her Seeker medallion had apparently given her some pretty good reflexes with the weapon. Still, she only managed to block half of his attacks before getting hit. He went again, and this time she blocked all ten.

Dio nodded…then attacked again.

The Seeker repeated all ten attacks…then kept going, hitting her with all-new strikes.

Clack clack clack!

The sound of their swords striking broke the silence, until Dio managed to hit her with his fourteenth attack. A thrust right into Sukri's already-tender belly.

"God *damn* it!" Sukri shouted, backing up and hunching over. She waited until the pain started to lessen, then stood up, glaring at Dio. "What the hell's wrong with you?"

Dio just stared at her, saying nothing. She sensed that same eerie calm emanating from him…and boredom.

"Lousy prick," she muttered utter her breath…and then moved to block another string of Dio's attacks. She managed to block the thrust this time, only to be smacked across the temple by his next attack.

That hurt.

"Fuck!" Sukri shouted, dropping her sword and stumbling to the side. She caught herself, rubbing her throbbing temple. "Goddamn asshole son-of-a-bitch!"

Still, Dio just stood there, his silver eyes unblinking.

"Bet you feel real…" Sukri began, but Dio struck again, and she was forced to concentrate on blocking his attacks. She did so, this time managing to block twenty attacks. Dio relented at that, stepping back, then nodding at her. He exchanged his longsword for the next weapon in the line then: a halberd. It was like a spear, but with a hook and an axe-like blade near the end, in addition to the point. He handed this to her, taking one for himself.

Then he walked up to her, settling into a fighting stance.

"Uh," Sukri stammered. "I don't know how to…"

And then he attacked.

She managed to block the first two attacks – awkwardly – but he hit her with the third. She grimaced, taking a step back, knowing that it was pointless to complain. Pointless to tell the bastard that she'd never used a damn halberd before. He was going to attack her, and if she didn't block his attacks, she was going to get hurt.

He went at it again.

This time, Sukri focused on each attack, using the halberd like she'd used her longsword. Both were two-handed weapons, but the halberd was considerably longer. She managed to block six attacks before getting hit. And then eight. And finally, after a few more tries, all ten. To her relief, Dio didn't go for the full twenty attacks; he placed the halberds back on the ground, grabbing the next weapon in the long row: a bo staff.

In this way, Dio and Sukri made their way through the entire row of weapons, ten in all. By the end, Sukri was sweating, out of breath, and had bruises pretty much all over her body. After a certain point, she'd gotten too tired to complain, focusing entirely on not getting hit. Each hit had hurt more than the last, her already-bruised flesh throbbing painfully with each subsequent blow.

When they were done, Dio reached down, grabbing the staff again and handing it to her. Sukri stared at it wearily.

"Again?" she groaned. Of course he didn't reply; she sighed, grabbing the staff and getting into a fighting stance. But Dio did not.

"Your weapon," he explained, gesturing at the staff. Then he began walking back toward the mansion. "We leave tonight," he added.

"What?" Sukri asked, watching him walk to the door leading back into the mansion. "Where are we going?"

"To the Kingdom," Dio answered, opening the door.

"I can't go back there," Sukri protested. "The guild will have me killed!"

Dio paused, turning to face Sukri, his unnerving silver eyes seeming to stare right through her.

"The Kingdom," he stated, "…of the Deep."

With that, he stepped through the door, letting it close behind him. Sukri stared at the door, her mind whirling.

The Kingdom of the Deep?

She sighed, turning to gaze out across the backyard of the Lady's mansion, at the wide river beyond. Then she looked down at the wooden staff Dio had given her. Her entire body was sore after the beating she'd gotten…and she knew damn well that it would only hurt worse tomorrow. She also knew that this was the way Dio was going to teach her from now on: learn, or get hit.

"Great," she muttered under her breath. "Just great."

A familiar glumness came over her, the same feeling she'd had ever since the day Gammon died. Since the day he was murdered. She closed her eyes, imagining him standing beside her. Imagining him putting a big hand on her shoulder, lending him that wonderful sense of peace he always seemed to have. At least before joining the Seekers. They'd taken that away from him, forcing him to become something else. He'd sensed it, and sensed the changes in her.

Gammon had known he was losing her, and that he was losing himself. That's why he'd taken off his Seeker medallion…and she'd nearly betrayed him and told Master Thorius.

She opened her eyes, looking down at her staff. Her knuckles were white; she loosened her grip, taking a deep breath in, then letting it out slowly. Gammon had lived for her, had sacrificed his soul for her, and had died for her.

Don't let them change you, he'd said. *Be the woman I loved.*

She took a deep, shuddering breath in, gripping her staff tightly. A vision of Gammon lying on the ground came to her, blood pouring from his neck. And Dio staring down at the man he'd killed with those soulless silver eyes.

Feeling nothing.

Sukri lifted her gaze to the river, gritting her teeth.

I'll make you feel something, she vowed.

She would play the Lady's game. She would practice day and night, devoting every waking second to getting better. It didn't matter how many bruises she got, or how painful it would be. Nothing could hurt her more than what he'd already done to her. She would train until she was good enough to stand toe-to-toe with Dio, no matter how long that took.

And when that time came, she would make him pay for what he'd done.

CHAPTER 34

Dominus's suite in the Acropolis was enormous, displaying the wealth and status of his position – second only in power to King Tykus himself – in spectacular fashion. His four-post bed was opulent and exceedingly comfortable, the other furniture equally well-made, designed to provide for his every need.

He stared at all of it despondently, feeling utterly trapped.

A fine prison, this.

He turned to face the only door in and out of the suite. Three armed guards stood there, and he knew there were more waiting on the other side of the door. If he'd been allowed to keep his cane, he would've made quick work of them. Unarmed, it was unlikely he would be able to defeat them.

What have I done?

He looked down at his own hands, studying them as if seeing them for the first time. As if they were someone else's. Everything he'd done, he'd done for the kingdom. He'd made it his life's work to protect Tykus, to preserve the greatest nation in existence, a beacon of humanity in this terrible world. And it had all come to this…a prisoner in his own home, doomed to die a despised criminal, labeled a traitor for all eternity.

A traitor that loved his country, and did everything in his power to serve it!

He laughed bitterly, causing one of the guards to glance at the others uneasily. Dominus went silent, knowing what it must look like to them, the great Duke of Wexford accused of high crimes, laughing to himself while pacing endlessly in his room. The actions of a madman, someone corrupted.

Someone guilty.

There was a *click*, and then the door opened, more guards entering the room. Duke Ratheburg followed closely behind, and Dominus's own private physician, a man in long red robes. Dominus stared at the two, swallowing past a sudden lump in his throat. He stood at his full height, refusing to appear anything less than what he was in front of these men. The Duke of Wexford, a man of confidence. Of impeccable moral fiber.

"Good evening, Dominus," Ratheburg greeted coolly. "It is time for your Test." He gestured at the assembled guards. "Hold him fast," he ordered. "Stand him up and force his right forearm outward."

The guards obeyed, surrounding Dominus at once. He resisted the urge to fight back, allowing the men to grab his limbs. They forced his forearm forward, so that his hand was palm-up.

"Doctor, if you would," Ratheburg continued, gesturing at Dominus. "An incision, from his wrist to his elbow. Through the skin only, so that the fat is exposed. Avoid vital structures, of course."

"Yes Duke Ratheburg," the doctor replied. He walked up to Dominus, reaching inside a pocket of his robes and retrieving a scalpel. Made of obsidian, Dominus knew it was so sharp that it would separate his flesh with the barest of effort. One guard brought a bucket, positioning this on the floor just below Dominus's forearm.

"Don't move now," the doctor urged, giving Dominus an apologetic look. Dominus glared at him.

"You used your scalpel to heal me once," he stated coolly. "Now you use it to harm me. Have you forgotten your vows?"

The doctor glanced back at Ratheburg, who gestured for him to continue. He turned back to Dominus, refusing to look him in the eye, instead focusing on Dominus's forearm. He pressed the scalpel onto the flesh there, just below the hollow at the front of the elbow. Dominus felt a slight pinch, and steeled himself for what was to come.

If you must die, he told himself, *die well.*

The doctor slid the scalpel downward, and Dominus flinched slightly, clenching his teeth at the sudden, sharp pain. His skin gaped open, the flesh parting quickly, crimson blood pouring from the wound. Yellow fat was exposed, its bumpy texture in stark contrast to his smooth skin. The doctor ended the incision at Dominus's wrist, then backed away quickly, returning to Ratheburg's side. Dominus stared down at his wound, watching as blood poured down the edges, dripping over his hand and dribbling into the bucket. He turned his gaze to Ratheburg then, staring at his fellow Duke unblinkingly. Ratheburg's expression was stony.

"Shall I apply a bandage?" the doctor inquired, wringing his hands. Ratheburg shook his head.

"No," he answered. "This room is contaminated," he added with a grimace. "It will be removed stone by stone, and replaced." He turned his gaze to Dominus. "His blood is of no consequence now." He nodded at the doctor, then at the guards. "Leave us."

"Your Grace," one of the guards protested, clearly hesitant to leave Ratheburg alone with Dominus.

"Now."

They exited the room, leaving the two dukes alone. Dominus ignored the throbbing pain in his forearm, knowing all-too-well that the wound was only temporary. It would heal, and when it did, it would reveal the corruption of his soul. Indeed, the bleeding was already slowing to a steady ooze.

"Ratheburg," Dominus began, but Ratheburg held up one hand.

"Please understand that I am completely aware that this is only a formality," he interrupted. "I saw your leg," he added, gesturing at Dominus's right leg. "You showed it to me yourself after you killed your son."

Dominus said nothing, knowing that the man was right. His foot had been partially amputated by his doctor, and despite this, had grown gangrenous and infected. He looked down at his own bare feet, seeing them utterly whole.

"The law requires a Test to confirm corruption," Ratheburg stated. "A Test we both know you'll fail."

"Rathe-"

"I'm disappointed in you," Ratheburg interjected. "I believed in you, Dominus. I believed you to be the best among us, the greatest man in the kingdom besides Tykus himself." His gaze hardened. "I looked up to you, Dominus."

"Let me explain," Dominus insisted.

"Explain what?" Ratheburg retorted. "What is there to explain?"

"This isn't my fault," Dominus replied. "I didn't choose this."

"Then who did?"

"My son," he answered. He shook his head bitterly. "Conlan…changed when he was a teenager. Starting having notions of 'improving' mankind. He wanted to use illegal artifacts to make us stronger…wanted us to be like the Kingdom of the Deep."

"He was corrupted?" Ratheburg asked, clearly surprised.

"He was," Dominus confirmed. "And his will was slightly more powerful than mine," he confessed. "I sent him here to cleanse him of these horrible thoughts, but it didn't work. And it was too late for me." He sighed, lowering his gaze to the floor. "He knew he'd corrupted me," he continued. "He told me right before he died."

Ratheburg considered this, staying silent for a long moment. Then he too sighed.

"If that's true," he replied, "…then I'm sorry, Dominus. I suspect it *is* true," he added. "It explains why you sent him away, and why he tried to destroy the Ossae of Tykus. But," he added, "…you should have notified the authorities instead of sending him to the Acropolis."

"You're right," Dominus admitted. "I should have."

"Why didn't you?"

Dominus shrugged.

"I loved my son," he confessed. "I knew what would happen to him if I outed him. Or maybe he'd already corrupted me."

"I suspect so," Ratheburg agreed. Then he frowned. "I don't understand. How did Conlan get led so far astray?"

"I don't know," Dominus admitted. "It happened when he was a teenager. He'd started traveling to the kingdom then, learning about the city."

"Someone corrupted him."

"Maybe," Dominus conceded. He'd never considered the possibility. It was stupid not to; given his station, corrupting Conlan would have proven a very effective way of corrupting *him.* He stood there silently, his mind reeling with the possibilities.

"Not maybe," Ratheburg countered. "Definitely."

Dominus nodded, swallowing past a lump in his throat. Ratheburg shook his head.

"This is tragic, Dominus," he stated wearily. "That a man such as you would have been taken down by his own son, through no fault of your own. Especially after what Conlan did…after what happened to your wife. Someone got to you through him. And we should all be terrified by that fact," he added. "If they got to you, they could get to any one of us."

"Agreed," Dominus stated. "But who in the kingdom would do such a thing?"

"Rest assured," Ratheburg replied, "…that I will do everything in my power to find out."

Dominus nodded, feeling some small consolation from that. Ratheburg was a man of his word; he would not rest until Dominus was avenged.

"Thank you, old friend."

"You were a great man," Ratheburg stated. "I find it monumentally depressing that that man is gone."

"I'm still that man," Dominus protested. Ratheburg raised an eyebrow. "For the most part," he corrected. "I still believe in the kingdom. I would still die to protect it."

"You will," Ratheburg replied coolly. Dominus grimaced.

"Everything I did, I did for the kingdom," he insisted.

"You're corrupted now," Ratheburg retorted. "You feel that you are still yourself, but this is merely an illusion, Dominus. You're lost now…and what remains of you is something that cannot be allowed to live."

"But…"

"You've become," Ratheburg interrupted, "…the very abomination your son strived for."

Dominus clenched and unclenched his fists, staring at Ratheburg, resisting the sudden anger that threatened to build within him. He had the sudden urge to kill the man, to snap his self-righteous neck. There was no doubt in his mind that he could do it, were he to try.

He let the emotion come, knowing that it would leave just as quickly. Moments later, it did so.

"I can still be saved," he insisted, forcing his voice to remain calm. "I can be the man I was before. I can be Cleansed." Ratheburg gave him a withering glare.

"No amount of Cleansing can save you now," he retorted. "Only the Ossae of Tykus could do that…and we all know how that turned out for Conlan."

"I would never *dare* to harm the Ossae!" Dominus nearly shouted. "How could you possibly…"

"No Dominus," Ratheburg retorted, raising his own voice. "How could *you*?"

"I…"

"You used your disease as an excuse to send your own son to be swallowed whole by Tykus!" Ratheburg shouted. "You *murdered* him, then neglected your duty to become Tykus *again*, all so you could dabble in wild artifacts to heal yourself!" He glared at Dominus, his lower lip trembling. "If you *really* cared about your duty, you would've healed yourself, then offered yourself to the crown and *become* Tykus. Tykus would have removed your corruption, and you would have served our kingdom well."

Dominus stared mutely at Ratheburg, unable to reply. There was nothing to say. The man was right.

"Goodbye," Ratheburg muttered, his voice almost too quiet to hear. "Whoever you are."

He turned to go, opening the door. Suddenly there was shouting. Dominus looked past Ratheburg, spotting guards rushing down the hallway toward them. The guards skid to a halt before Ratheburg, their brows dripping with sweat.

"Your Grace!" one of them blurted out. There was panic in his voice.

"What's going on?" Ratheburg demanded.

"The kingdom," the guard replied. "It's under attack!"

Chapter 35

Vincent glanced through the long vertical bars at the cell beyond, eyeing the tall man seated cross-legged on the gray stone floor. The man stared back at him silently, hardly seeming to blink. Vincent shifted his weight from foot to foot, his hand going to the hilt of his sword sheathed at his hip. He knew the prisoner couldn't possibly get out of his cell, not to mention the fact that the guy was unarmed. But he also knew who the man was.

High Seeker Zeno, the leader of the Guild of Seekers.

Vincent turned, glancing at Thomas, his fellow guard. Thomas looked bored, leaning against the wall behind him, his eyes half-closed. Vincent nudged him.

"Wake up," he said. Thomas jerked awake, glaring at him.

"The hell," Thomas grumbled. "I was sleeping, asshole."

"Not on the job you're not," Vincent retorted. Thomas glanced at Zeno, then gave Vincent a look.

"What's the guy gonna do," he replied. "Spit on us to death?"

"You're a guard," Vincent countered. "We don't get paid to sleep."

"*I* do," Thomas retorted.

"Yeah, well not with this guy," Vincent shot back. "You know who he is, right?"

Zeno continued to stare at them. If he minded them talking about him, hardly showed it. The man was like a statue.

"Doesn't matter who he is," Thomas replied. "He's in there, and we're out here." He gestured at the cell. "See those bars?" he asked. "He's gonna have to lose a lotta weight to squeeze through 'em."

"Yeah, well I don't want you sleeping," Vincent insisted, eyeing Zeno uneasily. The guy freaked him out.

"Fine," Thomas muttered. He crossed his arms over his leather uniform. "But I'm transferring to a different wing," he muttered. "Fucking hate working with assholes like you."

"Shut up," Vincent retorted. "And do your goddamn job."

Thomas rolled his eyes, but didn't try to go back to sleep, to Vincent's relief. He knew that Thomas was right, but he also knew that he didn't want to be the only one awake working this shift.

"I hear this guy's supposed to be a badass," Vincent ventured. Thomas snorted.

"Doesn't look so tough to me."

"Easy for you to say," Vincent grumbled.

"Yup," Thomas agreed. "I'm on this side of those bars."

Vincent said nothing, his eyes returning to Zeno. The guy was still looking right at him. Just sitting there. He wondered what the man was thinking. He knew the charges against Zeno, knew that the man was almost certainly going to get the death penalty. But what if he didn't? What if Zeno was declared innocent, and went free? He was the head of the Seekers, after all. He could have Vincent and Thomas murdered…and he'd probably get away with it too.

Fuck, he swore under his breath. He had a kid on the way, after all. His first kid. Hopefully it was a girl…he'd always wanted a girl. His cousin's daughter'd just turned two, and she was frickin' adorable.

"God this job sucks," Thomas grumbled.

"Every job sucks," Vincent retorted, irritated that Thomas had interrupted his train of thought. "If it didn't suck, they wouldn't pay us."

"They practically don't."

"I got another mouth to feed on the way," Vincent shot back, "…and you don't see me complaining. This is overtime for me."

"Shoulda pulled out," Thomas muttered.

"Go to hell."

"Already here."

Vincent sighed, shaking his head. How he'd gotten stuck with this asshole was beyond him.

"You know…" he began, but he was cut off by the sound of a bell ringing in the distance. It was incredibly loud, loud enough to hurt his ears, even through his helmet.

"What the hell?" Thomas blurted out.

"The alarm," Vincent stated, his heart leaping into his throat. He grabbed the hilt of his sword. "Shit."

"Probably just a drill," Thomas ventured. Vincent glared at him.

"And what if it isn't?" he shot back. The alarm meant one of two things: either a prisoner was trying to escape, or…

"Stay here," Thomas ordered. "I'll check it out."

"Hey," Vincent complained. "You can't leave your post!"

Thomas ignored him, unsheathing his sword and jogging down the hallway. He reached the end of it, turning right and vanishing from sight. Vincent watched him go, then glanced at Zeno, who hadn't moved so much as a centimeter. He wondered if the guy was even breathing. Still, Zeno was staring at him.

Fuck.

The bell continued to toll, the sound echoing through the prison. Vincent stared at Zeno, then looked down the long, empty hallway, wiping sweaty palms on his pants. He gripped the hilt of his sword, switching his weight from one foot to the other.

Come on Thomas, he thought.

He glanced at Zeno, who still hadn't moved. If the guy was perturbed, or even curious, he certainly didn't show it. Vincent turned away from him, glancing down the hallway again.

Where in the hell are you man?

He heard shouting, then the ringing of metal on metal. A blood-curdling scream echoed down the hallway.

Shit!

Vincent drew his sword, holding it out before him, and took a step back. Suddenly he saw guards backpedaling into view at the end of the hallway, their swords drawn. One of them shouted, then lurched backward as a long, thin blade impaled him through the belly. Men in black and gold uniforms came into view, spilling past the remaining prison guards and rushing down the hallway toward Vincent.

Seekers!

"Stop them!" one of the guards shouted, swinging his sword at one of the Seekers. But the Seeker blocked the attack easily, slashing the man's throat in one smooth motion. The guard fell backward, slamming into the leftmost wall of the hallway, then slumping to his butt. The remaining guard – it was Thomas, Vincent realized – sprinted madly down the hallway toward him, the Seekers right behind the man.

"Vincent!" Thomas shouted. "Don't…"

A Seeker leapt on Thomas's back, knocking him to the ground. Thomas slid a few meters, then scrambled to get to his feet. But the Seeker raised his sword above his head, thrusting it downward, straight into Thomas's back.

Thomas gasped, his eyes going wide open, his mouth open in a silent scream.

The Seeker yanked their blade out of Thomas's back, the metal slick with crimson blood. Thomas lay there on the floor in a rapidly expanding pool of blood, his eyes staring vacantly at Vincent.

Before Vincent could react, the Seekers were rushing toward him, at least five of them, their blades gleaming in the light cast by the lanterns on the walls. He stumbled backward, his back striking the wall at the end of the hallway.

"Open the damn cell!" one of the Seekers ordered, pointing right at him.

Vincent nodded mutely, reaching into one of his pockets and retrieving a ring of keys. He held them out to the Seeker, his hand trembling so badly that the keys jingled.

"*You* open it!" the Seeker shouted. Vincent nodded again, walking up to Zeno's cell and fumbling for the right key. He found it, then put the key in the keyhole, turning it. There was a *click* as the lock opened. He stepped back then, giving the Seekers wide berth. They ignored him, opening the cell door and bowing to Zeno, who was still – *still* – sitting cross-legged on the floor.

"High Seeker," one of the Seekers greeted. Zeno turned to the man, nodding once. Then he got to his feet in one smooth movement, brushing the dust from his prison uniform. The Seekers backed up, giving him room to exit the cell; he did so slowly, almost casually, stepping into the hallway. Then Zeno turned to Vincent, those terrible eyes locking on his.

Vincent realized he was still holding his sword, and dropped it to the floor, backing up a step.

"Just…go," he stammered. "I won't stop you."

Zeno paused, then stepped up to him. Vincent took another step back, putting his hands in front of him.

"I don't want…" he began, but Zeno raised a finger to his lips. Vincent's jaw snapped shut.

"Go," the High Seeker stated. "Be with your family."

Vincent hesitated, then nodded, relief coursing through him. Zeno stepped to the side to let him pass, and he did so, eyeing the Seekers as he did so.

Then he felt hands grab his head from behind.

The world spun madly, and he heard a loud *crack*. Before he knew it, he was on the floor, laying on his back. He saw Zeno come into view, standing over him. Staring down at him.

Then the High Seeker stepped over him, walking down the hallway with his Seekers ahead of him.

Vincent followed them with his eyes, then tried to get up.

Nothing happened.

He stared up at the ceiling, willing his body to move. Still nothing. He couldn't even feel his arms, or his legs. Or his chest. Nothing.

It took him a moment to realize he wasn't breathing.

A surge of terror came over him, and he opened his mouth, struggling to get a breath in.

Nothing.

He lay there, willing his body to obey him. Willing air to come into his lungs. But his body would not obey.

Oh god oh god…

His vision began to blacken, the world fading from view.

And the last thing he saw before death claimed him was his wife lying in bed at home, holding a baby girl, and smiling at him.

* * *

High Seeker Zeno strode down the hallway away from his prison cell, leaving the trail of dead guards behind him. His Seekers led the way, as much to shield him from any attack as to show him the way out. One of the Seekers handed him a sword and a sheath, and he took these, strapping the sheath to his waist. They turned the corner at the end of the hallway, continuing down another one.

More bodies littering the floor. All of them guards.

Zeno stepped over these, allowing himself to be led through the maze-like halls of the prison. There was no resistance to his passage. No guards that swarmed the hallways to stop him. His Seekers had killed them all.

And they would kill so many more.

After a few minutes, they reached the exit, emerging from the prison into the large prison yard beyond. High stone walls surrounded it, guard towers rising above even them. Empty guard towers, of course. And the front gate of the wall was closed in the distance, the city guards not having yet responded to the prison bell. They would mobilize if the alarm did not stop soon. Zeno knew his time was limited.

Moonlight cast the yard's crushed stone surface in silver light, and it crunched underfoot as Zeno continued forward, his men fanning out around him.

The prison bell tolled once more, then went silent.

They reached the gate quickly, and Zeno found more Seekers standing in a large group before it. A very familiar woman broke off from them, walking up to him.

"Grand Councilor Nova," he greeted, nodding at her. She gave him a relieved smile.

"High Seeker!" she exclaimed. She bowed quickly. "It's good to see you."

"And you," he replied. "What's our status?"

"Everything according to plan," she answered. "We have Seekers in position and ready to strike all targets."

"Synchronize the attacks," he ordered. "Don't give them time to organize."

"Yes High Seeker."

"Good work, Nova."

"Thank you High Seeker," she replied, clearly pleased. She hesitated, glancing at his prison uniform. "Shall we recover your uniform?" she asked.

"Don't bother," he answered. "I'm going underground."
"What about the Founder's medallion?"
"Retrieve it if possible," he replied. "Keep it in a neutral room."
"Yes High Seeker."
"And Nova," he continued, putting a hand on her shoulder. "Make the Founder proud. It's up to you now."
"High Seeker?" she asked, looking confused. "You're not…?"
"I have a higher purpose now," he explained. "I must complete the final step of the Ascension."
"But…"
"Alone," he interjected. Nova swallowed visibly, then bowed again.
"Yes High Seeker."
"You retrieved what I asked for?" he inquired. Nova nodded, handing him a pack that had been set on the ground beside her. He looked inside briefly, then slung it over his shoulders. He gazed up at the night sky, noting the position of the stars. It was nearing midnight.
"Send the signal," he ordered.
"At once," Nova replied.
"Goodbye Nova."
He nodded at one of the other Seekers, who looked up, waving at a shadowy figure crouching on top of the wall. The figure waved their arms in turn, and within moments, the front gate of the prison yard began to open, the huge doors swinging inward slowly. Beyond them lay the ramshackle buildings of Lowtown, its streets cast in shadow. The night air was still, the city asleep despite the recent tolling of the prison bell.
A lone, golden light shot up between the buildings nestled on the hill beyond Lowtown in the distance, flying high into the air above the city. Moments later, it exploded, sending countless smaller lights shooting outward in all directions. They fell to the earth slowly, winking out after a few seconds. Moments later, Zeno heard a *boom*, the sound echoing off of the buildings of Lowtown.
The group of Seekers split, one faction staying with Nova, the other moving forward through the gate. Zeno followed them, making his way through the city quickly and quietly. Making his way to the secret, vast underground network of tunnels that would lead him outside of the kingdom, beneath the great wall. His Seekers would leave him then, and he would continue forward alone.
To the Deadlands, and far, far beyond.
He felt a chill pass through him, and allowed himself a smile. A new day was coming. The Founder's great mission – centuries after his death – would finally be complete.

CHAPTER 36

The King's Road curved gently leftward, a wide stone bridge supported by rows of massive wooden columns rising twenty feet above the forest floor. Light from the three moons above cast it in a bright silver glow, making it easily visible as it cut through the trees a half-mile to the right of where Hunter walked. He stared at it, remembering the first time he'd seen it. The day he'd arrived in this strange world, only to be chased by a huge, deadly monster.

He glanced to his left, seeing that same monster walking alongside him, its mane glowing brightly in the darkness. To think that it was his brother – that it'd been his brother all along – still blew his mind. He wondered what would've happened if he'd gone with Xerxes that day. If he'd never gone into the kingdom. He would never had had to deal with Trixie, would never have joined the Seekers. And he would never have met Vi.

"Lost in thought?" Vi asked. He looked past Xerxes, seeing Vi walking alongside the big guy. She grinned at Hunter. "Can't say I'm surprised," she added. "Easy to get lost when you're in an unfamiliar place."

"I've spent plenty of time in the forest, thank you," Hunter retorted.

"I meant in thought," she quipped.

Hunter rolled his eyes, not bothering to reply. She'd been needling him the whole trip, of course. It'd been welcome banter for the first few hours, but now he was exhausted. Vi never seemed to get tired, which was annoying. Neither did Xerxes, for that matter. It probably had something to do with the fact that he healed so quickly. After all, how could his muscles ever get sore if they could completely regenerate so quickly?

At least Xerxes is quiet, he muttered to himself. Xerxes hadn't said much of anything since they started the journey, communicating mostly in grunts and gestures…as usual. He often wondered what the big guy was thinking.

Was he quiet because it hurt to speak? Or was it because he didn't feel like talking?

"Hey Blue," Vi said, looking up at Xerxes. "What's your plan when we get to the castle?" Xerxes grunted, turning his black eyes to her.

"KILL" he growled.

"Well yeah," Vi replied.

"…EVERYONE," he finished.

"Wow," Vi stated, raising her eyebrows. "That might be the most detailed and well-thought-out plan I've ever heard. I can see why your mother made you her second-in-command. Goddamn strategic mastermind here."

Xerxes glared at her.

"WHAT…YOURS?"

Vi considered this, rubbing her chin. Then she shrugged.

"Eh, we'll go with that," she answered. She turned to Hunter. "Ever seen Blue fight?"

"Only when he fought you," Hunter replied.

"That doesn't count," she retorted. Then she grinned. "It's *real* fun to watch. Might just have to stand back and let it happen."

"What's it like?"

"Wait and see," she answered. "Wait and see."

They walked in silence for a while, following the path of the King's Road in the distance, walking parallel to it. Vi swung her pack off her shoulder, reaching inside and pulling out a hunk of dried meat. She bit into it, then offered Xerxes a bite. He grunted, clearly not interested in it. Hunter's stomach growled – he hadn't eaten since that morning – and he felt his mouth watering.

"Can I have some?" he asked.

"Nope."

"Why the hell not?" he pressed, feeling even more annoyed. "Just give me some."

"Gotta keep you hungry," she explained. "We're going to need Zagamar."

Hunter grimaced, feeling his stomach growl again, complaining bitterly.

"You just had to say his name," he grumbled. But to his relief, that didn't seem to trigger anything. It was getting a little easier to suppress the Legend, he realized. Maybe he just wasn't hungry enough yet…or maybe he was actually getting a little better at holding the guy at bay. Either way, the thought of letting Z loose was hardly something he looked forward to. If it was in the heat of battle, and he couldn't keep things under control…

"Why aren't you eating, Xerxes?" he asked, glancing up at his brother. Xerxes just grunted. "What *do* you eat, anyway?" he pressed. He thought back to all those human skeletons embedded into the walls of the caves, and the heaps of skeletons lining the perimeter of his mother's cavern. "Is that why you had all those skeletons in Mom's place? You eat people?"

"NOT FOR…FOOD," Xerxes answered.

Hunter stared at Xerxes, not sure how to take this.

"Those skeletons are there to help the Ironclad keep their humanity," Vi explained. "They drag any humans they kill and bring them back to their caves. Build them right into the walls, and pile 'em up near your mommy."

"Oh."

"They take shifts," Vi continued. "The ones that are in danger of becoming the Lost are transferred to your Mom's chamber for a while, to keep guard there."

"The Lost?"

"Ironclad that lose too much of their humanity," Vi clarified. "And don't end up getting it back. Ironclad have human brains, mostly. When they start to go all insect-like, they have to be taken care of."

"Taken care of?"

"Put down," she clarified.

"Ah."

Hunter walked silently for a moment, then glanced up at Xerxes again.

"You said you guys don't eat humans for food," he stated. "So you *do* eat them?" Xerxes nodded. "What for?"

"DESSERT."

Hunter blinked, then glanced questioningly at Vi. A low rumbling sound came from deep within Xerxes' chest, sounding suspiciously like a chuckle.

"Ooo," Vi piped in. "Blue made a funny!"

"Ha ha," Hunter grumbled. "But seriously, do you really eat humans?"

"NOT…ME," Xerxes answered.

"What he means is some Ironclad do," Vi offered. "When they're close to being Lost, they'll eat human flesh to try to regain their humanity. You know, like you drank Zagamar's…essence."

"It was *brains*," Hunter retorted rather hotly. He felt his cheeks flushing, and Vi grinned at him.

"Mmm hmm," she replied. "Sure it was."

"Does it work?" Hunter asked Xerxes, ignoring her.

"SOMETIMES."

Hunter glanced at Vi, who bit into her meat, chewing it absently.

"So what *do* you eat, big guy?"

"PLANTS," Xerxes answered. "MUSH…ROOMS."

"Gross," Hunter replied. He hated fungi of all kinds, just like his dad. The idea of eating anything that could grow on his feet…

"They *love* mushrooms," Vi piped in, biting off another hunk of meat. "Must be the beetle in them. They frickin' fight over that shit. Look like they're having an orgasm every time they eat it."

"There's a visual," Hunter muttered.

"Hey, that's a good question," Vi realized. "Blue, you guys have sex?"

"YES."

"Bet you're just swimming in beetle pussy," she guessed. "Being second-in-command and all."

Xerxes smirked at her.

"How do you guys do it, anyway?" she pressed. "You got a penis in there somewhere?"

"YES."

"How big is it?" she inquired. He raised two hands, spreading them out a disconcertingly large distance apart. Vi's eyebrows rose, and she let out a low whistle.

"Damn," she muttered. She grinned at Hunter. "Looks like you got the short end of the stick, kiddo."

"Oh Vi," Hunter replied. "You'll never know." Vi chuckled.

"Touché kid."

They fell into a comfortable silence then, trekking through the forest. Vi set a quick pace, but for once Hunter could keep up without too much difficulty. He was getting stronger, that was for sure. Xerxes, being nearly nine feet tall, had no problem keeping up with either of them. They continued to follow the King's Road in the distance; after what seemed like an hour, Hunter saw it turn more sharply leftward, descending gradually through the trees until it ended in a large clearing about a mile ahead. Vi led them toward the clearing, and as they grew nearer, Hunter spotted something through the trees. A tall stone wall far beyond the clearing, twin spires of a large castle rising above it.

"There it is," Vi declared, gesturing at the castle.

"You mean…?" Hunter asked. Vi nodded.

"Behold," she exclaimed with a dramatic flair. "The Castle Wexford!"

* * *

Hunter crouched a few dozen yards before the end of the forest ahead, gazing across the huge clearing at the Castle Wexford. He glanced at Vi and Xerxes; Vi was crouching as well, but Xerxes was standing at full height.

"What now?" Hunter asked.

"Now we have to get inside the outer castle wall," Vi answered. "It's not like they're gonna open the gate for us."

Hunter nodded, studying the wall. It extended over a hundred yards in either direction, a single closed, wooden drawbridge in the middle. A wide moat surrounded the wall, undoubtedly as much to prevent the build-up of unwanted influences as it was to act as a physical barrier to entry.

"You're saying we have to swim across the moat," Hunter stated, "…then climb up a sheer wall, then somehow drop forty feet to the ground?"

"And fight a few hundred soldiers," Vi added. "Yup, pretty much sums it up."

"Yeah, I changed my mind," Hunter quipped. "You guys go ahead, I don't need revenge that badly."

"Getting cold feet?" Vi asked with a grin.

"Maybe I'll let Zaggie handle this one," Hunter muttered. Vi arched an eyebrow.

"Zaggie?"

"Doesn't trigger the bastard when I say it," he explained. Vi shrugged.

"Zaggie it is," she replied. "Alright, enough bullshitting. Blue, can you swim across that moat?"

"SINK."

"Got it," Vi replied. "So we'll need to lower the drawbridge for him. Hunter, you suck at life, so I'll have to swim across and scale the wall. Then I'll drop down, kill the guards inside, and lower the drawbridge for you."

"Kinda hoping you die," Hunter grumbled.

"Once the drawbridge is down, you and Blue run across. Blue, I'll need you to execute some very specific instructions then."

Xerxes frowned.

"Kill everything but us," she ordered.

He grunted, giving her a horrid smile.

"Hunter, the minute you cross the drawbridge, I'm gonna need you to summon Zaggie if I ask," she continued. "Keep the bastard on task though. I don't wanna have to knock you out while a couple hundred guys are trying to kill us."

"I'll do my best," Hunter promised.

"In that case," she replied, "...you wanna be buried or cremated?"

"Ass."

"The hardest part," Vi explained, "...other than being outnumbered hundreds to one, is going to be finding the damn vault. It'll be underground, to prevent surface contamination and to hide it from aerial surveillance. It should be accessible from the castle itself, probably the basement levels."

"Not a problem," Hunter replied. "Just bring me some of Dominus's stuff and I'll swipe his memories."

"His bedroom'll be the best bet," Vi guessed. "Considering he spends a third of his life there. I'll help you get there, and Blue, you just make sure anyone who tries to get to us dies."

Xerxes nodded agreeably.

"Any questions?" Vi asked.

"I got one," Hunter replied, raising his hand. "How exactly are you planning on killing hundreds of soldiers?"

"Easy," Vi answered. "Xerxes will kill a few dozen, you'll kill one or two, and I'll kill the rest." She smiled. "Ready?"

Xerxes grunted, and Hunter nodded reluctantly.

Vi got to her feet, sprinting through the forest, closing the distance to the tree line with remarkable speed. Hunter watched her as she ran across the clearing beyond, toward the leftmost corner of the castle wall. He supposed it made sense; guards were more likely to see her if she went right for the gate. With her dark uniform, she blended into the night fairly well; hopefully they wouldn't spot her.

And if they did, well, he was pretty sure she'd figure something out.

Vi kept running, until eventually Hunter lost track of her in the darkness. He glanced at Xerxes, who was peering into the darkness as well, his mane and tail glowing brightly.

"Do you see her?" he asked.

"YES."

"You see better than I do," Hunter grumbled.

"SEE GOOD…IN DARK," Xerxes explained.

Hunter stared at his brother, realizing that – with his glowing mane – the guards weren't going to have a particularly hard time seeing *him*.

"You're going to stick out like a sore thumb," he warned. Xerxes smirked.

"GOOD."

Hunter shook his head, smiling despite himself. He had to give it to Vi and Xerxes…they had no shortage of confidence. He supposed being able to have your head cut off and still live to tell the tale made one less concerned about being hurt.

"Hey," he asked. "When I uh, shot you in the face…sorry about that, by the way. But when I did, why didn't you just heal immediately and get up and pound those soldiers?"

"LOST…FLESH," Xerxes explained. "HEAL SLOWER. NO LOSE…FLESH, HEAL…FAST."

"Makes sense."

He stared off into the distance, wondering if he spotted a shadow climbing the far-left side of the wall. He squinted, but couldn't see anything.

"What's she doing?" he asked. But Xerxes ignored the question. Minutes passed, and Hunter shifted his weight. His legs were starting to go numb from crouching too long. He stood up; Xerxes was a nine-foot-tall night-light. If anyone was going to see them, it'd be because of him.

Hunter spotted movement in his peripheral vision, and realized the drawbridge had started lowering itself slowly to the ground.

"Yes!" he exclaimed.

And then Xerxes burst forward, sprinting across the clearing.

Hunter cursed, running after the big lug. It was no use trying to keep up, however; Xerxes ran just as fast as Vi – maybe even faster – barreling across the clearing. The drawbridge continued to descend until it lowered itself completely, spanning the wide moat…and providing entry through the wall into the outer courtyard of the castle beyond. Xerxes reached the drawbridge far before Hunter, stomping across it. From this distance, he was a bright blue light shining in the darkness, streaking toward the entrance.

Hunter pushed himself, running as fast as he could. He reached the drawbridge, his boots *clunking* on the thick wood as he sprinted across. He spotted Vi ahead, standing just inside the entrance; Xerxes ran right past her, charging into the courtyard beyond. Hunter saw shadows spilling out of the castle toward Xerxes, and heard shouting ahead.

"Stay back," Vi ordered as he reached her. He slid to a stop, leaning over to catch his breath…and watching as the first of the soldiers ran up to Xerxes.

"Ironclad!" one of them cried out. "Get your hammers!"

The soldiers scattered before Xerxes, giving him wide berth – and switching to the warhammers strapped to their backs. They surrounded Xerxes, who continued running, slamming into one of the guards and throwing him a good twenty feet backward. Xerxes continued forward, leaping on the fallen soldier and slamming his four fists into the man, one after the other. Over and over again.

The other soldiers ran after Xerxes, the nearest one swinging his warhammer over his head and smashing it down on Xerxes' back. Xerxes took the blow, then turned and swung one huge fist, backfisting the soldier across the temple. The guy flew to the side, landing on the ground in a heap.

Two more soldiers ran up to Xerxes, swinging their hammers wildly. He took both blows, stumbling backward, then rushing forward and grabbing one of them by both arms and lifting them off the ground.

He *pulled.*

The soldier screamed as his shoulders popped out of their sockets, and Xerxes slammed his forehead into the soldier's face, then tossed him right at the second soldier. They collided, tumbling to the ground in a tangle of limbs. Xerxes leapt on top of them, tenderizing both of them with his huge fists until they stopped screaming.

"Archer above!" Vi warned.

Hunter ducked reflexively, hearing a *thunk* as an arrow embedded itself in the ground a few feet away. He grabbed his bow, nocking an arrow and looking up. He saw an archer standing in the guard tower, aiming right at him. Hunter held his breath, then let the arrow fly, watching as it sailed upward, slamming right into the guy's forehead.

"Whoa," Vi exclaimed. "Nice shot kiddo."

"Told you I've been practicing," he quipped. "We need to get in the castle," he added, looking past Xerxes – who was busy ripping various limbs off the remaining soldiers around him – to the front double doors. "I'm gonna guess those doors are locked."

"And well-reinforced," Vi agreed. Hunter nodded, spotting another archer aiming at them through one of the third-story windows of the castle.

He shoved Vi to the side, then dodged away himself…just as an arrow passed right between them. He nocked an arrow, aiming and letting it fly. It flew right through the window, slamming into the archer, who vanished from sight.

"You didn't have to push me," Vi grumbled. "I would've dodged it you know."

"You're welcome," he shot back. "Don't see you doing anything."

"My job's to keep you alive, remember?"

"Uh huh."

"And believe me," she added, patting him on the back. "That's gonna be a full-time job."

"Can you get up there?" he asked, pointing at the open window he'd shot the archer through. Vi looked up at it, then nodded.

"I'll run through and open the doors," she stated. "You stay here and help your brother. And Hunter," she added, putting a hand on his shoulder.

"Yeah?"

"Don't die."

"Right," he grumbled. She ran off, ignoring the guards fighting Xerxes, reaching the wall of the castle. She began scaling it, doing so with surprising ease. Hunter shook his head.

One day, he thought, *I'm gonna be just like you.*

Vi had reached the second story when she let go of the wall with one hand, lurching to the left. An arrow slammed into the wall inches from where she'd been, ricocheting off and falling to the ground.

"Little help here!" she yelled.

Hunter cursed, turning around and looking up at the guard tower. No one was there; he scanned the top of the wall, spotting an archer perched atop it. From this close to the wall, Hunter didn't have a clear shot; he ran toward the castle, taking cover behind a statue, then nocking an arrow. He looked up, spotting the archer aiming right at him, arrow drawn back. But the guy didn't fire.

Damn, he thought. *He's pinning me.* Which meant that there was probably another archer.

Vi scrambled upward, lurching to the side again to narrowly dodge another arrow…then lobbed some colorful language Hunter's way.

Yup.

He nocked an arrow, then emerged from cover…and went right back behind the statue. An arrow whizzed by, and he emerged again, aiming, then firing. His arrow flew wide of the target, and he cursed, nocking another arrow and letting it fly, then immediately ducking behind cover again. Another arrow slammed into the ground a few yards away.

He heard a scream, followed moments later by a *thud.* He smiled, then felt a sudden terror grip him. He looked back, spotting Vi still climbing the wall, and breathed a sigh of relief.

One more to go.

Hunter nocked another arrow, peering from behind the statue, studying the wall. There was another archer there, but they were crouched down, only their head visible. Hunter waited; if he could pin the guy down long enough for Vi to reach the window…

"I'm in," he heard her shout from above. He glanced back, seeing her vanish through the window. Which was great for her…but the archer was still up there. He couldn't exactly stay behind this statue forever.

He glanced at Xerxes, who was busy finishing off the one remaining soldier that had attacked him. The big guy swung a warhammer at the soldier, clipping him in the jaw. The soldier spun about, landing on the ground, out cold. Xerxes stomped up to him, swinging the hammer above his head, then chopping downward in a vicious arc, flattening the guy's skull with a sickening *crunch.* Then he tossed the hammer aside, gazing at the carnage around him.

A dozen or so soldiers were lying in various stages of dismemberment around him, their blood soaking the ground. Xerxes stood in the middle of them, his shoulders heaving with each breath, his huge body spattered with blood. He was smiling like a kid on Christmas.

Then an arrow bounced off Xerxes' armored chest, and his smile vanished. He glared up at the archer atop the wall.

Oops.

Hunter followed his brother's gaze, the archer already having ducked out of view again. He heard Xerxes' heavy foot stomps to his right, and glanced at his brother, who stopped at his side.

"COME," Xerxes urged. "I…SHIELD."

"Gotcha," Hunter replied. He got behind Xerxes – just as another arrow ricocheted off the guy's armor. Xerxes ignored the attack, striding toward the double-doors of the castle ahead. Hunter followed alongside him, spotting more guards rushing toward them to the left, and swore. There were at least twenty of them, if not more.

"Incoming!" he warned.

Xerxes grunted, facing the soldiers, his four hands clenched into fists. Hunter nocked an arrow, aiming it at the incoming soldiers and letting it fly. One of them fell, an arrow protruding from his face. Hunter glanced at the double-doors of the castle, which were still closed.

Come on, Vi!

"STAY…CLOSE," Xerxes urged. As if on cue, another arrow slammed into Xerxes, less than a foot from Hunter's head. Hunter ducked down low, making sure his brother was between him and the archer. He heard shouting, and then the guards were upon them!

They surrounded Hunter and Xerxes, keeping their distance, their eyes going to Xerxes, then the shattered bodies of their comrades strewn around him. Some wielded longswords, others warhammers. Hunter put his bow away, drawing his longsword and pressing his back against Xerxes', his eyes flitting from soldier to soldier. One of the soldiers stared at something to Hunter's left, then nodded. Then Hunter heard a shout from behind him, and glanced back, seeing two soldiers rush in at Xerxes, swinging their warhammers wildly!

Xerxes grabbed one of the hammers in mid-swing, tearing it out of the soldier's hands even as the other soldier's hammer struck him in the shoulder. The first soldier stumbled past Xerxes, falling onto the ground to Hunter's right…just as one of the soldiers facing Hunter lunged forward, thrusting their sword at him!

Hunter blocked, then slashed at the soldier's face. But the soldier was quick on his feet, dodging back just out of reach. Another soldier chucked a rock at Hunter's head; Hunter dodged out of the way…and right into the path of the first soldier's sword thrust.

He parried frantically, barely deflecting the blade in time, and felt a sharp stinging sensation in his left flank. He ignored it, lunging at the soldier and stabbing the man right through the heart. Or rather, he would have, if it hadn't been for the guy's metal breastplate. The tip of his sword bounced off harmlessly, and Hunter stumbled backward, nearly losing his grip on his weapon. The soldier who'd thrown the rock charged at him, raising his sword high, then chopping downward at Hunter's left shoulder. Hunter tried to get his sword up to intercept the blow, but he was too slow.

He didn't even have time to scream.

A huge black arm came between his shoulder and the blade, the soldier's sword ricocheting off harmlessly. Hunter blinked, taking a moment to realize that Xerxes had saved him. Then he ducked under his brother's arm, slashing at the soldier's throat as the man stumbled backward. The soldier's neck gaped open in a spray of blood, a gurgling sound coming from his severed windpipe.

More soldiers replaced him, squaring off against Hunter, who backpedaled, going back-to-back with Xerxes once again.

"Thanks bro," he offered, and heard Xerxes grunt. And then heard a loud *crack*. Hunter glanced back, realizing Xerxes had been struck in the chest with a warhammer. Xerxes stumbled backward, shoving Hunter forward and to the side. He felt something *whiz* by his right ear, and saw an arrow bury itself into the ground a few feet away.

That damn archer!

Hunter backed up into Xerxes again, glancing up at the wall. The archer was still there, no longer crouching low, busy nocking another arrow. Hunter cursed, positioning himself so his brother was shielding him…and turned forward to see one of the soldiers lunge forward, swinging their huge warhammer down at his skull!

Hunter dodged to the side, the hammer striking Xerxes in the lower back. Xerxes spun around, glaring down at the soldier, then boxed the man's ears. Or at least, that's what would've happened if a human had struck the guy; with Xerxes' incredible strength, the guy's head practically exploded.

The remaining soldiers backed away from Xerxes, eyeing the huge Ironclad with newfound respect.

"Don't let them pick you off one-by-one," one of the soldiers shouted. "All at once now," he ordered. "Charge!"

The soldiers cried out in unison, charging at Hunter and Xerxes from all sides. Hunter stumbled backward as swords came at him, swinging his longsword to bat them away. He felt a sudden pain in his shoulder as a blade got through, and cried out, feeling his back strike Xerxes. Still the soldiers ran in, crushing against him, pinning his sword against him. He felt a sharp pain in his thigh, and pulled his leg back, then twisted to the side just as one soldier tried stabbing him in the gut with a dagger. The blade sliced his lower back.

"Xerxes!" he screamed.

Hunter saw huge arms wrap around him then, felt a tremendous weight shoving him belly-first onto the ground. Within seconds, he was covered in a cocoon of black armor, Xerxes having laid on top of him, shielding Hunter with his massive body. Hunter saw the soldiers swarming all around his brother through the small gaps between Xerxes' arms, felt his brother's body jerk with each *thump* of the soldiers' warhammers on the big guy's armored back.

He heard a loud *crack*, heard Xerxes grunt as the hammers broke through his armor, pulverizing his flesh.

"Xerxes," he gasped, hearing another *crack*, then another. Blood poured down Xerxes' flanks, dripping onto the ground...and mingling with bright blue fluid that came in a sudden gush. "No!"

A warhammer struck Xerxes' head with a terrible *crack*, leaving a dent in his temple. Hunter saw his brother's eyes glaze over, felt Xerxes' tremendous weight press harder on his back.

Still the blows came, pulverizing Xerxes' back, a rapidly growing pool of blood soaking through Hunter's clothes. Hunter gasped as Xerxes went limp, his enormous weight shoving Hunter's chest into the dirt and forcing the air out of his lungs. Hunter struggled to push himself off the ground, but it was no use. Xerxes was too heavy.

Hunter gasped for air, but no air came. He lay there, feeling blow after blow raining down on Xerxes, his lungs on fire. Then he heard soldiers shouting, felt the weight on him subside. The soldiers were rolling Xerxes off of him!

He sucked air into his lungs, pulling his arms and legs beneath him to get up, then felt someone kick him in the flank…hard. He grunted, rolling onto his back – and saw a dozen men standing over him, blood-soaked weapons in their hands.

"Kill the fucker!" one of the soldiers screamed.

And then he spotted movement to his left, and saw the front doors of the castle swinging open…and someone very familiar stepping through.

"I leave you two alone for *one* minute," Vi groused, unsheathing her longsword. All eyes went to her.

And then people started dying.

Vi sprinted at the soldiers, and the nearest one swung at her with his longsword. She parried without so much as looking at him, blocking the blow and slicing through his neck in one effortless movement. Before his body hit the ground, she was already upon the soldiers surrounding Hunter, a whirlwind of death.

Her blade flashed in the moonlight, over and over, moving so quickly it was a blur. One-by-one the soldiers fell, their screams echoing through the night air.

Within seconds, it was over.

Vi stood there before Hunter, her longsword somehow already back in its sheath, her entire body covered in other people's blood…and none of it was hers.

"Hey…" she began, then dodged to the side abruptly. An arrow slammed into the ground a few yards away, and she followed it back to its source – the archer on top of the wall, already crouching safely behind it. Vi grabbed her bow, nocking an arrow and firing it in one rapid movement.

The arrow flew into the air toward the archer, but went far too high, sailing above him. And then, impossibly, it curved *downward*, plunging right into the archer's head.

Hunter heard a scream and then there was silence.

"Fucker," Vi grumbled, her bow somehow already on her back again. She crouched down, grabbing Hunter's arms and hauling him to his feet. "Any of that blood yours?" she asked, eyeing him critically.

"Some of it," he admitted, staring up at the wall, then at her. "How did…?"

"You think I taught you *all* my tricks?" she replied, giving him a look. "Please. You haven't seen shit."

Hunter shook his head, then turned to Xerxes. Incredibly, the big guy was on his hands and knees. Xerxes got to his feet, his armor slick with his own blood. His mane had already healed…as had the wounds to his head.

"Xerxes!" Hunter cried, running up to his brother. "You alright?"

"SOON," Xerxes replied. And it was true; as Hunter watched, the rest of Xerxes wounds began to close, the flesh knitting itself back together. "YOU?"

"I'll live," Hunter answered, looking down at himself. He had a gash in his shoulder, and another in his thigh, and his lower back. But they all seemed to be pretty superficial. "Thanks bro," he added, smiling at Xerxes. "I owe you one."

Xerxes grunted, slapping him on the back with one big hand…and nearly toppling him in the process.

"WE…FAMILY."

Then the big guy turned around, stomping up to a small puddle of blue goo on the ground, and promptly knelt to pick it up…and ate it.

"Nasty," Vi muttered.

"Why…?" Hunter asked.

"Your brother doesn't want the enemy to get ahold of his goo," she explained. "Kinda like you didn't want Lady Camilla to…"

"Oh let it go," Hunter interrupted, glaring at her.

"I will," she replied, "…once you grow some balls and do something about it."

"One thing at a time," Hunter shot back. "Kinda busy right now if you didn't notice."

"Busy getting your ass kicked," she retorted. But she grinned, slapping him on the back – the lower back, the bitch – and gesturing at the open double-doors. "After you," she offered.

"Ladies first," he shot back, crossing his arms over his chest.

"Ooo, a gentleman," Vi observed. She took him up on the offer, striding up to the entrance and stepping through. Hunter sighed, watching as Xerxes followed behind her. He followed suit, stepping through the doors and into the magnificent foyer of the castle. "Close the doors on your way in," she added without looking back.

"Yes master," he grumbled, doing just that. He could almost *feel* her smiling.

"You're learning," she replied.

Chapter 37

Duke Ratheburg stared at the guards standing before him, a look of shock on his face. Dominus stepped forward, glaring at the guard who'd just spoken.

"Under attack?" he stated. "By whom?" But Ratheburg shot him a withering glare.

"I'll take care of this, thank you," he snapped. He returned his gaze to the guard. "Explain yourself, and do it quickly." The guard swallowed visibly, glancing from Dominus to Ratheburg.

"It started with an attack on the prison," he explained. "Seekers swarmed the place. Now they're attacking everything else."

"You're sure they're Seekers?" Ratheburg pressed.

"They're dressed like Seekers," the guard replied. "And apparently they fight like them too."

"I need specifics," Ratheburg urged. "Where are they exactly, and what have they attacked?" The guard shifted his weight from foot to foot, looking profoundly uneasy.

"Everything," he answered. "Hightown, Lowtown. The inner and outer gates. The guards on the wall." He shrugged. "Everything."

Ratheburg swore, glancing at Dominus, then at the guard.

"Assemble the dukes," he commanded. "And King Tykus. We meet in the Hall of Tykus. *Now.*"

He strode toward the door of Dominus's suite, and Dominus moved to intercept him.

"Wait," he insisted. "If the kingdom is under attack, you'll need my help. You have to let me go!" Ratheburg stopped to glare at him.

"I don't *have* to do anything," he retorted. "And I won't tolerate your corruption spreading all over the Acropolis."

"I'm still Duke of Wexford," Dominus reminded him. "The law says I'm innocent until proven guilty. You have to let me help!"

"The law *also* says you're to be detained until your Test is complete," Ratheburg reminded him icily. "I think you've 'helped' quite enough."

With that, Ratheburg stepped around Dominus, following the guards out of the room. A few remained, standing between Dominus and the door. Dominus cursed, turning about striding up to one of the large windows on the far wall. He peered into the darkness, seeing the stately buildings of Hightown beyond the wall surrounding the Acropolis, the coarser buildings on the lower slopes of the hill leading to the slums of Lowtown. Bright tongues of flame licked a few of the larger buildings…the Royal Bank, the prison, a few of the guardhouses…consuming them greedily.

A chill ran through Dominus, his guts squirming in terror.

The kingdom is under attack, he thought. *And without me…*

He gripped the windowsill so hard his knuckles turned white, grinding his teeth together. If it was truly the Seekers attacking the kingdom – and the fact that the attack began on the prison where Zeno was being held made that very likely – then the kingdom was in greater trouble than Ratheburg could imagine.

Dominus turned away from the window, eyeing the three guards blocking the door. Their body language was relaxed, casual. They had no fear of him attacking them; he was an elderly, unarmed man. A danger to no one.

You're a dead man either way, he told himself.

He thought back to the last conversation he'd had with King Tykus, the last words he'd spoken to the great man before they'd said goodbye.

Then I'll die as I lived. For the kingdom.

"So be it," he whispered.

He took a deep breath in, then bolted toward the guards. He was almost upon them before they reacted, taking far too long to realize what was about to happen. Dominus reached the nearest guard in seconds, shoving him backward into the wall, then reaching for his sword.

"Hey!" the guard shouted.

One of the other guards grabbed Dominus by the wrist, trying to yank him away. Dominus resisted, grabbing at the first guard's belt frantically. His fingers closed on the hilt of a dagger, and he pulled it free from its sheath.

"Drop it!" a guard shouted, yanking him backward. Dominus stumbled, but managed to keep his balance, his superior reflexes kicking in. He spun around, slashing at the guard's face, making a deep gash just above the man's eyebrows. The guard jerked backward, letting go of Dominus and clutching at his bloodied face.

"Fuck!" the guard shouted. He unsheathed his sword, thrusting blindly at Dominus, who dodged to the side. The guard's blade continued past

Dominus, burying itself into the belly of the guard whose dagger he'd stolen.

Dominus slashed the former's guard's wrist, then grabbed the sword from his hands, yanking the blade out of the other guard's belly. Then he spun in a half-circle, slashing both guards' necks in a single blow.

The third guard cried out, unsheathing his sword and slashing at Dominus!

Dominus's reflexes took over, parrying the blow effortlessly, and a split-second later, his sword was buried in the guard's neck.

He withdrew his blade, and the guard slumped to the floor, grasping at his throat, his eyes wide with terror.

Then the door opened.

Dominus hid behind the door, pressing his back against the wall. He saw more guards rush into the room, their backs to him. They saw the bodies of their comrades on the floor, and swore, unsheathing their swords.

Or at least they tried to.

Dominus lunged at them, letting his body take over. Not resisting the reflexes he'd absorbed over the years, the centuries of expertise he'd acquired.

Within seconds, it was done.

Dominus stood over the bodies of the guards, blood still pumping from their bodies. Still alive, but already dead. He crouched before one, removing their belt and strapping it to his own waist. He sheathed his sword, then paused, looking through the open doorway to the long hall beyond. It was deserted…which meant he had time.

He shut the door, considering his options. There was no point in trying to get to the Hall of Tykus and help the other dukes plan the defense of the city. They would reject him, and summon more guards to subdue him…or even kill him outright for his newest crimes.

But he *had* to help save the kingdom!

If it was truly the Seekers attacking the kingdom, they would prove to be extremely dangerous opponents. Who knew what illegal artifacts they'd hidden away over the centuries, augmenting their abilities? It would take his own abilities – equally illegal – to fight them.

Which meant that he had to get out of the Acropolis…and somehow, someway, through the wall surrounding the great fortress.

He knelt down, unfastening the breastplate from one of the guards – the one with the least blood on them – then pulling off their clothes. He changed into them quickly, then put on the breastplate, and their helmet. He went to the mirror at one corner of the room then, gazing at himself. The helmet covered much of his face; it was enough to make him difficult to recognize, certainly at first glance. As long as no one looked too closely…

He turned toward the door, taking a deep breath in, then walking up to it, swinging it open and striding into the hallway. He made his way quickly down it, amazed that he could do so easily, without even losing his breath. A few days ago, he'd struggled to walk more than a few meters. He reached the end, turning left, then continuing down another long hallway, which opened up into a large room ahead. He heard shouting, and saw guards running across that room from right to left, vanishing from sight.

Dominus slowed, but the guards hadn't noticed him.

He continued forward, striding into the room ahead; huge stone statues of Tykus's twin son and daughter stood in the center of it, a wide set of stone steps leading down to the first floor on his right. He made his way down them, reaching the bottom. Another large room…with hallways to his left and right, each lined by rows of closed doors. Going left would lead him to the entrance to the Acropolis. Going right, to the Hall of Tykus. He spotted a group of guards rushing down the leftmost hallway toward him, and froze, his heart pounding in his chest. He reached for his sword.

But the guards rushed past him toward the hallway to the right.

"Come on!" one of them shouted at him, gesturing for him to follow. "We have to protect the king!"

What?

Dominus hesitated, then ran after the guards, following them down the hallway. They rushed past closed doors on either side of the hall, making their way toward the stairwell at the far end some forty meters ahead. The stairwell that would lead them to the Hall of Tykus.

Why would the king need protection? Dominus wondered. It didn't make any sense…no one could get into the Acropolis. There was only one way in: through the gate.

Suddenly the doors on either side of the hallway ahead burst open, and men in black and gold uniforms spilled out of them!

"Seekers!" one guard shouted. The Seekers charged at the guards, even as more Seekers rushed out of the doors, sprinting past the guards toward the stairwell ahead. "Don't let them…"

The sentence ended in a scream as a Seeker ran the guard through the belly with his longsword, the tip of the blade protruding from the guard's back.

The dukes, Dominus thought, breaking out into an all-out run after the Seekers rushing for the stairwell. *The king!*

A Seeker rushed to intercept him, slashing at his face, and Dominus's blade was in his hand instantly, moving so quickly it was a blur. The Seeker's hand – and sword – went flying, blood spurting from the stump of his wrist…and a gaping wound in his belly.

Dominus ran past the doomed Seeker, sprinting to catch up to the Seekers ahead. He heard one of the guards shout for help, and ignored the man, watching in horror as the Seekers reached the stairwell, leaping down it.

Tykus!

The dukes and the king weren't armed; it was forbidden to carry weapons into the Hall of Tykus. If the Seekers reached them before he did…

Dominus ran as fast as he could, barreling down the hallway, ignoring the screams echoing down the hallway behind him. He reached the stairwell at last, leaping the ten stairs going downward, then turning and leaping down the second set. He heard shouting ahead, following by a blood-curdling scream. A scream that cut to his very soul.

No!

He sprinted down a short hallway, spotting the heavy platinum double-doors leading to the Hall of Tykus ahead. Already open, with the last of the Seekers rushing through.

"Stop!" Dominus ordered, running after them. His breath came in short gasps, his lungs burning with the effort. He made it to the doors, bursting through…and felt his heart leap in his throat. Time slowed, each horrible second seeming to take minutes to pass.

The Hall of Tykus stood before him, the long table fashioned of human bones in its center, set upon a floor of solid, transparent crystal. The five dukes were gathered around the table, some still sitting in their chairs, others rising from them, shocked expressions on their faces.

And at the far end of the room, seated in his chair of platinum-coated bone – the bones of his children and grandchildren – was King Tykus himself.

The first of the Seekers reached the nearest end of the table, grabbing Duke Mezgar from behind and drawing their blade across the man's throat. Blood spurted from the wound, Mezgar's eyes going wide with horror. He fell face-first onto the table, grasping at his throat, his lifeblood spilling between his fingers.

Dominus reached the nearest Seeker, thrusting his sword through the man's back…and watched as another Seeker ran up to Duke David, thrusting their sword into the man's chest.

"Stop!" Dominus cried, rushing forward and running another Seeker through. But the Seekers ignored him, continuing down the table. He saw Duke Ratheburg back away from his seat, heard him shout something unintelligible.

A Seeker ran toward Duke Klassen, who was rising from his chair, a bewildered look on his face. The Seeker swung his sword as he passed, the wicked blade flashing in the lantern-light from above. Dominus watched helplessly as Klassen's head separated from his shoulders, tumbling to the ground. As his body fell with it.

And as the rest of the Seekers continued forward toward the end of the table. Toward Ratheburg…and the king, still sitting in his chair.

Dominus rushed forward, nearly at the opposite end of the table now. He impaled yet another Seeker from behind, pushing past the man toward Ratheburg and the king.

And watched helplessly as a Seeker rushed up to King Tykus, thrusting their sword into the great man's chest!

Chapter 38

The grand foyer of the Castle Wexford stood before Hunter, opulent beyond anything he had ever seen. White granite floors polished to a mirror shine, thick granite columns rising to the painted ceiling thirty feet above, intricate carvings of men and women winding their way up them. Statues of older, stately-looking men standing by the walls on either side, wrought of what looked to be pure gold. Ahead of him was a wide staircase leading upward to a second story balcony of sorts, and on either side of this stairway, arched doorways leading to long hallways.

And everywhere he looked, there were bodies.

Strewn across the stairs. Lying in heaps on the floor ahead. Curled up at the foot of one of the columns. Blood streaked the polished floor, the awful smell of it thick in the air.

Hunter glanced at Vi, who stood beside him, her hands on her hips.

"Took long enough to open those doors," he grumbled.

She arched an eyebrow, gesturing at the bodies all around them.

"Sorry if I was a little too busy to babysit you two," she shot back. Xerxes glared down at her, shoving her with one big hand. Or at least he tried to; she dodged out of the way effortlessly.

"So what now?" Hunter inquired. They could either take the hallway to the left or to the right, or go up the stairs.

"Well, Dominus's bedroom could be anywhere," Vi reasoned. "The longer it takes us to find it, the more organized those guards are gonna get." She shook her head. "I'm good, but even I can't fight an army."

Xerxes grunted, crossing one pair of arms over his chest.

"Neither can you, meat-shield," she added. "Point is, the faster we find it, the better."

Hunter nodded, glancing down at one of the guards.

"Maybe they know," he offered. He walked up to one, taking off his helmet and kneeling to lower his forehead to theirs. He grimaced; their skin was already cool. Images flashed in his mind's eye, and he let them, not bothering to try to make sense of them. Then he got to his feet, putting his helmet back on and looking up at the second story.

"I think it's upstairs," he ventured.

"You 'think?'" Vi asked.

"Memories aren't like reading a book," he retorted. "They're vague, incomplete. They give me a kind of intuition." He gestured up the stairs. "We can go up, and my gut will tell me where to go from there."

"How reassuring."

"I found Camilla's place that way," he reminded her. "From a piece of paper, mind you." She smirked, and was about to open her mouth when he gave her a look. "Don't even think about it," he warned.

"Too late," she replied with a wink. "Already did."

Hunter heard sudden shouting from ahead, and looked up to see soldiers on the second story, running for the stairs. He unsheathed his longsword, then spotted two men carrying crossbows among the soldiers. He swore, running for one of the columns and taking cover behind it.

"Crossbows," he warned.

"See them," Vi shouted back.

One of the crossbowmen hid behind a column on the second story, while the other crouched, aiming at Vi while the other guards rushed down the stairs. Hunter grabbed his bow, nocking an arrow and firing it at the crossbowman; the arrow struck the guy's helmet, ricocheting off and snapping the guy's head back. Another arrow buried itself into the guy's neck; Hunter glanced at Vi, who was standing out in the open, her bow in her hands. She winked at him.

"Show-off," he grumbled.

The other soldiers were halfway down the stairs now; they spotted Xerxes standing in the center of the foyer, and slowed, eyeing the massive Ironclad warily. The second crossbowman leaned out from behind the column, firing down at Vi, who dodged the bolt, nocking an arrow of her own. She held the bow sideways, firing at the guy. But the arrow went far wide of the target, sailing to the right of the column the man was hiding behind.

And then it curved in mid-air, arcing *around* the column and striking the crossbowman in the shoulder!

"How in the…" Hunter blurted out, staring at Vi in disbelief. "You can *do* that?"

"Oh yeah," she replied, flashing a grin.

She put her bow away then, unsheathing her mace and rushing toward the foot of the stairs…and at the guards still standing in the middle of them.

But Xerxes held out one hand, blocking her way. She skidded to a stop, glancing up at the big guy.

"All right, have some fun," she muttered, gesturing up the stairs.

Xerxes grinned, then charged up the stairs.

The soldiers cried out, running back *up* the stairs, but Xerxes was too quick for them. He went after them, reaching the closest two and grabbing them by the backs of their uniforms, tossing them down the stairs. The remaining guards turned on him, slashing at him with their swords. He grabbed their blades with his bare hands, ripping them from their grasps, then pummeling them with their own weapons, using the hilts to bash their skulls. He threw the swords away, then grabbed a soldier in each of his four hands, holding them by their necks and lifting them high in to the air.

Then he *squeezed.*

Muffled *cracks* echoed through the large foyer, and Xerxes tossed the four men down the stairs. They fell like rag-dolls, rolling down the last of the steps and stopping in a heap at the bottom.

Vi stepped over them, making her way up the stairs to his side.

"Feel better?" she inquired. He looked down at her, his lips curling into a smirk.

"MUCH."

"Must've hurt your feelings," she ventured, "…getting your ass kicked like that earlier." She patted him on one of his arms. "You're a good little brother, Blue."

Hunter smiled at that, joining them in the middle of the stairs.

"Damn right," he agreed. "I have a hard time thinking of you as 'little' though," he added, craning his neck back to look up at Xerxes. "I guess technically I'm older."

"Not really," Vi countered. "You're like what, almost fifty Blue?" Xerxes nodded.

"Ah, right," Hunter muttered. He'd forgotten about the time difference between here and Earth.

"Lead the way," Vi told Hunter, gesturing for him to continue up the stairs. Hunter did so, reaching the top of the stairs and turning right. The balcony led to a hallway to the left and one straight ahead; he turned left. Not because he knew where to go, but because it felt right. Still, it felt strange trusting in someone else's memories, not even really aware of the details of them. He supposed it made sense; he never really had to think about where he was going when he knew where to go. Never had to pause in thought to get through his house back on Earth. It was all automatic…and it made sense that it would be for other people's memories, too.

"You sure you're going the right way?" Vi asked from behind.

"Nope."

He led them down a long hallway, nearly as ornate as the foyer had been. They passed door after door on either side; Hunter kept his longsword in his hands, all-too-aware that there had to be guards all over the huge castle. Damn place had to have over a hundred rooms, if not more. He heard the sudden sound of a bell tolling in the distance, and glanced questioningly at Vi.

"Alarm," she explained.

As if on cue, one of the doors ahead opened, three more soldiers rushing into the hallway. They saw Hunter, unsheathing their swords…and then spotted Xerxes behind him, their eyes going wide, their jaws dropping.

Hunter rushed them, knocking the nearest soldier's blade to the side, then slashing at his face. He screamed, dropping his sword and clutching at his bloodied face, stumbling backward into his fellow soldiers. Hunter kicked the soldier, knocking all three of them down…then ended them one-by-one.

"Aww," Vi said as Hunter stepped over their bodies, pretending to wipe away a tear. "Kids…they grow up so fast."

"I'll take that as a compliment," Hunter replied. Vi and Xerxes followed him further down the hallway, which ended quickly, branching to the left and right. He hesitated, suddenly unsure of where to go.

"What's up?" Vi asked. Hunter sighed, shaking his head.

"That fight screwed me up," he admitted. "Now I'm thinking too much…not sure where to go." He glanced back the way they'd come. "I need to get in the zone again."

"In the zone?"

"Figure of speech," he explained. "Means I gotta…" He paused. "Just trust me." He stepped back over the guards, going back down the hallway. There was shouting in the distance, the bell still tolling. "Whose genius idea was it to go through the front door, anyway?" he grumbled.

"I'm sorry, did you prefer the back door?" she inquired with a grin.

"Camilla did," he shot back.

"Thought that was a sensitive subject."

"Well," he replied, continuing down the hallway, "…it was consensual the first time. And besides," he added, "…I've decided I'm going to kill the bitch."

"Tsk tsk," Vi scolded. "You don't have to kill *everyone* that crosses you."

"Maybe I'll just maim her then."

"You hurt her, she'll try to hurt you back," Vi replied. "Focus on becoming someone she'd never want to mess with again. Then maybe you'll be able to stop her from screwing with anyone else."

"Fine then," he agreed, reaching the end of the hallway, then turning around. "Now shut up and let me do my thing."

"Yes master."

"You're learning," Hunter quipped, winking at her. He took a deep breath in then, letting it out and staring down the hallway. He started forward again, trying his best to ignore his brain's chatter. He passed door after door, stepping over the guards again, then reaching the end of the hallway…and turned left.

"This way," he informed Vi and Xerxes.

He continued down yet another hallway, spotting an ornate door at the end of it. It was, he knew, the door to Dominus's bedroom.

"Bingo," he declared.

"You always say that when you succeed," Vi observed. Then she smirked. "Which explains why it's only the second time I've heard it."

"Ha ha."

Hunter walked toward the door, then felt a big hand on his shoulder. He stopped, and Xerxes squeezed past him, walking up to the door and opening it…and revealing two guards on the other side. They shouted, then promptly died.

Xerxes stepped over their bodies, gesturing for Hunter and Vi to follow.

"Do your thing," Vi ordered. Hunter walked up to Dominus's bed, lowering his forehead to the pillow there. He figured it was where the duke's brain was closest to a third of each day, and therefore the best place to extract the man's memories. He closed his eyes, images zipping by in his mind's eye, not bothering to try to analyze them. After a moment, he stood up, then walked to one of the windows, peering out of it.

"The entrance to the vault is underground at some shrine," he stated. "But it's not in the castle…it's outside, in the gardens."

"Alright," Vi replied. "Let's go."

They made their way out of the room and back down the hallway, retracing their steps…and running into a few soldiers along the way. Xerxes made quick work of them, making fresh holes in the walls with their heads. It wasn't long before they'd returned to the foyer, descending the stairs and walking through the front doors. Hunter led them leftward, hugging the side of the castle as he went. They reached the gardens, taking a cobblestone path between the lush vegetation. The pungent odor of flowers was almost overwhelming.

"It's up ahead," Hunter notified, pointing off into the distance. There was a clearing there, and large wooden pallets lying on the ground, dozens of wooden crates stacked on top of them. He got close, then stopped, peering at them. There were insects buzzing around them…they looked like bees.

"What?" Vi asked.

"Bees," Hunter muttered, grimacing in distaste. "I hate bees."

"So where's the damn entrance?" Vi pressed. She grabbed her bow then, aiming toward the castle and firing off an arrow. It flew into an open window on the fourth floor, and Hunter heard a scream.

"Under that pallet," he answered, pointing to the leftmost one.

"Alright," she stated. "What're you waiting for?"

"I ain't messing with those goddamn bees," Hunter replied. He'd have to take all the crates off first…and he knew damn well – probably from Dominus's memories – that those crates contained beehives. Lots of beehives.

Xerxes pushed past him, striding up to the pallet and reaching down to lift up one side. The crates slid off, tumbling onto the ground…and releasing a swarm of angry bees. They flew straight for Xerxes, covering the big guy in the least comfortable blanket Hunter could imagine. Xerxes, of course, hardly minded the swarm; even if their stingers could've gotten through his armor, he'd heal instantly.

Xerxes flipped the pallet over, revealing a large circle of dirt below.

"So where exactly is this entrance?" Vi inquired, arching one eyebrow at Hunter.

"Under that dirt," he answered. Xerxes grunted, kneeling down and brushing the dirt aside…revealing gray stone beneath. It was a hatch, Hunter realized.

"Let me guess," Vi stated. "Bingo?"

"Yup," Hunter agreed. "Hey bro, think you can kill those bees for me?"

Xerxes nodded, flopping onto his back and rolling around on the ground, crushing the bees that were crawling on him. Then he got up, shaking their tiny corpses off. At length, the rest of the bees dissipated.

"All right, let's move before more soldiers find us," Vi ordered. Hunter walked up to the hatch, studying it. There were three circular rings in the center, like the rings on a dartboard. Symbols were carved into each of them at regular intervals.

"It's a combination lock," Hunter explained. He knelt down, pressing down on the outermost ring, then sliding his hand to the side. The ring rotated; he kept going until the symbol of a bee was facing a small notch in the stone beyond the ring.

"Little obvious," Vi opined.

Hunter moved the middle ring, rotating it in the opposite direction, until a symbol of a skull was lined up below the bee. Then he rotated the innermost ring, stopping at a symbol of a castle. There was a *click*, and he stood up.

"Done," he proclaimed. "It should swing open."

Xerxes did the honors, digging his fingertips under the hatch, then lifting upward…and revealing a deep cylindrical hole in the ground, with walls of stone. There was a ladder leading down it.

"The third rung down is booby-trapped," Hunter warned. "Skip it."

"Sure thing," Vi replied…and promptly jumped down the shaft, vanishing into the darkness beyond. Hunter shook his head, then used the ladder, avoiding the third rung. Then he glanced up at his brother.

"ME…GUARD," Xerxes stated.

"Gotcha," Hunter replied. "Thanks bro…and be careful, okay?" Xerxes only grinned, making it obvious that he had no intention of following Hunter's advice.

Hunter made his way down the ladder, darkness enveloping him as he descended. He reached the bottom of the shaft some ten feet down, and turned around, peering into the utter darkness.

"Vi?"

He saw a flash of light, then spotted Vi ahead of him, standing in a small tunnel with irregular stone walls. She was carrying a short torch.

"Where'd you get *that*?" he asked.

"Always prepared," she stated, grinning at him. "It's a woman thing."

"Be careful," he warned, peering down the tunnel. "This place is full of booby-traps."

"Not surprising," she replied. "Having people break into his family's shrine is Dominus's worst nightmare. His family goes all the way back to the original Tykus's lifetime…six thousand years ago."

"Damn."

"The oldest family in the kingdom," she informed. "And most prestigious, other than Tykus's, of course. We're almost certainly the first people other than Dominus's ancestors to ever be inside this place."

"I'm honored," Hunter grumbled.

"Yeah, well let's not spend too much time here," Vi stated. "Gotta be some real powerful wills in here. I don't want Dominus inside of me."

"Me neither," Hunter agreed. Vi grinned.

"There's a visual."

He ignored her, walking past her down the tunnel, stepping over one part of the floor. A pressure-activated plate, he knew; one that, when stepped on, would result in something terrible happening to whoever did so. Dominus's memories didn't say what exactly, but he knew well enough to avoid it. He didn't even have to tell Vi what to do; she copied his movements exactly, following a few feet behind. They continued onward, and he walked around another invisible pressure-plate, hugging the wall. He slowed then.

"Duck," he warned. Then he took a step forward, following his own advice. He heard a *click*, and something shot through the air above his head from behind, flying down the tunnel and vanishing into the darkness beyond.

"Bet he has to reset that trap every time he comes down here," Vi guessed. Hunter nodded.

"Yup."

"Must be weird having all those memories inside you," she mused. "Ever get confused which ones are yours?"

"Sometimes."

Onward they went, until the tunnel curved suddenly to the left. He spotted a small metal bolt on the ground near the wall ahead; it looked like a crossbow bolt. He had the urge to pick it up so that he could re-arm the trap on the way back, but ignored it. He turned left with the tunnel, spotting a closed wrought-iron door ahead.

"It's locked," he warned, stepping up to it. There was a small lever where a door handle would be. He pushed inward, feeling it sink into the door a little, then pulled to the right, then rotated it upward forty-five degrees…and not an inch farther. Failure to unlock the door properly would result in it locking permanently.

The door swung open.

"Damn Hunter," Vi murmured. "You got a hell of a gift."

He went through the doorway, being sure not to close it behind him. Doing so would activate another trap. He had to give Dominus credit…without the man's memories, it'd be damn near impossible to get to the shrine intact.

"Keep it open," he told Vi as she passed through. She nodded. They continued down another long tunnel, avoiding more traps, until they reached another door at the end. Hunter unlocked this as well, using another series of movements that no one could have guessed. It opened, and he stepped through into the large underground chamber beyond.

"And here we are," he murmured, waiting for Vi's torchlight to illuminate the room as she stepped through the doorway. "Whoa," he breathed, looking ahead, his jaw dropping. "God damn."

"Holy shit," Vi exclaimed.

Chapter 39

Dominus yanked his sword from the back of the Seeker he'd impaled, sprinting toward the long table in the center of the Hall of Tykus. He watched in horror as the lives of four of the six dukes of Tykus were snuffed out, as their murderers – the remaining four Seekers – ran toward Duke Ratheburg and King Tykus himself, their swords glimmering in the lantern-light.

And watched helplessly as a Seeker reached the end of the table, lunging at King Tykus, still seated in his chair. As the Seeker's blade went right for Tykus's heart. If Dominus could have shouted, he would have. But terror gripped his throat, no sound able to pass through its grasp.

Ratheburg leaped through the air in front of the king, knocking the Seeker to the side at the last minute. Ratheburg landed on the edge of the table, the Seeker flying over the tabletop, well clear of Tykus, and landing headfirst onto the floor with a *thump*.

The other two Seekers shouted, charging at Ratheburg and the king!

Dominus ran after them, sprinting to the left of the long table. One of the Seekers lunged at Ratheburg, still lying over the table, slashing at the old man. Ratheburg rolled out of the way just in time, the Seeker's sword *clanging* as it ricocheted off the tabletop. Dominus caught up to the other Seeker, burying his blade into their back. He withdrew his blade, watching as the remaining Seeker recovered, glancing at Ratheburg, then Dominus…and then lunging for the king!

"No!" Dominus shouted.

Ratheburg leapt at the Seeker, yanking him backward by the shoulders and throwing him to the floor. The Seeker rolled, springing to his feet and slashing at Ratheburg, who hopped backward, the blade nicking the duke's belly. A bloodstain grew quickly on the fine cloth, crimson against pure white.

Dominus reached the Seeker, thrusting at the man's flank.

The Seeker spun to face Dominus, parrying the blow expertly, then jabbing at his belly. Dominus's blade moved in a blur, his reflexes taking over. Metal rang on metal, the sound reverberating in the small room.

And then it was over.

The Seeker stared at Dominus, his sword falling from his hand. And then his head tipped backward, falling clean off his shoulders, his body joining it on the floor.

Dominus gazed down at the dead Seeker, his sword already back in its blood-stained sheath.

"Thank god!" Ratheburg blurted out, rushing up to Dominus and grabbing him by the shoulders. "Thank…"

He froze, staring at Dominus, his eyes widening. Then he jerked back, shaking his head, his mouth opening in shock.

"You!" he gasped.

"You're welcome," Dominus grumbled. He took off his helmet, tossing it aside, then turned to King Tykus, who was still sitting in his chair calmly, as he had from the beginning. Watching them both serenely, as if nothing of importance had happened. "Your Highness!" he cried. "Are you all right?"

"Of course," Tykus replied.

"Leave at once," Ratheburg ordered, stepping between Dominus and the king. "You have no right to be in this sacred place!"

"He saved your life," Tykus reminded him. Ratheburg glanced at the king, then grimaced.

"He did," he conceded. "And I am thankful. But every minute he stands here, he's corrupting this Hall!"

"Not likely," Tykus replied calmly. "I doubt the wild wills inside of him are stronger than the wills within this room."

"Even so," Ratheburg insisted, "…he is being Tested. And we both know he'll fail that Test."

"He already has," Tykus replied. Ratheburg blinked, and Tykus gestured at Dominus's forearm. The forearm the doctor had sliced open. Dominus looked down, realizing that the wound had already partially closed, no longer gaping. He looked up, seeing Ratheburg staring at him, his mouth set in a grim line.

"Then I have no choice," Ratheburg declared. "Dominus, I find you guilty of corrupting yourself with wild Ossae. As the sole remaining duke of Tykus, I hereby sentence you to death."

"Now is not the time," Dominus shot back. "In case you didn't notice, the kingdom is under attack. I can help you."

"The king will be quite safe in his chambers," Ratheburg retorted. "The Seekers don't stand a chance against the Royal Guard."

"Oh really," Dominus stated. "And how exactly are you going to make it there?"

Ratheburg reached down, retrieving a sword from one of the fallen Seekers.

"I'll escort the king there myself," he replied coolly.

Tykus sighed, pushing his chair back, then standing. Both men turned to face the king.

"Dominus," he stated, "…give me your sword."

Dominus hesitated for only a moment, then complied, handing his sword to the king. Tykus held it in one hand, kicking off his boots and standing – barefoot – on the crystalline floor.

"I'd like it very much if you would take a walk with me back to my chambers, Dominus," he declared.

Ratheburg's mouth fell open, and he glanced from Tykus to Dominus.

"What?"

"Yes your Majesty," Dominus replied, bowing deeply. Tykus glanced down at Dominus's feet, then back into his eyes, raising one eyebrow. Dominus smiled, removing his own boots. The floor was cool and slick under his feet…a sensation he'd never felt before.

"But your Highness," Ratheburg interjected. "He's a criminal!" He gestured at Dominus in disgust. "He's defied our laws…he's let nature corrupt him!"

"That," Tykus countered gently, "…is exactly the type of man I'd like to take a walk with."

"I don't understand…"

"You wouldn't," Tykus agreed. "You still have your boots on."

Ratheburg blinked, looking down at his own feet, utterly confused. Tykus walked up to Dominus, grabbing him by the elbow.

"Come, Dominus," he urged, pulling Dominus toward the stairs leading out of the Hall of Tykus. Ratheburg intercepted them, standing before Dominus and pointing the tip of his sword at Dominus's chest.

"I can't let him go, your Highness," Ratheburg stated. Tykus sighed.

"I know," he replied. "You're just like your father," he added. "And your grandfather, and every other duke in your family." He smiled. "A perfect replica of one of the finest men in the kingdom…as I'm sure your successor will be."

"Thank you, your Highness."

"I look forward to working with him."

Tykus lunged forward, knocking Ratheburg's sword to the side with his own, then plunging his blade into Ratheburg's chest. The fine steel sank into the duke's flesh, just to the left of his breastbone.

Ratheburg gasped, his eyes going wide, his mouth open in a silent "O."

King Tykus withdrew the sword, handing it back to Dominus, then gesturing for Dominus to walk with him. They made their way toward the stairs going upward, their bare feet padding silently on the cool crystalline floor, mere centimeters above the countless skeletons embedded within. Countless generations of the dead, men of the highest virtue, paragons of the kingdom's values. They mounted the stairs, leaving the Hall of Tykus behind.

Duke Ratheburg fell to his knees, then face-first onto the crystalline floor, joining his fellow dukes. And the great Hall of Tykus gained five more souls that day, every one of them a worthy addition to the hallowed room.

* * *

Dominus reached the top of the stairs, striding into the hallway, King Tykus at his side. They walked forward together, side-by-side, neither man speaking. Dominus heard shouting in the distance, and the *clang* of metal on metal. Then a scream, followed by silence.

"There are more of them, your Highness," Dominus warned.

"I know," Tykus replied.

"We need to figure out how the Seekers got into the Acropolis," he pressed.

"Oh, I already know all that," Tykus replied dismissively. Dominus stopped abruptly, turning to face the king. Tykus stopped as well, giving Dominus a conspiratorial smile.

"You do?"

"They took the underground tunnels from their guild," Tykus explained.

"There are…"

"Oh yes," Tykus interjected, gesturing all around. "Tunnels throughout the city. Older than the Acropolis itself, you know. One of my predecessors had all records of them destroyed a few millennia ago."

"But why?" Dominus demanded. "It's a security risk!"

"Clearly," Tykus agreed.

"I don't understand," Dominus pressed. "Why…"

He paused then, staring at the king, his eyes widening.

"You *wanted* this," he realized. Tykus chuckled, resuming walking. Dominus did as well, catching up to the man. "But your Majesty, why?"

"Every one of my predecessors was tasked to create a single stone tablet," Tykus explained, "…upon which he would carve the most important lessons he had learned in his life. No one has ever looked at them but me….and my predecessors, of course. There are nearly two hundred of them now…the accumulated wisdom of a life spanning over six thousand years."

Dominus just stared at Tykus as they walked.

"I'll spare you the details," Tykus continued. "But suffice it to say that in that great expanse of time, I've apparently come to the same conclusion over and over again."

"And what is that?"

"That all of this," Tykus answered, spreading his arms out wide, "…is a great evil."

"But my liege!"

"Now now," Tykus admonished. "Don't be so alarmed. I've been telling you this all along."

"You have?"

"Have you spared any thought to our conversations?" Tykus inquired. Dominus nodded.

"A great deal, your Highness."

"Then recall what I said about nature," he stated. "That Man believes he is separate from it. That he learns – from a very young age – to believe he is a being *within* nature, rather than nature itself."

"But we are not a part of this world," Dominus countered. "Humans came through the Gate."

"And yet you were born here," Tykus replied, "…and the substance of your flesh is the substance of this world. Therefore you are of this world, and the world is you."

Dominus was about to reply, but Tykus raised one hand to stop him.

"Dominus, you hate nature because it might change you," he stated. "You fear that it will steal your humanity – who you are – and turn you into something else. You value your identity, no?"

"Of course."

"What of the people?" Tykus pressed. "The generation after generation of people we force to absorb our wills, transforming them into pale imitations of us? What of *their* identities?"

"They want to be like us," Dominus retorted.

"Do they ever have a choice?" Tykus asked.

"No."

"Then how are we better than nature," he stated, "…when we steal men's souls just as we fear nature will steal ours?"

Dominus said nothing. Could think of nothing to say.

"We aren't human, Dominus," Tykus insisted. "I was, before I came to this world. But the moment my flesh converted to the substance of this place – the moment I gained the power of a Legend – was the moment I became something else. Something *more* than human. Humans cannot change others with their wills, or absorb each other's memories. We're not human, Dominus. And you," he added, jabbing a finger at Dominus's chest, "…never were."

"Then we preserve what humanity we have left," Dominus replied.

"Yes," Tykus agreed. "And there is something to this, I think. This kingdom should exist for as long as it can, to provide a safe haven for the humans that come through the Gate. To preserve our wisdom, and our history."

"But you just said…"

"That it was a great evil?" Tykus finished. "Yes. But a necessary one. The nature of this world demands it."

"Then why risk the kingdom?" Dominus asked. "Why let the Seekers gain power, and leave the tunnels open to the Acropolis?"

"Are the tunnels a vulnerability if I've already planned for their use?" Tykus inquired.

"Look around you," Dominus answered, gesturing at the bodies of guards strewn across the floor.

"And yet we've exposed the true nature of the Seekers," Tykus pointed out, "…and my Royal Guard is well aware of the danger, and will destroy them." His eyes twinkled. "And this kingdom will never forget the guild's treachery," he added. "Monopolies such as theirs will never be allowed to exist again."

"But the dukes are dead!" Dominus shot back.

"And their replacements will be utterly identical."

"Like me," Dominus muttered. Tykus chuckled, patting Dominus on the shoulder.

"Oh Dominus," he chided. "You're something else entirely! Do you know, that in six thousand years, not a single duke has ever strayed as you have?"

Dominus nodded, feeling shame come over him. He was the first to allow corruption into his soul. All because of his son…a fool that he'd all but disowned far too late.

"What a marvelous creature you are!" Tykus exclaimed. "Dabbling in wild artifacts, yet still so dedicated to your people. You're proof, Dominus, that nature is not to be feared. You've maintained your wisdom – your humanity, I might add – all the while gaining something incredible."

"I did it for the kingdom," Dominus stated.

"Bullshit," Tykus scoffed. "You did it for *you*."

"That's not…"

"You should have died," Tykus interrupted. "You should have left your Duchy to an heir, and let your disease take your life. As your father and his father and his father before him had."

Dominus lowered his gaze. There was no denying it…Tykus was right.

"You did this for *you*," Tykus insisted. "Because *you* wanted to be the one to protect the kingdom…not some replica. Because *you* wanted to endure. You loved us so much you couldn't leave it to anyone else…not even a replica of yourself."

"I didn't trust anyone else," Dominus admitted. Tykus raised an eyebrow.

"You trust me."

"You're Tykus," Dominus replied with a shrug.

"I've given you a reason to trust me, Dominus. Because I let you in. I let you see me for who I am. Because I have none of the walls that you've built around yourself."

"You don't need them," Dominus realized.

"Neither do you," Tykus replied. "So go outside these walls," he added, "...and step outside of your own. Live your life, Dominus. Protect us...protect *me*...from the outside, as your family always has. Be what I can never be...eternal, one life extending forever into the future, gathering the wisdom we so desperately need."

"But your Highness, I'm not..."

"You *are*," Tykus insisted. "Look at you," he added, smiling broadly at Dominus. "Younger with every passing day!" He shook his head. "You're like her now."

"Like who?"

"Why, Neesha," Tykus answered. "The queen of the Ironclad."

Dominus's eyes widened, and he drew in a sharp breath, taking a step backward involuntarily.

"*What?*"

"Oh yes," Tykus stated, clearly amused at Dominus's consternation. "She's their leader, you see. And you're in possession of her son's head."

Dominus just shook his head, feeling numb.

"How..."

"Do you ever wonder why Neesha fled the kingdom?" Tykus inquired. "Why she just up and left...right when the Acropolis was in her sights?"

"We defeated her army," Dominus answered. Tykus snorted.

"Not hardly," he retorted. "And as a Legend, she could have simply converted our soldiers to her cause. No Dominus, she left quite voluntarily, I assure you."

"But why?"

"Because I spoke with her," Tykus answered. "Or at least one of my predecessors did. A fascinating woman, really. A student of history. She even knew of my father." He smiled. "Do you know they still speak of him, on Miogaror? I believe they call it 'Earth' now. Anyway, he's become a kind of legend himself."

"How did you speak with her?" Dominus demanded. "She never reached the Acropolis!"

"Ah, but remember the tunnels," Tykus replied with a wink. "They go all the way past the Deadlands, you see."

"*You* went to her?"

"I did," Tykus confirmed. "She was as shocked as you are, believe me. We walked together for a long time," he added. "With our boots off, I might add. She understood the importance of connecting with nature better than anyone I'd ever met."

Dominus shook his head, hardly believing what he was hearing.

"How did you get her to flee?"

"I gave her my perspective," Tykus answered. "As a Legend."

"That's it?"

"That's it," Tykus agreed. "A shame the dukes were so insistent on hunting her down, and her people. Eventually I managed to convince them she was dead. I visited her a few times over the years, after the war…and saw her transformation."

"Nature corrupted her," Dominus guessed. Tykus shrugged.

"She let nature into her," he countered. "And lost some of her humanity. But she gained something else…the same gift you now possess, in far weaker form."

Dominus looked down at his own hands, seeing the smoothness of the skin there, no longer so dry and wrinkled from age.

"How convenient," Tykus added with a conspiratorial smile, "…that everyone that knows of your corruption is dead, and that the kingdom is too distracted to consider a war on the Ironclad."

Dominus stared at Tykus mutely, a chill running through him.

"You *planned* this?"

Tykus chuckled, patting Dominus on the arm.

"In any case, Neesha is cursed," he continued. "As all Legends are. But you are not a Legend, my friend. You can make far more of your gift than she'll ever be able to. Don't waste it, Dominus."

"But the Duchy," Dominus protested.

"I will choose your heir," Tykus stated. "He will continue as your ancestors have, as you did. You, on the other hand, will stand outside the kingdom, its eternal champion. You will ensure that we endure, that *I* endure. And that the kingdom will remain limited, never daring to engage in conquest and expansion. That we allow the rest of the world to live as they want, as nature intended."

Dominus swallowed past a lump in his throat, then nodded.

I am the beekeeper.

"I instructed my Royal Guard to clear the tunnels after the Seekers made it through," Tykus stated. "Go outside of the Royal Chambers, and they will direct you to the tunnel that will take you to the Fringe."

"But what about you?" Dominus asked. Tykus smiled.

"I'll be fine."

"But you almost died," Dominus protested. "The Seekers nearly killed you!"

"You forget, Dominus," Tykus replied, spreading his arms out wide. "I'm in infinite supply!"

"But if you'd died…"

"Then one of the Royal Guard would have entered my chamber and become me," Tykus interrupted. "Go Dominus," he added. "You know the way."

"I can't leave you, your Highness," Dominus insisted. Tykus smiled, reaching in and embracing Dominus, then stepping back, keeping his hands on Dominus's shoulders.

"There is always a path back to me," he replied. "Through the tunnels." He let his hands drop from Dominus's shoulders. "I look forward to our walks together, Dominus."

Dominus smiled, moisture blurring his vision. He bowed deeply.

"Thank you, your Highness."

"No need for titles," Tykus countered. "You are no longer Duke of Wexford. Tykus will do."

"Thank you, Ty…Tykus," Dominus replied, stumbling on the word. "For everything." Tykus winked at him.

"You're welcome."

CHAPTER 40

Hunter's eyes widened as he stepped into the large room housing the Shrine of Wexford, his jaw dropping. He heard a sharp intake of breath behind him, and glanced back to see Vi standing behind him, the flame from her torch dancing in a slight breeze. The light shone throughout the shrine, casting it in a golden hue.

"Damn," Vi breathed.

A large fountain stood before them, a bowl made entirely of human skeletons, their bones cemented together with a silver metal. It was at least ten feet in diameter, the lip of the bowl rising to Hunter's waist-level. In the center of that bowl, rising from the ever-flowing water, more skeletons stood, crawling over one another to form a tapering column that nearly reached the domed ceiling some twenty feet above his head. Water flowed from the top of that column, dribbling down the skeletons, flowing over their bones to reach the bottom.

Skeletons spread outward from the bottom of the fountain, forming a floor made entirely of bones. Walls – also made entirely of skeletons, rose upward toward the ceiling above, arcing inward to form a large, unholy dome.

"Jesus," Hunter swore. The entire room was made of skeletons…a shrine not just *to* the dead, but *of* the dead. "Are all shrines like this?"

"Hell no," Vi replied. "This is…" She trailed off, studying the room. "I've never seen anything like this. Dominus's family is the oldest in the kingdom, as old as the kingdom itself." She gestured at the skeletons all around them. "And you're looking at them."

"These are his relatives?"

"Yep," she confirmed. "Every single one of them. Only the men, of course."

"Damn."

"Come on," she urged, striding forward, going around the fountain. "There's some pretty damn strong wills here. We can't afford to stay any longer than we have to."

Hunter followed her around the fountain, spotting a door on the other side of it. Vi reached it, then glanced at Hunter.

"Am I gonna die if I open this?" she asked.

"No, you're good," he reassured. She opened it, stepping through into the room beyond. Hunter followed her, finding himself in a long rectangular room. Unlike the shrine, the walls were made of plain gray bricks; there were several rows of square pools of water set into the floor, like a grid of tiny indoor swimming pools. Set on an underwater platform in the center of each pool were what looked like treasure chests made of black stone.

"This must be where he keeps his best artifacts," Vi guessed. "Each of these pools is like my storehouse back home. Water flows through each of the pools, absorbing the wills stored within each artifact on the center platform. Then it flows out of the room, carried underground…probably to a stream far from the castle, or to the moat around it."

"Huh."

"So which one's got your brother's head in it?" Vi asked. Hunter frowned, walking forward slowly, scanning each obsidian chest as he went down the long room. He stopped before the fourth one, pointing to it.

"That one."

Vi walked up to it, kneeling down and leaning over to grab the chest. She lifted it, putting it down on the ground beside the pool, then opened the lid. She stared inside, then glanced up at Hunter.

"Empty," she stated.

Hunter frowned, looking inside. She was right…it *was* empty.

"Well what the hell," he muttered.

"Try again."

He did so, walking around the room, then coming back to the one he had before.

"That's it," he insisted. "I remember putting it there."

"You remember *Dominus* putting it there," Vi corrected. "Come on, let's check all of them." She walked to the next one, and Hunter went to the chest after that, retrieving it and opening it up. There was an Ossae inside of Hunter's – a skull – but it was clearly human. He glanced up at Vi, who looked in her own chest, then shook her head.

"Mine neither," he admitted. They walked around the room, opening all the chests, but none of them contained Xerxes' head.

"Well shit," Vi swore. "You're sure he didn't take it back out?"

"Positive."

"Maybe he did," she countered. "If he removed it later, he might not have stayed around long enough for the chest to absorb the memory."

"True," Hunter conceded. Then he frowned. "But what if it did?" He walked up to the chest, kneeling before it and lowering his forehead until it rested on the lid. Then he stood.

"Anything?" Vi asked.

"Someone did take it out," he revealed, his mouth set in a grim line. "Some guy named Farkus. I think he's a servant or something."

"All right then," she decided. "We find Farkus and get him to tell us where it is."

"And if he doesn't talk?"

"Then you rip the memory out of him."

* * *

Hunter and Vi left the Shrine of Wexford, closing the door behind them, then tracing their steps back through the series of tunnels leading to the surface. Hunter avoided the numerous traps expertly, Vi mimicking his every move. They reached the end of the last tunnel, with the ladder going up to the stone hatch above.

"After you," Hunter offered, gesturing at the ladder.

"Such a gentleman," Vi replied. "You just want to look at my ass, don't you."

"That's not why I offered," Hunter retorted. Then he grinned. "But yes, now that you mention it, I do."

"Enjoy," she replied, smirking at him and climbing up the ladder. He gazed upward, watching her ascend.

"It's very nice," he called out after her.

"It's goddamn spectacular," Vi shot back. Hunter chuckled, grabbing onto the ladder and climbing up after her. She reached the hatch…but it was closed. She was about to open it when she froze, cocking her head to the side, as if she was listening. The she swore.

"What's wrong?" Hunter asked.

"Get ready to fight," she warned. Then she dropped her torch, shoving the hatch open and bursting out of the shaft. Hunter climbed after her, emerging into the cool night air above…and froze.

There were dozens of soldiers all around them, swarming toward a huge black figure some thirty feet away. A black shadow with a glowing blue stripe running down its back, with countless bodies strewn across the grass all around it.

Xerxes!

Soldiers leapt on his brother's back, while others swung their hammers and swords at him, chopping at his legs. Xerxes threw one of the soldiers off, punching another one, but there were too many of them. The armor on his knee split open under a warhammer's blow, blood gushing from the wound. Xerxes fell to his hands and knees, more soldiers leaping atop him.

It was then that Hunter realized one of Xerxes' arms was missing, cut off just above the elbow. And his glowing mane was deflated, blue gel leaking from a tear in it dribbling down his flanks.

"We have to help him!" Hunter cried. But there were too many soldiers between them and his brother. One of them turned, noticing them.

"Hey!" he shouted, pointing at Hunter and Vi.

"Back to back!" Vi ordered, grabbing her mace and pressing her back against his. She kept to the edge of the open shaft, blocking the guards from reaching them from that side. Hunter heard footsteps behind him, and glanced back to see a bunch of guards rushing at them.

"Incoming," Hunter warned.

"Focus on your side," Vi scolded. Hunter obeyed, unsheathing his longsword…and spotting two guards rushing at him, warhammers in their hands. One of them reached him, chopping down at his skull. If he dodged, it'd hit Vi; he swung his sword as hard as he could, the blade smacking into the warhammer's long shaft. The hammer buried itself into the ground right next to Hunter, so close he could feel the breeze from its passage.

Hunter chopped at the man's extended arm as hard as he could, severing it at the elbow.

The second soldier reached Hunter, swinging his hammer like a baseball bat. Hunter leapt *into* the swing, past the head of the hammer. Its shaft slammed into his flank, forcing him to stumble to the side. Somehow he managed to keep his balance, twisting his hips and swinging at the man's legs, making a deep gash in the man's upper thigh.

The soldier went down screaming, clutching at his half-severed leg.

He felt something slam into him from behind, and turned to see Vi pressing her back against him again.

"What'd I say?" she grumbled.

"I can't block a damn warhammer with my longsword," he retorted. "Want me to dodge and let you get creamed?"

"Take this," Vi offered, handing him her mace. "We need to get to Xerxes," she added. Then she drew her longsword, decapitating one of the soldiers in front of her…all in one motion. Hunter sheathed his sword and gripped the mace, feeling its unfamiliar weight in his hands.

All right then, he muttered to himself.

Another soldier rushed him, swinging their warhammer at his legs. His reflexes kicked in, making him leap over the attack. As he fell, he chopped down at the soldier's head. Their metal helm crumpled under the blow, blood gushing down their forehead and into their eyes.

They dropped like a stone.

Hunter heard shouting to his left, and turned to see soldiers carrying a large bucket running toward Xerxes. The soldiers on top of the big guy scrambled off, fleeing just as the soldiers with the bucket reached his brother. They heaved the bucket at Xerxes, black fluid flying outward at him, splashing on his back. A few soldiers were caught in the deluge as they attempted to run.

"Now!" one of the soldiers screamed.

Hunter turned to see an archer in the distance, a flaming arrow nocked in his bow.

No!

Hunter dropped his mace, reaching for the bow on his back with one hand, and an arrow with the other. He nocked an arrow and let it fly in one smooth motion…just as the flaming arrow shot out of the archer's bow.

Hunter's arrow slammed into the archer's eye socket…right as the archer's arrow struck Xerxes.

Flames spread across Xerxes' body, engulfing him instantly.

"Xerxes!" Hunter shouted. He unsheathed his sword, then sidestepped toward his brother, keeping his back pressed against Vi's. Tongues of flame licked at Xerxes' armored flesh, consuming him…and the soldiers unlucky enough to be too close to him. The ground all around him was in flames, thick black smoke rising into the air. "We've got to help him!"

"No shit," Vi shot back. She severed one guard's arm, then another's head, her blade a blur as she fought. Two more guards rushed Hunter with longswords, thrusting at the same time. He managed to block both blades to the side, slashing at the soldiers' throats. One of the soldiers fell, clutching at their severed windpipe. But the other soldier dodged back, then thrust forward again, striking Hunter in the chest!

Hunter grunted, the force of the blow shoving him back against Vi. He looked down, expecting to see the blade sticking through his chest, but his breastplate had deflected it. He batted the man's sword aside, slashing at their belly. The cold steel sliced through the soldier's flesh, intestines spilling out of a gaping wound there.

The soldier screamed, clutching at their guts, stumbling backward. But three more took his place, charging Hunter!

"Vi!" Hunter warned…and then felt his right shoulder jerk back with a *thunk*. He stumbled, nearly losing his balance, and saw an arrow sticking out of his shoulder.

Fuck!

He tried to raise his longsword, but lifting his right arm sent a horrible pain shooting through his shoulder, and he cried out, nearly dropping his sword. The three soldiers reached him, slashing at him with their swords!

Hunter felt arms shoving him to the side, then saw Vi turn to face the soldiers, parrying their attacks with one swing of her sword. She crouched down low then, cutting at their knees…while ducking another attack from a soldier behind her. She spun in a half-circle, thrusting upward, her blade passing right underneath that soldier's chin, burying itself into his skull.

And then an arrow flew right into her lower back.

Vi cried out, jerking her blade free from the soldier's chin, then spinning around, her bow appearing in her hands, an arrow nocked and fired before Hunter could even register what had happened. Her arrow shot over the heads of the soldiers swarming the garden, slamming into an archer standing just inside a second-story window of the castle. She put her bow away, reaching down to help Hunter up. He gasped, clutching at his throbbing right shoulder.

"I can't move it," he blurted out. Another arrow zipped past his ear, missing him by mere inches. He ducked down. "God *damn* it!"

Vi stood beside Hunter, ending the lives of two more soldiers that got too close. But more were coming…far too many more. And in the distance, Xerxes stumbled onto his hands and knees, an inferno engulfing him. Then he collapsed onto the ground, crawling forward on his belly. The flames reached so high and burned so hot that the soldiers surrounding him had to keep back a few yards.

We're not going to make it, Hunter realized, watching as Vi shot an arrow at the archer who'd shot at them, then turned and impaled another soldier rushing at her.

Another soldier ran at Hunter, swinging their warhammer at his left flank. Hunter dodged, but the hammer clipped him on the hip, sending him flying to the ground…and landing directly on his injured shoulder.

He *howled.*

Scrambling to his feet, Hunter saw the soldier lunge for him again, swinging their warhammer in a vicious arc, aiming again for his left flank. This time, he didn't even have time to react.

And then he saw Vi leap between him and the soldier, putting herself right in the path of that deadly hammer. It struck her in the back, sending her flying into Hunter. They tumbled to the ground, Vi sprawled on top of him.

Hunter heard footsteps approaching, saw the soldier standing over them, his lips contorted into a grim smirk.

"Vi!" Hunter shouted, shaking her with his good arm. She groaned, but didn't move. He saw the soldier gazing down at him, planting his feet in a wide stance. The man lifted his hammer high in the air, the weapon a black shadow against the moons above.

Hunter smelled the smoke in the air, heard the shouting. The screams. He felt something stirring within him, something demanding release.

Za-ga-mar!

An image of the tomb came to him, the giant statue rising from the base of the skull, arms held high in triumph. He knew at once what it meant. The great Legend reborn from the substance he had consumed, from the skull of Zagamar himself.

I am the Legend reborn, he thought. *I am…*

Time slowed, the soldier's warhammer seeming to pause in midair above his head, his face contorted into an awful grimace, the veins on his temples bulging grotesquely.

Za-ga-mar!

Hunter felt the Legend waking within him, stirring from its ancient slumber. It came faster and more powerfully than he had ever experienced. He resisted it, suddenly terrified of its raw power. Terrified that this time, it might consume him.

Still it came, overwhelming his will, a force that could not be denied. A raging river of power, its current threatening to sweep him away. To pull him under and drown him.

I am ZAGAMAR!

Time stopped, the world sharpening, every detail coming into focus. The sweat dripping from the soldier's brow, the pulse of blood in the vessels of his neck. The soldiers all around them, seeming to have been frozen in time. An arrow suspended in mid-air high above his head.

The unstoppable force of Zagamar's will engulfed him, crashing over him like a tidal wave.

No.

He let it surround him, but stepped *outside* of it, watching from the periphery of his own consciousness.

I am Hunter, he told himself. *And Vi. And Mom, and Dominus. And Zagamar.*

He let go of his grip on his soul then, realizing with a sudden, utter certainty that, in this world, he could never be just himself. That he had become a combination of everyone he'd met here. A community in one flesh.

I am *Zagamar!*

Time flowed with graceful slowness, the soldier's hammer falling gradually toward him. He stared at it without fear, his mind racing, thoughts spilling over each other in rapid succession. Fear paralyzed the mind, making men into fools. They reacted instead of acting…and died.

But *he* was not a fool.

Potential actions and their consequences branched out before his mind's eye, all of the possible futures spread out before him. The soldier's hammer had only moved a few centimeters by the time Zagamar made up his mind. He looked down at the soldier's legs, spread wide, feet planted on either side of Hunter's legs.

All force is exerted from the ground. Disconnect the object from the ground, nullify the attack. Swing already begun; momentum achieved. Have to redirect.

He hooked his foot around the back of the soldier's right knee, pulling at it, forcing it to bend. At the same time, he kicked the soldier's other knee backward, locking it. The soldier's hips rotated to the left, his whole body twisting, the hammer falling at an angle now.

Just enough to miss.

Zagamar was already rolling away from the blow, shoving the woman off of him. He jumped to his feet, watching as the hammer sank into the ground, the soldier wielding it thrown off-balance. Zagamar tore the hammer from the man's grasp, spinning in a circle, taking stock of everything around him. Every soldier. Every archer hiding in the castle nearby. The great black beast, burning to death ten-and-a-half meters away.

All moving in slow-motion, none of them knowing who he was, or what he could do.

None of them realizing they were already dead.

He swung his hammer in a wide circle, planting his feet, then twisting his hips. He felt the power come from the earth, traveling up his legs, directed by his hips…and then expressed in his hands, transmitted to the cool metal shaft of the warhammer.

The head of the warhammer smashed into the nearest guard's temple, his skull caving in with the sheer power of the blow. The soldier flew to the side, and Zagamar used the momentum of his swing, redirecting the weapon up over his head and sending it crashing down on another guard's skull. He took a step back then, watching as an arrow flew in front of his face, missing it by mere centimeters. He was already reaching up with one hand; he plucked the arrow out of the air, placing it in his quiver.

All according to plan.

He turned, spotting a soldier rushing at him with their longsword. It was obvious from their posture that they were going to thrust; he threw his hammer at the soldier's face, then dodged to the side, watching as their blade passed slowly by him. He grabbed the sword by the blade with his palms, tearing it from the soldier's grasp…then swung it – by the blade – so that the cross-guard slammed into another soldier's face.

More soldiers rushed in at him…and at the woman, Vi. She was rising up onto her hands and knees, clearly in a great deal of pain.

He felt this body's mind – the boy named Hunter – nudging at him.

We need her alive, he pressed. *And the beast.*

Zagamar felt a flash of irritation, but knew immediately that he would have to obey… that for now, this body was not fully his. The boy would be foolish enough to let his feelings for Vi make him force Zagamar out…unless he complied.

Fine.

He let go of the blade of his longsword, using the momentum from his earlier swing to spin it in a half-circle in midair in front of him. He grabbed the hilt then, lunging at the guards threatening Vi…and slicing both of their throats open.

He saw Vi rising to her feet, moving faster than everyone around her. Saw her eyes flit from soldier to soldier around her, calculating. Planning.

And then she burst into action, a whirlwind of death, moving even faster than him. Moving faster than anyone he'd ever seen. She ended three soldiers' lives in rapid succession, then dodged to the side of an arrow, grabbing it out of the air and twisting around to plunge it into a fourth guard's eye socket…then dodging a fifth guard's sword thrust, at the same time swinging her sword to decapitate him.

At that moment, Zagamar felt an emotion so unfamiliar that it took him a moment to realize what it was.

Awe.

Told you so, he felt the boy think.

He smirked, dodging another soldier's attack and lopping off the man's arm. Then he followed Vi as she pushed toward the beast – the thing they called Xerxes – murdering everyone who got in her way. But he noticed her grimacing in pain every time she twisted her torso. The blow to her spine had injured her.

Then she jerked backward as an arrow buried itself into her belly, falling onto her back amidst the soldiers.

Zagamar sheathed his sword, grabbing his bow and yanking out the arrow still embedded in his shoulder, then nocking it. He aimed at the archer who'd shot Vi, high up in a castle window, and let the arrow fly.

A testament to this body's skill that the arrow flew true, ending the archer's life.

Zagamar rushed at the men surrounding Vi, throwing his bow high into the air, then unsheathing his sword and attacking them. One-by-one they fell, helpless against him, tumbling to the ground in slow-motion. None of them even registering that they were already dead.

He sheathed his sword then, catching his bow as it fell, then scanning the area. He spotted men rushing through a fresh group of soldiers toward him and Vi, holding a barrel filled with oil. He glanced upward, spotting an archer in the distance, a flaming arrow nocked in their bow…aiming right at him.

Zagamar nocked an arrow, shooting it at one of the men holding the barrel. It struck the man right through the eye socket, and the barrel fell to the ground, the oil spilling on the grass under the group of soldiers there. He was already nocking another arrow, and let it fly…right at the archer with the flaming arrow.

It struck the archer in the shin, locking the man's leg…and forcing his hips to bend, his bow lowering slightly. The archer let go of his bowstring, the flaming arrow shooting downward…and slamming right into the oil-soaked ground ahead of Zagamar.

The grass burst into flames, engulfing the group of soldiers.

Zagamar strode up to Vi, ignoring the screams of the burning men. She'd already ripped the arrow from her own belly, blood dripping from the wound. Far less blood than expected.

She's healing.

He offered a hand, and she grabbed it, letting herself be hauled to her feet.

"Thanks," she said.

Then she burst forward to the ring of soldiers surrounding Xerxes, murdering them one-by-one. Zagamar followed her, taking down a few soldiers of his own. Xerxes had stopped crawling, lying motionless on the charred grass, dying flames licking at his body. Zagamar felt Hunter's fear, and ignored it.

Vi limped up to Xerxes, ignoring the flames and bending over to roll him.

"Get my back!" she shouted, each word seeming to take an eternity to come from her mouth. Zagamar complied, attacking any soldier that got too close. They were more hesitant now, he observed. Watching so many of their fellow soldiers get slaughtered had taught them to fear him.

An entirely appropriate emotion.

Vi rolled Xerxes onto his side, then his back, smothering the last of the flames. The creature's back was badly burned, its armor there shrunken and cracked, exposing seared flesh underneath. The front of its body had been relatively spared, but it appeared to be dead. Its lay there, utterly limp, its black eyes staring lifelessly upward.

"Leave him," he told Vi. She shot him a glare.

"Fuck you, Zagamar," she shot back. A few soldiers gathered the courage to rush in at her, and she spun to face them, longsword in hand. They promptly rushed back, eyeing each other nervously. "Hunter, kick that asshole out."

Zagamar felt this body's will collect itself, felt it rising within him, threatening to overtake him. He resisted, but it was no use. He was too small a part of the boy's mind…for now. He acquiesced, feeling his consciousness *shift*, that greater part of this body's mind taking over.

I am Hunter.

And suddenly he *was* Hunter, that familiar and comforting sense of *self* returning. As if everything that had happened when he was Zagamar had been a dream. His sensation of time normalized, seeming to move far too quickly now. And the hunger – that horrible hunger – returned.

"All right," Hunter stated, eyeing the soldiers surrounding them. They all stayed a healthy distance away, no one volunteering to be the first to die. "What now?"

"Now we get out of here," she answered. "And kill everyone that gets in our way."

"But what about…" he began, glancing back at Xerxes. To his surprise, his brother was moving, rolling onto his belly, a low rattle coming from his throat. He grunted, pushing himself to his hands and knees; a sliver of blue light shone from his charred and torn mane, growing brighter and thicker as Hunter watched.

The soldiers around them shouted, rushing inward at Xerxes. And then Xerxes got to his feet, rising to his full height, towering over them. One arm was still missing, ash falling from his charred back.

He roared.

The soldiers had a sudden change of heart, backing away quickly.

"We need to find Farkus," Hunter told Vi as he backed up to stand at Xerxes' side. But Vi shook her head.

"Too late kiddo," she replied grimly. "There's too many of them."

"But..."

"We need to leave," she interrupted. "Now."

There was a shout, and Hunter looked beyond the soldiers around them, spotting more of them rushing through the gardens toward them. Like fifty more.

"Right then," Hunter agreed. "Lead the way."

Vi pointed at the inner wall surrounding the castle in the distance, nudging Xerxes, who lumbered forward...right toward the guards surrounding them. The nearest guards backed away quickly, but not quickly enough. Xerxes kicked one in the chest, sending him flying backward into the guards behind him. They toppled like bowling pins, and Xerxes continued forward, trampling them under his armored feet, ignoring their screams as they were crushed by his massive weight.

"Stop that thing!" one of the soldiers cried, rushing at Xerxes and swinging their warhammer at his flank. Vi intercepted them, decapitating the soldier with one swing of her longsword.

"Anyone else wanna try?" she inquired, following Xerxes as he trampled his way through the crowd of soldiers. Anyone that got too close to Xerxes was grabbed and promptly turned into abstract art. Hunter followed behind Vi and Xerxes, facing backward, gripping his longsword tightly. A few soldiers eyed him, but kept their distance, no doubt remembering what he'd done as Zagamar...and believing him still capable of fighting like the long-dead Legend. Hunter wasn't about to disabuse them of that notion.

They made their way quickly through the guards in this way, breaking through and sprinting down a narrow path through the vegetation parallel to the inner wall. Vi pointed to the drawbridge in the distance, which was still open. Hunter saw the large clearing beyond, leading to the King's Road...and the forest.

"Close the drawbridge!" someone behind them shouted.

Hunter looked back, spotting the fresh group of guards rushing toward them...and more than a few archers among them.

"Archers!" Hunter warned.

"Take them out," Vi shouted. He grabbed his bow, nocking an arrow and shooting it at the nearest archer, who dropped like a stone. But he had to slow down to aim, making him fall behind Vi and Xerxes. And the soldiers were catching up to him.

He turned to run and catch up with his friends, and saw an arrow fly over his head, ricocheting off Xerxes' back.

"I said *take them out,*" Vi yelled. She twisted around, her bow somehow appearing in her hands, and shot three arrows in rapid succession, not even seeming to pause to aim. Three archers fell, causing the soldiers behind them to trip over them.

"Showoff," he grumbled, catching up to Vi, then turning around to fire another arrow. It missed, flying over another archer…who promptly shot an arrow at *him.* He swore, ducking his head…and felt the breeze of the arrow passing right over him, slamming into Xerxes' back. This time it struck his mane, puncturing it. Blue gel oozed from the wound.

Xerxes glanced back, glaring at Hunter.

"Damn it," Hunter swore, nocking another arrow, then turning and focusing. He fired, and this time the arrow flew true, embedding itself right into the archer's forehead.

Yes!

"Come on!" Vi urged. He turned forward, realizing he'd fallen behind again. They were only thirty yards from the drawbridge now. But something was wrong.

It was starting to rise.

Hunter cursed, pumping his legs as fast as he could…and still barely able to match Xerxes' and Vi's pace. Another arrow flew over his right shoulder, barely missing Vi ahead. The drawbridge angled steadily upward, the end already five feet above the ground.

"Go go go!" Vi shouted.

Xerxes burst forward, running even faster than Vi, reaching the start of the drawbridge. She reached it moments later, her boots *thumping* on the thick wood. Hunter trailed behind, still a good ten feet from the drawbridge.

And then he felt a sudden pain in his right calf, and his leg gave out beneath him, sending him tumbling to the ground.

"Vi!" he cried out, scrambling to his feet. He limped forward, looking down to see an arrow sticking out of his calf. He heard shouting from behind, and saw the soldiers charging after him, only thirty feet behind…and closing in fast. He reached the drawbridge, limping up it as fast as he could, swearing as pain shot up his leg with each step. Vi skid to a stop, rushing back toward him, her bow in her hands. She shot the archer who'd shot him, then grabbed his arm, yanking him forward. He stumbled, nearly falling again. The soldiers behind him were only a dozen feet away now.

"Hunter," Vi stated, her tone ice cold. She glared at him with her green eyes. "Run or die."

Hunter felt an eerie calm come over him, and he focused on the end of the rising drawbridge ahead, now ten feet off the ground.

He ran.

Another arrow flew past him, slamming into the drawbridge ahead. He ignored it, running as fast as he could, ignoring the horrible pain in his calf. It didn't matter anymore. Nothing mattered except the end of the drawbridge twenty feet ahead.

Run or die.

Vi ran beside him, gripping his arm tightly. Their boots struck the drawbridge in unison, the sound drowned out by the soldiers closing in behind them. The steeper the drawbridge became, the harder it was to keep going. If he fell, he'd slide backward…right into the soldiers.

Ten feet.

He heard the footsteps behind him getting closer, then felt a hand grab his shoulder from behind. He pulled away, his eyes glued to the end of the drawbridge. They were easily a dozen feet off the ground now…and rising quickly. Below, he saw the dark water of the moat, its surface glittering in the moonlight.

Five feet.

He felt Vi let go of his arm, saw her leap off the end of the drawbridge, careening through the air above the moat. He reached the end of it, jumping off with his good leg…and felt someone grab his ankle from behind. He fell forward, his shin slamming into the edge of the drawbridge. Then he plummeted toward the water far below. He entered into free-fall, the water rising up to meet him. He saw Vi plunge into the water ahead of him…and then he struck the water.

Ice-cold darkness surrounded him, and he felt something slam on top of him from above, blasting the air from his lungs. He panicked, clawing upward through the blackness. But his armor and weapons dragged him downward, making it impossible to swim to the surface. He grabbed at his belt, struggling with the clasp, feeling himself sinking even faster. The belt came loose, the weight of his weapons vanishing, and he swam upward, his lungs starting to burn.

Come on…

He felt something grab at his ankle, and kicked, feeling his foot strike something hard. The grip on his ankle let go, and he clawed his way upward, the urge to breathe becoming stronger with every stroke.

Suddenly he burst through the surface!

Hunter gasped for air, spotting Vi swimming ahead of him…and Xerxes beyond her, standing at the shore of the moat.

Then he felt an arm wrap around his neck from behind, pulling him below the surface!

He grabbed at the arm, trying desperately to pry it off his neck, but it was no use. He reached back, feeling blindly with his fingers, and felt a nose, then eyelids. He hooked his fingers into his attacker's eye socket, then pulled as hard as he could.

There was a *pop*.

The arm around his neck slipped away, and Hunter kicked away from the soldier behind him, swimming upward. His head burst through the surface, and he took deep, gasping breaths, swimming as quickly as he could toward the shore. Vi was already there; Hunter swam up to her, and she and Xerxes grabbed his arms, hauling him out of the water.

He glanced back, seeing the drawbridge nearly closed. Soldiers slid backward on it, many of them tumbling off the sides to the water below.

"Hold him," Vi told Xerxes. Xerxes grabbed Hunter by the shoulders, and Vi knelt down, grabbing the arrow stuck in Hunter's calf. She yanked on it…hard.

"Ow!" Hunter cried as the arrow tore free. Blood oozed out of the wound, staining his pants. "Damn it!"

Xerxes turned Hunter around to face him, then knelt down, studying the wound on Hunter's shoulder. The big guy reached back to his tail, pinching it. Blue goo oozed out onto his fingers, and he pressed it into the hole in Hunter's shoulder. Hunter bit back a yell, at the sudden pain, but Xerxes went right for Hunter's leg, putting some goo in the wound there too.

"HELP…HEAL," he explained.

"Let's go," Vi stated, grabbing Hunter's arm and slinging it over her shoulder. He leaned on her, limping toward the tree line in the distance.

"What about the Ossae?" he asked. Vi shook her head, her expression grim.

"It's too late," she replied. "Wherever it is, they'll make sure to move it somewhere we'll never find it."

"But…"

"We failed," Vi interjected. "Dominus has your brother's head, and knowing him, he's going to use it."

"Which means…"

"Which means the chances of us winning a war against Tykus," she replied, "…just got a whole lot smaller."

CHAPTER 41

The grand hallways of the Acropolis were silent by the time Nova strode through them, two dozen of her finest Seekers at her side. Bodies lay strewn across the floor, Seekers and guards both. The smell of blood hung in the air, thick and pungent. The smell of death.

And from that death, Nova knew, would come the rebirth of Man. The dukes were dead, save for Dominus. Her men had confirmed the bodies of the five dukes in the Hall of Tykus. The king, however, had made it out alive, retreating to the King's Chambers.

Nova reached stairs going downward, taking them two at a time, her Seekers following close behind her. A wide hallway continued forward as far as the eye could see, tall statues lining either wall. Statues of King Tykus in various poses. A hallway of vanity, of false worship. For the king was merely a man, inferior to the Legend that the Founder had discovered.

Inferior to the greatest Legend that had ever existed, older than civilization itself.

Nova jogged down the hallway, spotting double-doors at the end of it. Doors wrought of pure platinum and gold, the fabled entry to the Great Hall before the Royal Chambers. She adjusted the mask she wore over her nose and mouth, a mask made of thick layers of fabric forming a tight seal over her lower face. A mask that every other Seeker around her wore. Then she unsheathed her longsword, knowing full well what lay beyond those doors.

The Royal Guard, personal defenders of the king. The most skilled warriors in the Acropolis, molded from childhood to serve as the last line of defense for the king.

This was her final test. The sacred duty High Seeker Zeno had entrusted her with.

I will not fail you, High Seeker.

She reached the massive double-doors, skidding to a halt before them. They were locked, she knew, and bolted shut. Even a battering ram might not succeed in opening them. And made of inert metals, they were impervious to acid, inflammable, and enormously heavy.

She gestured to her Seekers, many of who were carrying crossbows on their backs, others carrying large packs. The latter lowered these packs carefully onto the floor before the doors, removing large sealed flasks from each. One Seeker lit a torch, while the others unsealed the flasks, tipping them over before the doors. A dark fluid flowed from each, flowing under the small gap between the bottom of the doors and the floor.

Then the Seekers backed far away from the doors, and Nova joined them. All except the one Seeker with the torch; he lowered the flame into the pool of dark fluid by the doors, igniting it instantly. Then he sprinted to join the rest of the Seekers, turning to watch.

Thick black smoke rose from the burning fluid, rising to the ceiling. A noxious plume, it would spread out relatively harmlessly in this huge space, and the masks she and her Seekers wore would protect them from its effects.

But within the sealed hall beyond, it would prove much more effective, choking the air from the guards' lungs…and preventing any guards from coming too close to the doors.

Nova heard shouting from beyond the doors, and smiled, shifting her weight from foot to foot, wiping a sweaty palm on her pants. She glanced at a group of four Seekers nearby, each carrying warhammers.

"On my order," she prompted.

"Yes High Councilor," they replied.

She waited for the fluid to finish burning, then nodded at the Seekers.

"Go."

The men rushed up to the double-doors, then swung their hammers at the granite floor before them. The granite shattered under their blows, and they continued, striking again and again, pulverizing the stone. When the men tired, four more Seekers replaced them, continuing to smash a hole through the floor. Nova watched them work, quickly widening and deepening the hole.

The doors were impervious, but the floor…

A stupid oversight, she knew. Had the floors been wrought of thick metal, this mission would have been over before it started.

Four more Seekers replaced the ones who had tired, the hole deepening and widening until it was deep enough to allow her men to slide under.

"On my order," Nova stated, making a chopping gesture at the doors. The Seekers drew their swords, the sound reverberating off the stone walls. She waited a moment, making sure her mask was sealed, then made the motion again.

And sprinted toward the doors, her Seekers at her sides.

The first of the Seekers slid into the hole in the floor, passing underneath the double-doors. More of her Seekers slid underneath, and she waited for all of them to do so before sliding under herself. She ducked under the thick metal doors, emerging on the other side.

Thick smoke hung in the air, a dark haze. Even with her mask, she could smell the noxious stuff. She peered down the short hallway through it, spotting guards huddled against the door at the opposite end, their weapons drawn.

The Royal Guard.

Her Seekers stood before her, raising their crossbows and firing them into the guards. The guards moved with remarkable agility, dodging and blocking the missiles expertly.

None fell.

The Seekers fired another volley, then another, managing to kill only one of the Royal Guard; the rest charged at the Seekers, their weapons held before them, their heavy boots *thumping* on the granite floor.

"For the Founder!" Nova cried, raising her sword high above her head.

The Seekers rushed forward through the haze, and Nova joined them, sprinting down the hallway toward the nearest guard. She reached inside her pocket, grabbing a small bottle and chucking it at the guy's chest. The guard slashed at the bottle with his sword, shattering it.

And releasing the acid within, splashing himself in the chest and face.

The guard howled, dropping his sword and clutching at his face. Nova dispatched him with a single thrust, sprinting to another guard and lobbing another bottle at him. He dodged it…and right into the path of her blade. He parried just in time, leaving his flank exposed…and Nova sank a dagger into it, burying it in his liver.

Two down.

Nova turned to another guard, watching as he slashed a Seeker's throat. She rushed at the falling Seeker, slamming into him…and sending him flying into the guard. They both tumbled to the floor, and Nova leapt on them, plunging the point of her blade through the Seeker's back…and impaling the guard trapped underneath.

Three down.

She jerked her sword from the two bodies, then spun around…just as another guard thrust at her belly. She twisted away, but was too slow; the blade grazed her flank. She ignored the pain, backpedaling quickly…and watching as one of her Seekers impaled the guard from behind.

And then was decapitated by another guard behind *him*.

Nova chucked her dagger at this new guard, rushing at him and reaching into her pocket again. He dodged out of the way of the dagger, and right into her last bottle of acid. It shattered on his forehead, liquifying his face and eyes.

Four down.

There was a loud *thunk*, and Nova turned to see the door to the Royal Chambers opening. There was only one guard – and one of her Seekers – left standing.

"For the Founder!" Nova cried, sprinting toward the opening door. A young man stepped through it. A tall man with long blond hair, a long beard, and striking blue eyes.

Tykus!

"Your Highness!" a guard shouted, rushing to intercept Nova. "Get back in your chambers!"

She rushed the guard, slashing at him. He parried easily, counterattacking with a vicious series of blows. Nova barely managed to hold her own against him, backpedaling quickly as she blocked each attack.

"Grand Councilor!" a Seeker shouted, rushing the guard and throwing himself on the man. The guard turned to impale the Seeker…allowing Nova to cut him down.

She faced Tykus then, watching as the king unsheathed a long silver sword. It was unlike any weapon she had seen…the Sword of Tykus.

"You must be Nova," Tykus stated. His voice was calm, without fear. Nova glanced around the room, realizing that all of her Seekers had fallen…as had the Royal Guard. She and the king were the only two left standing.

"You must be Tykus," she shot back, holding her blade before her.

"I've heard of you," Tykus admitted. "Zeno's prized swordswoman." He nodded at her. "You fight well."

"You should be afraid then," Nova stated, stepping toward him. He sidestepped, circling around her, until his back was to the double-doors the Seekers had come through.

"Why?" he inquired.

"Because you're about to die."

"Perhaps," he conceded. She closed the distance between him, and to his credit, he did not back away. "But I'm an old man," he added. "And I've already died once."

Nova leapt at Tykus, thrusting at his chest…then jerked back at the last minute.

He did not react.

Interesting, Nova thought. Nearly all men who'd absorbed the skills of other warriors had uncontrollable reflexes. It made sense that Tykus, a Legend, would have none. Legends were the only men that remained wholly themselves.

"The thing about dying," Tykus continued, "…is that we fear it because it is the last great unknown." He smiled. "Having experienced it, I've found it nothing to be afraid of."

"The end of your kingdom is," she retorted.

"All things end eventually," he replied. "And when my kingdom falls, all of the wisdom I've collected – hundreds of lifetimes' worth – will be casually destroyed." He sighed. "That," he added, "…is my greatest fear. And it will be Man's greatest loss."

She lunged forward again, this time not pulling back. He parried the blow, and the next one, and the next one. But he did not counterattack.

"Afraid to fight back?" she taunted.

"My father taught me how to use a sword," Tykus answered. She attacked again, and again he parried. "And when not to."

"Then lower it," she retorted. "And stop wasting my time."

Nova attacked again, feinting, then slashing at Tykus's sword arm. Her blade cut a deep gash in his forearm, and he grimaced, his sword dropping from his hand. It fell with a clatter on the granite floor.

Nova flashed him a grim smile, pressing the tip of her sword against his chest, right below the breastbone. A bloodstain grew where the tip punctured his fine shirt.

"Your kingdom is ours now," she declared. "Your bones will be ground up and thrown into the sea. Your books will be burned, your people slaughtered."

"So be it," he replied, lowering his hands to his sides. "You've done well, Nova. In six thousand years, no man – or woman – has ever made it this far. Zeno would be proud of you."

Nova regarded the king for a moment, unable to help herself from admiring the man's courage. He betrayed absolutely no fear. No regret. He did not beg for his life like so many lesser men.

"I'll make your death quick," she promised. He nodded gravely.

"A kindness I appreciate."

And then she lunged forward, thrusting her sword through his heart.

Tykus gasped, his eyes going wide, his hands gripping her shoulders. She pressed inward, shoving the blade deeper, until the hilt rested against his chest.

He hunched over, gripping her shoulders tightly, his face twisting in pain. Then his face relaxed, and he looked directly into her eyes.

"Thank…you," he gasped.

And then his eyes rolled back into his head, a final, rattling breath escaping his lips.

Nova shoved him away with one boot, yanking her sword from his chest. He fell to the floor, staring sightlessly at the ceiling far above, a rapidly expanding pool of blood forming on his chest. She stared at him, holding her bloodied sword in one hand, a chill running down her spine.

Tykus, the great king, ruler of the kingdom that bore his name for six thousand years, was dead. His endless cycle of death and rebirth was finally over.

"For the Founder," Nova whispered.

She turned away from him, toward the door to the Royal Chambers, and felt something kick in her the chest like a horse.

Nova flew backward, landing on her butt on the cold granite floor. She gasped, staring at the door to the Royal Chambers. At a figure standing before it, ten meters away from her, obscured by the smoke suspended in the air.

She looked down, seeing the feathered fletching of an arrow sticking out of the right side of her chest.

Nova grimaced, dropping her sword and gripping the arrow with both hands. She tried pulling on it, but doing so sent a fresh jolt of agony through her chest and back.

The figure by the door stepped forward through the haze. It was a man, she realized. Holding a bow. A man in a white, blue and gold uniform.

Nova's eyes widened, her jaw going slack.

"You…!" she gasped.

The man strode toward her, stopping three meters away. He stared at her with sky-blue eyes, his handsome face framed by long golden hair.

"You're dead!" Nova blurted out. "I just killed you!"

King Tykus gave her a wry smile, tossing his bow aside. He stepped up to her, unsheathing a sword at his left hip.

"Apparently I," he replied calmly, "…am in infinite supply."

Nova scrambled backward, turning to crawl on her hands and knees away from him…and saw Tykus's body blocking the way. Her eyes went to his sword lying on the floor beside him; she lunged for it, grabbing the hilt and spinning around.

…and saw her hand separate from her arm in a flash of silver.

Nova stared at the stump of her right wrist, at the twin jets of blood spurting from it. King Tykus stood over her, his blade dripping with blood, his blue eyes locked on hers.

"A Legend never dies," he stated, pressing the tip of his sword under her breastbone.

She felt a sharp pinch there, and grimaced, gripping the blade with her left hand.

"You, on the other hand," Tykus continued, "…never lived."

Nova felt her body jerk, felt a horrible pain in her chest. And then her vision blackened, her world fading into oblivion.

CHAPTER 42

Lady Camilla sighed, stepping into to the huge walk-in closet adjacent to her master bedroom. She had countless shelves and drawers filled with clothes, many of them the elaborate – and highly expensive – gowns she'd designed herself. Clothes meant to show off her figure, to dazzle her company, her guards…and her lovers.

For the latter, of course, the clothes rarely stayed on for long.

Camilla felt a presence behind her, in her master bedroom. She heard no footsteps – there were never any to hear – but knew without a doubt that Dio was standing there, watching her. She reached back at the hooks holding her corset together…but did not turn around. Moments later, she felt the heat of his body behind her, felt him removing her corset expertly.

She smiled.

Her corset fell to the floor, and she let it, her breasts and belly left exposed. She slipped out of the rest of her clothes, standing there utterly naked, her back still to Dio. She reached for a simple nightgown, pulling it on slowly, knowing that he was watching. It was very nearly sheer, and low-cut enough to be scandalous, even for her.

She turned around.

"You're upset," she murmured, staring into his exquisite silver eyes. His gaze lifted to meet hers, and she noted a slight change in his expression, even with his face hidden behind his mask.

"The girl," he muttered, his tone as flat as ever.

"You resent having to train her," Camilla guessed. She arched an eyebrow. "Would you have me force someone else to do it?"

"No my Lady."

"I want the best," Camilla stated, flashing him a little smile. "And with Vi dead, that's you, my dear."

Dio stiffened ever-so-slightly, and she sensed a slight perturbation in his customary icy calm. He hated being compared to Vi, she knew.

"She reminds you of her," Dio muttered.

"And?"

"Is that why you're doing this?" Dio asked. Camilla tilted her head slightly, eyeing him with an amused look on her face.

"Have you ever known me to be a fool, Dio?"

"No my Lady."

"Then trust me."

"I tested her yesterday," Dio pressed. "The girl is worthless."

"No one is worthless," Camilla scolded, shooting him a glare. She knew he was grimacing behind the mask. "Everyone has their use, my dear. You just have to be…open to finding it."

"But I need to stay here, my Lady," Dio insisted. "To protect you."

Camilla smiled, knowing that *this* was the true reason why Dio was upset. She leaned in, putting a hand on his mask, where his cheek would be. Let her gaze fall to his chest, which was full and chiseled under his tight leather armor. Admired his abs. He was a specimen of a man, with a body and mind forged by a discipline few possessed.

She slid her hand down to his chest, her fingers trailing down his abdomen. Still lower she went, taking her time, until at last she stopped at his groin. She cupped it gently, feeling the swell of his manhood there. The heat of it.

"Oh Dio," she murmured, leaning in, her lips brushing against his ear. "So protective of me."

She reached around with her other hand, sliding it down his spine, all the way to his buttocks. Held him there, one hand in front, the other behind. She waited, feeling him growing against her palm in regular pulses, until he could grow no more. Then she pulled away, smiling up at him.

"I'll be careful," she promised. Dio cleared his throat.

"If she dies?" he asked.

"Make sure she doesn't."

Dio hesitated, then bowed before her.

"Yes my Lady."

"Tsk tsk," Camilla scolded, putting a hand on his chest. "So formal, Dio. We're not in public, you know."

Dio bowed again, but to his credit it was not quite as deep as before.

"Run along," Camilla ordered, waving him away. "Come back to me when it is done." She gave him a smile, letting her gaze drop to his groin. "Then I'll give you your reward."

"Yes mother," Dio replied.

Chapter 43

The deep forest was still as Hunter, Vi, and Xerxes hiked back to Ironclad territory, the late-afternoon sun hidden behind somber gray clouds high above their heads. The only sound was of leaves and twigs crunching underfoot. None of the three had said much of anything since their escape from the Castle Wexford. There wasn't much to say.

Hunter stared at his feet as he walked, kicking a small rock on the forest floor.

We failed.

He grimaced, glancing at Vi and Xerxes, who were a few feet ahead. To think that, after everything he'd been through, he'd failed to get Xerxes' head back, failed to get revenge on Dominus and the Seekers…it was monumentally depressing. And now there was nothing he could do. They had no idea where Dominus had taken the head, and the duke was still alive and well.

And very soon now, the kingdom would send their armies against his own mother.

Hunter sighed, kicking another rock.

"Geez kiddo," Vi stated, slowing down to walk by Hunter's side. "You're depressing the shit out of me."

"Why *shouldn't* we be depressed?" Hunter shot back, irritated at her tone. As usual, she wasn't taking anything seriously. "We failed. We're done for."

"We're not done for until we're dead," Vi retorted. "We're alive, which means we get to fight another day."

"Yeah, well," Hunter grumbled. "Maybe if I'd been better, we coulda killed those soldiers and searched the rest of the castle."

"Probably."

"Stop it," he shot back angrily. "Just stop it, okay? Why don't you take something seriously for once in your goddamn life?"

"And end up like you?" she replied. "No thanks."

"We're as good as dead," Hunter complained, "…and all you can do is joke around!"

"Hunter," Vi began, but he cut her off.

"I don't wanna hear it."

"We failed," she said. "Oh well. But it doesn't matter," she added. "We can't focus on the past. We have to concentrate on what do to next."

"What can we do?"

"Well, for one, you can stop obsessing about getting revenge," Vi stated. Hunter glared at her.

"Really?"

"Really," Vi insisted. "Hunter, you've been itching to get back at Dominus and the Seekers ever since Traven bashed my skull in."

"So?" Hunter pressed. "You're saying I should just let it go? Let them do whatever they want and get away with it?"

"Please," Vi retorted. "Do you even know me?" She shook her head. "You're doing things for the wrong reason, Hunter. You need to focus on what's important."

"Like what?"

"Your family," she answered. "And me. And the Ironclad. You know, the people you care about."

Hunter turned away from her, his eyes on the forest floor as he walked.

"It's not just about getting back at the people you hate," she continued. "Revenge is based off of hate. It's poison, Hunter. It might get you to hurt your enemies, but it's going to hurt you too."

"Bullshit."

"Look at what you did for Camilla," Vi ventured. "You did anything she wanted, just for the promise of getting help with your revenge. You risked your life – your *soul* – for a chance at getting back at Dominus and the Seekers."

Hunter said nothing, knowing that Vi was right. He would've done a hell of a lot more, too.

"You hurt yourself just for a chance to hurt someone else," Vi insisted.

"I get it," he muttered glumly.

"I don't get revenge," Vi explained. "I protect what I care about: me, and the people I love. I don't let shit eat me up inside." She put a hand on his shoulder. "Remember my uncle?"

"Yeah."

"I spent almost a decade fantasizing about murdering that bastard," she explained. "Trained all day, every day. And after all those years, you know what? I *did* kill him. Thought I'd feel great afterward. And I did, for a few minutes."

"And?"

"And then I just felt lost," Vi continued. "Empty. Lonely. That's revenge, Hunter. It doesn't fill you up…it drains you. You've got family now, Hunter. Protect them. Get stronger, be smarter. Don't waste your life hating people. Just make sure you become someone they would never dare to cross."

Hunter sighed, knowing that she was right. He glanced at Vi, seeing her smiling at him. He smiled back grudgingly, putting an arm around her waist and pulling her to his side.

"Thanks Vi," he mumbled. "And…sorry."

"You should be," Vi replied. "You're an insufferable little bitch sometimes, you know that?"

"Uh huh."

"I asked your mom who you got that from," she continued. "She said your dad was a little bitch sometimes too."

"That's true."

"At least you're not the only one," Vi added, turning to Xerxes. "Good job getting the shit beaten out of you back there, Blue."

"HOW…MANY YOU…KILL?" Xerxes asked.

"I dunno," she replied. "Lost count."

"ME…FIFTY-SIX," the big guy growled, thumping his chest with one big fist.

"Damn," Vi swore. "I take it back. Maybe you two had different dads or something. Might wanna ask your mom about that when you get home, Hunter."

"Kinda wishing you'd die again," Hunter grumbled.

"Speaking of home," Vi continued, "…looks like we made it."

Hunter looked forward, realizing that Vi was right. The grass here was black, and crunched underfoot. And ahead, maybe a quarter mile away, he spotted the entrance to the main Ironclad lair.

They were home.

Xerxes led Hunter and Vi up to the cave entrance, then through the maze-like tunnels and rooms leading to the Queen's chamber. After what seemed like an eternity, they finally made it, the last of the long tunnels opening up into the huge underground cavern. The roar of the waterfall cascading down into the pool in the center of the cavern drowned out every other sound, a cool breeze whipping through Hunter's hair.

Xerxes gestured for them to walk up to the edge of the pool, then stopped there. He opened his mouth, emitting a deep, mournful wailing sound. Moments later, a figure emerged through the waterfall, stepping into the pool below. An Ironclad taller even than Xerxes, her armored body glowing a bright blue.

"You kept your promise," Neesha stated, nodding at Vi, then turning to face Hunter. "Welcome home, son."

"Hey," Hunter mumbled. Mom eyed him for a moment, then turned her gaze back to Vi.

"You failed."

"Yep," Vi confirmed. "It wasn't in the vault, and we were too overwhelmed to continue searching for it."

Mom took a deep breath in, then sighed.

"I see."

"I don't think Dominus was in Wexford," Vi continued. "My guess is he went back to the kingdom."

"Then he may already be dead," Mom replied. Vi frowned.

"Excuse me?"

"The kingdom was attacked," Neesha explained. "My scouts heard the alarm bells ringing from the Deadlands. The attack came last night. Much of the city is in flames."

"Well shit."

"Who attacked them?" Hunter asked. Mom turned to him.

"We don't know," she admitted. "But we do know that the soldiers at the military base in the Deadlands tried to come to their aid. The gate protecting the outer wall remained closed, barring them from entering."

"So it was an inside job," Vi deduced.

"Very likely."

"Interesting," Vi murmured.

"My scouts are keeping a close eye on the situation," Neesha stated. "Time will tell if the kingdom falls…or if it manages to survive."

"Guess they won't be attacking us any time soon then," Vi ventured. Neesha nodded.

"Agreed. We have little to fear at this point."

"So what now?" Hunter asked. Xerxes turned to face him, his inky black lips curled into a smile.

"ATTACK."

"What?"

"Blue's right," Vi agreed. "The kingdom is vulnerable. Weakened."

"Exactly," Neesha agreed. "We may never get a chance like this again."

"Wait, you're saying you want to attack the kingdom?" Hunter pressed. "Like, go to war?"

"Would you prefer sitting here waiting for them to recover, then try to wipe us out?" Vi retorted. "We have to strike while the iron is hot."

"Agreed," Neesha concurred. "And we will. My Ironclad are making preparations as we speak. They're building siege equipment to get over the wall, gathering weapons, armor, equipment. Food and other supplies."

Hunter glanced at Vi, flashing her a grin.

"Guess I get to have revenge after all," he quipped.

"No Hunter," Mom countered. "You're not going with them."

"What? Why not?"

"Because we need to save you first," she answered. "With every passing day, Zagamar is growing inside of you. Taking over, bit by bit. We need to stop him before we lose you to him."

Hunter swallowed, glancing at Vi.

"So we're going to the Deep," he stated. Vi glanced at Neesha, who shook her head.

"Vi stays here," she corrected. "I'll need her expertise to help plan the attack on Tykus. Xerxes, you'll accompany your brother to the Deep."

"YES…MOTHER," Xerxes growled, bowing before her. He stepped up to Hunter, putting a heavy hand on Hunter's shoulder. "SAFE WITH…ME."

"Don't doubt it for a second," Hunter replied, smiling up at his brother. "Thanks bro."

"Once Hunter's done," Neesha stated, "…bring him back here. We'll initiate the attack then."

Xerxes nodded, turning away from Mom and walking back toward the tunnel they'd come in through. He pulled Hunter with him, forcing Hunter to struggle to keep up with the big brute.

"Wait," Hunter protested, glancing back at Vi and Neesha. "We're leaving now?"

"No time to waste," Neesha explained. "Go quickly. We need Xerxes back to lead my armies."

"But…"

"We have packs for you both, filled with the supplies you'll need," Mom informed him. "Go to the Kingdom of the Deep first to get permission to enter the Deep."

Vi jogged up to Hunter then, grabbing his shoulder.

"Hold up Blue," she requested. Xerxes did so, letting go of Hunter's arm and stopping where he was. "Good luck, kiddo. Stay safe, alright?"

"I'll try," Hunter mumbled.

"You'd better," Vi shot back, grinning at him and tousling his hair affectionately. "Despite your personality, I kinda like you."

"Gee thanks," Hunter grumbled. "Love you too, Vi."

Vi winked, then leaned in, giving Hunter a hug. She held him for a long moment, then pulled away. Xerxes resumed walking, pulling Hunter along with him. Vi watched them go, waving goodbye.

"Hey Blue!" she called out after them. Xerxes paused, turning to look at her. "You better bring him back alive," she warned. "Or I'll cut your head off again." She flashed him a shit-eating grin then. "Both of them."

Xerxes raised his hands, extending all four middle fingers at her.

Vi laughed, the sound echoing off the cavern walls and down the tunnel Xerxes led Hunter down. Hunter smiled, shaking his head, then glanced sidelong at his brother, reaching up to pat him on the lower back.

“Guess it’s just you and me now, little brother,” he said. Xerxes grunted, smiling down at Hunter.

“BIG…LITTLE BROTHER.”

“Yeah, well,” Hunter stated, “…if we’re going to be spending a lot of time with each other, you might as well teach me that sign-language you use. Don’t want to wear out your voice.”

Xerxes nodded, beaming down at him.

“I…TEACH.”

“Appreciate it,” Hunter replied. “You know, I might just enjoy this trip. I always wanted a brother.”

“ME…TOO,” Xerxes agreed. “WAITED LONG…TIME.”

“I know,” Hunter stated. “I promise I’ll try to be the brother you deserve,” he added. “I don’t wanna let you down.”

“YOU HERE,” Xerxes stated, gesturing at Hunter. Then he thumped his chest with one fist. “ALL…I WANT.” He tousled Hunter’s hair. “FAMILY.”

Hunter nodded, feeling a sudden affection for the guy. He patted Xerxes on the arm, following his big little brother down the tunnel, toward the exit to the Ironclad lair. He remembered what Vi had told him, and took a deep breath in, letting it out slowly.

“Family,” he agreed.

CHAPTER 44

The sun shone in the west, its rays sending long shadows of the King's Road over the grassy plains half a kilometer from the Castle Wexford. The day was nearly over; in less than an hour, the sun would dip below the horizon, leaving the world in murky darkness. A cool breeze whipped over the grass, slowly sapping the ground of the heat the sun had baked into it during the day.

Duke Dominus walked on the grass to one side of the suspended road, shivering in the cool of the coming night. He leaned on his cane as he walked, more out of habit than anything else, thankful that Tykus had returned the cane to him before he'd made his escape, if only for sentimental reasons. He peered at his home in the distance, wanting nothing more than to lay in his bed. It'd been a long journey from the underground tunnels below the Acropolis to the Fringe, and then the deep forest. A journey that had taken him days.

Days of no food, and of little water. And even less sleep. For he had never imagined that he'd be forced to journey through the forest, exposing himself to the twisted wills of nature. What dire effects they'd had on him, he wasn't sure; he didn't *feel* any different, but he knew now that this was not a reliable measure of the state of his soul.

I am Dominus, he thought. *I am the beekeeper.*

That, he knew, was all that truly mattered. That he remained in service to Tykus, loyal to the great king's vision. A new Duke of Wexford would replace him, carrying out the duties that had once been his. He would gather the necessary belongings, and travel to one of the small towns to the south. There were many of them, islands of humanity loyal to the kingdom, scattered amidst the forest.

A new life awaited. A life, if king Tykus was correct, that would be without end.

Dominus reached the end of the King's Road, continuing onward toward the high walls of the Castle Wexford. The drawbridge was up, the waters of the moat surrounding it glittering in the fading sunlight.

Almost there, he thought.

Eventually he made it to the edge of the moat, glancing up at the guard towers flanking the drawbridge. He waved at them, knowing that his soldiers were watching, and would be peering through spyglasses to identify him. A moment later, he was proven correct; the drawbridge began to fall, angling downward until it spanned the moat, resting on the ground beyond. He strode across it, his stomach complaining bitterly. Much as the urge to empty one's bladder grew unbearable the closer one got to the bathroom, his hunger grew more insistent with the thought of his impending meal.

He crossed the drawbridge, making it to the other side, and spotted numerous guards standing close beyond, on the path leading to the castle itself. Their expressions were stony…and Dominus soon discovered why. Blood stained the grass in numerous locations, its pungent odor thick in the air.

"What's going on here?" he demanded of the nearest guard, stopping before them.

"We were attacked, your Grace," the guard answered.

"When?"

"Last night," the guard replied.

"By whom?" Dominus snapped.

"An Ironclad," the guard revealed. "And a man with brown skin. And Vi."

"*What?*" Dominus blurted out. Vi was dead…Vi *had* to be dead.

"They came in the middle of the night," the guard explained. "A big Ironclad with a blue mane that glowed in the dark, the brown man, and Vi. They killed ninety-three of our men."

"You're sure it was Vi?" Dominus pressed. The guard nodded.

"Yes," he replied. "Your Grace."

Dominus grimaced, turning away from the guard and staring at the nearest bloodstain on the ground.

She's alive.

He felt a chill run through him, and clenched his fists. If Vi was alive, then that was very bad indeed. She'd almost certainly come here to repay him for double-crossing her. It'd been sheer dumb luck that he hadn't been home; if he had, she would certainly have found him. And despite the treasure trove of artifacts he'd accumulated – the vast number of wills he'd absorbed, improving his skill with the sword beyond nearly any man in the known world – he knew that he was no match for her.

If he'd been here, she would have killed him.

"I take it they made it out alive," Dominus guessed. The guard nodded. Dominus sighed, facing the guard once again. "Get me the captain of the guard," he ordered. The man hesitated.

"One more thing," he stated.

"One more thing *your Grace*," Dominus corrected, feeling another flash of irritation. A lack of respect for his office was not to be tolerated. Normally he would have a man whipped for such insolence, but given the recent attack – with its inevitable effect on morale – he would have to be careful about punishing his men.

"My apologies," the guard murmured, bowing before Dominus. "Your Grace, the enemy was seen exiting a shaft in the ground, just beneath your beehives."

Dominus's breath caught in his throat, and he stared at the guard mutely, terror gripping him.

The shrine!

"We surrounded them," the guard continued, "...but they managed to escape."

Dominus nodded absently, his mind reeling at the revelation. No one outside of his family – and Farkus, regrettably – had dared enter the shrine in the last six thousand years.

They couldn't possibly have made it past its defenses, he reasoned. *They couldn't possibly have...*

Dominus strode past the guard, walking quickly down the path toward his gardens, his heart hammering in his chest. He made it quickly through the lush vegetation of his carefully maintained gardens, reaching his beehives.

He froze, his heart nearly stopping.

One of the wooden pallets his hives had stood upon had been tossed aside, the boxes within which his bees lived scattered across the ground. Shattered. The corpses of countless bees lay strewn across the grass, smashed into oblivion.

My bees!

He stared at the carnage, his fists clenching, then unclenching, his breaths coming in rapid gulps. His head swam sickeningly, his whole body feeling hot. He stumbled forward, feeling as if he might pass out.

My bees!

Dominus made it up to the beehives, staring at them, suddenly wanting to weep. They'd destroyed his bees...half a century of care, of daily effort. Colonies as close to perfect as any had ever been.

It's only a single pallet, he told himself, willing his breathing to slow. *They didn't destroy all of them.*

He grit his teeth, taking a deep breath in, then letting it out. His eyes fell to the exposed stone hatch ahead, still open. The once-secret entrance to the shrine of his forbearers, the sacred shrine to the Dukes of Wexford.

How Vi managed to find it was beyond him; no one knew of the entrance…except for Farkus, of course. But Farkus would never have given up the location, not even under threat of torture. After decades of being exposed to Dominus's will, the man was nearly identical to him. Still, he would have to question his trusty servant, assuming he was still alive.

Dominus walked up to the open shaft, dropping his cane on the ground next to it, then lowering himself to the ladder. He climbed down to the bottom, striding down the dark tunnel beyond. It was pitch black ahead, but he was not concerned. He could navigate these tunnels blindfolded, so often had he visited them. He avoided the numerous traps expertly, making his way past each locked door. It wasn't long before he reached the door to the shrine itself; he unlocked it, feeling it swing open, and the cool breeze created by the flow of water in the fountain ahead.

He reached for the lantern he knew hung to his right, igniting it.

The Shrine of Wexford appeared before him, bathed in the soft glow of the lantern-light. He studied the bones of his ancestors, scanning the sacred chamber carefully. He let out a breath he hadn't realized he'd been holding.

Not a single skeleton out of place.

He focused inward, studying his feelings, walking forward into the room, circling the fountain in the center. There was no sense of corruption, no foreign wills or emotions. Either Vi's will hadn't been powerful enough to corrupt this place, or she hadn't spent enough time here to make any significant impact. Or perhaps she hadn't made it into this room at all.

Thank god.

He turned his attention to the door leading to his vault, where he kept his most secret artifacts and Ossae. It was, to his dismay, open.

They made it inside, he realized, a chill running through him.

He stepped through the door into the room beyond, holding his lantern before him. Obsidian chests lay partially submerged on underwater platforms in neat rows beyond. All of which were open.

His guts squirmed, his heart starting to race again.

Dominus hurried up to the chest that contained the Ironclad's head, ignoring the others. He knelt before it, his fingers trembling as he grasped the edge of the chest, peering inside.

Empty.

He cursed, bolting upright, scanning the other chests quickly. They were all full, none of the other artifacts taken.

She stole it.

Dominus stood there, his heart pounding, staring off at nothing in particular.

She got her revenge, he knew. *She's sending me a message.*

The fact that she was still alive…that she'd somehow survived her fatal wounds, and recovered enough to slaughter so many of his men…was ominous indeed. Dominus had absorbed the talents of countless warriors over the decades, his skill with a sword unmatched by anyone in the known world. Anyone, that was, but Vi. He had no illusions of what might happen if he'd been here when she'd attacked. If she'd found him, he would not have stood a chance against her. It was pure dumb luck that he'd been away at the time…or maybe it wasn't.

Maybe Vi wanted Dominus alive. Wanted him to suffer.

He immediately dismissed the thought. If Vi had *truly* wanted to hurt him, she would have destroyed the shrine. But it was intact, and only one of the artifacts in his vault was missing. Which meant that she'd been after the Ironclad's head, not Dominus.

The Ironclad.

Dominus thought back to what the guard had told him. There'd been three attackers…Vi, a brown man that had to be the Original, and an Ironclad. An Ironclad with a glowing blue mane.

It can't be the same one Vi killed, he reasoned. *She cut off his head.*

Unless…

He spun around, striding quickly out of the vault and through the shrine, reaching the door on the other end. He turned off the lantern, hanging it back in its original spot, then passing through the doorway and closing the door behind him. He backtracked through the tunnels, reaching the ladder at the end and climbing up. Reaching the surface, he closed the hatch, locking it.

"Your Grace," a voice greeted.

Dominus spun around…and saw Farkus standing before him. His servant was stooped over, resting his weight on Dominus's cane. Farkus bowed.

"Good evening, Farkus," Dominus greeted, relieved to see his trusty servant. "I heard what happened."

"A tragedy, your Grace," Farkus opined. Not for the first time, Dominus was struck by the man's appearance, so similar to his own. It had never been more apparent than now; if Farkus hadn't been older and stooped, and had possessed a beard, an observer would not have been able to tell them apart. Dominus frowned, noting some scruff on the man's face. Servants were not allowed to grow beards, of course. Only the aristocracy had that right. Of course, the man could not be chastised for this, given the recent events.

"Indeed," Dominus agreed. "I hear it was Vi and the Original who attacked us," he added. "And an Ironclad."

"Yes, your Grace," Farkus confirmed. "Unfortunately they managed to escape alive."

"They stole an artifact from the vault," Dominus informed him. Farkus raised an eyebrow.

"What artifact?"

"The Ossae that Seeker brought me," Dominus answered. "The head of the Ironclad I was…studying."

"They did?" Farkus inquired.

"Yes," Dominus confirmed. "It's missing."

"They weren't seeing leaving with it," Farkus countered. "As I was informed, they left empty-handed, your Grace."

"You're sure?"

"As sure as I can be," Farkus answered. Dominus frowned, lowering his gaze; if Vi hadn't taken the head, then who had? No one knew the location of the entrance to the shrine, much less how to get past the traps leading up to it. But somehow Vi had found it…which meant that someone must have exposed the entrance *before* the attack, and taken the head before Vi even got there.

But the only person who'd ever been in the vault was…

He glanced up at Farkus, staring at the old man. His blood ran cold.

"What did you do?" he demanded.

"What do you mean, your Grace?" Farkus inquired. His tone was calm, even casual.

"You helped me get to the shrine before, when I was…sick," Dominus explained. "You're the only one who would know how to get to the shrine, and the vault."

"As you say, your Grace."

"So *you* took the head?"

"I did," Farkus agreed. Dominus stared at the servant, hardly believing his ears.

"But why?" he managed.

"The Ironclad's head was a wild Ossae," Farkus answered. "You know that's forbidden."

"It was a new species," Dominus protested. "I had to study it, to…"

"I didn't make the rules," Farkus interjected calmly. Dominus's jaw snapped shut, taken aback by his servant's rudeness. To dare interrupt a duke!

"The rules…"

"Are all that keep this kingdom from anarchy," Farkus stated. "From the corruption of nature."

"I didn't have a choice," Dominus retorted. Farkus arched one eyebrow.

"You *chose* to prolong your own life instead of ceding the Duchy to an heir," Farkus countered. "You *chose* to break the law, corrupting your own humanity."

"I'm still human," Dominus retorted. "And I don't answer to *you*," he added icily.

"But you do have to answer to the law," Farkus replied.

"Do I?" Dominus retorted. "I'll have you know I'm ceding the Duchy to an heir…and that Tykus will choose him. *That's* my choice."

"But you still broke the law."

"And I will preserve the law," Dominus insisted. "In my own way, with the blessing of the king."

"The Duke of Wexford will preserve the law," Farkus retorted. "Not you."

"You're complicit in this," Dominus warned, pointing a finger at Farkus. "You knew what I was doing, using forbidden artifacts. You *helped* me." He sneered at the man. "You're a hypocrite, Farkus!"

"I absorbed your will," Farkus replied calmly. "Your corruption. I was...temporarily affected by it."

"You still are," Dominus retorted. Farkus smiled.

"Hardly," he countered. "You see, after I gave the Ironclad head to the Seekers to dispose of, I Cleansed myself at the shrine."

"You *what?*" Dominus nearly shouted. "You are forbidden from entering into *my* family's..."

"You're corrupt," Farkus interjected, pointing the butt of Dominus's cane at Dominus's chest.

"I am the Duke of Wexford!"

"No, Dominus," Farkus replied. "You aren't...not anymore."

"Are you trying to threaten me?" Dominus shot back. "You insolent *peasant.* I'll have you drawn and quartered!" He stormed away, walking quickly up to a few guards in the distance. One of them, he realized with satisfaction, was his Captain of the Guard. He strode up to the man, stopping before him.

"You," he growled, pointing at the captain. "It appears my *servant* has turned on me. I want him beheaded." He glanced at the captain's sword, reaching for it. "In fact, I want to do it myself," he added. But the captain stepped back, leaving his sword out of reach. Dominus lifted his gaze, staring at the captain incredulously. "What..."

And then he felt his body jerk forward, a sharp pain lancing through his back and chest. He gasped, looking down at himself...and seeing the tip of a sword protruding from his chest, coated with blood.

Dominus stood there, his jaw hanging open, watching as a red stain spread outward from around the blade.

He felt a tugging sensation, felt the blade withdraw from his body. His legs gave out beneath him, dropping him to his knees on the grass below.

A man came into view then, circling around him from behind. It was Farkus, holding Dominus's cane-sword in his right hand, the silver metal coated with crimson blood. The servant stared down at Dominus, his expression stony.

"How..." Dominus croaked. He coughed, blood flying out of his mouth and dribbling down his chin. His chest was on fire, his breathing coming in short gasps. He couldn't take a deep breath, no matter how hard he tried.

"You betrayed the kingdom," Farkus stated coldly. "What was I supposed to do?"

"I am…your Duke!" he gasped.

"You *were*," Farkus retorted.

Dominus stared up at the old man, his head starting to swim sickeningly. He dropped to his hands and knees on the grass, gritting his teeth against the awful pain in his chest, each breath sending a stabbing sensation through to his back. He coughed again, blood spewing from his mouth, and nearly choked on the thick, metallic fluid. Then he fell onto his side on the cool grass, rolling onto his back. He struggled for air, feeling as if he were drowning.

"Captain," he heard Farkus say. "See to it that this man's body is disposed of."

"With pleasure," the captain replied.

Dominus stared up at the night sky, the first of the stars' pure white light piercing through the black veil of space. They vanished as his vision blackened, the world starting to fade away. He felt his consciousness slipping, and clung to it desperately, hearing the sound of his cane-sword being sheathed.

"And captain," he heard Farkus add.

"Yes?"

"Burn the body," Farkus requested. "Please."

Epilogue

High Seeker Zeno hiked through the dense foliage of the deep forest, his shoulders chafing under the straps of the pack he carried on his back. He ignored the discomfort, focusing on putting one foot in front of the other. Days of travel had left him stiff and sore. He hardly minded, knowing that this discomfort was temporary. It would all be over soon now.

He peered ahead, spotting the telltale sign of the ground sloping upward toward the mountain in the distance, and an abrupt change in the trees a quarter kilometer away. Their bark was black, unlike the dull brown of the trees around him, and their trunks were more spindly. They grew taller than their counterparts, however, their branches twisting up toward the heavens, the few that remained alive sporting dark green leaves.

It wasn't long before Zeno reached these trees, his boots sinking into a dense carpet of dead branches and leaves underfoot. The trees ended abruptly perhaps a hundred meters ahead, giving way to a rocky plain…and the base of the mountain.

Almost there.

He trudged through the black forest, a sudden twinge of fear gripping him. He ignored it, decades of training kicking in. Studied it dispassionately, seeing it immediately for what it was. The Founder had observed this same emotion, he knew. The wills of madmen, their bones buried beneath this very soil, tainting everything in their vicinity.

The first of Zagamar's Trials.

He continued forward confidently, having trained for this ever since the day he earned the status of High Seeker. Every High Seeker before him had done the same, in preparation for the Ascension. They had not been given the opportunity to utilize this training, of course. He felt a giddy sensation come over him, piercing through the fear.

How glorious that *he* should be the one to make this pilgrimage!

Zeno passed through the black trees, emerging from them and continuing forward on the rocky terrain beyond. The ground sloped upward at a sharper angle, a narrow dirt path visible in the distance. He made his way to it, following it as wound up the base of the mountain. Short rock walls flanked the path, growing taller as he walked. The path – and the top of the rocky walls – was littered with sun-bleached bones. Some, he knew, were human; most were not.

Another twinge of fear struck him, and he ignored it, forging on.

The path was some three meters wide here, the rock walls on either side taller than he was. The sun beat on Zeno's back mercilessly, his skin red and sore with sunburn. This only made the chafing of his pack's straps on his shoulders all the more uncomfortable. He shifted one of the straps to a slightly more comfortable position, then swatted absently at an insect that had landed on his cheek.

Then he stopped in his tracks, feeling a chill run down his spine.

The second Trial.

He steeled himself, then continued onward, recalling the entry he'd read countless times in the Founder's diary. Of the many defenses protecting the Crypt of Zagamar from would-be intruders. Defenses that, in the end, not even the Founder had been able to overcome completely.

Of course, everything was different now. Someone *had* overcome them. Had gained access to the great Legend's tomb.

He felt another insect land on him, and resisted the urge to swat it away. It wasn't real, he knew. It was another delusion, originally that of madmen Zagamar had killed, scattering their bones over this path. Undoubtedly Legends, these madman, those with that curious affliction of the brain that made them convinced that their flesh was infested with bugs. A rather common delusion, Zeno knew…and utterly incurable.

Zeno felt another insect land on him, felt them crawling over his skin. He imagined them burrowing into his flesh, tunneling through his body, and had the sudden urge to rake at his skin with his fingernails.

Emotion is temporary, he recited. *Action is forever.*

He focused on the *crunch, crunch* of his boots on the fragments of bone underfoot, following the path ever-upward. However, he couldn't help but notice tiny black spots crawling over these bones, hundreds…no, *thousands*…of the illusory creatures blanketing the path.

Fear gripped him, more powerfully this time. He recited the mantra again, forcing himself to step outside of his own mind, observing himself. It came easily, this state of dissociation. Countless hours of practice were serving him well.

He ignored the crawling sensation running up his legs, refusing to look down, to give in to the delusion. Onward he went, until at last he saw the gaping maw of the entrance to the Crypt of Zagamar ahead, a huge tunnel carved into the base of the mountain.

Zeno smiled, feeling elation come over him, for a brief moment obliterating the mounting fear that threatened to overtake him. He knew at this moment that he was standing where the Founder had stood – where Zagamar himself had once stood – on the path leading to his crypt. A powerful sense of history came over him, of the vast expanse of time that had passed since Zagamar had been taken to his final resting place.

He realized he was walking more quickly now, a fresh wave of energy invigorating his tired limbs. He made it quickly to the entrance, passing into the shadow of the tunnel…and feeling the fear, and the sensation of bugs crawling all over him, fade away. The stone floor of the tunnel was littered with skeletons, the walls on either side also made of stone. Zeno retrieved a lantern from his pack, lighting it and continuing forward toward a set of massive double-doors. One of them had been opened slightly…just enough for him to squeeze through. Beyond, there was a narrow hallway, skeletons piled up against the inside of the doors. He waded through them, ignoring a sudden jolt of terror as he did so, continuing forward until the hallway ended, only darkness visible beyond. Zeno knew from the Founder's diary that there was a pit of spikes beyond…and that there were narrow ledges to the left and right. He went left, knowing that this was the correct way…and that he would soon suffer from fear embedded within the wall to his left.

Zeno followed the ledge, turning right down a narrow hallway, passing tall statues on his left. The hallway turned right again, then left, leading to stairs going downward. He followed them, reaching the end of another hallway, which branched left and right. He went left again, following the instructions from the Founder's diary. The hallway turned left twice, then opened up into a narrow ledge with a wall to his right and the spike-laden pit to his left.

The third Trial awaited, he knew. The last one that the Founder had passed. A delusion that the wall opposite the spike-laden pit would move, pushing him off the ledge.

He took a deep breath, then strode forward…and heard a rumbling sound. He tried to ignore it…and the illusion that the wall was moving, the ledge getting narrower with every step he took.

It isn't real, he reminded himself.

Knowing this was one thing…but seeing the wall moving – *seeing* it with his own eyes – was impossible to ignore. He quickened his pace, looking down, forcing himself to walk in a straight line, well away from the edge of the ledge. The wall moved ever leftward, the ledge now less than a meter wide. He realized he was stepping closer to the edge of the pit, and panicked, sprinting toward a narrow staircase ahead and to the left. He felt the wall pressing against his side, and leapt the last meter, landing at the top of the staircase.

Zeno stood there for a long moment, sweat trickling down his forehead, his heart pounding. Relief washed over him.

The third Trial, he thought. *I did it!*

He had done as the Founder had done…completing three trials. The trials the Guild of Seekers had based *their* three Trials on. A symbolic representation of the accomplishments of the Founder.

But he knew there was another Trial …one the Founder had failed to pass.

He made his way down the stairs, following them as they spiraled downward. Reaching the bottom, he found himself in a dark chamber, the uneven rocky floor covered with a dense layer of skeletons…all human, he noted.

Zeno strode through the blackness surrounding him, eventually reaching a stone wall curving slightly inward as it went upward. There were symbols carved into its surface at regular intervals; he ignored these, walking parallel to the wall.

The Founder had failed the fourth Trial, and Zeno knew very well that he would have failed it as well…had it not been for the Original. The boy who'd been the first to gain entrance into the tomb of Zagamar.

Zeno spotted an opening in the wall ahead…a passage one meter squared. He reached it, peering through, holding his lantern before him.

And smiled.

The Founder had described this room – this wall – in excruciating detail. His diary had never mentioned this.

The Original had paved the way, opening the door to the tomb.

He ducked through the passaged, finding himself in a large domed room. The ceiling was shrouded in darkness; ahead, the floor sloped sharply downward to a pool of dark water. Zeno felt fear grip him suddenly…and knew immediately that the emotion was his this time. It was the fear of the unknown. There was no way to know what lay ahead. No diary entry for this section of the crypt.

Zeno studied his surroundings, focusing his mind. Reason would cut through his fear, would provide him a path forward. This room was a dome, which meant that he could circle around the perimeter, or wade through the pool to the center.

He did the former, soon finding himself back where he started.

The center of the pool then.

He stepped up to the edge of the water, dipping his boot into it, then waiting. No sizzling of a strong acid. He dipped a finger in, then rubbed the liquid between his fingertips. It was not overly slippery, as a strong alkaline solution would be. He smelled it, noting a musty odor. But there was no pain, no burning of his flesh. It was harmless, most likely water.

He slid his pack from his shoulders, holding it and the lantern over his head, then wading into the pool. The bottom sloped downward gradually, until the water was at his waist. He continued forward, spotting a large circular platform ahead. There was a ramp leading from the pool up to it; Zeno took this, noting life-size statues of human-like creatures lining the periphery of the platform.

The Svartálfar, he knew. The Founder had written of them. Wretched souls carrying the curse of Zagamar.

He threw his pack over his shoulder, squeezing past two of the statues and continuing forward toward the center of the platform. Toward a massive statue, a skull wrought of black stone, its cranium missing. From it rose a tall statue, nearly ten meters in height. A statue of a nude creature, humanoid, its muscled arms rising to a "V" high above its head.

A pose of victory, Zeno knew, a veritable god reborn, emerging from his own dead flesh. The symbolism was obvious. He felt goosebumps on his arms, and knew that *this* was Zagamar. The Legend himself. Zeno studied the statue, ignoring a sudden pang of hunger. Zagamar appeared human at first glance, but there was something…off about him. His limbs were too long, his face gaunt and cheekbones high and sharp.

He was not just inhuman, Zeno knew. He was *beyond* human.

Zeno's eyes went to a large stone bowl positioned just below the engorged phallus of the statue; there was a human skull embedded in a block of transparent crystal there. He felt another pang of hunger, this one much more insistent, and grimaced, doing his best to ignore it. He had not eaten in some time, but this usually did not bother him. Zeno ate to live, not the other way around.

It was a compulsion, he knew. Absorbed from the will of Zagamar himself. A compulsion to take in the liquid of this skull's contents, the flesh of the Legend, as the Original had done.

Za-ga-mar!

He heard voices chanting the name, felt a chill run through him. He was absorbing the memories of the Legend…in a way the Founder never had.

I have eclipsed him.

Zeno stepped toward the bowl, reaching out to the skull within. His hunger intensified, insatiable now. If he drank, he would become Zagamar, his body serving as the vessel by which the ancient Legend would return to this world. An honor beyond imagination, one that would secure his name in the annals of history forever.

He pulled his hand back, his jawline rippling.

Remember your mission.

Zeno slipped his pack from his shoulders, setting it on the ground before him. He opened it then, reaching in to retrieve what lay inside. The precious artifact that he'd managed, at great cost, to possess.

The head of the Ironclad.

He stared at the thing, remarking on how, weeks after its death, it had not begun to decompose. Its mane, once flaccid and emptied of its glowing gel, was now full again. Turning it over, he spotted new tissue growing at the severed stump of its neck. He allowed himself a smile.

The experiment had been a success.

He set the head inside the bowl, then pulled a long, thin crystal tube from the pack. Each end of the tube was sharpened; he lifted the top of the skull, which was hinged like a chest, seeing a dark liquid inside. He was immediately relieved; the boy had not drank much of the Legend's essence.

Zeno punctured the Ironclad's glowing mane, holding the head over the skull. The glowing gel oozed into the skull, mixing with the dark liquid there. It overflowed, spilling down the skull itself and dripping into the bowl.

Still Zeno poured, until there was no gel left.

He watched as the thick translucent membrane of the mane sealed itself, healing rapidly. Then he located the large artery at the base of the Ironclad's neck, puncturing it with one end of the sharpened crystalline tube. He brought the other end of the tube to his own arm then, puncturing a vein there. Crimson fluid flowed down the tube, entering the beast.

Za-ga-mar!

He watched as his lifeblood drained into the creature, watched as glowing gel slowly refilled its collapsed mane. Then he gazed up at the statue of Zagamar, at its face contorted into a silent, eternal scream.

The Seekers were irrelevant now. The *kingdom* was irrelevant. Whether Nova had succeeded in her mission to murder King Tykus and the dukes was a matter of little consequence.

The Ascension of Man was coming...and no one would be able to stop it now.

www.ingramcontent.com/pod-product-compliance
Lightning Source LLC
Chambersburg PA
CBHW030420310726
48979CB00009B/1540/J

* 9 7 8 1 9 4 8 4 9 7 0 2 2 *